Looking *for* Leon

SHIRLEY BENTON

POOLBEG

Published 2011
by Poolbeg Press Ltd
123 Grange Hill, Baldoyle
Dublin 13, Ireland
E-mail: poolbeg@poolbeg.com
www.poolbeg.com

1

A catalogue record for this book is available from the British Library.

ISBN 978-1-84223-469-3

Typeset by Patricia Hope in Sabon 11/15
Printed and bound in the UK by CPI Mackays, Chatham ME5 8TD

www.poolbeg.com

About the author

Shirley Benton is originally from Tipperary but now lives in Dublin with her husband and daughter. Educated at Mary Immaculate College of Education, Limerick and NUI Galway, she worked full-time in IT for ten years before leaving the industry in 2009 to pursue her dream of becoming a writer whilst working part-time as a freelance editor. When she is not writing or working, she reads, spends too much time on property websites and watches more *Deal or No Deal* than any thirty-something woman should. *Looking for Leon* is her first novel.

To my lovely husband Michael for accepting my extra-marital relationship with my laptop so gracefully

Acknowledgements

Writing my first set of acknowledgements reminds me of doing out a list of invitees to my child's christening – I'm slightly scared that I'll leave someone out. In truth, there are so, so many people that I could thank that Poolbeg would go bankrupt from the cost of printing this book if I made the list as long as I could potentially make it, so in the interests of me not being responsible for that, I'll make it brief. (If anyone is highly insulted at their omission, I should point out that I'm writing this with only five weeks of pregnancy left – so it's all down to pregnancy brain!)

The other half, Michael, is doing well and getting the book dedicated to him, but he has to be thanked hugely for being completely fine with having an absentee wife during the many hours per day when I'm holed up in our home office. (Maybe I should be concerned about just how fine he is about getting rid of me, but that's a worry for another day.) As for the firstborn – well, she can't read very well yet, but when she can, I want her to know that she made it extremely easy for a new mother to write a book. I don't know what I did to deserve a child who sleeps all night every night, but I would swear she was rooting for me to succeed with this book in her own little way. (And, Aoibheann, whatever the trick is to your unbroken-sleep thing, please teach it to your brother as well when he comes along – cheers.)

Our house in Tipperary when I was growing up was like a refuge for unwanted books – books that the neighbours had read and were about to set fire to were salvaged, books left over at the end of the village jumble sales were bought for 5p each just to give them a home – in short, no book was ever turned away from our door. My mother and my sister deserve a big thanks for putting up with having their home turned into a library because of my book obsession. The foundations of the house might be crumbling year on year under the collective weight of my collection, but not one has ever been chucked out to this day (of course, they are in storage there because my own house in Dublin is an even bigger library).

I am lucky enough to have *the best* friends in the world. I think you're lucky if you make a few true friends in life, but I have been blessed with more than my fair share and I am so, so grateful for that. Your constant support, enthusiasm and interest in my writing never ceases to make me feel like the luckiest friend in the world. You all know me well enough by now to know I'm not great on the old gushing front, but suffice it to say that I'm thrilled to have you all in my life. Which leads me on nicely to the *WriteOn* site, a place where I found many new friends years ago. The support I've had from the girls on that site over the years as I've endeavoured to become a published author is nothing short of incredible. Thanks particularly to Oonagh Considine for the brainstorming lunches, Megan Wynne for her constant online positivity and encouragement, Fionnuala McGoldrick for being so generous with her advice, and Claire Prins and Susan Flood for being generally brilliant throughout the years. And about five years ago, I remember making contact with Sarah Webb for advice about writing, whereupon she rang me and told me absolutely everything and anything I wanted to know. I remember being blown away by her generosity to someone she'd never met. Sarah, I've never forgotten that conversation and want to thank you for being so kind to a newbie.

I don't know if Poolbeg have any idea just how ecstatic I am to have this opportunity to work with them – so, guys, just so you know, I'm ecstatic and cannot wait for what's to come! Thanks for taking a chance on me at a time when I know it's never been more difficult to break into the industry. And to Gaye Shortland, you have made this book a much shinier, happier version of what it was

– your eye for detail is amazing, and I'm not only appreciative but slightly jealous of your talent! My agents, Prizeman Kinsella, have been a joy to work with from day one. The second I met Patricia and Yvonne, I felt like we were already friends. Girls, I trust you 100% and it's a great feeling – I'm so looking forward to everything we'll do together.

Was that brief? I don't know. But there is just one more thank-you – I wanted to keep my biggest thanks for you, the reader. All any writer can hope for is that readers will enjoy their work. I'm thrilled that you've taken the time to read this book and I really, really hope you enjoy it.

Chapter One

The *shame*.

There I was on the front page, flashing my knickers.

It all made sense now. Why my normally laid-back mother had suddenly developed chest pains and had to hang up when I rang home from Las Vegas and innocently asked, "Any news?". Why my brother had laughed hysterically when I rang back, worried sick, to ask if Mum was still alive. As for Dad, he'd just hung up immediately when it was his turn to pick up the phone, but he was known to do that kind of thing so I hadn't been worried.

I should have been.

A drunken flashback that I'd been trying to evict from my brain suddenly came flooding back. Oh God, oh God. I tore open the red-top newspaper that my brother had kept for me while I was in Las Vegas and seen fit to slip under my door that morning, so I would see it just before my return to work – his idea of a joke. Please don't let them have pictures of . . .

I squeezed my eyes shut and pulled my jumper over my head. Then I fumbled for the beanie hat that I'd abandoned on the table only seconds before, and yanked that over my bejumpered skull too – but it only reminded me of exactly what I was hiding from, so I flung it across the room instead.

I wanted to launch into a self-indulgent rant about soulless photographers and ruthless journalists, but being one myself – a journo, that is, not ruthless or a photographer, soulless or otherwise – I knew how the game worked. Besides, there was nobody in the room to listen to the rant, and God knows I was enough of a freak now without talking to myself as well.

The knickers-flashing front-pager had been taken in the wee hours of the night before I went on holidays, when I'd stumbled – okay, crashed – onto the pavement as I'd attempted to hail a taxi. Where the camera had come from, I have no idea – although, with the state I was in, I'd probably thought the flashbulbs were people flashing their car-lights at me to say hello as they drove past. Sorry if that sounds vain – it's just that it happens a lot to me. But how the pictures inside the club had been taken, I just don't know. When I'd spotted the ladder in my tights while out dancing with the gang, it had seemed like the most sensible thing in the world to rip them off right there and then. As we just happened to be dancing beside a pole, it would have been rude not to do a little dance around it while I was ripping the aforementioned tights off. And everyone knows that a pair of tights make the world's funniest balaclava, so it had made perfect sense to pull the tights over my head and demand free drink at the bar . . .

I was absolutely ruined in this town.

I pulled my jumper back down so that I could breathe again and ran to my laptop for salvation. My online bank account was the only thing that could save me. The only logical thing to do was to fly back to Vegas as soon as possible, a place where people had a sense of humour about those kinds of things – you did something like that in Vegas, and you ended up with your own show. Over here, you just made a show of yourself. I swallowed hard. My credit-card transactions had stacked up . . . how could a bit of shopping possibly have come to that amount?

I slammed the laptop shut. The only way I'd be flying was by the seat of my pants when it came to talking my way out of this.

But God, the Devil, or whoever else was pulling the cosmic

2

strings, wasn't finished with me yet. As I ripped the incriminating pages out of the paper to tear them to shreds, I spotted a picture on the next page. Well, I didn't so much spot it as it jumped out at me, really. My heart thumped. Johnny, the guy I'd broken up with shortly before I went on holidays, was staring down the top of some sequined scrap of a woman, with the obligatory perma-tan and tattooed lips – her, not him – although I wouldn't be surprised if he had them too. The caption under the picture flashed across my eyes, but I had to read it a second time to take it in. What the hell . . . ?

> Johnny Meagher, Éire TV news anchor, enjoying the company of a luscious lady after breaking up with Andie Appleton recently.

After breaking up with *me*? I broke it off with *him*! Our relationship had been a disaster from day one, and I couldn't wait to get the hell out of it. How could anyone think that *he'd* done the breaking up? The man had followed me around like a chewing-gum stuck to the sole of my shoe for months!

I was so busy stamping on the paper while shouting obscenities that I didn't hear Mum come into the room.

"You'd want to stop jumping on the paper, or you'll be late for work," she said, as if I was just drinking a cup of coffee or something. "Oh, and I'll be driving you in today."

I stood still, all the fight gone out of me. "Look, Mum, it's nice of you to try to cheer me up, but it's going to take more than a lift to work for me to get over this!"

"Oh, that's not why I'm doing it. You just can't drive yourself to work."

"What, you think I was out last night and I'm still drunk? Just because I got caught once acting a little tipsy doesn't mean I'm an alcoholic!"

"Oh, don't be daft. Now, come on before the traffic gets too bad."

I looked at my shaking hands, and realised that driving in my state of shock might not be such a good idea.

I allowed myself to be shooed into Mum's car, thinking that when I got home from work that night I'd definitely take my own one out of the garage for a spin. I did love cars, and my Merc was my pride and joy. I'd spent an absolute fortune on it and I hadn't even driven it to the airport when I went to Vegas in case someone reversed into it in the airport car park. It was much safer in Mum and Dad's cosy garage.

I settled down into the passenger seat, and tried not to cringe anytime we drove past a woman wearing tights. This too would pass; I, of all people, should know that. As the gossip columnist for a newspaper, I knew how fast big news was replaced by the next drama on the so-called celebrity circuit.

Mum hadn't reprimanded me for my nightclub antics, and I was grateful for that. Still, that was Mum. Some would call her accepting. Some would call her just plain away with the fairies. No matter what happened, she would glide serenely through it all, leaving you to wonder if she was really taking it all in. Her other-worldliness had its moments, and this was one of them.

"Now, dear," she said as she pulled up in front of the offices of my newspaper, "here we are."

"Thanks, Mum. It was nice to get a lift today. I'll drive myself in tomorrow though, so don't worry – it'll be back to normal for you."

"No, Andrea, dear, that won't be possible." She never normally called me by my full name. My full name meant big trouble. "You see, your car . . . met another car, shall we say, and now it's more of an accordion than a car." She smiled, looking rather pleased with her pretty description of what sounded suspiciously like a written-off car.

"But, Mum," I said in a low voice, "how could my car meet another car when it was in the garage all the time I was away?"

"Well, it wouldn't have if it was in the garage, of course. But when your brother took it out . . . well, there was every chance it would encounter other cars on the road, as cars do. And you know Adam – he was never even any good at that Operation game years

4

ago, so a steady hand on the steering wheel is slightly beyond his capabilities." She looked out the window thoughtfully. "Or maybe it was the speeding. One or the other."

"What? How did Adam get the keys of my car?" I yelled when I finally recovered the power of speech.

"Good Lord, there's no need to shout! He took them from the key-box, of course. What do you expect when you left them in such an obvious place? What if we'd had a burglar? You might as well leave the keys in the ignition as in the key-box. You'll have to take this up with your brother. He'll be back from his holiday in Spain in about two weeks, he said. Got some last-minute deal for a song and flew out this morning." She looked at her watch. "Speaking of flying, I must fly myself. Go on, get out!"

Mum shoved me out of the car, and then drove back to whatever planet she was on today (I was now firmly in the 'away with the fairies' camp).

I physically shook myself. If only I'd stayed asleep that morning . . . a few hours ago I was dreaming about being reunited with that impossibly charismatic man that I'd met in Vegas. A few hours ago, I was happy and had some hope. And now look at the mess that constituted my life . . . everyone in the office had better have the sense to leave me alone today.

I somehow managed to drag myself to the front door of my office's building, where I met Jason, my least favourite colleague.

"Hey, Andie, was that you I saw on *Crimecall* last night with the balaclava? *Ahahahahaha*!"

And so it began.

If only things had worked out in Vegas, it could all have been so different . . .

Chapter Two

Las Vegas, Last Week

"So, you wanna lay?"

"Excuse me?"

"A bet." Leon pointed to the endless rows of roulette, blackjack and craps tables before us. He looked bewildered at my enquiring expression.

"Oh." I didn't know if I was embarrassed or disappointed.

It had all been going so well. I was on the last night of my two-week holiday to Vegas, and I still hadn't gambled. You see, I had a hundred-euro bet on with my friend, Roseanne – and, yes, I can see the irony – that I'd last the fortnight without coming in contact with a croupier, unless he was handing me a free drink. What was the point, when I hadn't a clue how to gamble and would only end up losing a fortune? But now, the cost of my lost bet with Roseanne seemed like a bargain. Besides, she'd gone out with a guy she'd met and left me on my own for the night, so what she didn't know wouldn't hurt her.

I made a beeline for a roulette table, where my lack of gambling skills wouldn't be so evident. As soon as we had ourselves settled at the table, a cocktail waitress came straight over to take our drinks order. I watched Leon out of the corner of my eye as he asked the waitress about the cocktail menu. God, he was really something. I could feel his presence from several feet away. He was the kind of person that made a solid wall of people part as he approached. Would you think I was rude if I said I couldn't help thinking that it probably wasn't the only thing he would part easily? Believe me, you'd have thought that too if you'd seen him.

I'd spotted him from miles back as he'd walked towards me in the MGM Grand Hotel. All I could think was that there was no way I could only glance at that face once and never see it again. I had to do something – but I couldn't think of anything. Thankfully, as he walked past me, something made him look up from the garish carpet and right into my eyes. His gaze travelled all over my body as it journeyed upwards. Not in a leery way – in fact, it was so subtle that I wouldn't even have noticed except I was looking out for it. Good God, I was *praying* for it. I searched his face for a sign that he was in some way impressed. A ghost of a tentative smile appeared on his face as we made eye contact. I returned it with a full-blown Cheshire grin. He looked relieved, and smiled back properly.

A single second of time can make a lifetime of a difference. The second after that smile was our chance to either make something of it, or walk out of each other's lives forever. I opened my mouth to say something – anything. But nothing came out except a croak. Trust me, it wasn't often someone stunned me into silence. I felt the blood rush up to my face and knew I was going purple, so I jerked my head in the opposite direction, absolutely mortified. When I looked back a second later, the guy had been eaten up by the crowd making their way along the hotel lobby.

I should have ploughed my way through everyone until I found him – that would be my style usually. I still don't know what it was that held me back, but the few seconds of hesitation were enough to let him drift away. I continued walking, not even knowing now where I was heading. I had a vague notion that it might be towards a bar, which wasn't altogether a bad thought.

If you've ever been to Vegas, you'll know that it takes a lot more than a spot of self-indulgent introspection to stop people approaching you. My head was hanging so low that I was practically getting carpet burn as I slouched aimlessly along, but that didn't stop an over-enthusiastic blonde girl with a wide mouth of bright teeth getting right in my face.

"Heeeeeey! You're just the person we're looking for!" She gesticulated wildly at a group of people that were wearing the same clothes as her – red T-shirt, black leather trousers, red shoes. "Everybody! I've found The One!" I suddenly felt like a lab animal as the group crowded around me and scrutinised me.

A tall guy nodded and said, "Yeah, she'll do."

Through my confusion, I found the head-space to be instantly insulted at his lack of enthusiasm for whatever it was I would 'do' for.

"Take her over," he said to the blonde.

She took my elbow, and led me off.

"Hang on a second! What's going on? Where are you trying to take me to?"

"A place where you'll make lots of money. You start gambling, you lose money. You stick with me, you'll make big bucks this evening. Sound good?"

"And what if I have plans?"

"Forget them. We're saving you the hangover," she said with a saccharine smile.

It was an amazing smile, in fairness – she reminded me of Julia Roberts – but it wasn't going to work on me. I curled my lip up.

"Oh, come on!" she said. "You looked depressed as hell before I stopped you. Guy trouble, huh?"

The lip hadn't worked, so I gave her my special evil look reserved for family members and boyfriends, but it didn't faze her in the slightest.

"I thought so. Why spend the evening drinking over some man who isn't worth it, when you could be having fun?"

"Having fun doing what?"

"How does hanging out in the shiniest set of wheels in this city grab ya?"

She'd found my weakness. Now, I was interested.

She stopped at a car that I had passed earlier on in the hotel. Yes, you read that correctly. The MGM was so big that it had show-cars dotted around the hotel for advertising purposes – brand-spanking-new cars that really made you want to be stinking rich. I could only imagine the effect they would have on the subconscious of hardened gamblers.

"We're doing a promotion for this particular model at the moment," she said, turning her back to reveal the brand and make of the car on the back of her T-shirt. The price was missing, not surprisingly. "What we need, though, is an extremely gorgeous couple to help us show it off!"

I frowned. "As you've already pointed out, I'm having man trouble, so I'm not a couple. I'm just a 'cou–'."

"A what? Oh, I get it." She waved dismissively. "That doesn't matter – we're sorting out a fantastic guy for you right now!"

Great. All I needed now was to spend the night in the company of some loser. "No. I'm not doing this."

Her sugary smile vanished. She suddenly looked quite scary, far scarier than my scary look would have been. "Well, can it make you any more miserable than you already are right now?"

She had a point. That didn't mean I had to admit it, though.

I was saved from having to come up with a witty retort by a protesting voice at the other side of the car. "Uh uh. Not interested."

"Come onnnn, sir! You'll be well compensated for just a few hours of your time – and you just wait until you see the beautiful lady we've got lined up to work with you!" A shaggy-haired guy who hadn't been part of the team that scrutinised me looked frantically around the side of the car to see if his colleagues had found anyone. He caught Julia Roberts' eye, looked me up and down, scrunched his face as if to say 'Can't you find anyone better than her?', then shrugged in acceptance.

"I don't care if she's Angelina Jolie," the voice said. "I have plans for tonight. I . . ."

Julia dragged me over, ignoring my demands that she should release my arm if she didn't want a whack from it.

The protester took one look at me, and suddenly shut up fairly lively. So, for that matter, did I.

"There was only ever one thing we would do with this twenty dollars," my partner in crime said as we walked towards my chosen roulette table.

I still couldn't believe it. Out of all the hundreds of people passing through the hotel, the gorgeous man I'd spotted earlier had been picked to be the other half of the happy car couple. That had to be more than a coincidence, surely? The rest of the hotel seemed to fade away as he told me his name. Leon. I was barely able to croak out my own in reply.

Our mission, which we were forced to accept, was to sell the dream of a supposedly beautiful, successful couple by drinking champagne, laughing loudly and making it look like we were having the time of our lives in our slinky, up-to-the-minute car, a new Lexus model. The logic of knocking back alcohol behind the wheel of a car, albeit an immobile one, was lost on me. Even if we were in Vegas, this was the land where people spat out an artery if they found their twenty-and-a-half-year-old drinking. But who was I to question the art of advertising?

Sipping champagne and clinking my glass delicately against my beau's, in celebration of our perfect lives, sounded like a simple task in theory, but the more I drank, the more difficult it got. Three sips in, I started gulping, which seamlessly progressed into me throwing the rest of my glass down my throat like any respectable woman would. One of Julia's colleagues refilled it, complete with a dirty look, and I promptly knocked that one back too. What else could I do to celebrate finding Leon? Okay, you might say it wasn't very ladylike – but to my delight, Leon was no gentleman either. He matched me drink for drink, and seemed thrilled and impressed to be in the company of someone who could keep up with him. I could see Julia and Shaggy frowning at each other as they watched us – but they needn't have worried. By the time Leon and I started our third bottle of champagne, we were laughing so raucously that we were attracting the attention of every single person that passed – which was exactly what they wanted, wasn't it?

And that was when it suddenly became a great idea to get up and dance. Well, why not? All the bar staff in a pub at the centre of the MGM had to abandon whatever it was they were doing when certain songs came on, and instantly jump up on the nearest table to shake their booties. We were now technically MGM staff, so wasn't it our duty to dance? The concert in the Grand Garden Arena had just ended, and music from the concert's artist was being pumped all over the hotel – probably to get the concert-goers to continue the party vibe with after-drinks.

"*Woooo!*" I pulled myself into an upright position. "*Come on, people!*" A hundred heads turned to look at me. Standing on my car seat, I flailed my arms in the air, roaring along with the song. Out of the side of my eye, I saw Leon standing up on his seat too. He threw his arm around my shoulders, and joined me in a raucous rendition of one of the artist's biggest hits. And incredibly, a crowd started to form around us to sing along. I could see Julia running over to get us to sit down, but Shaggy stopped her, no doubt sensing an opportunity to jump up when the crowd was big enough and start his sales pitch about the car.

It was an accident waiting to happen. We'd reached the crescendo of the song when I turned sideways on one of my heels, stumbling on top of Leon, who dropped the champagne bottle that he'd been holding to his mouth like a wino. Of course, this eejit here made a dive for it as it fell. And as I did so, I totally lost my balance and . . . stuck my other heeled foot right through the windscreen of the car.

Everyone stopped singing.

The T-shirt gang was frozen in horror. Not at the thought of me being maimed for life, of course – their concern was entirely for the car. Luckily for me, the shoe had taken all the impact, and I was able to slip my uninjured foot out of it. I tugged the shoe out of the glass: the heel was somewhat mangled but miraculously still attached to the shoe, if slightly wobbly. The whole scene was actually quite artistic, you know. The glass hadn't shattered – the heel of the shoe had created a dainty little hole, and great big cracks had erupted from the centre and spread to the corners of the windscreen. It was like a sunflower, for all the world.

Leon tried to recover the situation. "Buy a Lexus, everyone! You'll have a *smashing* time!" He erupted into fits of laughter at his attempt to be witty, but unlike with the songs, nobody joined in. Even I didn't laugh – I knew a predictable joke when I heard one – but the whole issue of almost putting my leg through the windscreen had quietened me down a bit anyway. If I'd fallen any harder, Leon's jokes wouldn't have been the only lame thing around here.

If you're one step ahead of me, you'll probably have worked out that our employment at the MGM ended abruptly. And that was how we ended up gambling the huge sum of twenty dollars that we'd earned after the cost of damages was taken from our wages, not to mention what we gambled from our own pockets.

Roulette was addictive. We bet on black, we bet on red. We played inside bets, we played outside bets – even though I had no idea of the lingo behind what we were doing at the time, and just nodded knowledgeably when Leon asked me if I thought we should play a corner. Our chips stacked up, then grew smaller. Before I knew it, two hours had passed. I could feel Leon's breath on my neck every time I leaned over the roulette table. As soon as we lost all of our chips, he put his hand on the small of my back, softly and tentatively, and whispered in my ear, "Gambling is thirsty work. Do you want to go to a bar?"

He had a full glass of drink in his hand as he said this, so I was hoping he just wanted to spend some time alone with me. I nodded, and we made our way to the bar with the table dancers. We settled in a cosy corner. A half-naked girl with an extremely flat stomach took our order, which Leon had paid for before I even had my wallet out. I didn't argue. It felt right.

I had ordered a strawberry daiquiri, and I sucked a long sup from it through my straw. Leon watched me, then laughed. "If I hadn't known you were Irish from your accent, I would have guessed it by the way you drink."

"They taught you to drink wherever it was that you grew up too, so I'm in good company."

"That's what a misspent youth in Arizona does to you. Vegas drinking is tame compared to what I'm used to in the wild lands of home." He rolled his eyes. "Nah. I'm from one of these towns where absolutely nothing ever happens. How about you?"

"I'm from Dublin – ever been there?"

"No, but I'm familiar with it from *Fair City*. My parents are Irish, you see – Mom's from Sligo, and Dad's from Galway – and they used to get videos of films and TV shows taped from the Irish national broadcaster and sent over years ago. I've seen far more begorrah films about turf and bogs than one man should see, but the early days of *Fair City* were also in the mix. And do you remember *Glenroe*? I must have seen every episode ever made of that!"

"No way!"

"I know. Imagine putting a young child through that in the name of culture. You Irish are cruel." He took a slug of his drink. "And crazy, too. I couldn't believe how fast you drank that champagne in the car."

"You were happy to join in my craziness. You actually drank faster than me, you know."

"I'm a closet crazy kid," said the clean-cut vision beside me.

"You don't look it. I thought you were as straight as they came when I first saw you. But then I saw your hidden depths when you knocked back the drinks with me. The Irish influence really makes sense!"

"I just need someone to be crazy with. Most of the women I meet are so . . . self-conscious. They don't let themselves go the way you did tonight – and I mean that in the best way possible. It's lovely to see a woman just be herself." He looked down at the table, suddenly looking self-conscious himself. "And . . . I really liked what I saw."

I shivered. Things were just getting better and better.

"Being with you tonight . . . it's made me feel like I've come back to being myself," he went on. "I used to be a different person, but stuff happened and . . . well, it changed me. You make me feel like I've just come home."

He smiled, shyly at first, but then it turned into a full-megawatt beam. I returned it. My heart felt like it was about to burst out of my chest. Something seriously special was happening here.

Before I knew it, I was telling Leon stuff I never told anyone. Serious, heavy stuff. The kind of stuff that would send most men running for the hills. I knew he wouldn't. Not him. I hadn't even realised I was going to say anything until it had come out, but I knew as I spoke that it wasn't a mistake to have opened my mouth.

The next two hours felt like they'd only lasted a few seconds. Despite the buzz of the hotel and the bar, it felt like we were the only two people in the entire world. It was magical . . . but then, nature had to ruin the spell, as I suddenly realised that I needed to use the bathroom.

I nodded in the direction of the restrooms, which were part of the hotel's main walkway outside of the bar. "I won't be long," I said, reluctantly getting myself up from the comfy yet trendy couch that had been swallowing me up.

"Take as long as you need. I'll be waiting." He smiled again, and something inside me exploded.

I couldn't stop myself from putting my hand on his shoulder as I walked past him, and squeezing it softly. He lifted his hand up to mine, took it from his shoulder and to his mouth, where he kissed it so tenderly that I instantly felt like crying with the beauty of the moment. It nearly killed me to take my hand away, but my bladder was winning the fight between body and soul.

I had to stop myself from skipping to the bathroom. How had I been lucky enough to bump into this guy? And unlucky enough to meet him on my last night here . . . The queue was ridiculously long. I eventually got a free stall, and was just washing my hands as fast as I could in my haste to get back to Leon when I heard the wail of a fire alarm. Being Irish, I didn't take a blind bit of notice of it. It had probably just been set off by accident.

"Hey, you! Quick, let's go!" An elderly lady beckoned to me as she ran towards the door.

"Don't worry, I'm sure some drunk just fell into a wall and set off an alarm or something." I thought of how much Leon and I had drunk, and hoped he wasn't responsible.

"Suit yourself. I'm outta here."

The lady opened the bathroom door. The smell of smoke immediately flooded in.

"On second thoughts, wait for me!"

The casino floor was in chaos. Black smoke had started to trickle through the hotel and people were racing towards the closest exits. I ran towards the bar to find Leon, but a harassed security guy was standing at one of the exits to the bar when I got there.

"No entry! Proceed to the emergency exit on your left *immediately*!"

"But I need to find a friend who was in there!"

"Everyone has been evacuated to the emergency exit on your left. Now *go*!"

I didn't need to be told twice. (Well, I had been told twice, but the first time didn't count.) I just had to find Leon. I joined everyone else in racing towards the exit, and then coming to an abrupt standstill as we joined the increasingly panicked crowd and shuffled our way outside.

Strangely enough, I wasn't one bit threatened by the fire that could potentially kill us all. My big worry was losing Leon – and as soon as I got outside, I could tell that it was a very valid worry. As the second biggest hotel in the world with over 5,000 rooms, the MGM's evacuation process had resulted in countless bodies being evicted onto the streets from every single one of the masses of exits in the hotel. The street was heaving with people, terrified people who had been separated from family members and friends. Names were being shouted up and down the street as people attempted to find others, people were pushing and shoving their way through the crowd, passers-by were stopping to see what was going on and making the crowd even bigger. I joined the second group – unpopular people who jostled their way through the crowd – and searched for

Leon. He was tall, which I had hoped would be an advantage, but it really meant nothing in a crowd of this magnitude.

The fire services arrived, and thankfully they got things under control. It hadn't been half as bad as the black smoke had led everyone to believe – in fact, it had been a relatively small fire, and nobody had been injured. We were informed that it had started in the north wing of the hotel and that the accommodation in the south wing was unaffected, but we would need to wait outside until the clean-up operation was complete. After a few sweltering hours on the street, we were allowed back into the hotel.

Although I had searched for Leon until I was black and blue from struggling through the crowd, I hadn't succeeded in finding him – but now that we were allowed back into the hotel, I felt a glimmer of hope. The bar we'd been drinking in had closed in the aftermath of the fire, so I walked back towards the table we'd been gambling at earlier. Surely if he wanted to find me as much as I wanted to find him, he'd think of coming back here? It was the only card I had up my sleeveless top, so I could only pray that it would work.

It didn't. I waited, and waited, and waited some more, for so long that I was sure I'd missed my flight home. I went to Reception and interrogated the staff to see if they had a guest called Leon staying in the hotel, but they told me where to go – albeit in the most polite way that you can possibly be told to feck off with yourself. At a loss as to what to do, I returned to the roulette table and stood there like a big eejit again. It got to the point where not only did I have to face the fact that Leon wasn't going to show, but my hangover was on the cusp of starting. I either had to get more alcohol or go to bed. I knew instantly which one was the more appealing option.

I texted Roseanne and asked her if she wouldn't mind awfully having a gatecrasher on her date. The phone rang immediately.

"Oh, thank God you texted. I have to get away from this lunatic. I was just trying to think of an excuse when I got your message. Where are you?"

"In the hotel."

"I'm in the Irish bar in New York-New York. Get over here, and come in wailing and bawling. I'll say you're having an emergency and I have to leave with you. Make sure you make it as dramatic as possible!"

"Okay." The way I was feeling, I wouldn't even have to act.

I made my way towards the west wing of the hotel and walked towards New York-New York via the overhead pedestrian bridge from the MGM. I looked down onto the Strip as I crossed over, wondering where Leon was out there.

As I entered New York-New York, the lights of the hotels lining each side of the Strip shone as brightly as ever, completely oblivious to how the light in my world had just dimmed.

Chapter Three

I couldn't believe I was back in work. Two glorious weeks away from it had nearly made it harder to step back into the madhouse instead of helping me to feel refreshed, and although I'd flown back from Vegas two days ago, I still hadn't recovered from my final night and day there.

After Roseanne and I made our great escape from New York-New York, we had done a casino-crawl until the wee hours of the morning, putting the world to rights along the way. I had asked at every hotel we had drunk in if they had a guest called Leon but, unsurprisingly, my success rate was no higher than in the MGM. I couldn't believe that after all the talking we'd done, Leon had never mentioned where he was staying, and I hadn't asked. But by the time I'd limped my way back to my hotel room in the MGM, shoes (one minus a heel by now) long since abandoned, I had a plan. Trouble was, I had very little time left to do it in, so I got up after only two hours of sleep with a thumping headache to put it into action. That was when I knew I really, really liked this guy. The suffering would have been worth it if I had actually found him, but I hadn't.

"Jesus, you look like shit." Not content with harassing me outside the office, Jason was determined to continue it inside as well.

"You shouldn't be so hard on yourself, Jason," I said. "Put away your mirror and you'll feel better."

He ignored my attempts to throw his insult back at him, and stuck his head in my face. "Christ, what were you up to in Vegas? You look about a decade older."

"Back away, smelly boy, and take your blackheads with you!" I shuddered.

Jason was truly loathsome. He never washed, and he knew it drove us all mental (because we told him straight out), but the more we complained, the smellier he would let himself get. He was just one of those people who didn't give a rat's ass what anyone thought of him.

"You had a shit time, then." He nodded knowledgeably.

I was sure I heard him mutter "Good" under his breath, but I didn't dare challenge him on it in case he came near me again. I felt nauseous enough as it was.

Luckily, Trevor walked in just then and plonked himself at his desk beside me amid hellos and enquiries about my holiday. If you saw Trevor walking towards you, you wouldn't feel quite so pleased to see him as I was. Trevor just had one of those heads you'd be scared of. He looked like he'd rob the dentures out of an old lady's mouth to sell on the Internet, eat babies' thighs with barbeque sauce, you name it. But the minute he opened his mouth, you'd instantly change your opinion of him. Not only was he the nicest, most decent guy you could ever meet, but he had a squeaky voice that meant you couldn't possibly find him threatening.

"Isolde missed you," he screeched when we'd finished the obligatory holiday recap palaver and a slagging about the newspaper pictures. "She never stopped talking about you." His rough head broke into a huge grin.

"Oh, great." I knew exactly what that meant. My boss, not to put too fine a point on it, hated my guts. Absence had clearly made the hatred grow stronger.

"Relax. She sent a mail saying she wouldn't be in until the afternoon, so you have the morning to catch up without her gawking at you."

Thea trudged in next, looking as wretched as ever. She didn't bother with the niceties of welcoming me back. "Andie, come over to my desk sometime in the next hour – Isolde wants us to work on an article together. I've to fill you in on what I've done so far – you're taking it over in one hour's time. Oh, but don't call over until you're caffeined up. You're too miserable without it." She scowled, then flumped into her seat.

I know, I know. Pot, kettle, black etc etc. But it's like when your mother gives out to you for eating fatty food while she's tucking into a scone dripping with jam and butter. You want to say something, but you know it's utterly pointless – she'll never see the similarity, only the difference. Thea, God love her, was someone who would remain oblivious to her miserable demeanour until her dying day. In her head, she was Barney-style happy, and everyone else had the blues.

You don't need me to tell you that we were a right motley crew. The only person I really got on with was Laura, who was thankfully making her way to her desk just as Thea finished her oration. Laura was the yang to Thea's yin – bright, affable and enthusiastic.

"Andie!" Big hug. "We missed you! How was the holiday?"

"Great, great."

"And did you meet anyone nice over there?"

"Well . . ."

"You did! I can tell by the head on you! Who was he?"

I decided to tell her about meeting Leon – God knows, I was only dying to talk about him, and we'd only end up talking about the pictures in the paper otherwise. As soon as I mentioned that there was a man involved, I could tell that the others were eavesdropping shamelessly. It wasn't long before they all started chiming in with questions about Leon – even Thea, although she was probably trying to ascertain that the whole outcome didn't have a happy ending and that I was miserable about it all.

"You mustn't have tried very hard to find him," Trevor shrilled.

"You reckon?"

Before I knew it, I was filling them in on my efforts to track Leon down. Might as well replace the talk of my public humiliation with –

well, humiliation abroad. I had them all in stitches within a few minutes, but I wasn't sure if that was a good thing or not.

I was just getting into the flow of my story about waddling up and down the Strip with a '*Do You Know Leon?*' sandwich-board when I heard the sound of an office door being ripped open. An innocuous sound to most, but not when you knew who was doing the ripping. Although I jerked my head around immediately, I felt like I was moving in slow motion as I turned to face bushy eyebrows, slitty eyes and a sour puss of an expression.

"Isolde! I thought you were away this morning . . ." Fuck, fuck, fuck. I couldn't have said anything that would make me sound guiltier.

"Evidently."

"So. *Ahem*. How are you?"

"All the better for having you back to do some work. Oh, wait. You're not. You're yapping."

"Just filling the gang in on my holiday," I said, sweeping my hand towards the aforementioned gang. I turned to find I was gesturing towards thin air. The yellow-bellies had all spirited themselves back into their cubicles, and were trying to look invisible in their seats. As you might have guessed, we were all terrified of Isolde. Nobody admitted it, but we didn't have to. We wore our fear all over our yellow faces.

"It was great. We get it. And now, it's over. We need a catch-up meeting, Andie. *Now*." She swivelled back into her office.

I swallowed hard as I walked – or, truth be told, semi-ran in the fashion of that Olympic event – to Isolde's office. I was only in the door ten minutes, and I was already being hauled off to the dungeon. At this rate, I'd be fired before the end of the day. I whacked my knees against Isolde's desk as I tried to position my legs in a ladylike, nonchalant, I've-done-nothing-wrong fashion.

"Any idea what you've done wrong this time?" Isolde said in a tired, almost bored voice.

"Okay, so maybe I distracted the guys with talk about my holiday – but they asked! I didn't come in here wanting to talk about it . . ."

She put her hand up to silence me. "Oh, forget it. We'll be here all day if we're waiting for you to work it out. Here." She threw a printed article across the desk at me. It was a piece I had written for my gossip column just before I went on holidays about how I had spotted two married government ministers canoodling in the VIP area of a top Dublin club. (I should point out that they were not married to each other – but even if they had been, it would still have been considered gossip – ministers and public displays of affection were not comfortable bedfellows.) It had been a midweek night, with not many people about, and they had obviously let their guard down.

She plonked another piece of paper in front of me. "And this is the letter we got from Mr Government Minister's solicitor, threatening to take a libel action against us. What do you make of that?"

"Well, of course they're going to try to deny it! They've been caught red-handed, but they're hardly going to pose for kinky pictures, are they? You knew something like this might happen before you agreed to run the story." I might have been afraid, terrified, petrified of Isolde and her temper, but when I'd brought the story to her, it had been her decision to run it. She had practically wet her knickers in her haste to get it printed up.

"Nothing like this has ever happened before, has it? And when it does, it has to involve you." She shook her head. "Give me one good reason why I shouldn't fire you right now."

I was too tired for all of this. "Because nobody else who would be willing to work for the pittance I earn here has the kind of contacts I have, that's why."

That shut her up. The last thing she expected was a back-answer. To be honest, it was the last thing I expected either. Nobody back-answered Isolde Huntingdon. And for some demented inner-rage-related reason, I just had. But I wasn't finished my attempt to annihilate my career. No, I had to make it worse.

"I will not be called a liar, Isolde. I know what I saw. Now, if you'll excuse me." I stood up, wearing what I hoped was a regal expression, and attempted to plod with dignity out the door – until her screech of "*Where do you think you are going?*" gave me such a fright that I stumbled and my entire body sprawled against the door that stood between me and escape.

I steadied myself, and somehow managed to stagger out and back to my desk for my handbag and coat. Strains of "*Hoy! Get back here!*" followed me. The yellow-bellies' faces were alive with the drama of it all. Drama at any time was good, but on a Monday morning . . . well, you couldn't pay for it. Isolde toddled after me on her stumpy little legs, but she hadn't a hope of catching up with me. As the glass lift in our building began to transport me downstairs to the freedom of the outside world, I saw her shaking her fist at me. Now, I told myself, that'll show her. Nobody – nobody – had ever stood up to her before.

I had a few glorious moments of self-congratulation before the reality sank in. When it did, I had to steady myself against a wall outside because my legs were shaking so much.

Oh God. What had I done?

Chapter Four

I suppose I should explain to you what I meant about my contacts, when I was giving guff back to Isolde. It's kind of embarrassing, actually, and it makes me sound like a right knob (or knobess, I suppose the technical term is). Actually, I'm quite grounded. How much more grounded can you get than being willing to wear a sandwich-board? I could barely move with the weight of that thing.

According to the tabloids, I am of that species that's known as an Irish celebrity. For anyone who doesn't know what that entails, it essentially means that pictures of my mush show up a lot in monthly style magazines and newspapers. I get invited to a lot of high-profile birthday bashes, charity lunches and balls, book launches, that kind of thing. And I suppose you're wondering what I've done to merit being a so-called celeb. To tell you the truth, I wonder the same thing myself. I never set out to be one, you know.

It started, as a lot of things do, with a man.

I was working as a part-time model to raise a bit of spare cash while studying journalism in college, but even though I was in the papers a lot advertising different things, nobody took much notice of me as a person. And then, I started seeing Graham. When I first met him through a model friend, I had no idea he was an up-and-coming football player. I was probably the only person in the city who didn't, judging by the showers of women who were following him around in Pied Piper fashion the night we met. Of course, the fact that his head could have fallen off his shoulders and I wouldn't have noticed instantly grabbed his attention. We eventually started dating, but we were only on the starters of our first dinner date when we were snapped. Or papped, Graham used to call it. I called it a damn nuisance. And then, out of nowhere, I couldn't go anywhere without my picture being in the paper the next day. If I was on my own, there would be a report under my picture saying that Graham and I had broken up. If I was sipping a drink, I was evidently drowning my sorrows. If I was scratching my nose, someone would be sent out to my mother's house to ask her how she felt about me taking cocaine as a result of the break-up – of course, my mum being my mum, she'd always say something bizarre that would convince the reporters that their fabricated story was actually true, that she was on it as well, and would they like to come in and have some?

It was all completely out of control, but it did open doors for me. When I finished college, having long since broken up with Graham after he started dating a millionaire's wife behind my back, I spent a few years in Paris teaching English. I thought everyone would have forgotten who I was when I returned, but to my surprise I landed a plum job as a reporter on an entertainment show called *Glitter* on an independent TV station called Éire TV. The hours were long, but I sometimes couldn't believe I got paid to do it – who wouldn't want to spend their days flying to London to interview stars on the red carpet at movie premiéres? And then . . . the station's broadcasting budget was cut dramatically, and our programme got the chop.

I'd hated every minute of modelling – well, would you want to do a photo shoot for bananas in a bikini on Grafton Street when it was only two degrees? (I was in the bikini, by the way – not the bananas.) Okay, so the sales of bananas soared in this country for months after the ad came out, but that was no use to my frostbitten feet – my toes looked like decayed mini-bananas themselves after that shoot. So, if I wasn't pictured looking like a sleepwalker as I left a nightclub, I was looking at my goose-bumped thighs over the breakfast table. No, there was no way I was going into modelling again – and I was several years older by then too. So the logical thing to do was what I was trained for. I would take over the world of journalism with my concise reporting on politics, global warming (I wasn't too sure that was happening at all after that freezing bikini incident) and world finance. And given my unblemished history of business travel for *Glitter*, I'd surely get sent to America as the US correspondent for big events, the whole hog!

I got a part-time job as an entertainment correspondent with a daily newspaper, the *Vicious Voice*. Well, you try getting taken seriously when the whole world has seen your bum cheeks. And the only reason I got it was because I knew half of Dublin from my modelling and reporter days. I had enough sense to know that I'd have to be careful about what I reported, but Isolde's idea was that I would blag my way into every event in town, fawn over everyone to their faces, and then tear them to shreds in my column. When that didn't happen, she took an irreversible dislike to me. Luckily for me, the public seemed to like my style, so she didn't fire me either. I also wrote a few controversial articles about my views on various things to redress the balance, and eventually Isolde allowed me to break into writing for other areas of the paper when my colleagues were out sick (aka nursing their hangovers at home). This eventually mutated into a full-time position with the paper, and a hard-fought-for one at that.

And now, I'd gone and walked away from it as if it had meant nothing. As jobs went, mine was right up there with pulling out eyelashes with a blunt tweezers on the painful scale, but I needed it. Not for the first time, I cursed the strokes of my pen the day I filled up my CAO form many years ago. I'd been oscillating between choosing teaching or journalism as my college course for months on end. I knew that becoming an English teacher was what I really wanted, but I had no confidence that I'd actually be any good at it. After many hours of pen-hovering, I eventually deemed journalism to be the better option. I was happy with my decision right up until the day I started my journalism course, at which point I commenced the process of spending the rest of my life to date wishing I'd chosen teaching instead. I was taking that process particularly seriously today. But it was too late to think like that now, and all I could do was salvage the wreckage of my career and get my job back. If I didn't, I was finished as a journalist. Isolde would blacken my name all over town – she was that kind of miserable old bag who was at her happiest when she was spreading poison (she and Thea got on very well, incidentally). There was nothing else for it. I'd have to go back in there tomorrow and grovel.

When tomorrow came, I stood outside the door of the building, summoning up my adrenalin to face the Wrath of Isolde. I was exhausted. I'd spent half the night worried sick, and the other half trawling the Internet in the vain hope of finding some dirt on Isolde to use against her – an affair with the husband of a mother of thirteen children and another one on the way would have done nicely – but there wasn't a hope of Isolde being involved in anything vaguely sexual. Without sounding mean, men (or women, for that matter) ran a mile from her.

Isolde, despite her rather grand name, could be described in one word as a bumpkin. She wore tweed suits that were at least thirty years old, presumed to be inherited from her mother, but nobody dared to ask. She alternated these with huge, baggy dresses made from curtains. Probably. She was too mean to spend money on material to make dresses, and God knows no clothes manufacturer would ever have made the junk she wore, even several decades ago. Two words summed up her head – Worzel and Gummidge. But she got away with it, purely because of her formidable personality.

There were times when I found her refreshing, because in her world PC referred to a police constable. She was so old-school that she had absolutely no grasp of political correctness, and it could be quite amusing sometimes. Unless, of course, she turned her non-PC ways on you and told you your arse looked fat (yes, it had happened – even to some of the men on our team).

Everyone gasped theatrically when they saw me march into the office with what they all knew was faux-confidence.

"Put your feet up, get the popcorn out, it's showtime!" Jason was first to get the ball rolling. Always the people's friend. He was soon drowned out by a cacophony of other voices telling me how completely screwed I was.

They all shut up pretty lively when Isolde threw her office door open and hollered a "*Shuddup!*" at them. If you're thinking our office sounds like a school that should have been closed down by the Department of Education, run by a teacher who should have been given her marching orders a long time ago, then you're really getting the picture of how things worked at the *Vicious Voice*. But it was Isolde's paper, and therefore Isolde's project to run as nastily and as childishly as she wished.

I often wondered how Isolde could be taken out in public. I mean, not just the state of her curtain clothing (as it happened, she had special navy curtains for big events that were marginally less scary – they were like one giant, ankle-length poncho with two holes for her hands to peep out), but because she was so intimidating that people tended to develop a pressing engagement at the bar/in the bathroom/under the table when she was around. But anytime I'd seen her in action, it seemed to work to her advantage. If she wanted information from anyone about rival newspapers, she was so relentless that people eventually gave it to her just to get the hell rid of her. Consequently, she had her finger on the pulse of what was going on pretty much all of the time.

I was almost glad Isolde came out of her office – it saved me having to summon up the courage to knock. When everyone was suitably quiet, she flicked her head at me. It reminded me of the way a snake moves before it attacks. I walked over to her. I was waiting for her to fire some vitriol at me, but instead she just stared. It was far, far worse than anything she could have said.

"Erm . . . Isolde . . . can we go into your office and talk?" I nodded my head at our captive audience, hoping she would take the hint. She didn't. Or, more likely, she did and chose to make me suffer. So we stood there, staring at each other. Someone had to do something, so I eventually dared to move past her into her office and take a seat. Then I rose about fifty feet off it when she slammed the door so hard I was sure I could hear the paperweight on my desk shatter. I hoped it had, actually. It had been a present, but who uses paperweights these days?

I decided to launch straight into it as she made her way behind her desk. "I'm sorry about yesterday, Isolde, but I saw with my own two eyes the event that I wrote about. There's nothing 'alleged' about this – it happened, end of story." Isolde's eyes narrowed. "It's just very . . . frustrating to be blamed for a situation that I didn't make the final decision on. It was an . . . editorial decision to allow that article to be printed."

"'An editorial decision', she says," Isolde muttered slowly. "Are you saying that I'm to blame here?" Before I could answer, she interrupted. "Think very carefully before you answer my question."

All my good, grovelling intentions went out the window. I couldn't help it. There she sat in her curtains, her face a mask of mockery and superiority, threatening me.

I stood up and pointed my finger at her like a policeman accusing a detainee of some heinous crime. "You couldn't be any more to blame if you tried! You encouraged me to write that article. You're the one that decides on what's too risky to print, and what isn't. You're the owner and editor of this paper and you earn the big bucks, so take a bit of responsibility and stop blaming me!"

My finger was still in mid-point when I finished talking. I flopped down on my seat, and wondered how long it would take to sort out a visa for Australia. I would have to start all over again in a city where nobody knew my name, or my bad reputation as a journalist. Actually, it wouldn't be such a bad idea to live in a place where I hadn't displayed my underwear to the nation . . .

"I'll go now and clear my desk," I said wearily.

I stood up to leave, but Isolde slammed her hand on the desk. "*Hoy! Sit!*"

I felt like a dog that had been to obedience training classes as my body jammed itself to the seat.

"Who would have thought you had it in you?" She shook her

head in amazement. "Do you know what sickens me about you lot out there?" She gestured in the direction of the office floor.

"Our drab dress sense?" I smiled, then dropped it immediately as she cut me with a look.

"You're such a pack of sheep that I'm surprised you can hear the telephone ringing over the sound of *baas*. Every one of you came into your interviews, all guns blazing, about to take over the world and all that horseshit talk. Then you get in here, and all I have to do is scream and you're all shitting your pants. Pathetic." She opened a drawer, and I honestly expected her to pull out a naggin of whiskey and start swigging from it, but she only produced a piece of paper. "I have a list here of people I want to interview for the weekend supplement, and I'm trying to decide who to pick for each job. What disgusts me is that I have no confidence that any of you have the balls to ask the hard questions." She threw the piece of paper down onto the table. "You were a goner yesterday until you walked out, you know. I had every intention of firing you until you impressed me by showing a bit of backbone, but then you ruined it by coming in here today acting like a lick-arse wimp with your apology. If you believed you were in the right, you shouldn't be apologising. The second you uttered the word 'Sorry', I was wondering how long it would take me to get your replacement in. But then, I caught a glimpse of what I wanted to see in the people in my team. I hadn't thought it would come from you, mind, but I'm not knocking it." She flicked her eyes dismissively towards the office. "It's a sad state of affairs when *you're* the gutsiest person I have working for me – I didn't see that coming – but I'll have to make the best of a bad situation."

"So . . . does that mean I still have my job?"

"Are you thick? Would I be wasting my time even talking to you if you didn't?"

"Thank you, Isolde, I mean it, this is great –"

"Shuddup!" She waved her hand in front of my face. "Don't make me change my mind."

"Thanks." I stood up. "I'd better head out and start my day's work, then!"

30

"Sit your arse down. I'm not finished."

I edged tentatively onto my seat. What now?

"Your writing is getting stale lately. I want you to work on something new."

"Oh?" This wasn't what I'd expected. I knew the reader feedback about my column was nothing but positive. "Do you want to get rid of my column?"

"No. The column stays. I'm talking about supplementary entertainment articles."

"Oh! Okay!" A smile spread across my face. "Reviews of the latest movies, checking out new restaurants, that kind of thing?"

Isolde smiled at me pityingly. "Riii-ght. How very original. Actually, you needn't tire your little brain out searching for ideas – I've already thought of something I want you to work on."

I held my tongue this time, wondering where this was going.

"I overheard you regaling the sheep with your tales of attempting to hunt down Mr Dreamy in Las Vegas."

I cringed.

"For the first time since I met you, I actually found something you said funny. I mean, who would believe that anyone would be ridiculous enough to do half of the things you said you did? I would have thought that you were making it all up, actually, but I know what you're like, so it must be true."

"Cheers, Isolde." I was starting to feel very nervous.

"What our paper is missing is humour. You all write like dead fish. We need to give our readers a laugh now and again. And more importantly, we need to give them a reason to buy the next edition of the paper. Something that they'll just have to find out the outcome to. Like this Mr Dreamy situation."

Now, I just felt downright scared. "But . . . there was no outcome to it . . . I didn't find him . . ."

"Fine. The public loves a good sob story."

"Yes, but . . ."

"So that's what we'll give them."

"Isolde, this is not a good idea. I'm not doing it. Why would I want to write a column that would make me sound desperate?"

31

"Oh, I don't know. How about – you like your job and you want to keep it?"

"No, Isolde. You're not making me do this. No way." There, I'd let her have it. It was time for my respect.

"But you *are* doing it, and we both know it."

I folded my arms across my chest. "What happened to kudos for my balls?"

"That's the beauty of being the boss. I can change the rules whenever I want. You're doing it, or you can go out there and pack up your desk after all."

As I buried my head in my hands, my mouth emitted a noise that sounded suspiciously like a *baa*.

Chapter Five

Eight Columns Later

The story so far:
Our gossip girl, Andie Appleton, met the man of her dreams in Las Vegas . . . then lost him over the roulette table. Not in a bet, but in a fire evacuation that separated her from someone she couldn't forget. In the final instalment of Looking for Leon, we find out how the story that everyone's been talking about ended . . .

I had thirty minutes.

I wasn't catching our flight until I'd tried one last thing. Okay, so shouting Leon's name into a megaphone while hanging out the window of a taxi going up and down the Strip hadn't worked. The LED billboard with a flashing "*Leon, phone Andie!*" sign and my mobile-phone number under it had only resulted in me getting the kinds of calls for sexual favours that would haunt me for the rest of my life. As for sneaking an "*Andie Thinks Leon Is Out of This World*" banner up to the top of the tallest structure in Las Vegas, the Stratosphere tower, and somehow managing to hang it off the side – well, that had been a big achievement for thirty seconds until the stupid thing had blown away into the desert. So, what could I possibly achieve in thirty minutes?

You'd be surprised.

(Note from Editor: If you knew Andie, you wouldn't. It took her less than ten minutes to burn an entire building to the ground once. But that's another story for another day.)

Thanks a lot, Isolde. Typical. Drag the arse out of it, why don't you? And I hadn't burnt a *building* down – it had just been our family home! She made it sound like I'd razed Trump Towers to the ground!

When I say "just our family home", I just mean "just" in terms of scale. Needless to say, the *'Four-Year-Old Burns Family Home to the Ground'* incident was somewhat of a big deal for my family at the time. But what had my parents expected, confiscating my toys for being bold and then leaving a box of matches lying around the place? One good thing did come of it though – both my parents gave up smoking afterwards. This was back in the day before the anti-smoking campaigns and the *'Smoking Kills'* stickers on packets of fags, when people could almost convince themselves that smoking was good for them when they had enough jars of porter in them, so it was quite an achievement on my part. Or maybe it was because my parents couldn't afford the smokes any more with the cost of a new house hanging around their necks, who knows?

Anyway . . .

After my stunts, I waited patiently for the call from LVTV, the Las Vegas TV station, to ask me what I was up to. But believe it or not, it didn't come – some lunatic from Utah who had a hate campaign going on against Elvis impersonators had escaped his asylum and attempted to shoot someone, so the TV crew was a bit busy that day.

Time was running out, and I had no time left to organise anything else – my friend had already abandoned me to my madness and made for the airport (having done all my packing for me, I hasten to add). But then, as I checked out of the hotel, I heard two of the receptionists talking about a TV interview that was going to be filmed in the lobby with a young singer who was staying there. He was getting big enough to merit an interview, but not so big that any guests in the lobby would pay a blind bit of notice, in a city that was host to more stars than the sky.

When the interview started, my suitcases and I were hovering in the background waiting for our opportunity. My plan was to jump in at the end of the interview, say my bit, and hope that the channel would see it as a quirky little incident that was funny enough to televise. If I jumped in during the interview, they'd only scrap my segment for stealing the singer's thunder. A well-thought-out plan by anyone's standards, wouldn't you say?

When it comes to never working with children or animals, scrap that. Never work with hungover, high young singers with a dose of the stutters. The idiot boy messed up one interview after the other, and I could almost feel the sand in my half-hourglass pouring over me as it seeped away. Twenty . . . fifteen . . . ten . . . five minutes left. I absolutely couldn't leave it any longer to get a taxi without missing the flight. And then, the miracle finally happened – the singer (I won't even bother telling you his name – trust me, he won't be around for long) managed to string a few sentences together. I waited until the presenter, Lindy, with huge relief in her voice, started on her "And that was Josh Feather (oops, so much for protecting his identity), the hottest young thing on the block at the moment" line, then abandoned my suitcases and literally leapt in front of the camera to reel off my own line.

"Hi, I'm Andie, I'm Irish, and I'm not mad, honest – not that Irish people are mad, you understand – I'm just looking for a man called Leon – not any old man called Leon, mind – no, my Leon is the loveliest guy from Arizona, and he's here on holiday at the moment – vacation, I should say . . ." I looked over at the presenter. "Actually, can I start again? This isn't going too well."

You'd think the security people in hotels would keep their strength for the high rollers who try to high-tail it out of the casinos with a big wad of cash, wouldn't you? You'd certainly never think they'd use it to wrestle a skinny woman to the ground. Yes – *they*! Not one, not two, but a rugby team of beefy security guys. They all looked so excited to actually have something to do that they attacked me like a starving dog devouring a fillet steak. We fell as a scrum on top of my neatly packed suitcases (my friend would have been disgusted to have seen all her good work go to waste). Clothes were squashed out, bottles burst and squirted all over the legs of passers-by, knickers landed on shoes, the whole hog.

I battled my way out of the scrum, and stuck my face in front of the camera again. "Leon, call me!" I rattled off my mobile number. I looked at my watch, which had miraculously survived the rugby. Minus four minutes. If I stopped to fix up my suitcases, I'd be singing on the street to drum up a new fare home. I grabbed my hand-luggage, made a run for it out the front door and practically leapt in front of a passing taxi.

Now, once I was safely on the plane (yes, I miraculously made it), I was thinking to myself that surely they'd show that footage, embarrassing and all as it was. First of all, there was no way they were going to go to the hassle of getting Mr Monotone to do yet another interview, and secondly, who wouldn't want to broadcast a lunatic making a show of herself? So the minute I got home, I logged onto the Internet and scoured LVTV's website to see what they'd broadcast on the TV.

Nothing.

I couldn't believe it. I found the interview they'd shown with the world's most boring singer alright, but they had cut out everything with me in it and reshot the end. What was wrong with them? Didn't they want any viewers?

And that, my friends, is where the story grinds to a horrible halt. I know nothing about Leon, except that he's Leon from Arizona. All I know is that if I don't meet a decent guy between now and a year's time, I'll be going back to Vegas on the same day next year.

Who knows, he might just be back . . .

"Andie! Your arse, my office, now!"

"I've been to more sophisticated marts than this place," Trevor muttered as I speed-walked towards Isolde's office after being summoned. Isolde's manner really grated on him. He was openly on the lookout for another job, supposedly because he couldn't stand working with someone as uncouth as Isolde, but we all knew it was down to his fear of her. Every time she called him, he jumped ten feet off his seat, and his heart couldn't take the strain of it all any more. He wouldn't live to see thirty at this rate.

Thankfully, I was feeling a lot less nervous than Trevor. I'd delivered the *Looking for Leon* series and, so far, it seemed that the public had taken to it. I wasn't sure what Isolde wanted to give out to me about now but, whatever it was, I was going to use the response on the column as leverage to get her to back off.

If people had previously suspected that I was a bit . . . eccentric, they now had their proof. Isolde had the memory of an elephant, and anytime I submitted a column in the series to her with my more embarrassing stunts left out, she reminded me of things I'd said to the team that hadn't made it into the article. I had to hand it to her – she had the art of punishment down to a tee. I'd never get another job now that I was known as someone who caused brawls in hotel lobbies. And I thought I was a laughing stock after the balaclava incident! I was expecting the police to show up at work to take my mugshots any minute.

I plonked myself in front of Isolde, waiting for the onslaught.

"I called you in here to tell you to put a bit of make-up on." She narrowed her eyes and peered at me. "For a former model, you don't make much of an effort, do you?"

I stared back. This was taking things too far. "You called me in here to tell me I look like crap, is that it?"

"Have you got voices in your head? I never said that, although you don't look great today, now that you mention it. You know, I'm glad you didn't catch up with Leon with that attitude; you'd have his heart broken. No, I said to put on make-up. We have your old Éire TV chums coming in here in about half an hour to do an interview with you about the column. See, I'm doing you a favour – you don't want to go on TV with a face the colour of chalk. Although it might fit in well with your new haunted, heartbroken persona, actually."

"What? Why do they want to do a report on the column?"

She pulled out a sheet of paper and handed it to me. It was circulation figures for the paper for the past few weeks. The sales of our paper had increased after the first column went out, and grew larger with each new column, which was published every second day.

"That's why. This column of yours has touched something in the public. I told you – people love a good sob story."

"But what do they want from me in this interview? I don't have anything new to say about it all. I didn't find him, end of story."

"Then repeat what you've already said. Just answer their questions. You're a journalist – supposedly – so you don't need me to tell you how this works." She looked at her watch. "Go get your face on."

I would have stayed and argued, but I knew I looked so tired that I needed every minute of that make-up time. This was disorientating. I was delighted that the column had been successful, but it had been hard to relive the whole thing again. It was one thing telling the funny stories to the lads in the office, but when I'd sat down to write the column, all I could think about was how strong the connection between Leon and me had been. And once I'd opened myself up to feeling it all over again, I felt worse than ever about it. I'd done my best to find him, it hadn't worked, and there was no way I'd find him now that I was back in Ireland. I just wanted to leave it behind me now and move on.

I cobbled together a presentable image from the mismatched make-up lying in the bottom of my handbag. When I returned to the office, I heard a loud, self-important voice booming orders. The TV crew had arrived, and there was Isolde in the middle of it all, dictating proceedings. The crew didn't have a second to get a word in, a situation they were clearly unhappy about, but were powerless to change.

Within seconds, I had been whisked off to a room in the office that we never used, and the cameraman, who I recognised from the TV station's canteen but didn't know personally, stuck his equipment in my face without introducing himself. I was used to the drill from my previous career incarnation, but right then I was in no mood for it.

"I'm Andie, by the way," I said pointedly as I swivelled my head around the side of the camera currently obscuring my vision. "And you are?"

"Colm Cannon," he said, glancing at me briefly before peering through the camera and adjusting it.

I instantly sniggered. "Nice try," I said. "Do many people fall for that?"

"For what?"

"Your fake surname. Colm Cannon the Cameraman. It has a ring to it, I suppose."

He frowned. "Cannon *is* my surname. Any camera-brand associations are purely coincidental."

"Sure. I believe you, Colm Cannon." I expected him to laugh politely, but instead he started fluttering his hands in a very disconcerting manner.

"Move," he eventually said. "I need all of you in front of the camera. I can't just film your chest, and that's all that I can see through the lens at the moment."

"My *chest*?"

"Your . . . torso, I mean. Upper body, whatever. Just stick your head back in, will you?"

I was about to stick my fingers into the camera instead of my head when a pretty girl approached us and introduced herself as Becky, my interviewer. She began to fill me in on how they planned to use our interview. I was happy to finally get some details, as Isolde had told me nothing. The station had recently launched a weekly half-hour programme reviewing quirky stories of the week, and apparently my story constituted one of those. Irish stories were favoured, but they used worldwide stories if they were short on Irish ones. And guess what, they'd had a slow week for Irish stories, so mine was going to be the headline act. Brilliant. I thought about running out of the room – but I knew that action would cost me my job. Isolde definitely wasn't going to take any more rebellion from me, so I decided to stay put. I was already the talk of the town, so what was another bit of mortification? No point in being mortified *and* fired.

The interview started tamely enough. Becky asked me to explain how I had met Leon, and to tell her about some of the escapades I'd been through hunting him down. We'd been talking for about ten minutes, and I was sure they must have everything they needed by now – even the longest segment on a half-hour show wouldn't exceed ten minutes. I started shuffling in my seat to give them the hint that I'd had enough.

"Okay, Andie, that's great. Before we finish, let me ask you one last question." She cocked her head sideways as the camera focused on her. "Just what was it about this guy that made him so special?"

The camera panned back to me. "Leon was . . ." I took a deep breath. It was hard to summarise everything that Leon was into a five-second soundbite. "Leon was my spirit in another person. We were two halves of the same entity." Christ, talk about melodramatic. Where had that come from? Maybe Isolde was right about the voice in my head . . .

And to my absolute horror, tears that I hadn't known were on the way started bubbling over the rims of my eyes. Becky looked dismayed and excited in equal measure, sensing that her story had just become a lot juicier but not quite sure how to handle the situation either. I gasped for air in an attempt to regulate my breathing, but ended up just catching my breath and sounding like I was about to choke on emotion. Something gave me the impression that my slot might just exceed ten minutes after all.

40

While all this was going on, Canteen Cameraman was hovering over me and getting closer and closer – and either he was unskilled or very cruel, because instead of using his zoom, he literally shoved the blasted camera onto my upper lip. The camera was the final straw in a day that refused to get any better. I shoved him out of my way (secretly hoping I might "accidentally" knock the camera to the ground and shatter it, so that the interview would never see the light of day), and raced out of the room and back to my desk. The sense of déjà vu was palpable as I grabbed my coat and handbag and ran out of the office with everyone staring at a blubbing me – only, this time, I had given them even more to stare at. They'd wear their tongues out talking about me. Thankfully, it was only five minutes away from our knocking-off time, so Isolde couldn't give me any hassle about leaving early. The fact that she could viably give me hassle about running out of an interview bawling was something my mind chose to gloss over. Things were bad enough without having to face yet another slice of reality.

Isn't it funny how the best-case scenario never works out? I visualised how the interview might look when it was transmitted and in my mind it wasn't too bad. You always saw interviews with people on the news pussing about this, that and the other. As usual, I had probably exaggerated the scale of the problem in my head.

I couldn't have imagined the worst-case scenario in my wildest dreams. We'd done the interview on a Wednesday, and it was due to be broadcast on the following Sunday. So imagine my surprise, and sheer distress, when I was greeted with the sight of my blotchy, mascara-streaked face during the ad break of *Corrie* on Friday. I'd been reading a magazine and ignoring the ads, when I suddenly heard the sound of my own voice. My *sobbing* voice. And then, *"It's the story everyone's talking about – and we've got the interview. Andie Appleton pours her heart out to us about her lost love on Sunday at five thirty."* I hadn't time to put down the magazine before the phone started ringing. I put it on silent, and ran straight to the drinks cabinet.

When *Corrie* finished, the ad came on again. And during the show after that. And during the nightly news. I got a duvet and sat in front of the TV with a bottle of Bacardi and two-litres of Coke, watching the whole thing unfold in the way that you would stay up all night waiting for the result of a presidential election. Every time the ad was shown, I poured a drink and knocked it back in one go. I lost count after seven drinks.

Never in my life was I so happy to pass out into oblivion.

Chapter Six

Three days later

The show had been broadcast the night before, but I'd refused to watch it. Mount Everest wouldn't have been large enough for me to hide behind and cringe, so I went out for a run while the show was on. I ran so hard and for so long that I was in terrible pain for the rest of the evening, which was great. It even took my mind off the whole thing for about five minutes at one stage. I had a bath and went to bed immediately afterwards, with my mobile turned off.

I was the first one into the office the next morning, which was hardly surprising after going to bed at half nine and waking up at half five.

Laura was next to land in.

"*Don't*," I said as she opened her mouth. "I don't want to know about it. Just say nothing."

"I was only going to say hello," she said, somewhat put out.

I didn't believe it for a second.

I went through this rigmarole with all the others when they came in too. Everyone wanted to talk to me just so that they could go home tonight and say they had. "Yeah, poor Andie, she's so embarrassed about the whole thing, *blah blah blah*!" We live in a world where everybody wants to be the first to have the fresh news, the one who knows everything about everything before anybody else, and nobody more so than journalists. Every single one of them bar Jason did a Laura and pretended they were only going to pass pleasantries.

"I can slag you now or slag you later, Appleton," Jason said. "You're only postponing the inevitable."

It was true for him. I couldn't bury my head in the sand forever – I had a meeting with Isolde that morning, and she was sure to bring the whole thing up in great detail. Still, I could try to avoid reality for as long as possible.

Isolde had other ideas.

"I'm bringing our meeting forward, come in now" flashed up as an instant message on my screen. This really bloody irritated me. She never even considered that I might be in the middle of something else. Everything was now, now, now when she wanted it to be now, now, now. And the cheeky cow couldn't even be bothered to get up off her seat and yell out the door for me any more – I was only worth an instant message that took two seconds of her time.

However, now (or even now, now, now) wasn't the time to point out those home truths. Not only was I still skating on thin ice, but I had no fight in me. Whenever I had entered Isolde's office recently, I'd seemed to slump down further in the seat each time.

I tried to gauge her mood. Hmm. She had the inscrutable face on today. This task was usually much easier, as she was just plain grumpy-looking most of the time.

"Do you have any idea what you've just done?" Her voice was low and, to my ears, menacing.

I decided to launch an appeasement bombardment. "I know, I know. I shouldn't have run out of the interview, and you've been good enough not to mention it before now – but it just got too much for me. If you'd have been in my position, you'd have done the same – well, maybe not, but you never know, you might."

She shook her head and looked at me with what I can only describe as a mixture of incredulity and contempt. "Every time I credit you with just the smallest amount of intelligence, you prove me wrong. You've missed the point entirely." She threw herself back in her seat

44

and swivelled. "You couldn't have dragged the arse out of this story any better if you'd planned that little bawling fit – which I presume you didn't. You're a right soft git, we all know that. And thanks to your little TV appearance, my phone hasn't stopped hopping since the broadcast last night."

I was taken aback. "Well, I'm glad to hear that . . . but does it really make any difference? The story has run its course, Isolde. There's nowhere else I can go with it."

Isolde grinned, a sly, knowing grin that spread all over her face. She should really have smiled more often – it made her look younger, less embittered.

"Oh, you're going somewhere alright." She grinned some more. "As you know, we like to maintain healthy professional relationships with our colleagues and friends in the media."

I frowned. She caught my look, threw her head back and cackled so coarsely it actually made her cough.

"I should have known I wouldn't get away with saying that crock of shit, even to you. Let me rephrase. Everyone knows that if you get a good opportunity, you grab it. And we've been offered an opportunity that will benefit an interested third party, you, and most importantly, the paper. As you of all people know, Éire TV are trying their damndest to get one over on the rival TV station. They need a big story to make people tune into their daily news show instead of the competition's. They had such a big response to the ad they showed of you being a sooky babby over Leon in advance of the show that they've come up with an idea, and they're sure they're onto a winner."

She reached into her sack of a handbag dramatically, almost theatrically. It would have been amusing to see her so animated if it was a different situation, but I was too busy being apprehensive to enjoy the moment.

"The public don't want this story to end. Everyone enjoyed the sheer embarrassment of your madcap antics when you were looking for Leon, and now they want to see new ones for themselves." She threw what she had fished out of her sack on the desk. It was an airline ticket. "Pack your suitcase. You're going back to Vegas to find Leon."

"*What?*"

"Don't even bother arguing. You know and I know that you'll do what I want you to in the end, so let's not waste our morning talking rings around it."

"But it didn't work out last time!"

"Last time, you had one day to make a few half-arsed attempts to find him. This time, you have a crew from Éire TV who are very good at liaising with other TV stations. They'll get you whatever local coverage you need. Just don't do anything too effective too soon. We want to drag the story out for a while."

"But . . . for how long? And how can you afford to give me the time off?"

"Time off? Are you crazy? You'll be sending me back a 1,000-word update every day for the paper, plus working on some of your other regular duties. We'll keep you over there for as long as there's still an appetite for the story. You'll need to make sure whatever you do to find him is zany and off-the-wall, but it's you, so that won't be a problem. And this time, give us a happy ending. We've got as much mileage as we could get out of the sob story, so it's time to change tactics."

"And what if there isn't a happy ending?"

"Andie, I'm going to say this to you once, and only once." She pulled her castor-seat over beside me using her feet to drag herself. She wasn't one for physical proximity usually. Was she going to impart some serious words of wisdom to me or what?

She leaned her head forward to whisper in my ear. "If you ever want to get another job in this country, you'll find the fucker."

There was no arguing with that. I was on the plane the next morning.

Chapter Seven

It was always the same dream.

She takes the shortcut. Safety is the last thing on her mind after what's just happened. All she wants is to get home, to get away from the place where everything fell apart. The distant sounds of the traffic whizzing past on the road behind the trees don't reach her ears. The memory of what she's just seen drowns out all of her senses.

When he grabs her, she's too shocked to even scream at first. By the time her brain kicks into action, it's too late. His hand is now over her mouth, tighter than a vice. His free arm is around her body. She feels like fresh tar has been poured all over her as she struggles like a newborn kitten would against an Alsatian attack.

By the time she gets the opportunity to scream, she's aware that it's too late. And now, she knows the answer to the age-old question of whether or not a tree falling in the woods makes a sound if no-one is there to hear it . . .

"Andie!"

I awoke with a jerk to see Colm's face hovering over mine. It made a change from his camera, but still not a welcome one.

"You were doing an odd little strangled-screaming type of thing in your sleep."

I put a hand on his chest and heaved him away. Personal-Space Invaders polled top of my list of pet hates, so I felt that a heave was appropriate in this instance. "I'm fine, I'm fine," I spluttered in a clearly-not-fine fashion. I was mortified. The dream usually happened at home. Just my luck for this to happen in a place where there was no escape for another – I glanced at my watch – six hours.

In a bid to save as much money as possible, the tight-fisted travel department in Éire TV had put two stopovers in our itinerary. We had to fly from Dublin to Heathrow, Heathrow to Atlanta, then Atlanta to Vegas. I had kicked up blue murder about it in the hope that they could somehow change the itinerary to have just one stopover, but it seemed that there really were no more direct flights left at such short notice. I still didn't buy it, but I hadn't time to go searching for cheaper flights myself with everything happening so fast. We were now on the Heathrow to Atlanta leg, the Dublin to Heathrow flight having mercifully passed in the blink of an eye. I'd been hoping I'd be able to sleep this one away, but my subconscious – and Colm – seemed to have other ideas.

"What?" I snapped at Colm, who was looking at me as if he expected an explanation. Possibly a reasonable expectation, but that didn't mean it was going to happen. I yanked the in-flight magazine out of the storage area in the seat in front of me, and buried my head in an article about rugby, a game I had minus-zero interest in. I could see out of the corner of my eye that Colm was still gawking at me, so I did what any mature woman would do in these circumstances and turned my back to him. I'd only known him a few hours, but Colm was already starting to get to me. I got the impression that he thought he owned all the space around him in a ten-mile radius. Have you ever met anyone who could smell like a month's worth of BO, or be going around with a runny nose or something, but they still wouldn't have a bit of shame about going up to the president of the country and sitting on her lap? He was one of those types. He didn't have BO, a snotty nose or a penchant for lap-perching (that I knew of, anyway), but it was the same principle. His personality apparently made him good at his job, or so I'd heard from an ex-colleague, but I couldn't share much enthusiasm about that either after the nasal-zoom incident. He was known to be fearless in his work, and I wondered briefly if Isolde had ever had a love child that she'd left on a doorstep thirty-odd years ago. Colm didn't look anything like Isolde though, thankfully. He had more of a . . . rusty look about him. He wasn't quite ginger, but he had a good schlep of red running through his otherwise brown hair. He also always seemed to have a few days of facial hair hanging around, but he got away with it because he was really tall and broad and it just fit in with his look somehow. That and the fact that he looked like someone who'd rip your head off if you dared to mention it.

I was forced to turn around when the air stewardesses came around with the in-flight drinks – there was no way I was letting that opportunity go.

Colm gave me what could only be described as a knowing smile when I ordered a white wine.

"Aren't you having one yourself?"

He shook his head. "I don't drink."

"Well, aren't you a good boy." I turned my back on him again, my precious alcohol secured in my grasp.

I had just taken my first relaxing sip of chardonnay when Colm piped up.

"So, you're a big rugby fan, then." The look he gave me after he said it was the observational equivalent of the world's loudest, most contemptuous guffaw into a loudspeaker.

"Yes." I adopted a brazen expression. "Why so surprised?"

"I didn't think *Glitter*-heads and rugby were good bedfellows."

"So, you think I could only possibly be interested in one thing?" Feck. That sounded really dodgy. "I mean, that I couldn't like sport because I am an entertainment correspondent?"

"I just thought soccer would be more your thing."

The *bastard*. I'd managed not to think about the Graham-and-the-married-woman incident for a long while, but now I was getting cream-pied in the face with it. And why? I didn't even know Colm – what did he have against me? Or maybe he was like this with everyone? The fact that Graham's betrayal squeeze had been a high-profile millionaire's wife meant that it had been big news at the time, so I wasn't surprised that Colm was aware of it – the surprise was that he would be so nasty as to use it against me.

I had to cut this kind of thing off at the pass – especially as I was going to be stuck in his company for the next few weeks, so I decided to go into psycho mode. I usually reserved it for after a feed of pints, but needs must. I had to go for the jugular with this guy to keep him out of my face. I did a bit of personal-body-space invasion myself before going in for the kill.

"If you have something to say to me, have the guts to say it straight out instead of inferring it," I said in a low, scratchy voice. I was quite pleased with it. That should do the trick.

He did this fake-surprise-look thing that made me want to leather him. "Calm down, Andie. I'm only making polite conversation. It's what colleagues do when they're stuck on a plane together. You should try it."

"And *you* need to learn some basic manners and re*spect*!" Okay, slightly OTT and game-show-contestant-esque, I'll admit. Heads all around us swivelled in my direction. I was half-expecting them to start chanting '*Jer-ry, Jer-ry, Jer-ry!*'. Colm had regained his composure and was now the picture of nonchalance, and looking at me as if I was crazy.

I cursed Amanda from Éire TV and her clumsiness. Isolde had signed us up for four half-hour episodes of the *Looking for Leon* documentary, with an option to extend the number of episodes on a rolling-contract basis if public interest in the story was still high after the fourth episode, and Amanda was originally supposed to have accompanied Colm and me on this trip as a storyboarder and editor for the show's footage. That was all well and good, until she broke her ankle in a supermarket. She'd seen a half-price offer advertised on the supermarket's own-brand breakfast cereal but, when she went in, all of the cheap cereal was on the top shelf, with the expensive brands layering the shelves that she could actually reach – and, of course, there wasn't a member of staff to be seen, or a random tall person for that matter. She got it into her head that the offer of cheap cereal was just a ploy to get people in and get them spending, because when most people had the more enticing, tastier brands within their reach, they wouldn't bother going to the effort of getting someone to take down the cheap cereal from the top shelf. But not our Amanda. In a fit of pique at the supermarket's cheek, she swept her arm across a row of Chocolate Swirl cereal to knock them off the shelf, then stacked them on top of each other in a makeshift set of stairs so that she could reach the top shelf. She'd just clasped hands on the cereal she wanted when a member of staff turned a corner, saw her and cried out *"Hey! Be careful, for the love of God!"* The voice startled Amanda. She lost her balance and toppled over, landing on her ankle. She said her leg and ankle looked just like a boomerang, that's how badly she broke it, and the staff member promptly puked all over the expensive boxes of Chocolate Swirl when she saw the ankle hanging uselessly to the side. Amanda never did get to buy her cheap cereal. I sent a curse up for her meanness too – we're talking about a saving of about seventy cents here.

The end result was that Éire TV had tasked me with the storyboarding, and Colm would do the editing. I wasn't tickled pink about this – I'd used up most of my tracking-down ideas the last time I was in Vegas, and I could have done with a pair of fresh eyes looking at the situation – which had been exactly Amanda's argument when she'd persuaded Éire TV to let her go on this junket. After all, the editing could easily have been done at home when Colm sent the footage through, but "You need to be in the thick of the action to storyboard effectively," according to Amanda. Realistically, she just wanted to live off expenses for a few weeks and save her wages, but she'd somehow managed to convince Éire TV to let her come. She used to reef the tea, coffee, biscuit and stationery supplies so much on a day-to-day basis that it probably amounted to the same cost to send her away anyway. But now that she'd cocked the whole thing up by getting injured, I'd really have to start thinking. I had a feeling that with an attitude like his, Colm wouldn't be much use to brainstorm with. Plus, he'd mentioned in the queue to board the flight that he worked as a project manager as well as a cameraman, and he was expected to keep things going remotely from a different timezone, so I had a feeling he wouldn't have a spare minute to help me even if he did have the inclination. I was essentially on my own. So much for the liaising Éire TV crew that Isolde had been on about.

Still, it would all be worth it if I found Leon. Okay, so that was a big 'if' . . . but even though it felt like Isolde was chucking me out of a plane without a parachute, at least I was doing something about the situation now instead of sitting around feeling pissed off about it. Guys like Leon were never on their own for long, and if I didn't act quickly, he'd be snapped up by another woman in no time. All I had to do now was work out how to find him in a country with a population of more than three hundred and ten million people before it was too late. Easy peasy.

"Beef or chicken?" The air stewardess was back.

"Chicken," Colm and I said in unison.

She buried her head in her trolley, then looked up with regret on her face. "I'm afraid I have only one chicken left."

"Did he say chicken? He meant beef." I patted Colm's head in what I hoped looked like an affectionate gesture. "He's been mixing up his words ever since he had a blow to his head a few years ago," I stage-whispered loudly. Out of the corner of my eye, I saw Colm throw me such a vicious look that I was actually a bit scared, but it was too late to stop now.

Believe me when I say that I would give the shirt off my back to absolutely anyone who passed me on the street who happened to be shirtless. It never happens – everyone seems to be in possession of shirts these days – but if it did, I would. But I was not giving that chicken to Colm Cannon. Not after that dig about Graham. I was ready for a fight, and I'd show him. I'd –

Colm cut across my thoughts. "I'll take the beef. I wouldn't want any of your passengers getting injured by the toys that'd be thrown out of the handbag if this one doesn't get her way."

The air stewardess giggled dutifully, then stopped when I gave her a look.

I'd won – well, I'd won the chicken, even if I had been insulted in the process – but I felt strangely deflated. He hadn't given me the fight I was all geared up for, which left me feeling like a bit of a fool. Of course, the chicken was vile. I had to fight the vomit down as I tucked into a medley of chicken and watery cabbage – always a popular combination. And for someone who hadn't wanted beef in the first place, Colm looked like he was quite enjoying his meal. And then, when he finished it, he fished into a ridiculous rucksack type of effort that he'd brought on as hand luggage, and pulled out some biscuits wrapped in tin foil. They looked distinctly like Mariettas, which I thought nobody ate any more unless they were over ninety. I took the opportunity to write my daily diary entry while he was distracted – I was convinced he'd be poking his nose into it to see what I was writing otherwise. No doubt there'd be some snide comment from him at some stage on this trip about how nobody kept diaries any more, but he managed to hold his tongue while it was wrapped around the Mariettas.

My diary entry for the day complete – and filled with complaints about nosey people who think they're God's gift – I turned my thoughts to work.

The night before my flight to Vegas, Isolde had called me while I was doing my packing. I took the call, even though it was outside work hours and I was up to my eyes in things to do, seeing as I had a last-minute transatlantic tenure to prepare for. Ignoring the call was never going to be an option.

"I've been thinking about the best way for you to write the column."

Heaven forbid that I might use a bit of originality and write it my own way . . .

"Now, I know you're not good with complex notions, so I'll make it easy for you and sum it up in one word. Cheese."

"Cheese. There are many different types of cheese, Isolde. Would you care to elaborate?"

"Types don't matter. That column just needs cheese, and lots of it. If your previous columns are anything to go by, you'll have no problem with that. Just ham it up a bit."

Ham and cheese now. I pursed my lips. "The *Vicious Voice* isn't exactly known for its cheese factor . . . I'm not sure how well throwing a block of cheddar into the mix every week will go down –"

"The fact that we have an entertainment column at all *is* cheese. *You* are the cheese in my paper. Didn't you know that already?"

I decided not to dignify that with a response.

"I'd prefer it if we didn't need to go near that stuff at all," Isolde continued, "but we do, and there's one very important reason why. Sales. A paper needs diversity in subject matter to appeal to as wide an audience as possible. As you know by now – although it's hard to tell sometimes with some of the rubbish you submit – I pride myself on maintaining the highest of writing standards in the *Vicious Voice*, and only letting the best writers work for me. But the reality is that there's no point in producing breathtaking writing if nobody is reading it. Popular entertainment and social-scene updates may be things I abhor, but articles about them bring the readers in. And everyone who buys the paper for entertainment news then also has access to our more high-quality editorial, so we're bringing our best work to a wider audience who might not otherwise have chosen our paper."

"Charming."

Isolde thought she was so high-brow, with her classical music CDs scattered all over her desk and a copy of whatever was the latest Booker Prize winner tucked under her arm as she walked out to lunch (or actually in her hand – she was one of those people who read books as they walked, the types who trampled on pets and young children and kept going without so much as a backwards glance). But I would bet anything that she went on furtive weekly expeditions into a supermarket where nobody knew her, and filled her trolley with copies of all of the latest gossip magazines.

"Charming, my arse. We all know you don't do the hard-hitting stuff well. Leave that to Jason. You worry about the fluff – it's what I pay you for. I want that column to convey lovesickness and romance – all that crap. That's what people want, and a good love saga is what'll bring the new readers in. Make sure you don't go overboard either, though. No '*Dear John*' type of columns. Get the balance right between cheese and not making a disgrace of yourself and the paper with bad writing."

'Here's a great idea – how about you just write the damn column for me altogether?' That was what I wanted to say. What I actually said was "Right. Okay." I would have agreed to write the next *War and Peace* if it meant I'd get off the phone. I'd had more than enough of this conversation.

The journey seemed to take forever. Thankfully, Colm had pulled out his laptop after the meal, and had buried his head in it for the rest of the Heathrow to Atlanta leg of the trip.

When we eventually arrived in Atlanta, we were due to have a two-hour stopover – but no sooner had I bagged a seat in the waiting area for the Vegas flight (having 'lost' Colm somewhere in the airport) than a big *Delayed* sign was projected into the boarding area. An announcement had been made that the flight would be at least an hour delayed due to T-storms in Vegas (thunderstorms to you and me), but that hour crept into two, three, four, five, until eventually we boarded six hours behind schedule. There was one small positive, which was that when Colm had made his way to the boarding area, there were no seats left and he'd had to slump against a wall far away from me to while away the hours – but it was scant solace as I tried to sleep while a middle-aged man's head continually dipped onto my shoulder.

Although I was seated beside Colm again for the Atlanta to Vegas leg of the journey, I managed to lose myself in the latest book from Daniel Larch, my favourite author, while Colm slept through most of the flight. Daniel Larch's fantasy novels were ostensibly for teenagers, but were a huge hit with adults all over the world too. I always felt a little better when I could escape into the magical worlds he created – and this was definitely a time when I needed a temporary escape.

There was a collective and unrehearsed whoop of delight when we eventually landed in McCarran airport. I'd felt a little thrill of anticipation as I looked out the window of the plane at the lights of the Strip. Okay, so I had my doubts about how effective this trip was going to be in finding Leon, but it was still a million times better being here than in Dublin where I had nothing to look forward to, annoying-Colm-presence or no annoying-Colm-presence.

I had to revise that line of thought when, a full hour later, Colm and I were filling in forms to have our lost luggage sent to our hotels in the eventuality that it might miraculously be found. At least in Dublin I had clean clothes. And as if not having our luggage wasn't bad enough, Colm seemed to have no grasp of the severity of the situation. As more and more people from our flight had sauntered away with their bags and suitcases, I'd become more convinced that ours wasn't coming through – but instead of getting upset about that like a normal person, Colm stayed infuriatingly calm. In fact, the more agitated I got, the less he seemed to care about his luggage. I could have sworn he was doing it just to annoy me.

The fact that, despite Daniel Larch, I was still shaken up after the dream wasn't helping matters either. If only Leon were here, he'd know exactly the right thing to say to make things better, just like he had in Vegas. I thought about how he'd reacted when I told him about all the stuff in my past . . .

"It sounds to me like you've been carrying a heavy load around with you for a very long time," he'd said when I wrapped things up after a good half an hour of non-stop talking.

"Well, it's nobody's fault but mine that I'm carrying it," I said. "If I hadn't done what I did –"

"No, Andie. Stop right there. I haven't known you for very long, but I already know that you're a good person. Sometimes, bad things happen to good people. When they do, we have to give ourselves a break."

"But I can't, Leon, not after what I did."

"Yes, you can. You need to forgive yourself. The only person who can give you absolution now is you. From what you've told me, I think that's something you've deserved for a very long time."

I shook my head.

He took my hands in his. "Please, Andie, just let it go. Don't let this eat you up and destroy you."

I shrugged. "It's too late. It already has."

"It's never too late to make a fresh start. Don't deny the world everything that you have to give. You're far too special for that."

He smiled, and suddenly I felt that I could conquer anything if I had him by my side . . .

"If you could just fill this in, Madam . . ."

The voice of the lady behind the lost-luggage desk brought me back to reality. I sighed, but took the pen to fill up the forms with a renewed vigour. If filling up a book's worth of forms brought me a step closer to Leon, then so be it. The pain of this journey, and the company, just might be all worth it.

Chapter Eight

An hour later, we grabbed a taxi and made our way to the hotel with our hands numb from all the form-filling. It was one I hadn't heard of, a low-budget hotel on the outskirts of the downtown area called Topple Town. I didn't expect much from it, and just prayed it wouldn't live up to my expectations.

The exterior of the hotel did nothing to allay my fears. The entire building looked like it was crumbling in upon itself. The top floors of the hotel seemed to hang significantly over the entrance, and the windows were positioned further and further to the left the higher up you looked. The hotel looked as if it had been built on quicksand that had been unsuccessfully cemented over. I swallowed, and prayed that my room would be on one of the lower floors. But even more worryingly, the hotel was practically located in the desert. It stood on its own on a dark street off Las Vegas Boulevard, with not another amenity of any type in sight, even a brothel. I flipped my head around to get my bearings. The reassuring lights of downtown were right behind me, and yet miles away on foot. It was the kind of hotel you'd only stay in if you were leaving the city the next day and wanted to avoid traffic in the morning – there seemed to be absolutely no other reason for this place to exist at all.

Colm strode off into the hotel as soon as he'd paid the taxi driver, so I followed. It wasn't the kind of street you hung out in on your own. Even the taxi driver looked relieved to be getting out of the vicinity – he was probably expecting his hubcaps to be ripped off if he stayed parked for long enough.

Despite seeing all the lights of the Strip and being dazzled by the slot machines as we walked through McCarran Airport, the lobby was a shock to the system. It was decorated in pure, unadulterated seventies-style garb, and was so bright as to be almost fluorescent. The walls were covered in orange wallpaper with a dreadful blue swirly design that burned your retinas if you looked at it too long. The desk was far bigger than it needed to be, and yet it was overcrowded with what looked like thirty years' worth of guest paperwork. The wood of the desk was missing chunks at intervals around the edges, as if it had been hacked by a chainsaw, and the resulting effect would frighten young children if this had been a family-friendly hotel – I could swear there were carvings of tortured faces in it when I looked for long enough. And the carpet – oh my God, the carpet. Twirls met whirls and waves met swirls, all in a regurgitated Shepherd's Pie colour. A few random slot machines were dotted around the lobby in a haphazard manner.

I looked around, expecting to see *A Clockwork Orange* or *Fear And Loathing In Las Vegas* playing on an ancient VCR somewhere – or were VCRs even invented back then? Everything looked so ancient that you could only assume that the hotel wasn't just going for some seventies chic look, but genuinely hadn't been decorated for several decades.

Colm seemed as if he was drinking in every inch of the place, though. He was gazing around the joint with a huge smile on his face, and the thought flashed through my mind that it was the first time I had ever seen him smile an authentic smile. It suited him to not look like a miserable bastard for a change, even if it was only for a few seconds.

In contrast to everything ancient, the guy working behind the desk looked about twelve. He barely glanced up when we landed in the lobby, so I eventually had to park my head on the twisted wood of the desk and stare him out of it.

"Yeah?" A bored glance upwards.

"Yeah, we're booked in to stay here." I slammed my documentation with my booking reference number onto the desk, hoping the ashes of some poor soul who'd died of old age while waiting for their room wouldn't rise up from the impact.

The youth flicked back his greasy mop and gave my A4 sheet the once-over. He turned to a PC, which I could have sworn was one of those old Wang models they stopped making in the nineties. He looked up at Colm. I took this to be as close as he was going to get to asking Colm for his check-in information, so I grabbed Colm's documentation from his fist and handed it over. Colm barely noticed, he was so busy gawping around the place. I wondered, not for the first time but more vehemently than before, what the hell was wrong with him.

"Your room is Number 25." The youth threw a key on the desk.

I wasn't sure which of us the room was for, but he seemed to be looking at both of us.

"What about the other one?"

"Only one key per room. You two will have to share it."

"No, I meant the other room!" I could barely hear my own voice for the alarm bells going off in my head.

"Have you two had a fight or something? Looks like you're gonna have to make up. We're fully booked." He sat back, with the attitude of someone who was about to enjoy the fireworks.

"We booked two separate rooms! We're *not a couple*!"

"According to the system, you only booked one room." He didn't even look surprised. I started to wonder if this happened a lot. The Wang, or whatever it was, whirred ominously as he spoke.

"Your system is like something from *The Flintstones*, and it's obviously got it wrong! We gave you printouts there with our booking reference numbers!"

"Number. You both had the same reference number."

I rounded on Colm, who was standing behind me looking worried. "Why did we have the same reference number?"

"Hey, don't ask me. One of the administrators in our place booked this trip. She's quite new, so maybe she made a mistake . . ."

"Oh, great. I knew I should have booked all of this myself, instead of relying on Éire TV!"

"Well, why didn't you, then?" He crossed his arms.

I looked away and resumed glaring at the youth. He'd obviously had a lot of experience at being glared at, because it didn't seem to perturb him in the slightest. It was as if we weren't even there.

"Check that thing again for another room," Colm told the youth. "And do it quick before it explodes."

I had to hand it to Colm – he had that quiet-sense-of-authority thing going on. The youth instantly started tapping on the keyboard, but he was shaking his head before he even touched a key.

"No rooms left," he eventually said after a long process of tapping and re-tapping. "You're booked in at the same time as the annual Retro Reunion party from the University of Nevada." He flicked a hand in the direction of the wall to his right, upon which lived a montage of curling photos of groups of fifty-somethings posing outside the hotel in their best 70s gear. "It's the class of '78 this year. We're all very excited about it."

"I'm sure you are." I started to warm to the youth. It wasn't his fault he worked in such a kip, and at least he had a healthy sense of irony.

"Are you being sarcastic? This is a family-run business, and if it's not good enough for you, I'm sure my dad won't be sorry to lose custom from people like you." He looked me up and down in my linen jacket and trousers as if I had been wearing a pelt of rotten potatoes. And he was eyeing the key on the desk as if he had plans for it. I no longer liked him.

"That's enough." Colm whipped up the key and whisked me away from the desk and towards the elevator in one fluid movement.

I stalled and folded my arms across my chest. "We're going to have to get somewhere else."

Colm pressed the elevator button. "We're miles from another

hotel. You fancy going for a two-mile walk, do you? Be my guest."

"Don't be ridiculous. I'll get a taxi." I went back to the desk to retrieve my abandoned hand luggage, glowering at the youth as I approached the desk. He glowered back, up for a fight.

Colm wiped a hand across his face. "It's five o'clock in the morning Irish time. I'm falling asleep standing up. If you want to go off and find somewhere else to stay, off you go – I'll take the room. Suits me great. But if you think I'm going out on the street to wait for a taxi to pass, you have another think coming."

I opened my mouth, but he pre-empted my words.

"Do you really think he's going to ring one for you after that little exchange?"

"Fine. I'll hail one myself." I picked up the handle of my little suitcase, flicked the case on its wheels and stormed out of the lobby. No sooner had I hit the street than I regretted my exit. It looked even dodgier without the back-up presence of the taxi driver and Colm – not that I trusted Colm to do anything if someone came along and murdered me anyway. He was one of those people who'd have no conscience about eating you if you got stuck in an *Alive* situation. But he was all I had in this place.

Three minutes and twenty-seven seconds passed without sight or sound of a taxi. Three minutes and twenty-seven seconds ago, the hooded figure that was making his way up the long street had seemed very far away. Now, I could practically smell his breath from where I stood. I hated judging people based on something as small as a hoodie, but I had a bad feeling about him. It wasn't a cold night. Why was he hiding his face under a hood? I turned the other way. If I got too scared, I could always forget my dignity and run back into the lobby. Yes, nothing to worry about. Although I didn't like the look of the silhouette that was ambling towards me in the opposite direction either . . . he was a very heavily-set man, the kind that could knock you out with his little finger. He could even have been a wrestler in a previous incarnation. What hope would I have against a wrestler? I couldn't even beat my little cousin at arm-wrestling, even when chocolate was the coveted main prize.

I swung around and looked back at the approaching hoodie who was now almost upon me.

Then a hand grabbed my shoulder.

I was so shocked, I couldn't even breathe for a few seconds. The wrestler. Oh God, he wanted my handbag. My company credit card. All my dollars. Not to mention my lovely Butlers Chocolates, purchased on the way over. All would be gone. In a twist of irony, I'd be completely dependent on Colm for everything, when all I'd been doing was trying to get away from him. I couldn't help it. I screamed so loud that Jim Morrison must have heard me in his grave in Paris. The scream was for the somewhat delayed realisation that my personal safety was now gravely at risk, and not for the threatened dependency on Colm, although that was something else to scream about at a later stage . . . There wasn't a sinner on the street, and doubtless the hoodie would be happy to watch me be mugged and maimed and tortured by this thug holding my shoulder . . .

"Andie, stop screaming, you lunatic! It's me! Jesus, do you scream as a hobby or something?"

"Colm! For God's sake, what are you doing grabbing me by the shoulder like that? Have you no sense!" I shrugged him off so hard that my shoulder hit my ear.

"I'm bringing you back in before you get attacked, that's what." He grabbed my case with one hand and my arm with the other. He had me yanked back into the lobby before I even knew it was happening.

"I don't know how people like you manage to cope from one day to the next. You're a liability to yourself." He pressed the button for the elevator. "Here's what's happening. We're sharing that room tonight. We flip a coin for who gets to sleep on the floor." The elevator arrived. "If I don't get some sleep soon, I'm going to kill someone in cold blood, but I can't sleep worrying about you gallivanting around the streets like a halfwit." I opened my mouth, but he put a hand up.

"No. I'm not listening to your nonsense."

The elevator door pinged open to reveal a dingy corridor with shabby brown wallpaper flecked with a rusty orange colour. As I left the elevator, I wondered what to do. The thought of going back out on the street wasn't appealing, but neither was spending the night in the same room as someone who was as dismissive of me as if I was a used tissue. Someone needed to tape him and let him listen to himself, with his patronising guff!

Room Number 25 was at the end of the corridor, as far away from the elevator as was possible. I yawned, and realised I was jaded myself. There was only one thing for it. I'd have to stay in the room, but I was getting the bed. I couldn't let someone as condescending as Colm have it, on pure principle.

I was pleasantly surprised by the room. Yes, the décor was as vile as expected, but it was warm and spacious. I instantly wanted to fling myself under the duvet and sleep for twelve hours. But the second Colm had dumped his bag, he plonked himself slap bang in the middle of the bed and rooted in his pocket for a coin.

"Heads, I get the bed." He threw the coin up in the air.

"No way! Who says you get to call?"

He did an annoying annoyed-exhale thing that people do when they're annoyed. "Fine. Call it."

"Tails."

"But that's what you would have had if . . ." He shook his head.

I enjoyed his exasperation.

He threw the coin, and smiled when it landed. "It's the floor for you, then."

I shook my head in disbelief. "What sort of a man makes a woman sleep on the floor?"

He walked over to the wardrobe. "There's a spare duvet in here. I'll use the bathroom while you get yourself ready."

"No, you will not!" I grabbed the duvet, and made a run for it into the bathroom. If I couldn't have the bed, he couldn't have the bog. Let him go down to the lobby. And as soon as he was gone, that bed would be mine. I ran into the bathroom and locked the door. Throwing the duvet over me, I sank to the floor and waited for Colm to come knocking and arguing with me to let him in. Then the strangest thing happened – I noticed how large the bath was, and it started to look appealing as a place to lie down. Just until I got the bed, of course. I threw off my shoes, wrapped myself in the duvet like a mummy, got into the bath and lay back in it. A dry bath. It was a new one on me.

As I waited, nothing happened. I started to get bored. There wasn't a peep out of him, and I had to conclude that he'd fallen asleep. In my bed!

Suddenly, I heard the sound of creaking, followed by a weird springing noise. Colm was obviously thrashing around the bed, trying to get comfortable. Enough was enough. I threw off the duvet and got out of the bath in a huge rage.

I stormed out of the bathroom ready to argue for the bed, but the sight of Colm standing beside it in only his boxers threw me. His hair was so tousled that it was touching the ceiling, his eyes were just a slit as they tried to keep the light out, and he had the confused look of someone who'd just woken up from sleepwalking.

"What were you doing in there?" he asked in a dazed voice.

"You want to see what I was doing? You come with me." I marched over to him and dragged him into the bathroom by the arm. It felt weird touching the naked skin of someone I barely knew, but I had a point to make. I gestured towards the bath in disgust. "You're a disgrace, making a woman take a duvet into a bath!"

He looked at me in total amazement. Then, to my astonishment, he got right into the bath and wrapped the duvet around him.

"You're right, you're right," he said in a voice so muffled with sleep that I could barely make out what he was saying. "You take the bed. It's all yours. Now goodnight."

He turned around in the bath, curled up, buried his head into the part of the duvet under him, and was snoring within seconds.

I was thrown. Colm being nice? He must have been feeling guilty for being so nasty to me earlier. Sometimes people do surprise you, don't they? I shrugged away my confusion and made my way towards the bed. I almost cried with happiness when I saw the crumpled-up duvet waiting for me. I caught a corner of it, threw myself under it, and . . .

Promptly found myself flat on the floor.

The bastard! The underside of the bed was torn and the mattress was dipping right onto the carpet! My arms and legs were jutting into the air, my torso, bum and thighs trapped.

"*Colllllmmmmmm!*"

I shouted and ranted and raved until the neighbours banged on the wall, and still I could hear the sound of Colm's oblivious snores.

As I finally managed to extricate myself from the mattress through a mixture of pulling, rolling and acrobatics, I knew that a war had officially started. Ironic, really, considering that I'd come to Vegas as a lover, not a fighter . . .

Chapter Nine

Where do you start when you're making a documentary? I'm fecked if I know. Interviewing drunken models (all of whom I knew from working with them) and football players (em . . . same story, different reason) was a far cry from planning an entire storyboard for how this show would pan out. Truth was, I hadn't a clue where to start when it came to finding Leon. Everyone seemed to have got carried away with what a fantastic idea this was, but nobody had put any planning into it. Whenever I complained to anyone in Éire TV about it, they'd be full of talk about how timing was everything – we had to move fast and get this filmed before the fickle public lost interest in it. Maybe that would have been a good thing, much and all as I wanted to see Leon again. Jesus, how did I get myself in these situations?

I'd been sitting on the hotel bed for the past half an hour with an A4 sheet of paper and a pen that kept drying up, trying to come up with content for the documentary. Every time I'd get anything that was approaching a good idea, the pen refused to write, and I'd have to scribble on the bottom of the page to get it working again. Maybe it was a sign. Éire TV wanted four half-hour shows, but I was worried I wouldn't be able to drag this out for five minutes.

Still, at least I now had a room of my own to come up with hopefully-good-ideas in. After a night on the floor, I went down to

Reception and ranted and raved at an elderly man in torn brown cords, who it transpired was the youth's granddad, Buck, and the founder of the family business. When I say ranted and raved, I did it in a nice way, because I couldn't possibly rant and rave nastily to an elderly man who looked as congenial and welcoming as this fellow did. He had the sunniest of smiles, crinkly eyes, and a general air of benevolence about him. I explained my predicament to him, and not only was he horrified that the bed had broken on us like that, but also that Colm had not just given me the bed in the first place. And then not to give me the bath when the bed snapped – well, he was obviously a bad egg, that Colm, according to my new best friend. Luckily, the class of '78 was checking out today, and Buck said he would give me the penthouse suite for the price of a single room to make up for my tribulations. He was almost foaming at the mouth in excitement as he described the room – king-sized bed, a VCR with a case full of VHS tapes of classic 70s movies, a vinyl record player with a stack of seven and twelve-inch records, an entire bookshelf full of 70s books, pictures of *Taxi Driver*, *The Godfather*, *Rocky* and other classics adorning the walls, etc. I heard the words "king-sized bed" and was happy with that. He also promised to give Colm dirty looks if he crossed his path, so overall I was happy with the outcome of my subdued ranting and raving.

And just as he handed me the key to my suite, the lost luggage that I'd written off as never to be seen again was delivered by taxi to Reception. Perhaps Buck was some sort of good luck charm.

I wasn't having much luck with this list though. My so-called good ideas were all absolute shite. I crumpled up the A4 sheet, fired it across the room and picked up the phone.

"Yes?"

"Friendly as ever, Colm. I hope you're not in a mood, because I want your help."

"With?"

I launched into my predicament. I'd grudgingly started speaking to Colm again after the bed incident, only to end up giving him the cold shoulder yet again when he told me, amid fits of laughter, that he'd been the one who'd recommended to Éire TV that we stay in this hotel, purely because he was into all things 70s (as if I hadn't known that from his clothes). Imagine, we could have been somewhere decent instead of this kip if he'd kept his gob shut. Now, though, I had no choice but to speak to him again for work-related reasons – plus, getting the penthouse suite had abated my anger somewhat.

"I have no idea where to start," I said when I'd finished explaining. "Any suggestions?"

"Here's an idea. Next time, don't agree to something unless you're happy with the conditions."

"Ah, Colm! I'm being serious – I need some clever ideas here!"

"I'm serious too. I have enough to do between the camerawork and different projects I have to manage remotely. You knew before you came out here that Amanda wouldn't be able to make it."

"Yeah, the day before we left! I could hardly back out then!"

"Of course you could have. You just chose not to."

"I chose to keep my job! Isolde would have my ass out on the street if I'd let her down after the flights were paid for!"

"You didn't even call her and discuss it."

"You don't bloody-well know Isolde!" I barked. "It would have been pointless. Just like this conversation." I banged the phone down. Jesus! He was unbelievable!

I was glad I was in the room of his dreams, while he'd been put in the smallest single room in the hotel.

 I flopped on the bed, and tried to put all thoughts of Colm and his negativity out of my mind. If only I knew a few people here, or had a few contacts that might help me to brainstorm. The only people I'd met here were that crazy crowd from LVTV, and I could hardly call them friends . . .

Hmm. A mad idea came to me. They might not be friends, but I'd be pretty confident that they would remember me all the same . . .

Several phone calls and long periods of time on hold later, I wasn't quite so confident. I'd eventually managed to get hold of Lindy's extension number, but it went straight to voicemail – and

I'd been given the distinct impression that she was available when I'd been put through to her department. I'd left a stumbling "It's your old friend Andie here – *surpriiiiise*!" type of message on her machine, and had asked her to call me – but chances were, she probably wouldn't. There was only one way to sort things out. I left the hotel and hailed a taxi.

Ten minutes later, I was at the entrance to the LVTV studios. It was located in a huge glassy office block at the north end of the Strip, the type that gives you vertigo looking up at it. A security guard nodded politely as I entered the foyer, using the opportunity of the nod to take in every last detail about me, no doubt. The foyer was divided into separate reception areas for each enterprise hosted by the office block. I saw a sign for LVTV over a reception area to my left, and made my way towards the receptionist.

As I approached, I grew nervous. If Lindy hadn't taken my call, she might well tell Reception not to let me through to her office either. If she didn't, that was it – my crazy plan was shot to shreds. I was getting quite fond of it, and didn't want it to end this way.

"Yes?" A snooty-looking bespectacled brunette eyed me.

"I'm here to be interviewed by Lindy," I said.

"And you are?"

"A singer." The words just fell out of my mouth.

"Ah, you're Misty!" The snooty looker suddenly became a smiler. "Misty, I gotta tell ya, I just adore your new single. So, this is what you look like!" Her smile faltered somewhat, as if I fell somewhat short of her expectations.

Something you should know about me is that I might be a former model, but I'm the most dishevelled-looking one anyone is ever likely to encounter. I just happen to be tall and I scrub up well, but that's where any resemblance to a model ends on a day-to-day basis. I usually wear flat shoes. I brush my hair back into a ponytail every morning, because it's easier to maintain that way. GHDs are a nuisance and a safety hazard, so I steer clear of them (a friend of mine had a car accident once when she turned around on her journey to work and drove home to make sure she'd unplugged her

GHD, and that was enough of a sign for me that they were bad news. Of course, she *had* unplugged the bloody thing). I never wore make-up, because that would mean I'd have to go to the effort of taking it off every night before I went to bed. Life was too short. So this look of disappointment was not one that was new to me. And obviously, a singer was expected to look a lot more glamorous than I was.

"Yes. Yes, this is me. Misty."

"Lindy's expecting you, but you're slightly early. But hey, I'll call her now, and I'm sure she'll be available."

I nodded. Yes, this was a good development. I'm sure if Lindy came face to face with me, she'd be more willing to give me a chance.

Snooty Smiler hung up the phone. "Lindy's actually away from her desk at the moment, but I left a message with her colleague to come down to you as soon as she gets back. Why don't you take a seat? And there are some cans of soda in the fridge to your left if you'd like refreshment."

"Thanks," I said, moving promptly to the fridge. "Do you have some chocolate too?" I know, it was cheeky, but I was starving.

"No." She had her snooty look back on again.

"Don't worry about it," I said innocently as I clicked open a can of Diet Pepsi.

"I'm not," she said.

I opened my mouth to explain that I'd meant no offence, but she'd buried her head in a document in a conversation-over manner. I had a feeling Snooty no longer cared for Misty's first single. Oops.

Seconds later, a door to my right burst open. A tall man with very big shoes and bulgy eyes made his way over to me, his hand outstretched.

"Misty." Another one who evidently had no idea what Misty looked like. "Nice to meet you. Come with me."

"Em . . . I'm here to see Lindy . . ."

"Yes, but as you've arrived early, we're changing the order of your schedule – Lindy's not free for another fifteen minutes. We were going to record your song for next week's *Top Pop* after your interview with Lindy, but we still have an audience here from another show we're recording, so let's just do it now and get it over with."

It wasn't an ask, but a command.

"But . . ."

"Misty, we're working to really tight schedules here." He held the door to the right open for me.

"Listen, em . . ." Feck, he hadn't even told me his name, and maybe I was supposed to know it. "There's something you should know . . ."

"Walk and talk, walk and talk." His manners were obviously on a timer, because it seemed he'd had enough of opening the door for me as he marched through it himself, leaving it swinging back in my face. I now either had to go through the blessed door to explain to him that I wasn't Misty, and hope he'd see the funny side, or make a run for it and lose my opportunity to meet Lindy.

I ran, but down the corridor after him instead of out of the building. And you needed to run after this guy – his long legs had already eaten up half the corridor. "Hang on, there's been –"

"Dave! Oh, thank God!" A small, tanned blonde almost knocked a door to the left of the corridor down flat in her haste to get through it. (Maybe it was a team-bonding thing they had going on here with their door-opening routine?) "Rita Ritchie's collapsed! She's due on *The Daily Dish* in two and a half minutes, and we've nobody to replace her!"

"What? Oh, look, just get Sandie to talk crap about something to fill in the time, Rachel. That's what I pay my presenters for. Now, I've got to go –"

"Rita vomited all over Sandie just before she collapsed – Sandie's had to go to get a change of clothes."

"But that'll only take a few minutes!"

Rachel looked increasingly nervous as she watched the seconds ticking away on her watch. "Oh come on, you know what Sandie is like – plus, Rita hurled all over Sandie's hair too. She's gonna be out of commission for at least twenty minutes. You gotta do something, Dave!"

Dave's face went purple. "What do I pay any of you for, if I have to sort everything out myself?" He turned his violet head on me.

I tried not to shrink backwards – the combination of his height, his temper and his purpleness was scary.

"Forget the recording. You're on now."

"*What?*"

"Look, nobody watches that show you were doing the recording for. You know it, I know it. This show is much more high profile." He looked me up and down. "Pity you've no time for hair and make-up, but we'll have to make do." He grabbed me by the shoulders and pushed me through the door Rachel had exploded from – manhandling law cases obviously being the furthest thing from his mind in a time of crisis.

"Rachel, get someone to put on Misty's backing track – it should be in the system as she was due on another show later. Quick! *Move, move, move!*"

"*No!*" I wriggled furiously away from his grasp. "You don't understand!"

"This is no time for nerves. Pull yourself together." He grabbed my shoulders again and forcibly led me onto the stage.

"Will you just let go and shut up for one second!" I made a run for it again, but he caught me and guided me back.

"Do you actually think you're going to have a long-term career if you act like this? Jeez. You're lucky I'm around to save you from yourself, young lady."

"And we're on in five – four – three – two –" Someone to the left of Rachel whispered the one, and Dave made a run for it off the stage.

"And now, a treat for all you fans of great new music! We have Misty Moore joining us in the studio today! And here she is, with her brand new song! Take it away, Misty!"

The camera panned onto me. I froze. I knew I needed to run like the clappers, but my legs just wouldn't work for me. And then, the song started, and guess what – I actually knew it. I'd heard it loads of times on the radio at home in the days before I left for Vegas without ever knowing who sang it, and Misty's debut song was actually as catchy as hell. It was destined to be a big hit. So I did the only thing I could do under the circumstances. I'd always been the first one to volunteer for karaoke . . .

"On the scene, I'm a boogie queen,
Gonna keep me lean, gonna keep them keen . . ."

I watched as one set of jaws after another dropped to the floor. I was totally and utterly useless at singing and I knew it, but that had never stopped me before, and besides, there was no going back now. They wanted me to sing, and sing I would.

I got about halfway through the song before I heard the whispers of an emergency ad break. The writing had been on the wall after someone called out, "She's not Misty!" and the audience started booing. I was only shocked that I'd managed to get halfway through the song before someone saw fit to stop me.

"Get her off!" Dave yelled at Rachel.

Rachel looked at me and swept her hands to the right in a brushing motion. Dave looked at her and threw his hands up in the air.

"Useless! You want a job done, you do it yourself."

He was lunging for my shoulders again. I swatted his approaching arms.

"Look here! You forced me up there! I was practically kicking you like a mule to get you to let me go – and we'll talk later about inappropriate physical contact, by the way – but you wouldn't feckin' listen. So get your paws off me and stop mauling me!"

"You're saying this is *my* fault?" He looked even more incredulous than he had while I'd been singing.

"Of course it is. You've brought this on yourself, you big lumbering eejit!"

Rachel started to snigger, although I doubted that either she or Dave knew what an eejit was.

Dave turned his ire on her. "What are you laughing at? Go and do some work! That's –"

"That's what you pay her for, am I right? Do you ever listen to yourself, Dave? Oh, I know you like the sound of your own voice, but do you ever actually listen to the rubbish that comes out of your mouth?" A part of me couldn't believe what was coming out of mine, but in for a penny . . . "I've only known you a few minutes, but I already know you're a bully."

His face was priceless. I was starting to enjoy this. It felt like a cameo in a soap. "And I don't associate myself with bullies!" I announced in the most dramatic voice I could conjure up. I thought it was quite impressive, actually. "Now, if you don't mind, I have to be somewhere." I finished my performance, my second in five minutes, with a faux-dignified flick of my hair over my shoulder, and clambered off the set.

Rachel winked at me as I walked past, and Dave just continued to stare at me in abject shock.

When I walked back out into the corridor, I had two options – go back the door I'd come through, or take another door at the opposite end and see where that led me. The adrenalin rush of my caterwauling episode made my mind up for me, and my feet carried me towards the other door – but as soon as I got there, I noticed that you had to swipe a card for access. Not much use when you were cardless. Now that I thought about it, I had vaguely noticed Rachel veering into the wall while Dave had been pushing me through the door – at the time, I had a notion that she must be of a sensitive disposition, and had found his behaviour too dreadful to watch. Now, it was clear she had been swiping her feckin' card to aid and abet his mission.

She must have sensed that I was on the brink of thinking some seriously evil thoughts about her because, when I turned around, she was making her way through the studio doors and towards me.

"That was brilliant –" she started.

I cut her off immediately. "Do you know Lindy?"

"Lindy? Yes, I –"

"Can you take me to her?"

"I . . . I shouldn't . . ." She took a look back towards the studio. When she turned around, her face was harder. "But fuck it. Come with me." She produced the magic swipe and bustled me through the door, looking back as she took her turn at manhandling me. Despite her bravado, she was still obviously shit-scared of Dave, but I was grateful that she was in the mood for rebellion.

She led me to a desk, where I saw the top of a spine over a chair, and a waterfall of glossy chestnut hair that looked familiar.

"Lindy, someone to see you." Rachel shot off to her desk, having done her bit and making it obvious that she was now abdicating from all responsibility.

Lindy narrowed her perfectly kohled eyes. In all the flurry of the news report, I hadn't really noticed how gorgeous she was first time around. Intimidatingly so, even for someone like me who used to work with the leggiest, toothiest girls in Dublin. She was all bright skin and strong-yet-delicate features, a look that evaded most models.

"*You.*" It was said with something akin to hatred.

"Now, before you say anything else, I can explain . . ." I launched into my story. Lindy's eyes narrowed further, so much so that I was sure she'd have a squint for the rest of her life after just a few minutes in my company. That, on top of the injuries she sustained in the bouncer brawl, surely wasn't going to endear me to her.

I continued regardless. ". . . and that's why I'm here."

She turned to her phone, then yelled over the partition. "Rachel! What's the number for security again?"

Rachel popped up over the partition. "No! Wait until you hear what she did!"

And so, Rachel relayed what I did. Fair play to her, she made it sound a million times better than it was. I had practically grown five feet during my metamorphosis from victim to hero, whilst Dave had shrunk to Tom Thumb proportions over the course of her recounting. I decided I liked Rachel.

Lindy turned her slits on me again. I felt a strange urge to check her desk for blue tack to hold her eyelids up. She was very annoying to look at. But suddenly, like a flower opening up in the first burst of spring sunshine, she popped her eyes open.

"Good for you. Dave can be a real crock of shit."

"Em . . . yeah, he can be, can't he?"

"You know what I like about you, Andie?"

I shrugged nonchalantly, and paused to accept whatever praise was coming my way.

"You have absolutely no qualms about making a complete and utter fool of yourself."

"Thanks." I smiled, but this time I was the one with slits where my lips used to be. Cheeky bitch.

"That's rare these days, you know. The whole world has taken extreme reticence to an unprecedented level."

She sounded like a younger, sophisticated, urbane version of Isolde when she was on her anti-PC rant. She was also coming across as a pain in the hole, just like Isolde, so I was starting to feel right at home in her company.

"When you say 'That's why I'm here', what exactly do you want from me?"

"Publicity." Okay, so she wasn't as bright as Isolde. "You're an interviewer, and I'm looking for an interview. Just a two-minute segment where you'd ask me about my search for Leon. Surely he'd see it and get in touch with me. I've heard everyone in this state and the neighbouring states watches your show."

"What's the name of my show?"

"Em . . ." Busted.

"I'd be surprised if they did, considering I don't have one. I'm an entertainment correspondent for the nightly news. That's the show I was supposed to be interviewing the real Misty for."

Ah, yes . . . now that I thought about it, the clip I'd found on the LVTV website of the interview with Josh Feather had been in an entertainment section of a news bulletin. Time for a swift recovery of the situation . . .

"Oh hey, I did something very similar!" I told her about my Éire TV days. This was good bonding material, surely.

Then Lindy's phone rang. She muttered "Shit," as she listened to the person on the other end, then her face brightened. "Rachel, be a doll and go down to Reception to explain everything to the real Misty. I'm kinda busy here."

"But –"

"No buts. Just go." She turned her back on Rachel and looked at me instead. I gave Rachel a sympathetic look as she left the office. I had a feeling the real Misty would be baying for my blood at having her slot stolen, to say nothing of being impersonated badly, but that was a worry for another time.

"You know, I'm actually starting to see the potential in this," Lindy said. "I could do a two-minute segment in the entertainment section about the mad girl from Ireland who's still on a desperate hunt for a man."

"What a delightful description." Cheeky and nasty too. Nice combination. She'd get her own show yet.

"I say 'still', because you did cause something of a stir with your ridiculous antics during my interview with the singer – you totally messed up our relationship with him, by the way. He's refusing to have anything more to do with us. When he hits the big-time, we're going to hold you responsible."

"Somehow I don't think I need to put a lawyer on speed-dial. But when you say it caused a stir, what do you mean? I saw the interview with the singer on your website, and there was no sign of me – I thought it hadn't been televised –"

"We broadcast it in a separate part of the bulletin. A kind of 'And finally, here are some of the weird things that are happening in the world today' type of segment at the end of the show."

"Oh wow. I didn't know." I instantly wondered if Leon had seen it.

"Are you free to be filmed now?"

"Yes."

She picked up the phone. "Let me call the cameraman."

I shuddered at the dirty word that reminded me of Colm, the auld bastard. Christ, but he was one streak of misery.

She put down the phone. "Right, he can't make it for another hour, so do you want to go to hair and make-up to kill the time?"

Why was everyone always telling me to go to hair and make-up before getting filmed? Was I that yukky-looking? Now, I have to tell you, I don't ever come out with the old "I was a model, you know" line, because a) I'd be slightly afraid they'd laugh in my face and go "*Ahahahaaa!* Good one!" and b) it's just plain arsey. But for the first time ever, I actually felt like spouting it. Yer one was pencilled, plucked and pansticked to within an inch of her life even though she would have looked amazing without any of it, and she actually made me want to go au naturel as much as possible.

"I'm fine, thanks." I raised my chin in defiance.

"You're not, you know. You look flushed and bedraggled. But hey, I suppose you've just been beamed to the nation looking like that, so hair and make-up is a bit pointless, really. You're right – don't waste your time."

Of course, now I wanted the bloody hair and make-up, but I couldn't give in and ask for it. "Is there a bathroom around here?"

Lindy gave me directions to the restroom, where I checked myself out in the mirror. God, she was right, and what's more, she was being kind. Flushed? I had the purple glow of a consummate alcoholic. Bedraggled? The knots in my hair from heat and sweat were tighter than those in a hammock – I'd have to cut the blessed things out.

Sometimes, good ideas are like buses. If I rang Colm and asked him to film this interview too, we'd have the beginnings of the footage we needed for our first episode of *Looking for Leon*, and what's more, he could bring my (small and limited) make-up bag with him. I'd have myself fixed up in ten minutes, whereas the hair and make-up department here would be primping and preening me for the full hour, not to mention the fact that I'd have to back down in front of Lindy. I'd given him a spare key for the penthouse when he'd come down to Reception to collect his luggage, purely because I was prone to losing things, drunk or sober – I suppose you'd already guessed that about me.

I pulled out my mobile, barked a few orders down the phone at Colm on the lines of "Taxi – LVTV – *now* – bring camera and make-up bag!" and made my way back into Lindy to make sure she was okay with having Colm film the interview too.

I smiled as I pictured the look of envy on Colm's face when he saw all the 70s goodies in the penthouse. What goes around comes around . . .

Chapter Ten

Colm was reading the paper at a table in the corner when I came down for breakfast the next morning. As soon as he saw me, he smirked.

I ignored him, and poured myself a bowl of clotting cornflakes. They looked like they'd been around for centuries. The young guy in Reception had probably robbed them from one of those window displays in shops where the logo on the cereal box has faded from being in the sun for years. Actually, that was something that always bothered me at home – and while it wasn't quite up there with Personal-Space Invaders, it was almost a pet hate. We never had any sunshine, yet every town or village you drove through had an old shop with a window full of faded cardboard. Does constant rain produce a glare, or have I missed something? Of course, that problem was being eliminated by the emergence of another one – the identikit grocery chain stores that were wiping out the little businesses. Those shops changed their displays about three times a day, even if it was only the same handful of old biddies that would ever notice. Mind you, I saw a group of them buying the latest Twirly Twist Limited Edition ice cream last week after a display went up in the window, so maybe it worked, who knows?

Tempted as I was to sit at a table at the opposite end of the room, I decided to be mature and join Colm. Besides, nosiness had got the better of me. He seemed very interested in that newspaper, and what was worse, he seemed to be laughing at me every time he looked up from it.

I sat down. "Anything good in the paper?" I took a spoon of cornflakes with what I hoped was an appropriate level of nonchalance. Christ on a bike, they tasted foul.

Colm looked into his bowl of fruit and speared a piece of shrivelled pear. I didn't know why he was bothering – there was no doubt in my mind but that the fruit had come from a tin, despite the handwritten 'Fresh Fruit' sign perching lazily beside the fruit bowl in the breakfast area. But it seemed that, despite his biscuit fixation, he tried to eat healthily most of the time – although he also had a fry on the table for after his fruit.

"Depends on your definition of good," he said.

"Throw it over here and I'll have a look."

"No, I'm not finished with it yet." He placed his cup of coffee on it.

"But you're not reading it at the moment!"

"I thought you came down here to eat breakfast?"

"I can eat and read at the same time – it's not that difficult!" I could feel the usual Colm-induced irritation rising in me. "Jesus, just hand it over, will you?"

"Are you sure you want to see it?"

"No. I want to smell it. Of course I bloody want to see it – why would I be asking for it otherwise?"

He lifted up his cup of coffee. "Okay, be my guest. But on your own head be it."

"I'm going to read a paper, Colm. It's not as if I'm going to play chase with lions or something. Stop being so damn dramatic." I grabbed the paper and browsed the cover, then flicked the page. "Oh my God!" I looked up at Colm in disbelief.

He raised an eyebrow. "Did you just say something about cutting down on the drama?"

"Oh, shut up! I'm all over the paper! What did you expect?"

"You're all over half of Page 3, you mean. There are other articles in the paper too, you know."

"Why did they put me on shagging Page 3 of a national newspaper, of all shagging pages?"

"It's a broadsheet. They don't have Page 3 girls in broadsheets. What difference does it make anyway?"

"It's the principle! It's the shagging association! Christ!"

At the top left of the page was a picture of me singing 'Boogie Queen' – and looking like I was quite into it, actually. To the right of the picture was an article about an Irishwoman's "infiltration" into the hallowed grounds of LVTV, accompanied by an interview from Dangly Dave.

> "This woman had an agenda," said Dave Dagenham, director of LVTV's programming schedules. "She violated our security procedures and purposely pretended to be someone she wasn't. My first thought was that she was a very disturbed woman."

"*A very disturbed woman!*"

Colm covered his ears as I shrieked.

"I did try to stop you reading the paper . . ."

"You made sure I read it by sniggering at me non-stop the minute I walked in here!"

I read on.

> "However, it transpired that her motive was in some way honorable. This lady is looking for the love of her life, a man called Leon from Arizona, and she's gone to some extraordinary lengths to find him. In fact, she's already featured on one of our previous bulletins in a former infiltration attempt, which you can now watch again on our website. Everyone's talking about her since she appeared on our show, but we're the only TV station she's chosen to talk to. Don't miss our exclusive interview with her on our entertainment show tonight at 18:30 PDT."

"My God, that was a bit of a surprise!"

"Oh, stop pretending you don't love all of this. Being in the paper is exactly what you want. The more publicity you can get, the more likely it is that you'll find Leon."

He had a point. I didn't have to admit that, though. "Hmmm. Do you want that toast?"

"No. I'm finished." He pushed his plate away, even though more than half of his eggs and bacon still sat on it. "See you later."

"That's fine, Colm, you just go and leave me sitting here on my own like an arsehole. Don't worry, I'll take it personally."

"I'd expect nothing less." He did that smirk again, but it was less malevolent this time.

"You might want to take your biscuits with you." I pointed to a cling-filmed stack of three biscuits that were peeking out from behind a teapot. They looked like raspberry creams.

"Oh, yeah." He grabbed them and stuffed them in his pocket.

"You do know they have biscuits over here too, don't you?"

"The biscuits here are shite. I always bring my own to have with a cup of tea."

It was my turn to smirk. It sounded like something my granny would say, if you took away the expletive. Well, no, actually. Granny was good for an auld curse too, when I thought about it.

"Did you bring a big stockpile of biscuits over in your suitcase then?"

"Yes, of course I did." He said it as if doing anything other than that would be completely mad. "Right. See you at three for our editing session." He took off, biscuits in tow.

I stuffed a corner of a piece of toast in my mouth, then walked away from the table too with the rest of the toast dangling from my lips and the paper in my hand. I had a column to write.

As I walked upstairs, I wondered if somewhere in the country Leon was choking on his cornflakes at the sight of me pretending to be Misty Moore. I really hoped so.

"And finally tonight, in Entertainment News, a video of an Irishwoman who stole the identity of singer Misty Moore on a TV show has become a huge Internet hit. Andie Appleton

duped staff here at LVTV into believing she was Misty, and appeared on a daytime show attempting to sing Misty's chart hit, 'Boogie Queen'. Staff on the show realised their error as soon as Ms Appleton opened her mouth, and an emergency ad break was taken to spare viewers from further aural distress, but the revelation of Andie's motives behind her deception has enthralled viewers. Former model Andie is on a one-woman crusade to find the love of her life, a man called Leon from Arizona who she met on a night out in the MGM Grand on the Vegas Strip three weeks ago, and was subsequently separated from. Leon, if you're watching, get in touch – we like a happy ending here at LVTV!"

I turned off the TV.

Sometimes, you just had to laugh. I wanted publicity to help me find Leon, and boy, had I got it.

It had been four days since my interview with Lindy was televised, and something about my story seemed to have captured the mood of the nation. In a world of Internet-dating, speed-dating, blind-dating, Frisky Fifties dating (such a thing exists, according to Mum's neighbour Eileen – she's abandoned the bingo entirely since she joined an online website) and so on, everyone was doing something to help them find love. My story was a little more extreme than what most people did, but the public just seemed to get it and relate to it. That, and the fact that Dave had been canny about exploiting the story for maximum publicity. It seemed there were no hard feelings between Dave and me – as soon as he sniffed the opportunity to make a story out of my appearance, he was all over me like that horrendous smell of chip-pan oil that permeates an entire house long after the chips have been devoured and forgotten. Even the real Misty was happy about the whole thing. She had enough sense to realise that there was no such thing as bad publicity, and her song had been flying up the charts ever since my TV appearance.

Since the footage had been broadcast, I had barely slept. Our half-an-hour interview, filmed by both LVTV and Colm, had been edited down into the promised two minutes for the entertainment show, but after it was broadcast LVTV were flooded with requests from viewers wanting more on the story. The next day, they broadcast fifteen minutes out of our half-hour interview on a daily entertainment show. Meanwhile, I got permission from LVTV to broadcast my singing escapades on Irish TV. Colm filmed some footage of me explaining how I had got myself in that situation, edited my interview with Lindy down to twenty minutes, and then filmed me sifting through the newspapers with articles about my search in them (minus the Page 3 article) – and hey presto, we had the first of the four episodes we were contractually obliged to produce. Colm emailed it to Éire TV and it had been broadcast at home the previous night, so now we just had to wait for the feedback on how it had been received. All in all, I certainly wasn't short of entries for my diary, if I only had time to keep it updated properly.

Dave had appointed Lindy as my unofficial agent, and she'd dragged me off to do interview after interview with radio stations, local newspapers, magazines, you name it, since the two-minute interview had been broadcast.

"Dave's been in a lot of hot water recently over flagging ratings for some of the shows he's involved in," Lindy told me and Colm over cocktails after my interview.

I was initially shocked that she'd invited us to go for a drink with her, but her motive soon became apparent as she threw long glances at Colm across the table in the trendy bar she'd brought us to.

"So anything that'll bring the spotlight back on him will be a feather in his cap," she went on.

"And he views me as a whole pillow's worth, I presume?"

She didn't bother confirming or denying that – she was far too busy making eyes at an unmoved, or possibly unaware, Colm.

When I'd told Lindy the first day that my cameraman would be arriving soon to film the first episode of *Looking for Leon* while she was interviewing me, she hadn't been one bit impressed at the prospect.

"That's quite a cheeky ask," she'd said in a sulky tone. "I'll have to speak to Dave about that."

"Can you speak to him now, so?"

"No."

"No?"

"No."

Good Lord. "I got that, but why?"

"Because he's not free right now."

"When will he be free?"

"Tomorrow. I know he has an important meeting downtown scheduled for right about now."

"So what does that mean when it comes to getting permission to do this today?"

"It means you have a problem on your hands."

I was about to ask her for Dave's number to ring him myself when Colm arrived. Lindy's face instantly took on a whole new expression. Quite simply, she suddenly looked as downright predatory as I've ever seen a woman look.

"Colm, Lindy, Lindy, Colm," I muttered.

"Well, hello." Lindy moved into vamp mode. She extended a perfectly manicured hand to Colm, and thrust her breasts out even further than her hand.

Colm did a one-second handshake and flicked her hand away as if he was tossing a stone into a well. Lindy didn't seem to mind. She responded by producing an even wider smile.

"I take it you've sorted out the permissions for me filming here?" Colm asked me.

"Well, actually, no. We need to get permission from Dave, but he's not free right now."

Colm's face clouded over. "So you mean I've had a wasted journey here today, then?"

"Oh, don't be getting silly and stressing about the little things, Andie," Lindy laughed. "Of course Colm can film here today!"

"But what about what you said about Dave?"

"You just let me handle Dave," Lindy purred. "Colm, you go right ahead and get yourself set up."

I shrugged. If Lindy flirting shamelessly with Colm was going to make my life easier, then I had no problem with it. It was about time he came in useful for something.

A really nice cherry on the cake that was my mission in Vegas was that the MGM had offered discounted accommodation to Colm and me, once they realised that theirs had been the turf upon which I had met Leon, and we'd moved there the day before. They got publicity out of it, we got a nicer and more central hotel (with me getting a suite again), so you'd think everyone would be happy – but, of course, Colm was loath to leave the 70s hotel. He did eventually, but it was a struggle to get him out of there. I thought he was going to stage a sit-in at one point, despite the fact that Buck had turned everyone that worked in the hotel against Colm, and he was practically being spat at in the corridors for his misogynistic ways. I had to promise that I'd go to a 70s club with him in a hotel near the MGM sometime in the future to even get him to begin the negotiation process, and I eventually got him out with promises of hiring out the most outlandish 70s costumes I could find for our night out – I hadn't a notion of going anywhere near that club, of course, but needs must. I was a bit sad to leave the hotel myself, truth be told – I'd grown fond of it since I'd struck up a friendship with Buck – but I was sure the MGM would plant some fake mould in the shower to make me feel at home if I missed it too much. Of course, I wouldn't have been that bothered if Colm had chosen to stay in the hotel on his own, but logistically it would have been a pain for us to get together in the evenings to work on our next episodes if we were in different hotels. It was also pretty handy to have Wi-Fi Internet access in our hotel rooms. So far, I'd been so busy during the day on all the activities Lindy had organised for me that I'd been doing all of my regular work for the paper at night. The 70s hotel had no Internet access, so that meant I'd been going into LVTV half an hour earlier than I could otherwise have been to email articles to Isolde.

It was all going according to plan (if I'd had a plan in the first place other than the great concept of finding Leon, and I can't say I had), but I couldn't help wondering though if all of this was going to send Leon running for the nearest plane out of the States. It was a reasonable assumption that some people might find all of this a little bit on the '*waaaaaayyy* too much' side . . . but then, I thought about Leon's enjoyment of me wrecking the windscreen of a car worth God only knew how much money, and I relaxed a little. He was zany, he'd get it. It was just a matter of finding him. And if I didn't do this, I'd never find him anyway, so why not give it a shot? I talked myself down. It would be fine.

Anyway, I had too much work to do to allow myself to get worried. Dave had also capitalised on me being a journalist, and had arranged for me to write articles for a women's magazine, a daily paper and a weekend supplement for one of the biggest-selling Sunday papers in Vegas. And, of course, I had my column to write and email to Isolde.

I took a quick walk around the hotel to clear my head before I tore into my work. As I passed Reception on my way back to my room, I saw my new best friend – my Buck replacement, if you will – one of the hotel porters, Philippe. When I'd arrived and checked in at the MGM, he'd escorted me and my luggage to the elevator where he'd proceeded to tell me his life story. He'd moved to Vegas from Paris thirty years ago to be with a local woman who he'd met while she was on holidays in France. They had married within a month of his arrival – the only surprise there being that they hadn't done it sooner, given the location – and they'd had a wonderful life.

Philippe and I were in my room by this time and he seemed to have no intention of leaving. On he went with his tale. When his wife died five years before, when he was fifty-three, he forced himself to go back into the workplace (after taking an early retirement from an administrative position at the age of fifty) so that he'd get out of the house and meet people instead of moping around. He was a people person, he said. He liked to talk, to get to know people, to help them if he could. I'd nodded and pressed a tip into his hand to try to close the conversation and get him out the door – he was a bit full-on for my liking. But anytime I'd seen him after that, I found that I liked having a friendly face greeting me. He also occasionally worked in Reception, covering shifts if anyone from the main reception team called in sick or had to absent themselves for a while, but whether he actually did any real work or not between all the idle chit-chat was questionable.

Today, he was only on porter duty and was currently hanging about Reception, looking like he hadn't a care in the world, while everyone else worked themselves into the ground.

"Andeee! Come over 'ere and 'ave a chat!" Even after thirty years, he still sounded very French when he spoke in English.

"I can't, Philippe. I have to work."

"But you've been working all day!"

"Yes, but I've more to do now. Anyway, aren't you supposed to be working yourself?"

"Pah!" He curled his lip dismissively. "A lot of the people who come 'ere are fat. They should carry their own luggage for exercise."

"Philippe!" I gave him a disapproving look.

"I am only saying out loud what everyone says behind the fat backs of fat people. Don't tell me you 'aven't noticed the overweight people who take those electronic buggies from the elevators to the breakfast buffets because they are too lazee to walk?"

He had me there. I had noticed it. I'd also noticed that Philippe was with Isolde in the non-PC club. He nodded, knowing my silence meant he'd made his point successfully.

"I have to go, Philippe."

"Okay. I will find something to get out of doing, then."

I smiled. "You do that."

I had so many emails that I didn't know where to start, but the one from Isolde with a big exclamation mark beside it to show that it was high priority would have the feedback on how the broadcast of the first show had gone, and was definitely being kept until last. If it hadn't gone well, my spirits would be too low to work through all the rest of the rubbish I had to attend to. I read all of the other nonsense, including one from Jason about the results of his monthly audit on the incorrect and inappropriate use of semicolons in all copy submitted for publication. I opened the spreadsheet of offenders, and found myself top of the list with five felonies. I pressed reply, typed the words **'Fuck; you; and; your; semicolons;'**, and just before I pressed the X on the top right of the email to get rid of it, I seriously thought about sending it this time. Every single month, I wrote a mail full of abuse to Jason when his monthly audit came out. It varied from telling him to go off and train to be an accountant if he wanted to do audits to outright plain abuse where I told him he stank and he needed an operation to get his ears pulled back (he did, honest). But I never sent them, because – well, I'm crippled by the rules of the workplace, just like everyone else is. But this time, I came very, very close. I felt like I was coaxing myself back from the edge of a cliff as I forced my shaking hand to move right and click on the X, as was customary. When the email was gone, I felt disappointed, and was tempted to go through the whole process one more time, but I really had too much to do that day to be dawdling around on work emails.

I suppose the fact that I hated ploughing through my work emails wasn't a good reflection on how happy I was in my job. In fact, I distinctly remembered telling Leon that I hated it.

"So how is it you're working in a job you hate instead of doing whatever it is you really want to do in life?" he'd asked me.

"How do you know there's something else I want to do in life?"

"Because everyone has dreams. What's yours?"

I smiled. "Well, I suppose there is something. It's not much of a dream, more a case of having made the wrong career choice. I think I should have trained to be a teacher instead of doing journalism."

"Okay, so how about retraining as a teacher now then?"

"I'm thirty, Leon. I'm far too old to retrain."

"Of course you're not. Think about it. You've got another thirty-five years of work ahead of you, maybe more. Do you want to spend those years doing something you can't stand?"

"But what if I retrained to be a teacher and discovered I didn't like it?"

"That's a risk you'd have to take. But wouldn't it be fun finding out? Life is all about finding what you're passionate about and then doing it." He shrugged. "That's my advice anyway, for all it's worth."

"And I appreciate it. How about I think about it over another round?"

I shook my head. Remembering the good times with Leon wouldn't clear my inbox. Time to read Isolde's missive and be done with it.

Andey, I said to myself as I opened it, Isolde here. Not only was she openly aggressive, but she did a great line in passive aggression too. Either that, or she really was the worst editor in the entire country.

From: **Isolde.Huntingdon@vicious.ie**
To: **Andie.Appleton@vicious.ie**

Andey,

Isolde here.

(I mean, who the hell else would it be from that email address? She might as well have said it was Isolde Huntingdon and be done with it, lest there was any confusion at all – who knew how many Isoldes there could be running around the place?)

Updating you on the reaction to what's been broadcast so far. Momentum is building. People were glued last night. We've been inundated –

(See? She could spell when she wanted to. And she always boasted that she never used the spellchecker on her computer.)

– this morning with emails to the info email address wishing you luck. KEEP IT UP. I'm doing a twice-weekly slot on the entertainment section of Éire TV's breakfast show where I give the nation a taster of what's to come in your column. Make sure you give me enough to talk about. I don't want to be sitting there like a turnip with nothing to say. Not that there is such a thing as a turnip that does have something to say. Anyway, I have work to do. Get your next column to me fast.

Kind regards,

Isolde

(The last three words were from her email signature, and were just there because of the necessity to email people outside of the company. The regards to people inside the company were neither kind nor existent.)

I sat back in my chair and exhaled. As Isolde's mails went, that was high praise indeed.

I flew through my first column and the articles I had to write, and then lay back on the hotel bed with the remote in my hand to chill out for the first time in days. Things were good. And I was shocked to realise that I'd almost forgotten about what had happened to Elaine for a while there. Almost.

Chapter Eleven

"Ms Appleton?"

"Yes?"

"This is Nicole in reception. We have a letter here for you. Will I send someone up with it?"

"No, I'll come down and collect it, thanks." Any excuse to get out and have a walk around the hotel. I felt I could live here for years and still marvel at how much it contained. It was like living inside a treasure chest.

"Okay, Ms Appleton. We'll have it waiting for you. Thank you!"

"No, no, no. Thank *you*!" I was in such a good mood that I could out-enthuse her no problem. I hung up, as there was silence at the other end of the phone. She could even have been wondering if I was taking the mick out of her. Or was that the Paddy?

"Ah, Andeeee! You 'ave come to collect your letter, yes?" Philippe stuck his hand behind the reception desk and fished it out, oblivious to or unperturbed by the disturbance he was causing to one of the receptionists who was trying to type a credit-card number in as he brushed his hand around her work area.

I examined the envelope when he handed it to me. It had nothing on it except my typed name – no stamp, no return address and nothing to indicate who it might be from.

"I didant see who dropped this in – I 'ave just started my sheeft," Philippe said.

"Don't worry, Philippe. I'm sure they left their name in the letter. That's what most people do when they write letters."

"Yes, but *I* don't know who they are yet. That is the problem. Open it up, queekly."

I shook my head. There was no point in calling him on his nosiness. He would just take it for granted that I should accept it. And, in a funny way, I did. Besides, I was a bit too curious myself about who the sender was to waste any time castigating him. I ripped the envelope open and read the typed letter.

```
Andie,
I've seen you on TV. You need to know that Leon
already has a girlfriend. You're wasting your time
over here. Do something useful with it and book your
trip home instead.
```

"What the . . . ? Philippe, is this your idea of a joke?"

"What?"

"Oh, come on. Mysterious letter mysteriously arrives for me – you just happen to be around when I open it to see my reaction – you're obviously even more bored than usual today!"

"What ehr you talking about? Show me!" He snapped the letter out of my hand. The second I saw his face as he read it, I knew he had nothing to do with it.

"Andee! This is nastee, no? I would nevare do this!" He looked quite hurt.

"Sorry, Philippe."

"'Ere is your letter. I am going to do some work alongside the people who trust me." He crumpled the letter into my hand and marched off.

"Ah, Philippe! Don't be like that!"

He treated me to a 'Talk to the hand' gesture. I decided to give him some space. I scanned the name badges on the four receptionists currently working in the reception area until I located Nicole. I introduced myself and asked her if she'd seen who left the letter in.

"I'm afraid not," she said with a smile. She looked like someone who didn't know how not to smile, but it was endearing rather than annoying even though what she was saying wasn't what I wanted to hear. "I just found it in my in-tray right here." She pointed to her in-tray, which was beside her computer in her position on the left-hand side of Reception.

"Do you think any of the other receptionists might have accepted it and put it there? I'm not trying to suggest that your colleagues are evil and foisting work onto you, by the way – I'm just wondering if that might have been possible?"

Nicole smiled politely. "Let me just check to see if they remember anyone delivering it."

All three shook their heads when asked if they'd been the recipient of a letter for Andie Appleton. I thanked Nicole for her time, gave her my widest smile (which still wasn't a patch on hers) and walked to the casino to gather my thoughts.

I put the letter in my handbag and sat down at a slot machine. I fed it with coins as I mused about the letter's origins. While the letter wasn't particularly nasty, it had shaken me up.

Maybe it was karma. When I was at school, I sent a poison-pen letter to a teacher once. She was a right wagon, but I didn't really even dislike her all that much – I had just seen the poison-pen letters in comics and on TV, and thought it would be cool to do one up. When Mum saw me cutting letters out of newspapers, I told her it was for my scrapbook of donkeys. I would glue the names of all the donkeys into the scrapbook. Mum thought it was a lovely idea, and I could see she thought I was great for partaking in such a creative activity for a change instead of beating up my brother. In fact, she was so content that she probably would have put the actual poison-pen letter together for me if it meant a night without the usual volley of abuse between my brother and me. She never liked this particular teacher much either. Anyway, I popped into the classroom before class began and left the letter on the teacher's desk, just so that I could see her reaction when she opened it. She was a right old cow, so I expected her to just grind her teeth and turn purple (our class had a competition going to see who could come up with the most inventive way to get this going on) – but I got the fright of my life when she burst out bawling the minute she read it. Now, I have to be honest, it was vicious – but so was she, so I thought I was matching like with like. It turned out that her sister had just been diagnosed with terminal cancer, so the letter caught her at a very bad moment. But I never admitted it had come from me, and to this day I still feel bad about seeing her purple face go all crumply.

So it looked like the time had come for payback. And as Mel Gibson said once, payback's a bitch.

But who the hell could it be from? Was it malicious bullshit or was it true? Had Leon started seeing someone since the night we'd met? Or maybe he'd been seeing someone before that . . . he certainly hadn't seemed like the type of guy who'd be flirting with other women if he was already taken, but that didn't mean it wasn't possible. Maybe it was his pyscho ex . . .

Leon and I had covered a lot of ground in the few hours we'd spent together, and it had transpired that he'd broken up with a woman called Germaine about a month before he came to Vegas. Her name alone would be enough reason for most men to hightail it, but Leon had stuck with her for two years. Apart from the incident where she'd spray-painted the front of his parents' house with the words '*Bastard within these walls!*' when Leon had been on a weekly visit home, and a drunken email where she'd warned him to expect trouble if he dared to start seeing someone else, it seemed that she'd taken it quite well. Or so Leon had thought, but the piece of paper that was fluttering in my clammy hand could suggest otherwise.

This was all Leon's mother's fault. I hadn't even met the woman, but already she was making my life a misery. From what Leon had told me, his mother, Bridget, was a bit of a livewire, and a sharp one to boot – so when she'd spotted Germaline (her pet name for the prospective daughter-in-law who she'd never liked) dousing her walls in red paint, she saw red herself. When she came outside and discovered that said prospective daughter-in-law was apparently calling her a bastard, she had her garden hose hooked up and ready for use within five seconds. Leon said she was like something from *Braveheart*, charging out into the front garden to launch herself and her hose on Germaline, who had moved on to spraying Leon's car with a '*Bastard within this car!*' message to keep in line with her theme. In another world, I think Germaline and I could have been friends – I quite liked her mad-yoke tendencies. Anyway, out came Leon's mother with her hose and, unfortunately for Germaline, Bridget had just had a new pump installed. The power of the hose had sent Germaline flying backwards out the driveway, right into the path of a group of kids on skateboards. They'd all ended up in a scrum on the pavement, and Germaline's leg was broken in two places.

Bridget had ignored Germaline's screams of pain as she turned her attention to trying – unsuccessfully, as it happened – to hose the graffiti off her house and Leon's car before it dried in.

Leon hadn't heard a thing from Germaline since his family had issued her with a bill for damages caused during the incident . . . but maybe she was now back on the scene and taking her anger out on me, thanks to Bridget? (Typical Irish mammy-in-law.) But then again, if she and Leon were no longer in contact, would she even know that he'd been to Vegas and make any connection between him and the Leon I was looking for? Unless, of course, it wasn't as over as he'd led me to believe . . .

As I inserted my last coin into the slot machine, I briefly considered asking Reception if they had CCTV footage that they could check out, before I dismissed the idea. It was a hotel, not Scotland Yard, and it wasn't as if anybody had just been murdered. I'd noticed that Nicole's in-tray was marked with a gigantic 'IN' sticker on the side, so maybe someone had just come up to the left-hand side of the reception desk and dropped it into her tray while her back was turned. As for who that someone was – well, in truth, it could be anyone. There were a lot of crazy people out there (some might say I was one of them, but that was beside the point). It could be as simple as a random person staying in this hotel taking a dislike to the look of me or what I was doing and dropping a letter into Reception, just to try and mess with my head. Or any member of the public in fact – it was no secret that I was staying in the place where I'd met Leon, after all. The best way to handle the whole thing was to try to put it out of my mind.

I got up and left the slot machine for some other poor sucker to take on. As I walked to the elevator, I tried to shake off the bad feeling the letter had left me with, but it was difficult to get rid of it. The last few years had been filled with nothing but negative vibes, and it was galling that no sooner had I left them all behind me in Ireland than more came my way over here.

That night, I had the dream again. And this time, it was a million times more graphic, more powerful and more upsetting than ever before.

Chapter Twelve

Elaine and I had been friends since before we were born, as our mothers had been best friends who were pregnant at the same time. My mother had been three weeks ahead of Elaine's mother Susan in her pregnancy, but Elaine couldn't wait to get out, and made her appearance at thirty-seven weeks. My mother thought she had been hallucinating with the pain when she'd seen Susan being carted into the pre-labour ward and plonked into a bed beside her. A few hours after I was born, Elaine joined the world. I often wondered if we had met for the first time at college or something, would we have decided we liked each other enough to become friends, but there was never a choice in the matter – we were pushed together for toddler play-dates, birthday parties, the whole shebang. Having sat beside each other throughout our entire schooling, we then plumped for the same college course in the same university. I had loads of people I considered good friends, but there was nobody quite like Elaine.

Having said all that, she could be a right cantankerous bitch at times. She loved the limelight, and couldn't handle it at all if she had to share it with anyone else – particularly me. The first time we got drunk together as teenagers, she told me that she felt like she'd spent her whole life catching up with me – I was born first, I walked first, I had a boyfriend before she did, etc etc. It was all maudlin, drunken talk that she dismissed and denied vehemently when I tried to speak to her about it when we were sober again but, as time went on, I could see that it was an issue for her. Once, when my mother had a massive bust-up with Susan after a neighbour reported back to her that Susan had called my brother Adam a bad influence on her son (she was 100% right, he was, but there was no telling Mum that), she spat out some venom about how Susan couldn't even let her have the limelight on the day of the birth of her child. Of course, it was never mentioned again after Mum and Susan made up over a bottle of Blue Nun and home-made scones, but her words had planted a seed in my head. How symbolic it was that Elaine had stolen my thunder on that day, seeing as she tried to make it a lifetime habit after that.

Our relationship during our entire college course was like a tennis match. Even though we would have dropped everything in the world for each other if either of us had been in trouble, there was still an undercurrent of points-scoring in our relationship. I often wondered if ours was one of those toxic friendships that you read about, and yet I was reluctant to discuss it with her. The whole thing was so deep-rooted that it would have been hugely traumatic to pull it up from where it lay. A symbiotic relationship like ours would have been too great a loss if we found ourselves unable to resolve our issues, so it was best all round to just keep things buried, right?

This theory worked well for me until Elaine snogged a guy I was seeing called Jay. When I look back on it, he was a tosser. His name wasn't even Jason, in which case I could have sort of condoned the pretentious Jay as an acceptable abbreviation – it was John. His name, and his pretentious nature, didn't bother me in the slightest for the first few weeks while I was still in the first flush of new love, but it didn't take long for his mannerisms to bug me. If someone was watching a repeat of an old sitcom, he'd have to say the lines along with the show, guffawing after every joke. If there was a big match on TV, he'd talk about transfer windows, goal history and upcoming fixtures all through the game until the person watching it was forced to tell him to shut up. I had a sneaking suspicion it was going nowhere by the time we hit week three, but I never got the chance to dump him. I had great aspirations to do so at a party we went to in one of the other student's houses, but when I slipped away to neck a bottle of beer before delivering the blow, I came back to find Elaine necking him.

The resulting hissy fit was a culmination of a decade's worth of repressed rage – I opened a can of cider belonging to God knows who and poured it all over her, I fired a platter of stale sandwiches in their direction, I yanked a canvas picture of the Pope down from the wall and crashed it over Jay's head, etc etc. All I needed was a cream pie to stick in her face to complete the effect, but there's never a spare cream pie just lying around when you need one. Of course, the party was the talk of the college, and photos of Jay with his head sticking out of the picture-frame kept popping up on the college notice boards for weeks (ah, the innocence of the pre-Internet days!), but his disgrace only made me feel marginally better – especially as most of the photos clearly showed me in the background with my arms flailing like a lunatic, and Elaine wearing a shocked expression as if she had been the innocent party in the whole thing.

Some of our mutual friends had separated us that night to prevent further fighting, but the next day we tore into the arguing when we met in the kitchen, both hungover. I swear to God, that fight went on longer than if all the episodes of *Countdown* ever made were broadcast back to back. Misdemeanours and perceived slights from eight years back were served over the net. Justifications were volleyed back. I felt it was Advantage Miss Appleton after what had happened the previous night, but Elaine was defending her behaviour to the end – I was making the matter worse by making such a big deal of it, that kind of thing. In the end, the net was torn down, and we advanced towards each other spouting the most unforgivable insults we could possibly muster. Elaine moved out the next day.

Eventually, after three months of a stalemate, we decided we had to put it behind us. Both of us did it grudgingly, and more because we were sick of avoiding each other when in the same group of friends or family than anything else. It was easier to go back to pretending again. But I never truly forgave her betrayal, and she never forgot some of the harsh words I had thrown at her during our argument. She'd given me a mouthful of them as well though and I felt we'd cancelled each other out on that score, which brought us back to her being the guilty party.

When Elaine met Eoghan, she became a different person. Although she'd gone out with plenty of guys in the past, none of them had ever made her blossom the way she did when she was with Eoghan. She was herself, but a happier, more colourful version – a better Elaine. Everything about her seemed to be illuminated. Eoghan was a new friend of her sister, Katy, and Elaine couldn't believe her luck when he asked her out – she fell hopelessly for him the second she laid eyes on him.

Problem was, so did I. As soon as they had established their couple status, Elaine couldn't wait to show him off to all of her friends. She had been quite secretive up to that and not even I had met the guy. She chose a twenty-first party of a friend of ours to do the unveiling. Perhaps it was my imagination, but it seemed that we had been invited to more parties than ever in the wake of our row – I couldn't help wondering if people were hoping for a repeat of the fireworks but, being a student at the time, I was more concerned about getting out there and having fun than motives.

The second I met him, I was bowled over. He had exactly the look I liked in a guy – tall, trendy, longish hair, but not too long – he was just my type. But he was exactly the opposite of Elaine's usual guy. She had always gone for the more sporty jocks (she'd made an exception for Jay, of course). I had a moment where I had to fight down one of those illogical rising resentments you get when you're well on the way to becoming plastered. This one was on the lines of 'There are enough jocks out there to choose from – why couldn't she leave someone like him for me?' My resentment rose even further as the night went on, and escalated into 'Well, if she was any sort of a friend at all, wouldn't she have kept me in mind and introduced him to me!' as I fell into full-blown drunkenness. I got through that night without causing any scenes, and I just hoped that the next time I saw him I wouldn't fancy him at all. But no, the fecker was still as gorgeous the next time Elaine paraded him around with her like a new handbag. As time went on and I got to know him, things got worse. It turned out that we had similar taste in pretty much everything. It was like he had been purpose-built to be my perfect partner. But he could never be that, so I just tried to stay out of his and Elaine's way as much as possible. If she noticed that I was doing that, she never mentioned it.

Whenever I did meet them, I noticed that Eoghan had started to act very strangely around me. It took me a while to work it out, and when I did, I wasn't sure if I was excited or horrified. He was behaving suspiciously as if he fancied me. There were blushes, there were stuttered words, there were awkward silences – and there were plenty of hard looks from Elaine whenever she came across this scene.

All of a sudden, she pretty much disappeared off my radar. Even though I'd been phasing her out since I developed feelings for Eoghan, it still felt very strange not to have her in my life at all. A part of me was angry at her. Another part not only understood, but was grateful.

We eventually all came face-to-face five weeks after Elaine had disappeared from my life, at a party I wish to God I'd never gone to. It's hard to think that something as innocuous and trivial as a party can change the outcome of your entire life. It's even harder to think that if I had behaved differently that night, it wouldn't have. Elaine hadn't expected me to be there, of course – if she had, she certainly wouldn't have been there herself. I'd gone along to the party with my cousin, but I had no idea how Elaine and Eoghan were connected to anyone or why they were there. Elaine did a dramatic, and pathetic, U-turn the second she clapped eyes on me across a crowded room, dragging Eoghan along with her. She was wasting her time. The house was too small to avoid anyone for more than thirty seconds. We passed each other at least five times, with Elaine all grim-faced and Eoghan all apologetic and confused nods, in the space of an hour. I resolved to stay away from her, no matter how drunk I got – I could see by the puss on her that she was in a mood.

If only she had been thinking along the same lines. She stumbled over to me halfway through the night, eyes glistening, face contorted in disdain.

"You're like my fucking shadow!"

A paradoxical statement on many levels, but now wasn't the time to point that out.

"Go away, Elaine. You're drunk. Go back and be your boyfriend's bodyguard." I couldn't help it. Even as I was trying to get rid of her, I was reeling her back in.

"Dyuh actshully think I don't know what you're playing at? You're interested in him!" She was spitting all over my face, her own face and probably everyone else's in the room as she attempted to speak. "The minute my back's turned, you're gonna go for it, aren'tcha? *Aren'tcha?*"

"Elaine, you know I could tear you apart when it comes to answering this question. You haven't a leg to stand on if we get into this argument. Do yourself a favour and get the hell out of my face before I start to lose my patience with you." In truth, I'd lost it several seconds ago, and was struggling hugely to keep my temper in check.

"Oh, I can just see it now. I go off to the bathroom, and I come back to find you on top of him."

It was as if I hadn't spoken.

I knew that saying anything else was pointless, not just because she wouldn't listen, but more so because her legs had given way under her as soon as she'd delivered her sentence, and she was now in a heap on the floor. When I tried to help her up, she suddenly regained the use of her legs as she kicked a foot back into my shin. Then she collapsed again, and seemed to go into a coma.

Eoghan came into the room just in time to see the kick and then the coma. He didn't seem too surprised to witness either event.

"She's been doing nothing but drinking over the past few weeks," he said.

"Call a taxi and get her home," I said to somewhere around his torso. I wouldn't, couldn't, look at him. This situation was bad enough as it was.

He got out his phone and made the requisite call. "Twenty minutes, they said."

"She can't stay lying on this floor for twenty minutes. Wait here with her. I'll sort something out."

I found the owner of the house, explained the situation, and once a bucket had been located was grudgingly allowed to carry/drag Elaine into a room rather than having her lying on the kitchen floor. Eoghan lifted her up under the arms and I picked up her feet. We laid her down on the bed, placed the bucket strategically in front of the locker and hoped for the best. I always thought buckets were a waste of time for drunk people – alcohol-induced pukes were usually of the projectile kind, so if you got one drop of the darned thing in the actual bucket, you'd be lucky. It was just one more thing to clean up afterwards, really.

When we had her settled on the bed, the inevitable awkward looks started between Eoghan and me.

"Come on, let's go back out to the party," I said. "We're no use to her standing here watching her."

I tried to lose him as I joined the crowd in the kitchen, but he seemed determined not to be shaken off.

"Did you and Elaine fall out over something?" he asked after about three aimless circuits of the kitchen.

I walked out into the garden and he followed.

"Well?" he said. "Did you? Did you fall out?"

"Hmm. What makes you think that?"

"She never makes arrangements to see you any more, never even mentions your name . . ."

My sarcasm had gone over his head. "Yes, we've fallen out,

Eoghan. There was nothing official, no big bust-up or anything like that, but we're definitely not on good terms."

"Is it something to do with me?"

I hadn't expected him to be so direct. I wasn't ready for it. "You give yourself a lot of credit, don't you?"

"I'm not saying it is, I'm just asking. I'm trying to work a lot of things out in my head at the moment. Elaine is a different person now to the girl I first met."

I said nothing.

"Something happened to change things shortly after I met you. Do you know what that might be?"

Jesus, he was really getting into the swing of the whole being-direct thing.

"No." That was true. I didn't know what it *might* be – I knew what it *was*. Pedantic, but a difference existed, so I wasn't lying. I wondered how long this school of thought would be able to get me through the conversation . . .

"Do you think she's afraid that there's something between us? Us as in you and me?"

I was no longer wondering. My tactic clearly wasn't working in the face of such directness.

"Why don't you ask her all of this, instead of asking me?"

"I've tried. You've no idea how many times I've asked her."

"And?" I knew what the 'and' was, but I didn't know what else to say.

"She went absolutely mental the first time I asked her if she wasn't talking to you any more. Then, when we talked about her going so mental, she said that you'd just grown apart – which really didn't justify her reaction. So I asked her straight out if she thought I fancied you, or that you fancied me. And if I thought she went mental the first time, you should have seen her reaction to this – which told me everything I needed to know, really."

"Which is what? That she thinks you fancy me, or that I fancy you?"

"One or the other."

"So you don't know which?"

"No . . ."

"So her reaction really didn't tell you everything you needed to know, then." I knew I was splitting hairs, but I had to swerve this conversation off course before I blurted out things that shouldn't ever go further than the back of my head. His physical proximity was wearing down my resolve to stay tight-lipped.

"It told me that she has a problem with you and me being around each other. She's afraid of what might happen."

"That's just silly."

"Is it?"

"Of course it is."

"Andie, I'm not being presumptuous here. There's a spark between us. Believe me, I'd prefer if there wasn't. It'd make my life a lot easier. I meet this girl I like, start seeing her and all is well, then I meet her friend, and . . . I can't stop thinking about her. About you, Andie."

"I preferred when you were talking about me as if I was someone else. It made this easier to listen to." I was lying. A part of me that was deeply ashamed of itself was loving every minute of hearing this.

"I don't want to feel like this about you, but there's nothing I can do about it."

"Here's one thing you can do, Eoghan. Forget about it." I was choking on the words, but they had to be said. "What do you think is going to happen – that you'll break up with Elaine, and then we'll just get together? Get real."

"It's over between Elaine and me – and it's nothing to do with you. I just can't be with the person I've discovered she really is."

"She's not that bad!"

"If you heard some of the things she's said about you, you might feel differently. She's full of venom and hatred, and I can't help her with that. She can't be happy with anyone until she's happy in her own skin."

My, someone was in a deep mood tonight.

"I know it's not fair to make comparisons, but I look at you and see someone who is happy and at ease with herself, and think 'That's the type of person I want to be with.'"

"Stop right there, Eoghan. I don't want to hear this."

"Well, tough, because I want to say it. We've been circling around each other since we first met. Whether it's terrible or not, the truth is that I'm crazy about you."

I shook my head, but he continued anyway.

"You know, when I asked Elaine if she thought I had feelings for you, I was going to admit to her that I did find you attractive, but it was her that I was in love with – and that much was true at the time. I did feel I loved her until she changed so much. You – well, I found you attractive, but in a vague way that I was never going to do anything about while I was with Elaine. I just wanted to be open with her, to have no secrets between us. But when she clammed up on me and closed herself off, I couldn't stop the thoughts of you creeping into my head."

"You don't even know me to be crazy about me. You've just built me up in your head, and now you have yourself convinced you're mad about me. Maybe you just want someone to be mad about, and now that it hasn't worked out with Elaine, you're turning to me –"

"All I know is I want to be with you. Give me a chance, Andie. I know there's something between us. Can you tell me I'm imagining it?"

"No, Eoghan, you're not imagining it. It's a very tangible thing. It's called 'Elaine'. How can you possibly think she's going to be okay with you and me being together?"

"Ah. You said that like it was a future probability. That's good."

I laughed. Just a little laugh, but it was enough encouragement for him. He covered my hands with his. I didn't shake them off. He stared into my eyes. I didn't look away. He inched his head forward towards mine, not close enough to kiss me, but close enough to test the waters and see if I would pull back. I didn't.

That was all that happened, but it was enough. The damage was done. We'd been too busy gawking at each other to notice Elaine approaching. We heard her before we saw her – a ferociously expletive-ridden wail was coming from the direction of the patio. I looked up and saw Elaine staggering out the kitchen door, sending people's drinks flying as she hopped off shoulders in her journey towards us.

"I *knew* it! You dirty whore! You ugly, selfish cow!" She lunged at me, caught me by the throat and shook me with a strength that only a mixture of alcohol and anger can provide.

I grasped her fingers and tried to pull them away from my neck, but they were buried in my skin. Just as I began to panic, Eoghan pulled Elaine backwards and deposited her on her arse on the grass.

"You're crazy, do you know that?" He looked at her with such contempt that I actually felt a little bit sorry for her. Only a little bit though, considering that she'd tried to strangle me.

"Don't you dare try to wangle out of this by turning things on me! I know what I saw!" She tried to stand, but she only got halfway up before she flopped down again.

"You're disturbed, Elaine," he said. "Do you have any idea how low you've let yourself go? You're eaten up inside by bitterness and hate. Look at you, making a show of yourself in front of everyone. And we know why, don't we? It's because you're so jealous of Andie that it's destroying you."

"Shut up! This is all her fault!" She tried to get up again, and this time she succeeded. She turned on me. "You can't let me have anything to myself!"

"She isn't trying to take me. I'm the one who's trying to talk her into giving me a chance. It's her I want, not you."

Elaine's face crumpled.

Pity for her, for the sadness inside her, unexpectedly filled me. "Eoghan, stop – she's not able to hear this right now . . . ."

"If she's able to dish it out, she's able to eat it too."

The girl who owned the house marched towards us. I braced myself to be kicked out of the party – she'd obviously had enough of us.

110

"Hey! That taxi you ordered for her is here." She pointed at Elaine. "Get her out of here now."

"I can hear, you know. Don't talk about me like I'm not here. I'll only be too glad to leave this poxy party."

"I preferred you when you were unconscious."

"I still would be, only your boyfriend came in and tried it on with me," said Elaine. "Don't worry, I didn't touch him. I have standards. Although you wouldn't think it to look at this creep." She matched Eoghan's earlier contemptuous look with one of her own as she stumbled to her feet.

"Get *out* of here, you cow!"

One of the girl's male friends came over to her and led her away, cajoling her with promises of a cocktail if she came inside.

"Go, Elaine," said Eoghan. "Your taxi is waiting. I'll walk you out."

When Eoghan moved towards her, she bristled and positively snarled. I was sure I was about to see foam dripping from her mouth.

"Touch me and I'll have you up for assault."

I touched my sure-to-be-bruised neck, and wondered if she was trying to be ironic in the midst of all this madness.

She flailed her arms. "Get the fuck away from me!"

Eoghan complied without putting up any more of a fight.

Before she left, she turned to me. "I'll never speak to you again, you bitch. You've ruined my whole life. It stops tonight. Our friendship is over."

"And good riddance to it! I don't care if I never see you again."

She gave me the benefit of her snarl too before she wobbled to the kitchen door.

I slumped onto the ground and sat cross-legged because my knees were shaking so much that I'd fall otherwise. And after Elaine's whole attempt-on-my-life fit, I was in a bad enough state for one night.

After Elaine left, people seemed to come out of the woodwork from everywhere to ask us what had just happened. Eoghan and I

111

fobbed them all off, but there had been enough witnesses to Elaine's attack for the story to spread like shingles anyway. Eoghan went into the kitchen, and returned with two blatantly stolen glasses of whiskey with only a dribble of lemonade mixed through them. I hated whiskey, but now wasn't the time to be choosy.

When we eventually got some peace and quiet, Eoghan put an arm around my shoulders. "I think I should take you home." When he realised what he'd just said, he pulled his arm away again. "No, not like that . . . I just mean that you've had a shock, and it'd be best for you to get out of here. I can walk you home if you like."

"No. I can take myself home." I got up and smoothed down the creases in my skirt, wishing I could wipe out the night's events as easily. "I'll call a taxi."

Eoghan made some wishy-washy attempts at insisting that he come with me, but I brushed them away easily enough. I suddenly didn't want to be in his company. I had a feeling mine was no longer so appealing either.

I found my cousin, and she decided to come home too, having declared the party shite. I made small talk with various people until the taxi arrived.

As soon as I got home, I tried to ring Elaine, as guilt over our fight had started to set in. She didn't answer. I texted her, asking her to give me a call the next day, then fell into a drunken sleep. When I checked my phone the next morning, she hadn't texted.

I got a call from her flatmate, Sorcha, at about three that afternoon, asking me if I knew where Elaine was. She hadn't come home. I told Sorcha that I didn't, and that Elaine had taken a taxi home at around one o'clock. Sorcha suggested that she might have gone to her parents' house, so she would ring them to see if she was there. I asked her to text me and let me know. Ten minutes later, my phone buzzed.

"Elaine's parents haven't seen or heard from her . . ."

Elaine's body was found in a shallow grave in the Wicklow Mountains two weeks later. She had been raped, beaten and suffocated to death. It transpired that she had asked the taxi driver to drop her off in Temple Bar in the city centre. The taxi driver, realising that she was drunk, had told her she'd be better off to go home, but she had insisted that she lived in an apartment in Temple Bar. She'd given the address of a set of apartments that a friend of ours had lived in a year previously. As soon as the taxi driver was out of sight, CCTV footage had shown her entering a nightclub, and leaving an hour later with a man. Elaine had been barely able to walk, and the man was half-carrying, half-dragging her out of the club. The same man was eventually found guilty of her murder, and was sentenced to life.

He wasn't the only one. It was eight years now since Elaine had been murdered, and although the rawness of the guilt I lived with had dulled, it never, ever went away. It filled my mind every morning, and was relentless in its ability to punish me, to colour every day with grey. I hadn't betrayed Elaine with Eoghan, but this was about more than him. Her death had come about as a result of our years and years of competition. If only I'd had the maturity to handle things better . . . if only I'd confronted her and never let things get as far as they did . . . with every year that passed after her death, I found new things to add to the 'if only' list. Eoghan blamed himself too, but he really had no idea of how insignificant his role was. No, the only person to blame for Elaine finding herself in the situation that she did was me.

I couldn't explain my guilt to anyone. Of course, lots of people noticed a change in me, but they put it down to me feeling guilty about fighting with Elaine before she left the party. I heard from a friend that some people, while supportive at the time of Elaine's funeral, were saying behind my back that her death was my fault because I shouldn't have let her leave the party on her own, taxi or no taxi. What they didn't understand was that it had started being my fault long before that. But the nature of my messed-up relationship with Elaine was one that was hard to put into words and explain logically, so I hugged the guilt to myself and let it fester. Somewhere along the line, it became a part of me.

So how do people deal with this kind of guilt? I only know what

I did to cope. I kept myself busy. For the past eight years, I'd thrown myself into things so fast and so hard that I hadn't had time to stop and see the bruises they caused. I didn't consider whether what I was doing was right for me or not – I just did them, and worried about the consequences later. Which was probably how I ended up in situations like being in Vegas looking for a man who everyone was starting to think was a figment of my imagination.

And yet, that man was the only person I'd truly confided in over the last eight years. And that was exactly why I was on this search.

Chapter Thirteen

It's funny. It's just one of those universal truths that no matter where you go in the world and hide, the Monday blues will always find you. I'd always thought there would only be shades of sunshine yellow in Vegas, but it seemed that Monday was Monday as long as you were working. Thankfully, it was almost time to go home – I'd had enough of LVTV in general, and Lindy in particular, for one day. Colm and I had been assigned temporary desks in the LVTV studios for the duration of Operation Arizona (as Dave had dubbed my attempt to locate Leon), where we had a wonderful view of the back of Lindy's head. She'd taken to raising her arms slowly to her head and shaking her mane nonchalantly yet furiously in a bid to gain Colm's attention, then slyly swivelling in her chair to see if he'd been looking at her. Invariably, he hadn't. Instead, she always caught me with what was no doubt an incredulous look on my face, while Colm remained blissfully unaware of her bids to catch his eye as he stared at something painfully interesting like a lens for a new camera or something equally trainspottingy. Her skirts and tops were getting skimpier each day, and her hair was so sleek that you could have ice-skated in it, but she still couldn't compete with the lure of nerdy stuff on the Internet.

I felt pretty lethargic after a weekend of pimping myself to the media. Lindy was in fifth gear with the publicity drive, and in fairness she was doing an amazing job of it. Of course, it was entirely for her own benefit. She'd plonked down beside Colm as he sat on his own having lunch in the LVTV canteen the previous day, and had bent his ear about her career ambitions. Apparently, she was ultimately working towards securing a position as a news anchor, and wanted to make a huge success of promoting my story to get her name out there, and show she had what it took to move things on to the next level. It sounded like she was trying to sell herself to him as an attractive proposition, but he hadn't given a toss. He'd been so annoyed at having his lunch interrupted by an unwelcome guest that he'd taken a huge dislike to her. And the reason I knew all of this was because his dislike of her was so huge that he, in turn, had bent my ear about how annoying Lindy was over dinner the previous night when we were supposed to be planning our next show for Éire TV. I can't say I blamed him – in fact, it was the first time we'd ever agreed about something – but she was certainly helping my cause, so I couldn't complain about her too much. Well, no, actually, I could. I could always complain. But she was doing a good job, even if the hectic schedule she was putting me through was making me feel like I'd just spent seventy-two hours straight cutting turf on the bog.

It didn't help either that my flipping laptop was operating so slowly this morning. Although, come to think of it, it'd been like this for quite a while now . . . I sighed. It was really that time of year again to delete all the unnecessary stuff on the hard drive. I decided to take a positive, effective approach and fly through the work. I quickly deleted a folder full of work files, bypassed my music folder and left its contents untouched, then deleted a few more work files for good measure. I went to all my temporary and local folders too, taking a quick look to see if there was anything I needed in them before purging them.

Ah. So that was where my instant messenger conversations saved to – the local folder. I took a quick through them, laughing at some old conversations that had been on the computer for yonks that I'd forgotten about.

Then, something *very* strange jumped out at me. So strange that I pushed my seat back from the computer . . . but when I'd recovered from the shock, I pressed my nose up against the screen to make sure I didn't miss a single word.

Christ. This was just too good not to share. I wished someone from the office was here, but in their absence, Colm would have to do.

He was in the middle of barking orders down a phone at someone in the Éire TV office. "Make sure you get that done before COB today . . . we need to hit that milestone . . . well, you'll just have to re-prioritise your other tasks, so. This is on the critical path . . ."

I yawned loudly as I waited for him to shut up. I had a feeling that the person on the other end of the phone was hoping he'd can it pretty soon too. Eventually, he hung up, cursing under his breath as he threw the phone back in its cradle.

"Colm!" I beckoned him over.

He gave me a disinterested look, but eventually sloped over, grabbing a biscuit off his desk before he made his move. Today's packet of choice were orange-flavoured custard creams. How they hadn't all been broken to bits in his suitcase on the way over was beyond me.

"Look at this."

He pulled up a chair, and started to read off my screen.

Isolde: You all set for tonight?

Martin: I suppose so. I just hope nobody sees me.

Isolde: Don't be such a friggin' wimp. I've been doing this for years. Once you get into it, you'll never want to stop.

Martin: I know. I really want to do it, but I feel so bad about lying to Valerie.

Isolde: Look, if you can't talk to your wife, that's your problem. It's not something I'm prepared to listen to you moaning about. You came to me and told me straight out what you wanted. I'm willing to give it to you.

Martin: I know, but it's not too late to put a halt to this. I haven't done anything yet. I shouldn't be lying to Valerie – she's a good woman, even if we haven't seen eye-to-eye about all this kind of stuff in the past.

Isolde: Stop pussyfooting about. You only get one chance with me. Do you want to do this, or don't you?

Martin: You know that I do. It's just going to be tricky, on so many levels.

Isolde: It'll become part of your life after a while, and it'll be as normal as breathing. I'll meet you at 7 outside Days Hotel. Of course, you do know that if you breathe a word to a soul about this, I'll grind every bone in your body to powder, yes? My private life stays private.

Martin: Well, I hardly want this coming out either. I feel so weak to need to do this in the first place. I wish I could control myself, but I can't.

Isolde: *Never* think you're weak because you need me. That's rule number one. So many people struggle with their needs, but they do nothing about it, and end up very unhappy because of it. At least you're doing something to help yourself. Now, go away and leave me alone so that I can get a bit of work done. I'm on someone else's computer while mine is getting an upgrade, and she'll need it back soon. She can be a right wagon when she's in a snit, which is a lot of the time, and I'm not in the mood for her today – so, good luck, see you later. And don't be late.

Martin: Okay. I'm getting a bit excited about it now, actually. It's the first step towards release.

Isolde: No need to be so melodramatic. Now go. Plenty of time for talking later.

I hovered over the email address associated with Martin's username, only to notice that it was an Éire TV address. "Do you know this Martin?" I squealed.

Colm looked at the email address. "Yes, I know him very well actually," he said. "What's this about?"

"Read the IM string and tell me what you think it's about."

I looked expectantly at Colm when he finished reading. He leaned back in his seat. "I'm not going to jump to any conclusions."

"Oh, neither am I."

"Good."

"I don't need to. It's obvious what's going on! Isolde's launching into an affair with a married man, and she's not even showing the slightest bit of remorse about it! The woman is heartless –"

"You don't know that for sure –"

"Oh, wake up! And the walking bitch called *me* a wagon! Me! *She's* the station-wagon of wagons! Well, if I am one, it's from hanging out with her for too long."

"Just forget you read that. Don't interfere in something that isn't your business –"

"So, you think it's okay that Martin is lying to his wife, then? You're going to condone it by keeping schtum about it all?"

"What do you want me to do? That IM conversation doesn't prove anything."

"This is exactly why people get away with things – people like you just can't be bothered disrupting their own lives to help someone else. Tell me, if you were being cheated on, wouldn't you want someone to tell you?"

"I don't know. I haven't been in that situation."

"Well then, you're very lucky. I have, and I wished afterwards that people who knew about it had had the decency to tell me, and stopped me looking like a total fool. But no, nobody wants to get involved, so they just let you go on being the only person who doesn't know about it."

"What good do you think it would do if I rang Valerie, and this guy she's only met a few times socially tells her that her husband is cheating on her?"

"Ah. So you agree that he's cheating on her, then? So much for not jumping to conclusions!"

He sighed deeply. "If he is, then I'm not the right person to tell her."

"So talk to Martin, then. Tell him that if he doesn't fess up, you'll tell his wife. That might make him see sense."

He shook his head. "I have enough to do trying to manage about ten different projects across an ocean and a timezone. I'm staying out of this, and you should too. It'll only do more harm than good to stick our noses in this, I'm telling you. It's probably nothing."

"You know it's not, but that's fine. You go away and pretend you know nothing."

I shook my head as he walked back to his desk. Mr High and Mighty I've-never-been-cheated-on. Wasn't it bloody well for some?

Just to fuel my fire, Lindy did an extra-long shake of her hair. My mood lifted slightly though when I saw the look of horror on her face as Colm remained oblivious to all of her efforts. Next thing, she'd be stripping in a bid to get his attention – although she was wearing so little as it was that he'd probably barely notice the difference.

That night, the dream changed.

She takes the shortcut. When he grabs her, her initial shock gives way to her survival instinct. She kicks and flails until she manages to get away from him for a few seconds. In those precious seconds, she screams at the top of her lungs, no longer constrained by the monster's grubby hand over her mouth. He gains ground on her attempt to escape, and soon she's knitted into his grip once more – but her time of freedom was long enough for someone to hear her plea for rescue. She doesn't see the man approach – but, more importantly, neither does her captor. The man hits the monster from behind with an object she can't see, but which makes a ferocious noise as it crushes her captor's skull. His hold on her instantly loosens, and she wriggles away just before he falls to the ground. She doesn't know if he is unconscious or dead, but she doesn't care. After what he's just tried to do to her, she hopes it's the latter.

"Are you alright?" the man says. "I called the police as soon as I heard you scream – they're on their way."

"Yeah, I'm okay now," she says. "Thank you so much for saving my life, em . . . ?"

"Leon," he says. "My name is Leon."

I woke up in a pool of sweat. This one had been far, far worse in its own way than the one where I lived through Elaine's death in every last gory detail. At least I was used to the pain of that one. This dream gave me hope, made me wake up feeling for just a nanosecond that everything was alright, then sent me crashing back to the reality of Elaine being dead.

Not to mention the fact that I'd now be haunted by Leon for the entire day.

I got up and threw myself into the shower, dressed in about two minutes flat and got to the office an hour earlier than usual. Isolde was still sending me loads of other work, so I had three articles to write this morning for the weekend editions of the paper. I kept my head down and worked solidly until lunchtime, then swallowed a sandwich in one bite and got back to work again. Lindy was out of the office in the morning, and Colm never spoke to me unless I spoke to him, so I had a gloriously quiet time until Lindy stormed in shortly after half one in a full-length black and white dress.

"Why are you still here?" This was aimed at me. Colm was privileged enough to get a nod from her.

"Where else would I be? We're not leaving for the launch party until three."

Lindy had wangled an invitation for us to attend the launch of a brand-new people-search website – a website for stalkers, to you and me. She'd been jumping out of her skin since she'd found out yesterday that we'd been put on the list – we probably had a cancellation slot and they just wanted to make up numbers, but she was acting as if Elvis was coming back from the dead just to meet us. The angle she was taking was that there were bound to be journalists there who wanted to talk to the hottest people-searcher of the moment (that's me, in case you're confused, but Lindy went to great pains to explain to me that it was my story that was hot, and not myself, not that I'd been in any doubt about that in the first place). My situation was so *relevant* and captured the *zeitgeist* of all the lonely people in the world . . . she didn't tell me straight out to use these words in an interview situation, but she didn't need to –

after the first twenty stressed references to all things zeitgeisty, I kinda got the hint. Sure, why wouldn't they be lining up to interview someone like me at such an event? So she'd warned me to be prepared – but I hadn't taken that to mean that I'd have to make my departure for the damn thing the night before.

"Exactly! We're leaving at three, and it's now one forty!"

"Which isn't three – what's the problem here?"

"Oh. My. *Gawd*. What is wrong with you?" She turned to Colm. "Are all Irish women this slovenly? No wonder you choose to be single." She took three seconds out of her rant to send a megawatt beam in Colm's direction, then she made her way over to me and slammed the lid down on my laptop.

"Taxi back to the hotel, quick. You too, Colm. Oh, and can you bring your camera to this event? We should probably film Andie at the launch talking about how lucky she is that a service like this exists – something like that. I'll make it up as I go along."

Colm shrugged. He always looked like he was lost without his camera anyway, so he was probably delighted to have an excuse to bring it.

An hour later, I was clad in a silk dress that I'd bought just before I came to Vegas. Lindy had pounced upon it midway through a fierce and uninvited rifle through my sparse wardrobe after she'd accompanied us back to the hotel. The bodice of the dress was silver and ruched, with delicate silver roses decorating the straps, but the knee-length skirt was a deep shade of amethyst. I'd bought it for a tenner in a closing-down sale in a boutique at home, but it was one of those gems that looked a million dollars when teamed up with a bit of jewellery. I'd matched it with silver pearl earrings, a chunky pearl bracelet and a silver pendant, and tied the look together with a pale mauve wrap and silver peep-toe shoes. I wondered idly if Leon would like it (or rather, if he'd like *me* in it. He'd given me no reason to believe that he was into wearing women's clothes).

Lindy hovered around me, nodding her head in approval and muttering randomly about how people should really stop being so lazy about making an effort. She seized upon the sparse contents of my make-up bag – a battered wand of supermarket-brand mascara, a stubby lipstick and some other basics, and got to work. Her twiggy fingers hovered in front of my eyes and my cheeks as she applied my make-up in vigorous strokes, her entire face a scowl of intense concentration. She then whipped out a hairbrush and a mini-can of hairspray from a handbag that looked compact but appeared to hold the contents of an entire department store, did some weird flicky thing with the layers of my hair, and within a few minutes, I suddenly looked quite sophisticated. This led to another rant about people who have great potential but don't use it – apparently there was nothing worse. Starving children and earthquake victims didn't seem to register in Lindy's universe, and I had enough sense to realise that right then wasn't a good time to fill her in on some of the other things that were going on in the world.

"Okay. You're ready."

I frowned at my reflection. "Aren't I a little overdressed for a website launch? I look like I'm going to a wedding!"

"No. Look at me. Am I overdressed?"

"Yes, but you overdress every day of the week, so that's normal. Me, well, even though this dress only cost a tenner, this is as dressed-up as it gets for me – and I just brought this over from Ireland because I shrank all my other ones in a dodgy tumble-drying cycle incident a few days before I came over here." An incident that I strongly suspected my mother had something to do with. She'd coincidentally been complaining that my lovely comfy black shift dress was too loose and baggy and did me no favours only hours before it came out of the tumble-dryer looking like something Barbie would struggle to get into.

"Thank the good Lord above for dodgy tumble-dryers, then, because this dress is amazing on you. But, whatever you do, do *not* tell anyone what it cost. You got it in a designer store in New York, okay?"

She shoved me out the door of my room and resumed her mutterings all the way downstairs, her specialist subject this time being the disgrace that was people who didn't buy matching handbags for beautiful dresses (her face had crumpled in disgust when she'd realised that the only handbag I had was the battered black one I always carried around with me). I was spared from having to go on a whistle-stop tour of the MGM shops in search of something silver and handbaggy by the sight of Colm with his camera waiting in Reception, dressed in a fresh set of clothes. He had the whole smart casual look going on in a light pair of brown chinos and a tan short-sleeved shirt. His presence had the effect of melting Lindy's face as effectively as ice-cream in a microwave. On paper, I suppose it wasn't such a hard thing to imagine happening. That whole big brown puppy-dog-eyed thing he had going on, teamed with an air of distance and a hint of unattainability that some women found quite a challenge, probably made him attractive to some. But, as Lindy practically purred as we walked towards Colm, it just felt really strange.

If Colm was aware of the vibes bursting out of Lindy, he didn't show it as she sidled up to him and gave him a coy "Hi, you." I wouldn't have been surprised if she'd wrapped her body around his like a snake right there and then in the middle of Reception.

"So, whaddya think of the finery?" she said.

Colm turned to me. "You look . . . really different," he said, drinking me in with a look on his face that was akin to shock.

Good God, surely I wasn't that much of a slob normally!

"I was talking about mine!" She gestured at her dress, then played with a coil of her hair and replaced her frown with a smile and a giggle.

"Oh – well, I saw yours already when you came into the office, remember? But yeah, you look great too."

Lindy looked distinctly unimpressed at Colm's half-hearted compliment, particularly as he had turned his attention from her to an elderly lady who was struggling to make it to the elevator under the weight of the bags she'd accumulated on a shopping trip, most likely to an outlet store.

"One second – I'll give this lady a hand."

He bounded off towards her, while Lindy stared in awe as if Colm had just rescued a newborn baby from the jaws of a shark.

Lindy exhaled a long, ragged breath, and closed her eyes. "Thank you, God. Thank you."

"Lindy, are you alright?" She seemed to have forgotten I was there.

"Oh, yes. Never better. Just giving thanks to the Lord that he's single. I don't know how, I don't know why, but I'm so happy he is."

"Why shouldn't he be single?"

"Why?" She looked at me as if I was a village idiot that she was afraid to talk to in case she would be contaminated by my stupidity. "Are you totally blind? Have you seen his pecs? And what about those eyes of his? Wow!" She took another deep, shivery breath. "It's a miracle. I thought there were no single guys like him left."

"Well, just because he's single doesn't mean you two are going to get together." I didn't know why I was arguing with her – it's not as if I cared whether they got together or not – but her certainty that she could have something just because she wanted it was not only astounding, but mildly infuriating.

"Oh, please. Why wouldn't we? We'd make a gorgeous couple."

Colm strode back to us. He was met with an immediate smile from Lindy and what doubtless looked like a scrutinising look from me, as I tried to see him through Lindy's eyes.

"Philippe needs to start sharing his wage packet with me," he said, more to me than to Lindy.

As far as she was concerned, though, I was invisible, so she fluttered her eyelashes and laughed dutifully at Colm's quip.

We made our way outside. I had assumed we were getting a taxi to the launch, but Lindy steered us away from the queue of waiting taxis and led us to an area on the left-hand side of the hotel, where a shiny black limousine awaited us. I don't know if my face betrayed my concern that my expenses for the week would be eaten up by my share in paying for the thing, but Lindy muttered "Don't worry, it's on LVTV" in my direction before we filed into its gigantic interior. Once I was ensconced on my very own leather sofa, Lindy having plopped down beside Colm, I looked around and took in every detail. Its array of services was dazzling – and completely unnecessary for such a short journey. DVD players (yes, plural), a wet bar (which I probably would use before the end of the short journey just to take my attention away from the sickening sight of Lindy trying to cuddle up to Colm – she obviously had limo fantasies, but I really didn't want to see them acted out in front of me), ice buckets flanking a gigantic champagne bucket which held an unopened bottle of very expensive-looking bubbly, and a selection of finger food that wouldn't look out of place at a wedding buffet. The launch party was on in a brand-new hotel at the opposite end of the Strip. It surely wouldn't take us longer than fifteen minutes to get there. LVTV were obviously doing well this year.

"So, do you think we'll manage to drink the entire bottle between us?" Lindy nodded her head towards the champagne and smiled up at Colm, who was looking around the limo in what looked like complete bemusement. "We can certainly have fun trying!" She extended her arm out towards the bottle.

"Colm doesn't drink," I said flatly. "But that's all the more for you and me."

"Oh." She yanked her hand back as if the bottle had burned her, and shrank back into the sofa. "Now that you mention it, Colm, I've never seen you drink."

"We Irish get such a bad name for boozing, but then when we don't, the whole world seems disappointed," Colm said. "Or just incredulous."

"Something tells me you're not a man who disappoints the ladies," Lindy said in a throaty voice that sounded more sick than seductive.

I had to fight the urge to rummage in my handbag for some spare cough sweets, while Colm stared at her as if she'd totally lost the plot.

Lindy folded her arms across her chest and looked up at the roof of the car with a sulky expression after his reaction, all thoughts of opening the bottle of champers forgotten when there was only boring old me to share it with. It was probably a good thing – if she was this full-on while sober, there wouldn't be anything left of Colm after she had alcohol in her – she'd eat him alive. I took pity on him, and decided to veer the conversation onto neutral ground before she thought up some new seduction plan.

"Tell us more about this website launch today," I said in a breezy voice.

Lindy pouted. "What do you want to know? It's a website. It's being launched. Today."

"But surely there are enough of those people-search websites out there already? What's the point in launching yet another one?"

"This isn't just any old new website being launched by just anyone. The person behind this is Rick Heidlbarge – the guy who created the social-networking site Headspace."

"I know who Rick Heidlbarge is," I snapped. Even the granny who lived down the road from me had seen that fecker on her twenty-something-year-old portable TV with a clothes hanger sticking out of the back of it. He was everywhere these days. A few years ago, he was a poor student who spent his spare time pottering around in his bedroom writing nerdy IT programs. He started Headspace as a college project, then had a light-bulb moment when he saw its potential as a way for people to keep in touch with many others in one handy location. Once the word was out about Headspace, investors were queuing up to pump their money into it. Now, Rick was one of the youngest billionaires in the world, and you couldn't pick up a paper without seeing his oblong smiley face beaming back at you. I'd be beaming too if I were him, of course.

"Well, then you'll know that he's one guy who has contacts – and who knows a good opportunity when he sees one. Have you ever tried to find anyone on Mantra?"

"Is that a rhetorical question?" I'd lost count of how many hours I'd spent typing "Leon from Arizona" into Mantra, the world's biggest search engine, knowing that it was a road to nowhere, but still praying that I'd miraculously find a photo of my Leon. The rest of this miracle involved finding his email address directly below the photo, me emailing him and him happening to be online at that precise moment, resulting in him emailing back a frantic 'What's your number? I need to call you!' message, and ultimately a tear-drenched reunion in the airport.

"Well, you might not have used Mantra to stalk Leon," she said haughtily. "There are other search engines out there. And you'd be better off using one of them for a people search – which is where Rick comes in. You see, Mantra has been trying to buy a people-search company for ages – they want to create a partnership with one of them and basically plug the functionality into the Mantra search engine. Problem is, they couldn't find one to meet their standards. So they approached Rick and asked him to create one."

"Just like that?"

"Just like that. And Rick being Rick, he came back to them with a spec for a people-search site that had a degree of functionality that the competition weren't anywhere near even dreaming about. This site is going to be *huge*, Andie. You have no idea how lucky you are that I've set this up for you."

"Steady on, Lindy. It's just an invite to a party! It's not as if the great Bargepole will even know I'm there!"

"Yes, well, there are opportunities in every situation," she said.

She looked a bit flushed. I wondered if she was planning on using this fancy-smanchy party as an opportunity to seduce Colm.

"You know, I think I'll open this champagne after all," she said. "You sure I can't tempt you out of your good ways?" She lowered her head and did the old staring-up-through-fluttering-eyelashes thing at Colm, obviously prepared to use every trick in the book if she had to.

"No. I'm fine, thanks." Colm sounded distracted and vaguely annoyed.

"Okay, then – have it your way! All the more for me!" She popped the bottle with a practised hand.

"Andie is in the car too, you know."

Lindy flushed again, a much deeper shade this time. "Oh, of course. I just meant . . . that I'd have your share, that's all. I know how fast Andie drinks – I've seen her in action, remember? It's a pity I won't be getting to see *you* in action today, Colm."

As she grudgingly poured a glass for me and handed it over, Colm threw his eyes up to heaven behind her back. I winked at him when Lindy wasn't looking. Boy, he'd really have to watch himself today with her around . . .

Chapter Fourteen

The limo pulled up outside the newly opened five-star Lightning Hotel. I'd seen pictures of it everywhere since I first arrived in Vegas, but no image could do this place justice. It was striking, not only because of the silver model of forked lightning on the hotel's roof that zigzagged its way three-hundred and fifty feet into the air, but because of its sheer scale – the hotel had over 4,500 suites spread over eight acres of prime Vegas land.

"Isn't it amazing? I'm *soooo* happy they've chosen this venue for the launch."

"It looks like an expensive venue to choose," Colm said.

"Oh, yes. Rick likes to make statements in everything he does."

"We could all make big statements if we were billionaires." It was my turn to sound sulky. Lindy's reverential tone when she spoke about Rick was getting on my nerves. She ignored me, being far too busy jumping out of the limousine without even thanking the driver, much less tipping him, to pay any heed to me. I grudgingly followed her, while Colm searched his pockets for the driver's tip.

A group of porters approached us in greeting as we made our way to the lobby. I half-expected them to offer to carry my handbag inside, such was their eagerness to please. Lindy dismissed them with a barely perceptible nod of her head, but I smiled a wide smile and asked them how they were, as if I'd known them for years. They looked discomfited at being asked anything about themselves, and looked at each other as if they were trying to work out how to deal with the situation. I moved on, not wanting to cause any trouble.

"This way," Lindy said, indicating a corridor that led to the hotel's conference rooms. "We're in the Staccato Room."

The corridor was so long that it could have done with an airport-style moving walkway (I made a mental note to look for a suggestions box in Reception later), and the Staccato was at the end of it. Once we entered the room, I blinked in disbelief.

The Staccato was as big as some counties in Ireland. It was a mammoth banqueting area extending to the right of the entrance. Although a huge crowd of guests was already present, it was so spacious that if you lost someone in here, you might never see them again – which, given my track record, was a very likely possibility. When I looked around to take in all the details, I actually gasped. I'd noticed an aquarium on the wall to the left as soon as I'd entered the room, but when I took a second look, I saw that it extended upwards and ran the entire length and breadth of the ceiling, finishing its journey on the room's opposite wall where another aquarium perfectly mirrored it (although the opposite wall was so far away that I could only just see it). Aquariums were nothing new – Vegas was swimming in them – but the scale of this one would make even the ocean weep. Every time I blinked, something new caught my eye and fought for my attention – the sweeping staircase that led to both indoor and outdoor balconies, the floor-to-ceiling windows that overlooked a huge lake at the back of the hotel, a tremendous floral arrangement in the centre of the room representing the most beautiful and prevalent flowers from all the continents of the world. A buffet that ran the length of the room in front of the windows was the only touch of normality in what felt like an alternate universe, but even that managed to look tantalising and exotic.

Waiters criss-crossed my path as they glided around the room, eagerly refilling champagne glasses – but, all of a sudden, the crowds parted and people seemed to melt backwards into the walls. I was having serious suspicions about what was in those champagne bottles until I realised what was going on: our host was coming through. It seemed everyone wanted to lay eyes on the man who'd made so much money at such a young age, as if they were hoping that his good fortune might be infectious if they just saw him in the flesh. The fact that we were going to have to spend God knows how long staring at him up on a podium seemed to have escaped everybody's awareness.

Lindy pinched my arm so hard that I suspected her fingers met in the middle.

"Isn't he just gorgeous?"

This, coming from the one that was lusting over Colm a while ago. "Has it been a while, Lindy?"

"Oh, stop it, you vulgar thing!" Her face glazed over. "He's something else!"

I took a long hard look to see if I could work out what she saw in him. Okay, she might have had a point, if he was my type, but he wasn't. All was fine in the looks department – thick black hair, sallow skin, way taller than average. But nothing turned me off as much as superiority complexes (it was on the pet-hate list), and this guy was looking around the room as if nobody else in it was worthy to be there. Cockiness seeped from him and lay on his shoulders like an invisible veil. It wasn't all that invisible to me – but I seemed to be the only one who could see it, if the adoring and admiring glances around the room were anything to go by.

"Fucking tosspot," Colm whispered in my ear as he pointed his camera in Rick's direction.

I turned around and gave Colm the biggest smile I'd ever given him – or perhaps it was the only one, I wasn't sure. He winked back at me, mirroring the wink I'd sent his way in the limo.

A huge round of applause went up as Rick made his way up to a jewel-encrusted podium. He greeted the crowd, then instantly launched into a monologue of how great it was that he was launching this site, how it would be the answer to the world's problems, and how he had just found the cure for cancer. Probably. I don't know, I stopped listening after he said hello. I went in search of one of those waiters and their hugely inviting trays.

"It's times like this that I wish I drank," Colm said when I returned.

Rick was meandering on about making your own opportunities and using the gifts God had given you, repeating the same points over and over as if nobody would notice. Someone should have given him the gift of a stopwatch.

"You will drink by the end of his speech," I said.

"And now, the moment you've all been waiting for . . . I'm ready to announce the winner of our hunt for the Face of People Search. The winner is someone that nobody knew up until recently, but now her name is the one on everyone's lips. I think she's shown us that when it comes to finding the one you love, you should use every resource available to you – and trust me, ladies and gentlemen, we're the best resource of them all. So, without further ado, the lucky lady joining our winning team, and the official Face of People Search, is . . . Ms Andie Appleton!"

"*Yes!*" Lindy punched the air.

"Oh my Gawd, isn't she that weirdo from Ireland that's stalking the guy from Arizona?" someone behind me said.

"Well done, Andie! I'm so proud of you!" Lindy was shrieking.

I looked around in confusion at everyone gawping at me. "Hold on, there must be some mistake . . ."

"No, no, no, you've won!" muttered Lindy. "Oh wow, what a prize this is!"

The only prize that I could see was myself – a prize idiot who hadn't the first clue what was going on. "I didn't enter this competition!"

"I enturrd dit for yoo." It was hard to make out Lindy's words while she kept a huge smile on her face and spoke through gritted teeth, but I got the gist of it. She'd entered me in this without even asking me!

"For God's sake, Lindy! You could have told me!"

"Come on up, Andie!" Rick flashed a menacing smile at me.

"I'm grand where I am!" I yelled back at Rick, feeling too blown away by this development to be able to move. What was I supposed to say if I went up on stage?

A few nervous titters could be heard in the audience. Rick's face hardened, then he pulled the fakest smile I've ever seen out of the bag – it made Lindy's ones seem amateurish.

"We've got a shy one here, folks!" More nervous titters. "Looks like I'll have to come down to get you!"

"No, you're grand where you are too . . ." My voice was lost amid the sound of clapping as Rick left the podium and stormed down towards me, the crowd parting before him again. He grabbed me and tugged me forward by the arm, with Lindy pushing me from behind like a car that had broken down. It felt like the singing incident all over again as I suddenly found myself standing on the stage.

"Here she is, everyone – the new Face of People Search! And what a beautiful face! How do you feel?"

"Like a magician's assistant," I said truthfully as I looked down at myself all dolled up in my best dress.

"Oh, listen to her, folks," Rick said, poking a finger in my ribs. "She's already sucking up to the boss! Calling me a magician, indeed!" Titters all round. "But hey, I've been called worse! So, Andie, how do you feel about being the winner of our three-month contract? Are you thrilled?"

I shrugged. "I would have expected a tiara to go with this prize, to be honest."

"Isn't she a riot, guys?" This time, he punched a fist in my ribs, guffawing as he did so. The warnings were getting clearer.

What I couldn't believe though was that anyone would take this twat seriously, with his game-show-host-for-the-over-60s style. He might have been clever, rich and good-looking, but he had a charm-deficit that no amount of money could fix.

And, to make matters worse, it seemed that it was time for part two of The Great Monologue. I stood beside him and smiled triumphantly as faces started to glaze over within the first few minutes. I had a feeling this was a networking event for most of the crowd, and while they wanted to be here because Rick was hot stuff within the social-networking industry, they didn't necessarily want to hear him spouting on about how he'd capitalised on his breaks and made himself very rich unless he was telling them exactly how they could do it too – which he wasn't. He was, in a word, boasting, and the crowd clearly wanted to get back to the business of making contacts. Arms extended frantically whenever a waiter passed but Rick was oblivious to the boredom in the room as he waxed lyrical about how great he was, how great his product was and how great the world would be now that it had People Search in it. Families would be reunited, children would be born as a result of lost loves finding each other – hell, the site would surely even put an end to wars all over the world. I felt sorry for Jerry Springer, whose show would surely be defunct and decommissioned after Rick's product was unleashed on the world and put it to rights.

It wasn't long before I'd had enough of standing on the stage beside Rick with absolutely nothing to do and no part to play in proceedings as he waffled on.

"Sorry to interrupt, but could I possibly get a chair, Rick? My legs are killing me, standing here for so long."

Rick turned his head very, very, *very* slowly towards me. Now, I wasn't easily intimidated, having spent so long dealing with Isolde and her strops, but this was one intimidating head-turn. It took so long that I had time to glance down at the audience and note a few looks of fear for my health and safety. It was also long enough to clock a look of pure rage from Lindy, who, no doubt, was furious at me for cocking up all of her hard work with my cheekiness. But I couldn't help myself – although I knew Rick could potentially be the one who held the key to reuniting me with Leon, it just wasn't in my nature to allow myself to be treated like an idiot. Rick had invited me up on stage and then blanked me and left me to rot while he talked about himself, and I wasn't going to let him away with it.

Rick gave me the full force of a horrible, hate-filled stare. It only lasted a millisecond before he put on his gameshow-host façade again – but it was long enough to get the message across that he was marking my cards.

"Ladies and gentlemen, it's time for me to take this lovely lady away and let her commence her duties. But before I do, I'd like you all to raise your glasses and toast People Search!"

"*People Search!*"

The toast was deafening, such was the relief amongst the crowd that the waffling was finally over. I noticed heartfelt smiles directed at me, as if I had pulled these people's children out of quicksand or something.

Rick put his hand on the small of my back, and pushed me in the direction of the sweeping staircase and up the steps. I resented the familiarity of his touch, but was slightly too concerned that he might push me over the side of the staircase to object to mere inappropriate contact.

"I can see you're pretty grateful for the opportunity I've given you," Rick said when we'd settled ourselves in two of the luscious velvet seats that lined the upper tier. His face was impassive, but his steely stare more than made up for any lack of expression.

I decided that the only way I could handle this was with honesty. "All of this is news to me, Rick. I didn't even know I was in the running to be the Face of People Search. If I appear less than enthusiastic, it's because this has come as a shock."

Rick frowned. "Hang on. I'm confused. Lindy told me that there was nothing in the world you wanted more than to become a household name in America. You fit the bill for what I was looking for, so I thought we could do each other a favour. You get more publicity for your cause, and I get a beautiful model to publicise my website. But you're telling me you knew nothing about this?"

"Not a thing – and for the record, I gave up modelling years ago. Did Lindy tell you I was still a model? If you think for *one* minute that you're going to have me out in bikinis branded with People Search logos, you're so mistaken!"

135

He raised an eyebrow. "How about just bikinis in the *colour* of the People Search logo, then?"

I got up to leave. He leapt up and stood up in front of me.

"Please don't go, Andie. We seem to have some wires crossed here, and we're not going to uncross them if you go storming off. Correct?"

Another pet hate – people saying "Correct?" when they're trying to win an argument with you. It was so patronising. But I could hardly retort with "Incorrect!" when Rick was indeed right. If I walked away now, I was walking away from what could be an amazing opportunity to gain more publicity for my cause. I took a deep breath and nodded, hoping the effort it took to concede that he was right wouldn't snap my neck. If this brought me closer to finding Leon, I'd be a fool to mess it up.

"Okay, so we've established that you knew nothing about potentially being the Face of People Search," Rick said. "But you know now that you've been chosen as the winner, so here's the big question. Are you saying that you don't *want* to be the Face of People Search?"

I thought about this. Well, there was only one answer, really – of course I did. Once I got over my fit of pique at Lindy not having mentioned the whole thing before, I knew I'd appreciate being involved in something like this. But before I could answer Rick, Lindy appeared, clunking up towards us in her high heels, brazen as you like. I suspected she was on a damage-limitation mission.

She smiled flirtatiously at Rick, but he was having none of it.

"Andie says she knew nothing about all of this," he said. "What's the deal? You said she wanted this more than anything in the world!"

"Oh, she does. She just needs a bit of a push."

"She's here, you know. Don't talk about her as if she's not even in the room. You've just put her in a terrible position – and even worse, you made me put her in a terrible position too. Whatever sort of a relationship you two have is your business, but don't drag *me* into things and make me look like a fool."

Mortification flooded Lindy's face. "Rick, I'm so sorry . . ."

"Andie, could you leave Lindy and me to talk alone, please?"

"Erm, okay." I hesitated, feeling slightly bad about leaving Lindy to the jaws of this particular shark. But then I said to myself, fuck it, she needs to learn her lesson.

As I walked down the staircase and noticed everyone gawping at me, my irritation at Lindy returned. She obviously had no respect for me, not to even give me a warning about what was going to happen. And it wasn't as if I would have said no – but some part of her that wanted to make sure everything went her way was too afraid to take that chance. But what could I do about it now? In fairness to her, she'd just orchestrated a brilliant move in our bid to find Leon – I just wished she could have handled it all differently. I wound around the bottom of the staircase feeling heartily sorry for myself. It wasn't just Lindy – the whole search was mentally tiring me out. The more it went on, the more I was starting to be tormented by thoughts that maybe Leon didn't want me to find him. It was getting harder to ignore the fact that despite the ease with which he could contact me through LVTV if he wanted to, there had been absolutely no word from him.

Colm ambled towards me as I was leaving the room.

"Listen, I'm going to walk back to the hotel, okay?" I said. "I'll see you later."

"In those shoes?"

He had a point – and so did they, four inches of a point to be precise. I took them off and hurled them into a champagne bucket that was sitting on a drinks table.

"I was always good at basketball," I said as I rummaged for a pair of soft black pumps that permanently resided somewhere in the depths of my handbag. I ignored the look of disgust that was coming my way from a waiter. Once I'd removed all of the random receipts that were sitting inside my pumps, I slipped them on.

"I'll see you later, Colm," I said as I walked away.

Colm followed me. "Are you sure about walking? This hotel must be at least four miles from ours –"

"Yes, I'm fine." I walked away even faster, needing to get out of this place.

"Okay, but before you go –"

"Sorry, Colm. I have to go now. We'll talk later, yeah?"

Colm continued to follow me. "But . . ." he said.

I spun around to him. "Seriously, Colm, can you just leave me alone?"

I turned and marched towards the front door, almost running towards it in my need for freedom from my search, my thoughts and most probably, from myself. Once I got outside, I instantly felt bad and looked back through the revolving glass door to see Colm still standing inside the reception area, staring at me and looking like I'd just kicked him. We held eye contact for a few seconds before he turned and walked out of my view, leaving me feeling like I'd just taken the prize for World's Biggest Bitch instead of the Face of People Search.

Chapter Fifteen

A few hours later as I lay on the bed and sulked between bouts of rubbing my sore feet, I decided to turn my phone on to play Pacman. I'd turned it off as soon as I'd left the hotel because I had a feeling Lindy was going to ring about the Rick situation, and it was probably best that we didn't have that conversation until I'd cajoled myself out of the bad mood I'd fallen into. As soon as the phone started up, a message came through from Colm that had been sent shortly after I had left him.

'**I was only going to ask you if you wanted to go for a drink tonight, that was all. You looked like you needed someone to talk to**.'

Oh, great. Why hadn't he called me a grumpy bitch or something? My conscience had been getting the better of me on the long walk home for snapping at him, and now I felt a million times worse after reading his text.

If I thought too much about what to do, I'd drive myself crazy, so I picked up the phone and dialled his extension straight away.

"Hello?"

"Colm, it's Andie. I'm sorry for being a grouch earlier. Do you fancy going for that drink after all?"

There was no answer for a good five seconds.

"I actually don't – I'm not feeling too good now."

"Oh?"

"Yeah. I feel like I'm coming down with something."

"But you were fine earlier!"

"I started feeling bad while I was editing the footage of the People Search launch for the second episode of the documentary a while ago. I just sent episode two back to Éire TV, by the way."

"Great – all the more reason to go out and celebrate!"

"No. I'm really not in the form for it now."

I took the hint. "Okay. I won't keep you, so. Get some rest, and I hope you feel better soon. Bye."

I slammed down the phone, furious at myself. How many more errors of judgement could I possibly make before the day was out? Colm was sulking, and I'd given him the chance to throw my apology back at me. I should have just kept my mouth shut.

My phone started to ring before I had a chance to berate myself any further. No number was displayed. I answered it out of sheer curiosity and boredom.

"Andie, don't hang up."

Surprise, surprise. I decided to make her suffer in the hope that she mightn't leave me out of the loop next time. "You have three seconds, Lindy. If you can't say something in three seconds that'll make up for what you put me through earlier, then it's goodbye."

"Okay." She sounded confident. "George Clooney."

"What?"

"You're going to meet him! How's that for three seconds?"

"What are you rabbiting on about?"

"Rick's got a lot of friends. Some of them are friends in high places. Which is another reason why you shouldn't get on his bad side, but it looks like you got away with your silly behaviour this time . . . anyway, it turns out that Rick's best friend is one of George's younger cousins, and George is going to be at the bash Rick has invited us to tomorrow night. I've managed to persuade Rick to wangle an introduction to George for us."

"*What?* Oh my God!"

"I'm as close to God as you're going to meet in this city, lady."

I bit my tongue, annoyed with myself for showing so much enthusiasm. The note of triumph in Lindy's voice was unmistakable. "You are not off the hook for what you did today. It was way out of line –"

"No, it wasn't. I'm trying to create a profile for you, and you're doing your best to sabotage it. So if anything, you're out of line. However, I'll allow you this transgression, but don't let it happen again."

"You what?"

"Oh, look, we're not going into the whole thing again. All I'll say is this – go shopping tomorrow. When our picture with George is plastered all over the newspapers, you'll want to be looking your best, won't you?"

"Who said it will be?"

"I said, of course. You hardly think I'd let an opportunity like this pass, do you?"

"But how did you talk Rick into doing that? He was as mad as hell with you when I left."

"I just have a winning way with men." When I said nothing in reply, she continued, "Oh, okay. I'll tell you, but don't go weird on me about this. Rick is willing to do this because he's into you. I think he was hamming up the anger at me to try to impress you."

"Rick *fancies* me?"

"It would appear so." She didn't sound too pleased about it. "How do you think you got this People Search gig so easily? Apparently, he saw you on the news and thought you were both mad and gorgeous – exactly what he looks for in a woman, according to him. You'd think he's Mister Square, but he has an eccentric streak, and madwomen are part of it. That rules me out, of course, but it leaves the door wide open for you."

"But if he fancies me, why is he setting up a meeting for me with George Clooney? Surely he knows that I wouldn't spare him a look when George is in the room!"

"Because he knows that George wouldn't spare you a look, of course, so he's no threat."

Fair point. "Have you ever thought about becoming a counsellor?"

"If you spent less time trying to think up of smart comments and more on dolling yourself up, you'd be a much happier and more fulfilled person."

Scarily, I think she actually meant that.

"Oh, and Rick said I should check to make sure you still want to be the Face of People Search. I said you would, of course, but he said to ask anyway."

"Oh, I suppose so . . ."

"See, I knew I didn't need to even ask. Okay, I'm off. I need to ring Colm and organise a way of getting what he filmed today from him so that we can broadcast it tomorrow, and you need to start thinking about what you're going to wear to the party. Make sure you get a magnificent dress so that you don't show me up." She hung up.

I was too thrilled to even be bothered by Lindy, for once. This was so exciting that I might even take up on Lindy's suggestion and go shopping for the first time since I got back to Vegas. I had the perfect dress but I needed to splash out on matching bag and shoes. I was going to meet George!

"Yeah . . . yeah . . . uh huh . . . mmmm . . . yeah . . ."

"Twenty-three," I mouthed to Colm. He threw a pen at me in response.

He'd been on the phone for only about four minutes, but he'd already managed to rack up an impressive number of yeahs. It didn't seem to matter how bored he sounded – and, in fairness, each subsequent yeah was even flatter than the previous in an attempt to get the hint across – the person on the other end just wouldn't shut up. I'd long since run out of fingers to count on, and was now marking each new yeah on a foolscap notepad with a stroke of my pen.

"Yeah . . . yeah . . . listen, I have to go soon, so let's get back to what I rang about. . . yeah . . . send that through to me as soon as you can, will you? . . . yeah . . . yeah . . . look, what you need to do is to talk to Valerie – there's no point is saying all of this to me instead of her . . . yeah . . . yeah, I know it's good to get a male perspective, but my advice is to speak to her . . . yeah . . . yeah . . . look, I really have to go, Martin . . . yeah . . . take care . . . yeah . . . alright, bye . . . yeah, yeah, yeah . . . bye." He hung up.

"Thirty-seven!" I said with a flourish. "That's an average of a little over nine yeahs a minute. Impressive."

"Give me my pen back." He coughed, then held his hand out for the pen he'd thrown at me.

"Not until you dish the dirt. What are Martin and Valerie fighting about?"

"None of your business."

"If he's messing around with my boss, then it becomes my business."

"You and I both know that nobody messes around with Isolde. The pen, please."

"What does he need to talk to Valerie about?"

"Buying a cheaper brand of teabags. *The pen*, for Christ's sake!"

"I presume you're talking about the pen that's going to be sticking out of your ass very soon if you don't tell me what the hell is going on between Martin and Valerie. She's found out he's having an affair, hasn't she?" I made the pen hover ominously over the partition that separated us.

"It's nothing to do with an affair. They're having other issues."

"Ah, but maybe she knows about the affair, and is biding her time so that she can lay traps for him to fall into! In the meantime, they're having rows about silly little things because she's so hurt by what he's done." I nodded knowledgably. "Martin is toast. She knows."

"No, she bloody well doesn't!"

"Oh, so you admit there's something to know about?"

He shook his head. "Give it up, Andie. It's not working."

"Well, if there's nothing going on, then it's no harm to tell me what Martin was complaining about on the phone there. Go on! I'm your only friend out here."

"Oh, thanks a lot." He coughed again. "Make a sick man feel worse, why don't you?"

"I'm no better – I don't have any friends out here either. Which means I can't tell anyone whatever it is that you're about to tell me."

"Philippe is your friend."

"Yes, but he doesn't know Martin."

"You know, it wouldn't surprise me if he did."

"It doesn't matter even if he does know him, because I'm not going to tell Philippe anything. Go on. You know you want to."

"What about your colleagues? I'm sure you'll be on email to them later."

"Oh, they hate me." Jason's ugly head flashed through my thoughts. "I wouldn't tell them anything."

Colm looked at me doubtfully, the doubt stemming from the latter part of my sentence, I would imagine, and not the former.

"Look, it's no big deal. He was just saying that Valerie has been moaning about them not spending enough time together lately, that's all."

I seized upon this piece of information like a hungry wolf. "There you go! He hasn't been spending time with Valerie because he's had his head buried in Isolde's curtains!"

"Curtains? What are you talking about?"

I decided not to clarify my statement. "The man's marriage is obviously falling apart. If you're his friend at all, you should let him know that the word is out about his antics."

"I can't just go making accusations without proof!"

"Fine. Let's get proof, so."

He gave me a dubious look. When he said nothing, I continued as if he'd asked me how.

"It's simple. All we have to do is pool our resources. You keep your ears open for any information from Martin, and I do the same for Isolde. We compare the stories we're hearing from each of them and assess them for any irregularities. Sooner or later, one of them is going to trip themselves up. My money's on Martin. So, really, you have the easy deal here. I'm the one taking one for the team. So, are you in?"

He was spared from having to give an answer by Lindy storming into the room in a cocoon of musky perfume and thunderous looks – until she saw Colm, of course. She waggled her fingers at him and said a breathy hi, ignoring me completely. Colm grunted a hi, then instantly concentrated on his computer screen. Lindy dumped her handbag on her desk, before stomping off to the canteen with a sulky puss for her morning espresso.

Colm's head appeared over the partition as he stood up, so slowly that he looked like an old man with arthritis. "I'm going back to the hotel. I feel awful."

"Oh yeah. A likely excuse. You're off to doss around in a casino for the afternoon, no doubt."

He grabbed a crumpled tissue from his desk and daubed at a trickle that was leaking from his nose. "Yeah, that's it. And then I'm going on the pull."

I felt a bit guilty for assuming he was sulking last night. He did look terrible. And he hadn't even eaten his morning biscuits – today's ones were Iced Gems.

"Will you be able to come to the ball tonight, do you think?"

"Only if they've changed the venue to the hospital." He turned towards the window and launched into a fit of sneezes. I stopped counting after the first ten.

"Oh, well, eight sneezes is the equivalent of an orgasm, they say. Every cloud and all that."

He turned his bloodshot eyes back to me, and looked at me as if I had gone mad. Then – and I wasn't sure if this was because of what I said, or the strain of all the sneezes – he started to blush furiously. Not one of those healthy-looking reddening-of-the-cheeks efforts, but one that crept up from wherever they started all the way up to the hairline. He looked away and started fussing with his paraphernalia, gathering it up into his arms furiously.

"See you tomorrow. Enjoy tonight."

He left in a blur of long strides and sniffles, leaving me

wondering what the hell all of that had been about. Why would someone as confident as Colm feel so threatened by the O word?

I was too excited at the thought of the ball to ponder the question for too long. That very night I'd be rubbing shoulders with George Clooney!

Chapter Sixteen

I felt a bit sorry for Colm, being stuck in bed all evening sick while the rest of us would be out boozing. I looked at my watch – I had an hour to get ready. I wouldn't need more than fifteen minutes, so I slipped on my pumps and made my way to the convenience store beside the hotel to buy Colm a few lads' magazines to pass the night for him.

While I was in there, I decided I might as well buy a whole get-well kit while I was at it. I filled a basket with paracetamol, throat-soothers, balsam tissues, energy drinks, chocolate bars and about ten packets of various biscuits that he'd probably turn his nose up at for being too new, then went to the men's magazine section of the store. I picked up one called *Axiom* and flicked through it – cars, check, gadgets, check, girls in bikinis, check. A music magazine called *Deafen* also looked like it would fit Colm's bill, plus I would have bought it for the name alone anyway. Finally, I threw a magazine about horses into my basket, purely for the randomocity of it. It was going to be a long night for Colm, and he might as well learn something new from it.

I walked briskly back to the hotel, and went up to Colm's room with my bag of tricks. I knocked until my knuckles were sore, but there was no answer. I looked at my watch – half an hour until it was time to meet Lindy. I went down the corridor to my room, wrote my daily diary entry in five minutes, then had a quick shower and got myself ready for the ball. Fifteen minutes later, my dress was on, my hair was brushed, and I'd even put a tiny bit of eye make-up and lipstick on. It suited me so much more than the trowel-loads I used to wear back in the modelling days. I twirled around to get a look at the back of my dress, and decided I was satisfied with how it looked. It was an unfussy dress – red, sleeveless, V-necked and to the knee – nothing special, but it looked a lot more expensive than it was, due to its classic design. I'd picked it up in a sale in some boutique in Paris a few years before, and I'd worn it at least eight times. It always made me feel comfortable in my own skin, and looked great with the red high heels I'd matched it with. I threw the few bits and bobs I'd need for the night into a small red handbag I'd also bought – it didn't exactly match, but nobody would notice – picked up the recovery-aid bag, and made my way back down to Colm's again.

I put my ear up against the door before I put my knuckles through another boxing match. The TV was definitely on, as it had been the last time. Colm was probably in another one of his antisocial moods and was just ignoring me. I'd soon sort that out. I took off one shoe and rapped it against the door. When there was no answer, I graduated from rapping to thumping at the risk of ending up in George's company wearing another heelless shoe. I was rewarded with the sound of shuffling at the other side of the door.

When he opened the door, I felt even more awful than he looked. His tousled hair and slitty eyes made it obvious that he'd been fast asleep.

"What's going on?" His voice came out as a croak.

"I just called to try to make you feel better," I said.

"I think sleep might help me," he said, frowning, but he held the door open to let me in. The room smelled musty and unhealthy.

"No, I mean . . . I brought you some stuff that might help you." I held up the bag. "I'm sorry, I should have realised you'd be trying to sleep . . ."

"Ah, it's fine. That was nice of you. Thanks."

I held out the bag for him to take, but just as he reached out for it, he seemed to lose his balance. He held his arms out to the wall for support, then crawled his arms down the wall and bent his knees until he was sitting on the carpet.

"Colm, what is it?"

He put his head between his knees and rubbed the back of his neck. "I'm fine. Just dizzy and my neck's a bit sore."

I knelt down beside him, and noticed beads of sweat in his hairline. Within seconds, I noticed them plopping from his forehead onto the carpet, where they were instantly sucked up.

"Did you go to the doctor after work?"

He shook his head. I put my hand on his forehead. It felt like a hob in a kitchen. It was then that I noticed a purple rash on the back of his neck. I put my hands on his neck and pulled the skin apart to see if the rash would blanch, having lots of practice at this from years of baby-sitting. It didn't fade at all. Colm didn't even react at my rough skin-pulling, and that, even more than the rash, told me that he was in trouble here.

"Colm, you need to go now! You're running a temperature and you're developing a rash on the back of your neck!"

"Not well enough to go. Can't move." His voice was more breathless now than it had been when he answered the door. He eased himself to one side and flopped onto the carpet, lying face down on it.

I let him lie there while I ran to the phone and rang Reception.

"'Allo? Reception."

"Philippe, we need a doctor. Colm is sick. Do you know of one that will call to Colm's hotel room?"

"What is wrong with 'im?"

"He's got a fever and a rash. He's in a bad way. Do you have the doctor's contact details to hand there?"

"What kind of a rash is it?"

"Just get me the contact details, please."

He continued as if I hadn't spoken at all. "Because it could just be 'eat rash, you know. You Irish are not equeeped to 'andle the 'eat –"

"*Philippe!* Just give me the goddamned phone number!"

There was a long pause. "You prove my point. The 'eat drives you people crazee. You cannot find your tempair when it is 'ot. Wait a second and I will get you the numbair." He crashed the phone onto the desk.

It took him a good six minutes to find the number, during which time Colm had moulded his body into the carpet and fallen into a fitful doze. His breathing was jagged and harsh.

"'Ere it ees." He called out the number. "You should ask the doctor to give you something too for your bad mood." He hung up.

I immediately rang the doctor's surgery. His receptionist informed me that the doctor wouldn't be available to do house calls for another five hours, but as their surgery was located only around the corner from the MGM, she suggested that we come in. The surgery was quiet at the moment, and the doctor would be able to see Colm straight away. I told her to expect us soon.

I walked over to Colm and shook him gently. "Right, mister. Up you get."

He rolled onto his back and looked up at me with wild eyes.

"You need to go to the doctor."

"No way . . . I'll be fine after a sleep . . ."

"You need medication. I'm bringing you to the doctor now, and that's that."

"I don't have the energy to go . . ."

"The doctor is just around the corner. So, come on – get up and let's go right now."

"But what about your ball?"

"Ah, I'll go later than planned. This won't take long."

"No. You go. I can go to the doctor's on my own."

"No way – if I leave here, you'll go straight back to bed. Then you'll be a million times worse tomorrow."

"I never knew you cared."

I shrugged. "We only have each other out here, so we have to look out for each other."

He looked a bit surprised when I said that. I meant it, though. He was a pain in the hole most of the time, but I was hardly going to leave him there to rot when he had nobody else to help him. There was an awkward silence, so I reverted back to the territory we knew how to handle. "Besides, it's not entirely selfless – I can't bear the thought of listening to Isolde going on and on if Éire TV contact her to say there's been a delay with the filming of the show. So, go on – get yourself cleaned up. I'll ring Lindy to tell her I'll see her later on."

While Colm went to the bathroom, I made a quick call to Lindy. I held the phone out from my ear as she ranted on about being there on her own, then I used Colm as an excuse to hang up as he came back out of the bathroom. He stumbled his way to the bed and lay down.

"No, you don't. Up up up!"

"Ah, Andie, I'm in bits here . . ."

"And you'll be a million times worse tomorrow if you don't get up. Not because you'll be even more sick, but because you'll have me to answer to. Now, shift!"

He sighed and gave me an evil look, but got himself into a vertical position. As I stood up to jolly him out the door, I realised that I'd have to lose the heels. I scanned the room and spotted Colm's flip-flops. I flicked my shoes off one by one, then crossed the room and slotted my feet into the flip-flops.

"They're too big for you!"

I waved his objections away. "Nah, they're fine."

"Why don't you go down to your room and get your own shoes?"

"Because if I leave you for so much as one second, you'll be wrapped up in that bed by the time I get back. We're going right now while I have you upright."

To my horror, the dreaded blush invaded his face again. I decided to put it down to his illness – it must have been causing hot flushes.

"And what about your dress? Do you want to get out of it?"

Once he realised what he'd said, the blush grew even deeper than the colour of the aforementioned dress. God, this hole was

151

getting deeper and deeper – I was going to start blushing myself if he didn't shut up.

"Nah, it'll save me time to just stay in it. Let's just go." I hurried him out the door.

We shuffled our way to the doctor's surgery, the three-minute walk taking at least twice that, between Colm's inability to walk fast and my feet wearing flip-flops that kept flopping off. I'd never noticed how big Colm's feet were before. We got a few strange looks along the way, but I wasn't sure if it was because Colm was stumbling along and leaning on me like a drunken old man after the pubs had closed, or if it was the combination of my choice of footwear and my cocktail dress. I hoped it was the latter. Colm's sickness was starting to scare me . . . I had an awful feeling that this wasn't just some flu.

"Good evening, how can I help you?" The receptionist was alert and in bring-it-on mode, something that I was happy about under the current circumstances.

"It looks like he has the flu, and needs to get some medication for it. Colm, why don't you sit down, and I'll do the paperwork bit for you?"

Colm looked only too happy to acquiesce – he was barely able to stand. Once he'd taken one of the few available seats at the back of the waiting area, I turned back to the receptionist. "Look, he has this weird purple rash," I said quietly. "I'm really worried it might be indicative of something a lot more serious than flu. Can you make sure we see the doctor immediately?"

"Yes, he's free now. Sit down, and I'll let him know what you've told me."

Within seconds, Colm was called in to the doctor.

"I'll go in with you," I said, feeling like his mother.

"What can I do for you?" the doctor asked.

"I think I have the flu," Colm muttered. His voice was so low that it was barely audible.

"What symptoms are you experiencing?"

"Just coughing, sneezing, high temperature. Bit of a fainting feeling too. And a headache."

"And what about the sore neck and the rash? Tell him about them!" I turned to the doctor. "He was complaining that his neck was sore earlier. Then, I noticed a gigantic purple rash on the back of his neck . . ."

"You never mentioned it was gigantic!" Colm suddenly sounded alive again, in an I'm-now-quite-scared kind of way.

"You didn't ask how big it was – it's not that big really. You know me, prone to exaggeration."

As the doctor got up from his desk to examine Colm, I moved my hands outwards and mouthed the word "huge" when Colm was looking the other way. The doctor put his hands on the back of Colm's neck, and pulled the skin apart with his thumbs. A frown flickered across the doctor's face – it barely registered, and he tucked it away immediately and resumed his inscrutable doctor's pose, but not before I had seen it. He then placed a thermometer in Colm's ear, but his face gave nothing away this time as he took the reading.

He picked up a doctor's torch, and shone it into Colm's eyes. Colm immediately recoiled.

As the doctor took Colm's blood pressure, Colm started to shake uncontrollably. The doctor hovered in front of him. "Colm, tell me how you're feeling right now."

"Freezing. It's so cold." Rivers of sweat ran down his forehead as he hugged himself.

I felt a chill run down my own back. This was not good.

Ten minutes later, we were in an ambulance on the way to the Desert Springs Hospital. According to the doctor, Colm was showing all the signs of meningitis. I trembled all the way to the hospital. Colm had made several attempts to fall asleep as soon as he got into the ambulance, and didn't seem to care what was wrong with him as long as he was allowed to sleep, but the staff used every means at their disposal to keep him awake and kept asking him questions.

When we arrived at the hospital, Colm was whisked away to ER. I was shown to a waiting area, and told that I'd be informed about what was going on as soon as tests had been performed.

It was only when I was left on my own that I had the headspace to turn my thoughts to Lindy. I pulled out my mobile to ring her, and saw that I had several text messages from her, and three missed calls.

I read the texts in order. First one: '**OMG! I've just spotted George!! Get here fast!**'

The second: '**Where are you?**'

The third: '**I just spoke to George! Oh my God! I can't believe you missed it!**'

My heart raced on the third one. Oh God! Lindy was chatting up my George! I rang her immediately.

"Andie!" Lindy already sounded pissed when she answered the phone. "Are you on the way?" she shouted, competing with a cacophony of voices, clinking glasses and general merriment in the background.

For a split second, I was tempted to say yes, to run out of this hospital in Colm's flip-flops and get a taxi to the ball – but there was no way in the world that I would do that to Colm. Even if I hated the grumpy old sod, he was still a sick man in a strange country with nobody else but me to help him.

"No." I explained the situation to Lindy.

"That is just terrible news. I really hope he's going to be okay. Can you let me know later how he is?"

"Yeah, I'll try to call if I can."

"Well, if you can't call, make sure you text me."

"Sure." Huh, if she really fancied him, she'd leave the party and come over to the hospital, I thought.

"Okay, well, I'll tell George you said hello when I bump into him again later!"

I tried to keep my disappointment and envy out of my voice. "I love how you said 'when' and not 'if' there, Lindy –"

"Oh, there's no chance of an 'if'. It's a 'when'. I'll make sure of that."

She would, too. "Enjoy the night." I hung up before my jealousy suffocated me. I couldn't believe that my opportunity to meet George was passing me by like this!

I focused my attention back on the hospital. I stared around the room, taking in the details of everything and anything to distract my thoughts from what I was missing. An elderly lady sitting across from me was knitting, her elbows resting on her round belly as her fingers worked furiously. I couldn't work out why anyone would need anything knitted in a place like Vegas where the dry heat would suffocate you, but I decided not to ask. Despite her innocent-grandma demeanour, she had the air of someone looking for a fight as her eyes darted from her needles to everyone else in the room. Hospitals never brought out the best in people. After that, I decided to just buy a few magazines and keep my head down. Besides, worrying about Colm would pass the time . . . the poor guy had looked in such a bad way.

An indeterminable amount of time later – I had somehow nodded off, in a narcoleptic manner, and only woke when I heard my name being yelled out – a doctor led me outside to a corridor for an update on Colm.

"Good news," he said. "It's looking like a viral infection but not meningitis. We did a CT scan upon Colm's admission, which showed no abnormalities or inflammation. We've also done some blood tests, and the results of those also indicate that he doesn't have meningitis. To be on the safe side, we just did a lumbar puncture, which is a very effective test in diagnosing meningitis. We're awaiting the results of that, but in the meantime please don't worry too much. We're quite confident at this stage that it's just a common viral infection."

"That's not good news – that's fantastic news!" I felt my whole body relax. I hadn't actually admitted to myself how worried I had been about Colm. It was strange – I'd been as concerned about him as I would have been about any of my really good friends, and I'd only known him a few weeks. But I supposed that's what happened when you spent so much time with one person – whether you liked them or not, you still grew to care about them, in a messed-up way.

"And, the even better news is that you can go in to see your boyfriend now, but just for a few minutes."

"Em – he's not my boyfriend."

"Oh, I do apologise. I just assumed he was, because . . ."

155

"Because what?"

"Oh . . . it's just that he was calling out for you at one stage when he woke up, that's all. We gave him some medication, and it's left him a bit confused . . . it'll wear off. Anyway, I can bring you in now to see your . . . ?"

"Colleague. We work together."

"I see. Come this way, please. Visiting hours actually finish up in ten minutes, so that's all you'll have – but at least you caught the end of visiting time."

Colm was in a public ward with about nineteen others. My heart went out to him as I walked towards him. He was lying in the bed all alone – not that I would have expected anyone to be in the bed with him – watching all of the other patients being comforted by their visitors. The din of chattering was overpowering, but none of it was directed at him. And then, he saw me approach, and his face lit up like I'd never seen it do before. He looked like a completely different person.

"Andie! Why are you here? What about the ball?"

"Oh, been to one ball, been to them all." I hoped I sounded convincing. "Speaking of balls, you sound pretty on the ball yourself now – a big improvement on the last time I saw you, at any rate."

"Will you stop – I sound like an alcoholic." His voice was slightly slurred from the medication.

"Well, a little bit. It suits you, though. Maybe you should start drinking."

"I think I have enough problems at the moment without adding hangovers to the list. Besides, these drugs are making me feel fairly drunk anyway."

I sat down on the side of his narrow bed. "How do you know what being drunk feels like, if you never drank?"

"I never said I never drank. I did, years ago. I gave it up when I was eighteen."

I nodded knowledgably. "Ah, so you were an underage drinker, and you gave it up when you got to the legal age. Very responsible of you."

"A model citizen, that's me."

We lapsed into silence. Then, out of nowhere, Colm grabbed my hand.

"Listen, thanks so much for helping me earlier . . . and now, you've missed the ball because of me, but I want you to know that I really appreciate it." He placed his other hand on top of our already clasped hands. It reminded me of something an old neighbour of ours, Maisie, did years ago, when Mum dragged me along to visit her in hospital. I was only about eight at the time, but even then, I had enough sense to know she was on her way out of the world. She'd gripped one of my hands between both of hers and squeezed it with a ferocity that you wouldn't expect from someone so old, frail and sick, and thanked me over and over again for coming to see her. The next day, she was dead. Colm obviously wasn't in that situation, but his brush with illness must have affected him – this behaviour was most un-Colm-esque. It was that, or the drugs the doctor had given him.

"No need to thank me. It's what anyone would have done."

"No, they friggin' well wouldn't have. I don't know many women who would sacrifice a night with George Clooney for one with me. Actually, I don't know *any* women who would."

"Ah, I've gone off George a bit recently."

He smiled. "Seriously, Andie, thank you. I won't forget this."

I shrugged, and withdrew my hand. "I'm just glad it's a viral infection, and not something more serious." I suddenly thought of something. "Hey, do you want me to call your parents and let them know that you're sick? You're probably not up to speaking to them right now, but you probably want them to know all the same?"

He turned his head away. "That won't be necessary."

"Okay, no worries. Just thought I'd ask in case you have one of those Irish mammies that need to hear from their sons every day or they have you written off as having fallen off a cliff or something –"

"My parents are dead."

That put a halt to my babbling pretty fast. "Oh, Colm, I'm sorry. I had no idea."

"How could you have?"

A nurse walked into the ward. "Right, everyone, visiting time is over *now*!" She poked her head into each cubicle and reiterated her message.

I stood up. "Did they tell you how long you'd be in here?"

"No – they're going to see how I am in the morning, and we should have a better idea then. Listen, Andie, I've a favour to ask. Could you get my health insurance documentation from the top drawer of the locker beside my bed, and if it isn't an awful pain, could you bring it in here tomorrow? Or maybe ask the hotel to fax it to the hospital if you're too busy to come in?"

"Don't be daft – of course I'll be coming in to see you tomorrow."

His face brightened again.

"I have the key to your room, by the way – I grabbed it from the desk as we were leaving."

"I was hoping you'd say that, because I had absolutely no idea where it was."

"And I'll ring Éire TV when I get back to the hotel and explain the situation to them. Don't worry, we'll work something out there."

"Are you sure you don't mind? I was going to ring them tomorrow when I felt a bit better."

"Don't even think about it. I'm on it."

The nurse stood at the foot of Colm's bed and glared at me. "I have to go. I'll see you tomorrow."

"Thanks, Andie, for everything. You're a real friend."

I smiled weakly before I left, the word "colleague" roaring in my head. It taunted me all the way to the elevator, mingling with the memory of Colm's grasp on my hand.

Chapter Seventeen

The next day, Colm was released from hospital. Confirmation had come back later the previous night that his lumbar puncture showed no signs of meningitis infection. Although he was free to leave, he was under strict orders to rest for at least a week. Most people would have been happy to take some time out to recover, but Colm wasn't most people.

"What am I supposed to do all day?" he said when I accompanied him back to his hotel room after he was discharged from hospital.

"You'll probably sleep most of the time. Your body needs time to recover."

"I won't sleep twenty-four hours a day!"

"So watch a movie or something!"

"I've watched all of the movies on demand that they have here already."

"So watch something on the Internet, then!"

"There's nothing I really want to watch at the moment."

"Well, I'm sure you could shuffle your way to the cinema – it's only around the corner and –"

"There's nothing on at the moment that I want to see."

"Colm, I'll put you back in hospital if you don't stop being so awkward."

"What about filming for this week though? My boss is going to have a fit when she hears we've no footage for Éire TV . . ."

"All sorted out. I've explained the situation to LVTV and they're willing to share whatever they film with us. They owe it to us after you gave them our People Search footage, remember?" I looked at my watch. "Sorry, but I'm going to have to go to work now."

"Oh, rub it in, why don't you?"

I shook my head. "There's a lot more to life than work, you know!"

"I know that. I'm just going to be bored, that's all."

"I wish I could trade places with you. Lindy has a live daytime TV interview organised for me this afternoon with this one called Dolly – I've seen her show, and she's a right pain."

"At least it's something to do. There's nothing like work to keep you going."

"Colm! Just enjoy being under orders to chill out for once. Your body gave you a hint that it wants you to slow down, so take it."

He shrugged, looking like he was having none of what I was saying.

"If you don't cheer up, I'll send Lindy around to do it for you."

"Oh God, no! You wouldn't." He smiled. "See. I'm happy again."

"Good. Keep it that way." I laughed to myself as I left his room. That was the first time either of us had made reference to Lindy's little crush. I know it was bitchy of me, but I was happy that Colm had more sense than to succumb to Lindy's charms. It was obvious that she was a thrill-of-the-chase type of girl.

When I arrived at the office, I made a list of everything I needed to do. I decided to tackle the *Looking for Leon* messages first. The previous week, Lindy had set up a website for me called *LookingForLeon.com* for members of the public to contact us. It was pretty basic – just a page containing the bones of my story, but most importantly, it had a box at the end of the page that would allow visitors to type in a message that would go directly to an email account that Lindy had set up. We both had access to it, and we'd set out a schedule for when each of us was responsible for checking it – and today was one of my days. So far, no leads had come in, but I'd received loads of messages of support, and they were always quite a nice read to finish the day with.

There were five emails waiting for me. Four were from various ladies who'd all been unlucky in love, and were hoping they'd see a shiny happy ending to my story. The fifth was an entirely different story. The name of the person who sent the email was 'Go Home'. Oh, lovely. Would it be from the person who'd sent the letter, or had I accrued another enemy? The increase in my media coverage was bound to bring a few ill-wishers my way – it came with the territory, so it wouldn't be surprising to find out that it was from someone new who was sick of the sight of me. But at the same time, I'd almost unconsciously been waiting to see if the letter sender would strike again too. Spoiled for choice . . . Swallowing hard, I double-clicked the mail, feeling nerves creep all over my body at the thought of what it might contain.

From: **gohomeandie@yahoo.com**
To: **lookingforleon@hotmail.com**

I've told you already that you need to stop this ridiculous crusade of yours. You're making an absolute fool of yourself. Leon is not interested. Go home.

My heart started to beat faster. Okay, so it was only an email, it couldn't hurt me, but it gave me the jitters all the same. The sender had obviously set up the email account just to email me, instead of mailing me from their own address. My finger was hovering over the delete key when something told me to keep the email. If I ever found Leon, this was something I'd want to show him. Or, worst-case scenario, I'd need this as evidence if this person continued to hassle me and I had to report it to the police. I knew, at a high level, that it was possible to specify where a person was located when they sent an email from their IP address, even if they had set up a fake email address. I couldn't risk Lindy seeing it, though – she'd only make a huge deal out of this if she knew about it – so I forwarded it to my personal mail, then deleted both the message itself and the forwarded mail from my sent items.

Then I tried to switch myself onto everything else I had to do, but the email kept replaying in my head. My brain seemed to be refusing to move on until I'd done something about it instead of just ignoring it. Okay, maybe it was just from some random person who'd taken against me for whatever reason, but the most likely scenario was that the communication was coming from someone who was close to Leon and who must know where he was. Maybe, instead of being a bad thing, this email was actually the key to finding him? If I could just engage this person in some sort of dialogue and try to get more information from them, it might bring me further in my search than anything else would. And much as I hated to admit it to myself, if this person was right and Leon actually wasn't interested, then I was making a gargantuan fool of myself. Maybe engaging in contact with Go Home was a risk, but I needed a lead.

I went into my personal mail and composed a new mail.

From: **andieappleton@hotmail.com**
To: **gohomeandie@yahoo.com**

Go Home,

Thank you for your email. If Leon isn't interested, then I'd really like to know why. Has he met someone else, or am I just not his type at all? I can't take your word for this. Until I hear from the horse's mouth that he's not interested, then I can't stop my search.

It seems to me that we both want something that neither of us are getting at the moment – but if we work together, we may actually get somewhere. If what you're saying is true, and you can prove it by getting me in direct contact with Leon and he tells me to my face that he doesn't want me in his life, then you've got what you want. I'll be going home. As for me, this may not be the outcome I want, but at least my search will be over and I'll have the answers I need. As you can see, you're getting the better end of the deal here really.

Perhaps you and I should talk about this instead of emailing? If you send me on your phone number, I will be happy to call you to discuss this further.

If I don't hear from you, then I'm afraid I can't take your email seriously and will most certainly be continuing my search.

Regards,

Andie

I read the mail back quickly and pressed the send button before I started to over-analyse my actions, then deleted it from the sent items. If anything came of it, I'd tell Lindy then, but it was best to keep this to myself until I had something concrete to go on.

I threw myself into the rest of the items on my list to try to settle myself down. Gradually, I managed to forget about the email and my reply to it as I worked my way through the deluge of things to do. Maybe Colm had a point about work.

"And now, Andie, we have a little surprise for you."

"Oh?" I plastered a polite smile on my face, but if anyone was watching me closely, they would have noticed me gripping the sides of my seat, and digging my fingernails into its plush velvet cover. My interview with Dolly on LVTV's daytime chat show was fully underway, and I'd just been quizzed about what I knew about Leon, what made me fall in love with him, and whether I believed he would come forward sometime soon. I trotted out the same lines I'd told everyone else who'd interviewed me, and realised that I was starting to get bored with my own story, not to mention the sound of my own voice. Still, if it brought me closer to finding Leon, it would be worth it.

"Yes. We may very well have your Leon in the studio here with us today!"

A whoop went up from the live 'stoodio' audience, while my intestines turned to liquid. I looked around frantically – which served to make Dolly grin inanely. Yes, I know, you're visualising a Dolly Parton lookalike whenever I mention her name, but in a cruel twist of fate, Dolly was fascinatingly flat-chested. Like, she didn't even have nipples. The area from her collarbone to her size-zero waist was as flat as an ironing board. Even more fascinating was the fact that she had an arse like two Frisbees – two huge butt-cheeks that spread out and curved in again to become part of her legs. It was seriously intriguing – I just could not understand how it could be physically possible to have that body shape, because surely to have a size-zero waist, you'd have to diet or eat nothing, and if you dieted or ate nothing, surely the weight would fall off the arse too? Anyway, it really didn't matter – her beautiful, flawless face made sure of that. She was seriously one of the most beautiful women I had ever met – tanned, poker-straight thick black glossy hair to her waist, huge, expressive eyes, gleaming white teeth, the lot. She made Lindy look like she'd just emerged from a cave. If Leon was here, he'd probably fancy Dolly.

Of course, there was no sign of him when I looked around, but there wouldn't be, would there? They'd have him hidden away backstage, then bring him out in a blaze of some cheesy love song . . . oh God . . . I wasn't ready for this. It was one thing talking about finding him, but actually finding him was something else entirely . . .

"Are you ready? Here come the Leons!"

The Leons? What the . . . ?

A group of men of various heights, ages and ethnicities trooped out wearing masks. They waved at the crowd as they made their way to a podium where any musical guests on the show would normally play, never once looking in my direction.

"Ladies and gentlemen, welcome to the Leon Line-up!"

So that's what it was. I was glad she'd decided to tell the audience what was going on, seeing as she'd failed to inform me.

"Yes, we put the word out on our website that we were looking for guys called Leon from Arizona to join us in our studio today! All of these hunks claim to know Andie . . . but are they just bluffing in a bid to capture the heart of this beautiful lady? Well, we're about to find out! Andie, come this way." She grabbed my wrist and yanked me down to the group of men, all of whom were throwing shapes and trying to outdo each other.

Lindy was a dead woman walking. She obviously knew about this and had kept it a secret – probably knowing full well that I wouldn't have anything to do with it if I'd known about it. Hell, what was I saying – it had probably been her idea!

"In a few seconds, Andie, these gorgeous guys are going to strip themselves of their masks, and reveal who they really are. If they're not Leon, you shake your head and move on to the next one. Got it?"

"Not quite. Can you repeat that?"

She gave me a funny look, then said, "No problem – it's loud in here, with all the cheering from those guys!" She raised her arms up to encourage the crowd to whoop again, which they obligingly did – I wondered briefly how much it had cost to fill them all with alcohol before the show began – and then went about repeating her sentence, at which point I explained that I had just been attempting a spot of sarcasm. I was rewarded with the briefest flash of an ugly look that destroyed her beautiful face. Within a millisecond, though, her professional front was back on again.

"Okay . . . and we're off!"

To my horror, 'You Can Leave Your Hat On' from *The Full Monty* was piped into the studio. Just as I was about to run, I realised that the only thing the guys were going to whip off was their masks – but with the way this day was going, I think I was justified in imagining that anything was possible. As the song began, they turned their backs to me, and then the first guy in the line-up turned around, and inched his mask off. He greeted me with a big cheesy grin, presenting a row of white teeth that were perfectly even, but terribly small and out of proportion with the rest of his meaty face. I shook my head.

"*Next!*" Dolly pushed me on to the next man, while Meathead pouted and raised his arms up in a "What can I do?" pose, generating a sympathy cheer from the audience. Scrap the drink theory – the

165

audience had definitely been given drugs before the show. Dolly had obviously helped herself too – she was now gyrating back and forth in time to the music, her arse wobbling hither and tither and looking like it was having a ball.

One by one, they whipped off their masks as I worked my way down the row of Leons as fast as possible. They really should have left them on. I wouldn't have been surprised if they wore the masks out in public on a day-to-day basis. Sorry, I know that's mean, but as I stood there with a big fake smile on my face, I was starting to get into a pretty mean mood. It wasn't fair of Lindy to have put me in this position. Okay, it might just have been a bit of fun that would raise my profile, but it felt like Dolly and her team were just taking the complete mick out of me, as each guy gyrated in front of me. One of them even flexed his muscles, and made a grinding motion with his hips. Where had they got these people?

Thankfully, I was on my last one now. It seemed to be a case of keeping the best until last – this guy was tall, and of a decent build. It would be vaguely interesting to see what he looked like . . .

When he whipped off his mask, it tipped a strange situation into the realms of the downright surreal. The guy smiled at the crowd, then leapt forward and threw his arms around me in a big bear hug.

"Say nothing," Colm whispered in my ear. "Play along."

"What . . ."

"Ooh, we've got a live one here, folks!" Dolly sidled up to us, smiling flirtatiously at Colm as if she wouldn't mind a bit of his hugging action herself. "He doesn't want to let her go! Could we have found Leon? Andie, is he the one? Have we found your man?"

A ripple of excitement went through the audience. I extricated myself from Colm's arms.

"I'm afraid he's not Leon, guys," I said, producing a huge groan from the audience. I wasn't sure if that was the answer Colm wanted me to give or not, but when I looked over at him, he gave me a barely perceptible nod.

"Gawd, *no*! And you looked so great together! Didn't they look great together?" Dolly asked the audience.

They clapped and whooped, while Colm raised his arms and shrugged his shoulders in a self-deprecating fashion. I, meanwhile, tried to glue my feet to the floor so that they wouldn't accidentally swing in the direction of Dolly's arse and kick her into the middle of next week.

"Andie, I'm sorry – we did our best for you. And I know you're probably sad now, and thinking that your love life is still in tatters . . . but guess what – all is not lost! We have another little surprise for you!"

I gritted my teeth. "I think I've had enough of your little surprises, Dolly . . ."

"Oh *no*! You're gonna *love* this one! You see, we want you to find love, Andie. And that's why we're offering you an all-expenses-paid meal for two for you and one of these awesome guys! All you have to do is choose a Leon, then let love blossom!"

Colm kicked the back of my foot.

For a few seconds, I actually thought about picking one of the other Leons just to foil his plan . . . but as I looked over at them, throwing shapes and desperately trying to get the limelight, I realised that I'd be up for homicide before the date was over if I had to spend too much time with any of those lunatics.

"Okay, well . . . after that hug Leon 8 gave me, I think he and I would have a lot to talk about, so I'm going to pick him."

The audience went mad, as did Dolly. "Oh my *God*! I just know you've made the right choice! And who knows? Maybe your Leon will go so wild with jealousy when he sees you enjoying dinner with someone else that he'll come forward! Wouldn't that be great?"

"Erm . . . what? Is he going to be sitting in a corner watching us through darkened glasses or something?"

She tapped my arm in an attempt to be playful, but it actually felt like a slap. Maybe it had been intended as such.

"Oh, Andie, you crack me up! No, silly. I meant that when he sees the footage of you and Leon 8 feeding each other food, well, it's bound to drive him crazy . . ." She turned her attention back to the camera and harnessed her best saccharine smile. "Yes, folks – next week, we'll be showing you the highlights of Andie and Leon 8's date!"

I could have sworn she had three sets of adult teeth in her mouth – she seemed to produce more and more as her smiles grew wider and faker. Conversely, I was finding her less attractive by the second.

"You just know it's going to be interesting, don't you? So whatever happens, make sure you don't miss next week's show to see how Andie and Leon got on! Folks, a big round of applause for Andie and the Leons!"

I took it that we were being dismissed. The Leons dragged the arse out of their final seconds of glory, shaking butts and blowing kisses to the audience all the way out of the studio. The second we got backstage, I pulled Colm into a corner.

He grinned. "What's this? Starting our date already?"

"What the *hell* are you doing here? What was that whole performance in aid of?"

"It wasn't a performance, my sweetheart. I meant every minute of it." He paused, then broke his arse laughing. "Your face when I took off the mask – priceless!"

"Colm. An explanation. *Now.*"

"Okay then. Check your phone."

"Oh, come on, stop playing games and just tell me!"

"Until you check your phone, I'm not saying another word."

"God, you are so childish!"

I pulled out my phone and turned it on. Within a few seconds, it started to beep furiously.

I read the first text message: '**Lindy has something lined up – literally – that you won't like. Ring me ASAP.**'

The next one said: '**Seriously, you need to ring me the second you get this text. Stop whatever it is you're doing and ring. You'll be glad you did, honestly.**'

The next one was more typical of Colm: '**What's the point in having a phone if you don't use it??????**'

The next text was a standard one from the phone network telling me I had a voicemail. I pressed the necessary digits to access it, while Colm fixed me with a smug look.

"*Andie, Colm here. Listen, Lindy just rang me to see how I am, but she let it slip that the show you're being interviewed on today has rounded up loads of freaks named Leon from all over Arizona in the hope that one of them is your Leon. Don't get your hopes up – they've all already admitted that they've never met you. It's just one of these so-called fun segments they do in the show. I bet not one single one of them is even called Leon. Anyway, Lindy said she's not telling you about it in case you get the hump and don't do the interview. I told her she was wrong not to tell you, but you know Lindy. So I'm telling you instead – or would be, if you'd answer your phone. I just thought you should know anyway before they throw you to the lions – or should that be the Leons? Okay. Bye."*

"I still don't know how you ended up in the line-up, though," I said.

He shrugged. "I came here to find you and warn you, seeing as your phone was turned off, but you were in the make-up room when I arrived. I waited around outside it to talk to you when you were finished, but then I overheard a bit of commotion – it transpired that one of the Leons had pulled out at the last minute, and the production team were looking for someone to step in and replace him. And, well, Lindy had mentioned that there'd be a date involved in this whole carry-on too, and I knew that would really drive you crazy – so I thought, why not beat these guys at their own game? They're taking the piss out of you, so we should do exactly the same thing right back to them."

"What if I hadn't selected you?"

"Well, there was that risk . . . but the competition wasn't up to much . . ."

"That's for sure. God, I can't believe Lindy put me through that nonsense! Christ, I'm going to gut Lindy and eat her for dinner when I catch up with her."

"No, you're not. Lindy is too much of a slippery fish to be caught and gutted. You know she'll talk her way out of it as soon as you confront her on it."

"She's one cheeky cow to have organised something like that. And as for you, mister, you're supposed to be resting!"

"I was going mad with boredom. You gave me an excuse to do something. And hey, let's look at it this way. You would have had to go through a date with some guy with plaited nostril hair if I hadn't been around. This way, we get a nice dinner and some good wine at the expense of the TV show, while also getting the chance to rip the absolute mick out of them while I prattle on in a truly woeful Arizona accent. If you're going to be set up, you might as well do the same thing back to them and see how it goes."

When he put it like that . . .

"Thanks, Colm. You didn't have to do that, but thanks."

He shrugged. "That turned out to be the most *craic* I've had since I came to this country, actually."

"I have a feeling Dolly wouldn't mind having a bit of *craic* with you, if you were on for it . . ."

He looked puzzled. "Me? No way. That was all just part of her act."

"You put up a pretty good act yourself."

As we walked away with big grins on our faces, I thought about just how true that statement was. Colm seemed to have more sides to him than a Rubik's cube . . .

Two nights later at dinner in the priciest restaurant in Vegas, I was glad Colm had disobeyed doctor's orders. My face ached for days afterwards from hours of trying to repress laughter as he kept up his truly awful American accent throughout the entire meal. It was a blessing that he didn't drink, as there was no way he would have been able to sustain the accent past the first few mouthfuls of a good wine – or a bad one, for that matter. The more I relaxed into the night and enjoyed it, the more I realised that I was veering dangerously close to liking someone I couldn't stand the sight of when I first met him. Fancy dinner and a chance to get out of the hotel or not, it was still decent of him to get involved and try to warn me about Lindy's plan. Maybe we could be friends after all . . .

Chapter Eighteen

From: **Isolde.Huntingdon@vicious.ie**
To: **Andie.Appleton@vicious.ie**

Andey,

Isolde here. Reaction to last night's show has been huge. All the major radio talk shows covered it this morning. That whole Leon Line-up thing gave good structure to the show, and gave people a water-cooler talking point. Keep things up at this rate and who knows, you might even pass your review this year.

I hope the plans are underway now for the next show. We need something explosive to keep the momentum going. Get thinking.

Kind regards,

Isolde

I clicked out of Isolde's email. Something explosive? What did she want me to do next, blow up the MGM because that was where I met Leon? She was right about one thing, though – it was time for me to get my thinking cap on for the next show. I had no idea what we were going to do next. Then again, Lindy probably would have something else up her sleeve to humiliate me with and make sure I stayed in the public eye, so I probably shouldn't get too worried about my own lack of ideas.

Colm interrupted my lack of a train of thought. "Andie, come over here. I want to show you something."

"Colm, that kind of talk could have you arrested."

I was getting cheekier with Colm since the Leon Line-up dinner. To my gratification, he didn't seem to know how to react whenever I threw a bit of guff his way, even though he'd been fairly cheeky himself the night of the Leon Line-up. He was a mass of contradictions. He'd been full of chat at the Leon reward dinner, but maybe that had been for the sake of the cameras, as he hadn't been as forthcoming since. I never quite knew where I stood with him. For now, though, it was enough that we were on better terms than before. It was exhausting working so closely with someone I didn't get on with. Whatever what we had now was, it was preferable to constantly being on the cusp of a run-in.

"Oh, whisht! Trust me, you'll want to see this."

"This better be good." I pushed my chair back and wandered over to Colm's ridiculously untidy desk. I would have bet my house that there were directions to the lost continent of Atlantis under his pile of rubble, if I had a house of my own to gamble on.

An email was open on his PC screen. It was from Martin. I read it as fast as I could, drinking in the details.

Hello Colm,

You're owed an apology. I know I rambled on and on the last time I rang you, but Jesus, Mary and Joseph, Valerie drives me gaga sometimes. And you're not helping matters, being over there in Vegas. Sure I've nobody to moan to here now – you couldn't tell these blabbermouths anything. The minute you get back, you're booked in for a night at the local – I need to get your advice on something women-related, so get your arse home soon. You might be useless with women yourself, but you do talk a bit of sense from time to time.

Martin

"So, what do you make of that?" Colm asked.

"He wants to get your opinion on whether or not he should leave Valerie for Isolde, by the sounds of it!"

Colm shook his head. "I'm still not convinced there's anything going on between them at all, but it does sound like there's something up with him and Valerie."

"Why did you call me over to read this so, if you still don't believe my Isolde theory?"

He shrugged. "Ah, I just thought you might be interested. It's a slow day today."

"Well, you've just given me even more reason to believe I'm right."

"But Martin is a total play-by-the rules type," Colm said. "He's the kind that'd want to pay for the free samples you get in supermarkets of new food or whatever. He makes life as difficult as possible for himself."

"I knew that – he's voluntarily hanging out with Isolde, for heaven's sake! And don't say he's not, because I know he is. In fact, I've had enough of just saying this. It's time to get proof. It shouldn't be too hard to organise . . ."

"Why, what do you have in mind?"

"A spy, my dear Watson. It's simple – we get someone to follow them some evening and take pictures of them together and that kind of thing."

"Who do you think is going to be crazy enough to follow Isolde around?"

"Someone who owes me a big, big favour. And luckily, I know someone who fits that bill."

Adam. I've already mentioned him – my smash-fetish brother.

You make it, he breaks it. So maybe he could do the same to Isolde and Martin – break them up by letting them know someone was on to them.

"No, Andie. Just leave it. I shouldn't have said anything . . ."

I ignored Colm and picked up the phone to ring home. I knew Adam would be there – it was five pm Irish time, so he'd be getting out of bed any minute now. Adam always went out on Thursday nights with a group of friends he'd known since college, then slept as late as possible on Friday to prepare his body for the weekend of carnage ahead. Adam, quite frankly, was a layabout. Mum and Dad didn't help matters either with their cosseting attitude. Adam had been a sick child, suffering from chronic asthma for years and years. He still had it, but he grew out of the worst of it and knew how to manage the bit that remained. He also knew how to manage the parents and to use the sick card to his advantage – and they, like eejits, fell for it every single time. That's why Adam would be living at home for God only knew how many more years, and the woman who ended up with him would have her heart broken trying to housetrain him. He was good-natured, though, just totally and utterly immature – so no different to any other man, really.

The phone rang twelve times before it was picked up.

"Yeah."

"Adam! What has you answering the phone?"

"The noise of it was going through my head. Why can't people respect the hangover?"

"No, I mean where's Mum to answer the phone for you?"

"She's gone out. She and Dad have got a new hobby."

"Please tell me it's not swinging or dogging or anything that'll shame us?" It was a reasonable thought. You never knew with those two.

"It's badminton."

"Oh, God. We'd better ring the sports shop and tell them to top up their supplies of cycling helmets."

A few years ago, Mum and Dad had dabbled in tennis. Dad was a natural, much to Mum's chagrin, as she was absolutely woeful at it. Her biggest problem was that she just couldn't get the serves right, which meant that she couldn't start a game, which meant that she pretty much couldn't play tennis at all. Something that she really couldn't do was accept this fact, so she dragged Dad out every day for weeks to stand at the other side of the net in the local tennis club, waiting for her to serve balls that never came his way. There was a period of a few months when nobody in the entire neighbourhood would talk to us, because the local kids weren't getting a chance on the court at all with Laurel and Hardy hogging it for the entire day. Anyway, that was all well and good until one of the local lads, Vincent, lost his patience and ran onto the court to show Mum where she was going wrong, so that order could be restored to the entire community. Dad, in the meantime, had given up standing like a statue on the far end of the court, and had retired to the umpire's chair with a newspaper and a Toffee Crisp. Nobody saw Vincent coming, and Mum had ignored the sounds of "Hey!" from behind her as Vincent heralded his arrival, dismissing it as the usual abuse she got at the tennis courts from onlookers. She threw the ball up defiantly, and, determined to get this one right and show them all, she viciously whipped the tennis racket backwards over her right shoulder – and buried it in the side of poor Vincent's skull. Quite typically of our lousy luck as a family, Vincent was going through a skinhead phase, so when a bump the size of a watermelon came up on his head, there was no hope of people passing off his uneven cranium as a rogue cow's lick.

Mum declared that she'd lost interest in tennis after that, not having the patience for it, seeing as Dad was so useless at it and was slowing her down. Dad was so relieved to get out of the wasted days and nights shuffling on the tarmacadam that he went along with her story. But it looked like she was ready to injure again, which meant that we'd have to send a press release out to the neighbours to take cover.

"It doesn't matter anyway – it was you I was looking for. How do you fancy a job as a spy?"

"A spy? Yeah, that sounds right up my alley. I'm all about action and adventure."

I held the phone away from my ear as he yawned.

"I could do with some dosh, as it happens."

"When I say job, it's the unpaid kind . . ."

"The kind of job that's a favour, in other words."

"You crashed my car! You owe me!"

"I was wondering when that was going to come up . . ."

"It will never be mentioned again as long as you do this." A lie, of course.

"Hmm. We'll see. What exactly do you want me to do, anyway?"

"Okay, well, you know what Isolde looks like."

"A curtain."

"Yes. We suspect The Curtain is having an affair."

"With what, a carpet?"

"More like an anorak."

I filled Adam in on the whole story.

"So what we're looking for is for someone to keep an eye out for Isolde's comings and goings after work, at lunchtime, that kind of thing, to see if she's meeting this fella Martin. I'll email a picture of him on to you, so you'll know who you're looking for."

"Lunchtime? I dunno about that. I need my beauty sleep."

"Well, tough. Isolde often works late, so you might be hanging around the bushes for ages in the evening. She always leaves the office for lunch at one on the dot, so lunchtime is your best bet."

"Slavedriver!"

"We're not all spoiled, you know. We're up at seven every morning here, and we don't finish work until all hours."

"What's all this 'we' business about, anyway? Who is 'we'?"

"Oh, just Colm and me. Colm's the cameraman that came over from the TV station – Colm Cannon."

"His professional name, I presume?"

"No, it's real."

"Ah, no way. That's a deed-poll name if ever I heard one."

"Yeah. Well, look, I have to go. We can't all sit around all day scratching our balls."

"Scratching your balls? I know people go a bit mad in Vegas, but a sex change was a bit dramatic, don't you think?"

"I think Mum and Dad have enough on their plate worrying about how to get you out of bed without me adding to their problems with sex changes. Right, head off there and log into the computer – I'll send you an email right now with that picture of Martin."

"Umm." Adam yawned again.

"You're going straight back to bed the minute I hang up, aren't you?"

"It's my morning, for Christ's sake! You're lucky I even answered the phone!"

"If I don't get a read receipt for this email, I'll be ringing you back. And if you plug out the landline, I'll ring your mobile."

"Don't bother, because I'll turn the mobile off if you do that."

"Turn off your life-support machine? Like fuck, you will."

He sighed. "Jaysis. I hate family."

I laughed, happy at having been proved right in my assumption. Adam was so predictable.

"Okay, I'm going. See ya."

"Bye, BB."

I chuckled as I hung up. 'BB' was Adam's long-standing nickname for me. In childhood, it stood for Bossy Boots, but over the years, Boots had been replaced by the inevitable Bitch. I never minded – I always knew I'd got the better of him when he called me that.

"What's the story?" Colm asked.

"He's in. I'm just going to email him the picture of Martin now."

"Right." Colm stood up and shook a packet of Mariettas at me. "I'm going for a coffee to have with these. Want one?"

"If I say yes, will you just tell me to go and get it myself so?"

Colm smiled. "Andie, despite what you seem to think of me, I'm really not that bad."

I smiled too as he walked over to the coffee dock. You know what, he was right. He actually wasn't half bad at all. I shook my head and turned it back to the PC to send Adam that email . . . I was getting soft in my old age. It usually took much longer for someone to change my opinion of them once I'd formed an initial impression, but the more time went on, the more I wondered if Colm was someone completely different from the person he projected himself to be. Or if I'd just been too quick to judge him in the first place.

Chapter Nineteen

Everyone Googles their friends these days, don't they? You need to know who you're hanging around with – especially when you're spending all day, every day with someone, and yet, you still know nothing at all about them except that they're partial to a Marietta biscuit. It'd been weeks now since Colm and I had our acquaintance forced on us, and despite us getting a lot friendlier, I still knew nothing about the guy. He had an uncanny knack for talking a lot without actually revealing a single thing. We'd had all of those getting-to-know-you conversations that you have with people you're stuck with for work reasons over dinner in our first week in Vegas, but they'd only served to make me severely hungover the next day, as I drank more through sheer frustration.

Our conversations would go a little something like this:

Me: So, where are you from?

Him: I thought it was pretty obvious that I'm Irish.

Me: Oh, ha ha. Let me rephrase so, if it helps you out. Whereabouts in Ireland are you from?

Him: Down south.

Me: Ah, the deep south. Which part?

Him: The part that rains all the time.

Me: That doesn't narrow it down. Which county?

Him: Em . . . Kerry. (Said in a whisper)

Me: Oh, great! I love Kerry. What part of it are you from?

Him: South Kerry.

Me: Oh, right. So where exactly is that?

Him: The part that's under the north.

Me: (Sighing) So we're talking the Kenmare direction, then?

Him: Christ, we're almost out of drink. Another? (Swift departure to the bar by the teetotaller.)

That was one of the first conversations we ever had after the bath debacle, and now, weeks later, I was still not getting much else out of him. To date, I had no idea where exactly Colm was from, how many siblings he had, where he went to college – you know, the kind of things that strangers sitting beside you on a train would tell you. It was enough to make me vaguely curious, so that night when I got home from work, I typed Colm's name into Google, clicked the search button, and didn't even feel remotely guilty. If he didn't want people Googling him, he'd talk more.

I found results for Colm Cannon straight away, but I had to sift through them to determine whether they were for him or not – he obviously wasn't the only Colm Cannon in the world. I refined my search to Colm Cannon, Kerry, selected 'Pages from Ireland' and hit search again. The first result was an article about Colm winning an award. He'd never mentioned that!

> Colm Cannon has been named Cameraperson of the Year in the national broadcasting awards. Cannon, a native of Kerry, beat stiff competition from veteran camera operators to win the coveted award for his coverage of the aftermath of Hurricane Katrina in New Orleans. A representative of the panel of judges said: "The depth of emotion and empathy in Cannon's coverage of the post-hurricane devastation was unprecedented and unsurpassed. This, merged with his technical talent and his storyboarding skills, made him our clear and unanimous winner."
>
> You can watch an excerpt of Cannon's work in New Orleans here.

There was obviously more than one Colm Cannon cameraman out there. Depth of emotion? Empathy? What? 'Be fair, Andie,' the good angel on one of my shoulders said – I was never sure whether the good one lived on the left or the right, but she was talking one way or the other – although maybe it was a he? Whatever the angel's gender was, it reminded me that I'd seen a new side to him recently. 'It's just a pity he didn't use his storyboarding skills a bit more when it came to thinking up of ideas of how to find Leon instead of leaving it all up to you,' the bad angel said. I told them both to shush. I reread the article. Wow, this was impressive stuff.

I clicked back, vaguely annoyed that the article I'd just read hadn't told me where exactly in Kerry Colm was from. I was going to find that out if it killed me. I went to the next link. It was about a different award that he'd won. Jaysis, he seemed to have won a lot of them. Who would have thought there'd have been so many cameramen awards? (Camera person, camera operator, whatever.) I browsed through the links, ignoring the ones that were repeats of what I'd just read. It was strange actually that he didn't have a social-networking account – I'd already asked him, and his response had been a curt "No way" to that.

I was just about to shut down the Colm Cannon browser when a link at the end of the page caught my eye. I clicked on it immediately, thinking that I must have misunderstood what I'd just read in the description.

I hadn't.

> A twenty-two-year-old Kerryman has been cleared of all charges of careless driving relating to an accident that caused the death of an elderly man last year.
>
> Colm Cannon, a native of Listowel, pleaded not guilty to careless driving on the Cahirdown Road in August of last year. Cannon collided with Edward Smith, 75, who had been walking home from a nearby public house to his roadside cottage at the time. Smith was killed instantly in the collision.
>
> One of the witnesses to the accident who testified in court said that Smith had stumbled off the pavement in front of Cannon's car. The witness reported that Cannon

swerved to avoid the man, but failed in his attempt to avoid Smith.

Judge John Dunphy said he was satisfied that that neither alcohol nor speed were responsible for the collision, and that the testimonies of several witnesses left him in no doubt that Cannon would have been unable to avoid Smith in any circumstance, as Smith's fall had occurred suddenly and without warning. A post-mortem on Smith after the accident showed high levels of alcohol in his system.

Smith's two sons shouted abuse at a visibly shaken Cannon as the verdict was read out. Jack and William Smith told the media after they left the court that justice had not been done for their father.

I must have read the article five times, but I still couldn't quite believe it. Colm had killed a man – he had to wake up every day of his life with the death of another human being on his conscience. We'd had our differences, but my heart suddenly went out to the twenty-two-year-old Colm Cannon . . . and even more so to the thirty-one-year-old one.

So many things about him started to make sense . . . no wonder he was so secretive, so focused on work, so determined to push everyone away . . .

I wondered if anyone in Éire TV knew. Probably not. I didn't remember hearing about Colm's case in the media nine years ago, and judging by the amount of coverage it had on the Internet, it hadn't been big news at the time. Of course, the Internet hadn't been quite the dominating factor nine years ago that it was today, but all the same, there still seemed to be sketchy coverage of the event.

I couldn't let him know that I'd found out about this. Without knowing a single thing about Colm, I knew him well enough by now to know how valuable his privacy was to him. It wouldn't be fair to drag up the past again – and, if things were sometimes a bit awkward between us, that was nothing compared to how they could be if he got sniffy about me knowing his secret. We still had to work together, and there was no telling how he'd react to knowing that the person he was spending most of his time with knew about something that he probably wanted to keep private.

I wasn't usually good at holding my tongue, but this was something I'd definitely have to make an exception for. That didn't mean it would be easy, though.

Chapter Twenty

Hi BB,

I think you're losing it. I've spent the last three days hovering around outside your building waiting for baggy trousers to go for lunch or to bog off home. Yesterday, she left the building for lunch at one o'clock, and – shock, horror! – went across the road to the shop, bought a salad – and went straight back into the building again! My heart nearly gave way under the strain of the excitement. I headed off for a while, then came back around five to monitor her departure. When she got into her car at seven o'clock (you really, really owe me), I followed her – and guess where she went? Home. Alone. Not a clandestine meeting in sight. And guess what she did today? The very same thing.

How much longer are you going to put me through this? I have to hand it to you – you are good. This whole punishment thing is really your forte.

I'm off now to put a heat pack on my legs – they're still all pins and needlesy from me kneeling in the ditch all day. And I bet you didn't even feel a single pang of remorse when you read that, heartless wench. I'd ask you where you got it from if I wasn't so well acquainted with the person we call Mum.

Adam

I sat on the bed after a long day at the end of a long week, replying to all of the emails that I hadn't had a chance to respond to earlier, and laughed as I read Adam's mail. I pressed the reply button and typed "Same time, same place tomorrow" and pressed send. There was no way he was getting out of all of this that easily. Even if he never busted Isolde and Martin together – and knowing Adam, he probably wouldn't – getting him to do my dirty work was way too much fun to give up on it just yet.

I had just settled into bed when the hotel phone rang. It was only going to be one of two people – Lindy or Philippe. I'd only spoken to Lindy fifteen minutes before, which made me think it would be Philippe – although it wouldn't be beyond the bounds of possibility that it would be Lindy again, ringing back to ask if Colm had said anything about her since we last spoke. I decided to take my chances on it being Philippe.

"*Bonsoir, mon petit choux-fleur,*" I rasped down the phone in what was meant to be a sexy, eighty-fags-a-day voice – although the image of eighty fags a day isn't even remotely sexy – but it just came out as a hocking sound that left spittle all over the phone. Still though, I knew Philippe would get a laugh out of being called a cauliflower – who wouldn't? It's amazing the stupid, random words you can remember from your school French. Ask me what's the French for something like Wednesday, and I wouldn't have a clue.

"Something stuck in your throat?"

"Oh . . . Colm. Didn't expect it to be you. What's up?"

"Nothing's up . . . I was just wondering what you're doing tomorrow."

Don't mention the accident, don't mention the accident. "Oh. Well, not much, apart from my daily game of dodge the publicist – my day is looking remarkably free, for once. Why?"

"I'm going on a desert drive tomorrow, if you're interested. I've hired out a car –"

"What kind of car is it?" I jumped in.

"It's a . . . why, does it matter?"

"Of course it does!"

184

"It's just your regular car-hire type of car."

"Oh."

"Why, what were you hoping for?"

"A Porsche would have been nice, but never mind. Anyway, go on."

"Go on, says the one who never lets anyone finish a sentence. I'll speak fast, so that I have some hope of getting this message across at all." He took a deep breath. "So, I'm picking up the car at eight tomorrow morning, then driving to Hoover Dam. It's a longish drive, I don't know anyone here, blah blah blah. See where I'm going with this?"

"You're stuck for company, so you're asking me along?"

"Something like that. So, is that an offer you can't refuse or what?"

"Hmm. I'll think about it."

"When you're finished thinking, set your alarm clock. See you at ten to eight in Reception." He hung up.

I rolled my eyes as I slammed the phone down. He was pretty sure of the lure of his company!

As I sank down on the bed, I had to admit I fancied a road trip. The last few days had been crazy as Lindy had continued her drive to push me down every publicity avenue imaginable. The Face of People Search thing had opened even more doors for us, and we'd taken every opportunity we were offered. There was still no sign of Leon, though, but I tried to put that out of my mind. If I thought too much about why he wasn't coming forward, I'd go mad, and after the week I'd just had, I hadn't the energy for madness. Plus I'd been in Vegas for weeks now, and it was starting to suffocate me in more ways than just the cloying heat. Every fecker in the hotel knew who I was, what I was up to each day, who I was up to it with, where it would be when I was up to it – they knew bloody more about me than I did myself. And okay, Colm was a pain, but at least he was an indifferent one.

It's strange, you know. Everybody wants to be somebody these days, but if they got their wish, they mightn't even like it. The taste

I'd had of notoriety at home was nothing compared to what I was experiencing over here, and having dipped my toe in the madness that surrounds being a known face in the States, I was feeling an urge to retreat and keep the rest of my foot dry. A day away from it all might do me good. The other side of that argument though was that I would be all alone in the middle of the desert for a whole day with someone that I knew a big secret about. When I know a big secret about somebody and really shouldn't say something about it, I always do. The odds of me getting through the day without letting what I knew slip in some way were slim, and then the rest of my time in Vegas with Colm would probably be unbearable. Maybe I'd be better off not going at all . . .

It was much of a muchness, and whenever I find myself in the muchness zone, there's only one thing for it. Time to take the scientific approach.

There were three music channels on the hotel TV. There were also three news channels. I would close my eyes, pick up the remote, and fumble with the buttons until I turned on a channel. If it was a news channel, I wouldn't go. If it was a music channel, I'd risk hanging out with the grouchball for the day. If it was any other type of channel, I would go to the next programme up until I hit either news or music.

I turned the TV off with the remote, then threw it on the bed and closed my eyes. I fumbled for it and pressed the first button my finger came in contact with. Music flooded the room. I opened my eyes to see if it was music on a news channel. It wasn't.

It looked like it was time to set the alarm clock.

As I got into bed, I had to admit that if I'd hit a news channel, I would have been slightly disappointed.

Chapter Twenty-one

I had to laugh when I saw the cut of Colm the next morning in Reception. Every other man in the city was doubtless wearing the lightest pair of shorts they could get their sweaty hands on to help them cope with the heat, but Colm was wearing a pair of brown cords that he'd sheared at the knees to create a pair of makeshift shorts. He'd coupled it with a tight brown T-shirt though, and somehow he managed to pull off the look and make it trendy. As usual, he was getting a few admiring glances from passing ladies in micro-skirts – at a time when he deserved looks of disbelief. You had to hand it to him. Presence was a great thing – you got away with murder if you had it.

He looked at his watch as I walked towards him. He was so engrossed in it that I knew he hadn't spotted me yet. Next thing I knew, he had turned on his heel and was making his way to the front door of the lobby.

"Colm!"

"Oh. You've decided to come. I thought you weren't, so I was just about to leave."

"I'm only . . ." I looked at my watch, "five minutes late!"

He shrugged. "Eight o'clock is eight o'clock. Right, well, you're here now, so let's go get this car."

I sat down in the waiting area of the car-hire shop while Colm collected the car keys at the counter, relieved to have a few moments of air-con. It was early, but the dry heat was already at feverish proportions. I hoped this car he'd hired had a nice big sunroof to help circulate air in the car.

Colm jangled a set of keys at me as he turned away from the counter. We walked outside towards the cars. I looked longingly around me at all of the amazing cars on the forecourt. This was my idea of heaven – not only were there the latest models of BMWs, Lexuses and Mercs, but a considerable portion of the forecourt was given over to classic convertible cars. I felt like a magnet was drawing me over towards the array of MGs, Triumphs and Buicks, and before I knew it, I was standing over beside them, identifying the model of each one. Colm could wait a few minutes, surely – it'd give him the opportunity to find his car and get it started.

I examined each and every one, touching the bonnets adoringly. But then, as I lovingly laid my hands on an Alfa Romeo Spider, I looked up, only to see Colm sitting behind the wheel and staring at me in amusement.

"Stop mauling my car, and get in, for the love of God." He was smirking and looking very pleased with himself.

"No way! *This* is your idea of a regular car-hire type of car, then?"

"This is a 'me' car."

"If this is you, then I like you very much." I jumped in, then sank back into my seat and inhaled the smell of the car, feeling deliriously happy. This day had started much better than I'd expected it to.

We set off, heading down Tropicana Avenue and leaving the rush of the Strip behind. I reached for the map and other documentation that Colm had thrown on the dashboard. The dam was about thirty miles from Vegas, which was far too short a distance to travel in a car like this. I looked at the route – we would be passing by Henderson, one of Vegas's best-known suburbs, and then Boulder City, before continuing up US 93 until we reached the dam.

"I read about Boulder City before I came over here," I said. "Do you know that gambling is prohibited there?"

"Yeah, it was made illegal by the government in the 1930s, when they built Boulder City to accommodate the workers who were constructing the Hoover Dam. Alcohol was illegal too – the government, quite naturally, didn't want anyone who'd been boozing and gambling all night in Vegas to be working on the dam. The residents of Boulder City were clean-living folks. The ideal employees."

"Alcohol was banned right up until 1969," I said. "I bet they had one hell of a party there when that ban was overturned."

Colm started to sing about partying like it was 1969, to the tune of Prince's '1999'. He hadn't a note in his head, but that fact was rendered unremarkable by the sheer fact of his random singing. Colm wasn't a random singer, not by a long shot.

"What amuses me is that Nevada allows some legal prostitution, but a town that's the throw of a poker chip away from Vegas prohibits gambling. It's a funny old world." There he was, talking away as if the random singing had never happened.

I nodded very emphatically. "It sure is," I said to the stranger that was evolving in the seat beside me.

Colm talked more on the way to the dam than he'd done in all the time we'd spent together. He reminded me of an old bachelor who used to live near us years ago, Fred. After Fred's brother died, the poor old man didn't see many people from one day to the next, except on pension day. So whenever any of us did run into him, he'd keep talking and talking non-stop about absolutely anything that came into his mind while he had the opportunity of conversing with another human being. Colm meandered from run-of-the-mill chitter-chatter about the scenery to whether Catch bars were better than Toffee Crisps without me having the faintest idea how we'd gone from one topic to the next (ah, Topics – I'd prefer them to Catch bars and Toffee Crisps put together, personally), then on to talk about driving down Route 66, which he'd done alone a few summers ago. And yes, we were sharing the same car and the same journey and all that, but it wasn't like being stuck in an elevator –

we had options to ignore each other if we wanted to. A loud radio usually solved that issue for me whenever I've been in it before. But Colm was like a bath unplugged, and it was strangely nice.

"Going on this trip has been one of the things I've wanted to do since I came here," he said as we got closer to the dam.

"It's definitely something we should see while we're in Vegas," I agreed. "We're lucky – this whole thing is a nice little junket, all the same."

"Yeah, it is. It still doesn't make up for the fact that I'm not in the job I want to be in, but it does help."

"How did you end up working for Éire TV?" I asked.

"I was just back from a stint in Australia when someone I knew in Éire TV asked me if he could refer me for the job. He was looking for the referral fee if I got hired, of course – it wasn't that he was all that concerned about me being in full-time employment – but it sounded like a decent enough job at the time."

"That was before they made you a jack of all trades, I presume?"

He nodded. "It's not just me – everyone in the company is doing several jobs now. There isn't the budget there to hire more people. I've complained, of course, and threatened to go to HR, the whole hog – but they're so smart about how they operate in Éire TV. They've make us sign role-related commitments, which means that in order to be deemed an effective worker in our positions, we have to meet a certain number of commitments for our jobs. If we don't meet them, they can give us warnings, and ultimately fire us. And then, of course, they twist all of these new responsibilities into somehow coming under one of the commitments we've signed up to."

"But project management is a completely different job to being a cameraman! Are you even qualified to do that? And I don't mean that in an offensive way, I'm just asking."

"Yes, I am. I've done a project-management course, but it was my fall-back plan in case I couldn't get a job as a cameraman. Let's face it, positions for cameramen – or people, whatever – aren't exactly falling out of the sky like raindrops in the West of Ireland on a winter's day. I certainly wasn't planning on doing the two jobs at once, though."

"Sounds like tough going."

"It is, but what job isn't these days?" He laughed. "Listen to me. All I need now is a pot-smoking hippy cap so that I can put it on and ask myself where it was along the way that I compromised on my dreams. I'd say you have a pretty rough time of it yourself with that old boot Isolde."

"Hey, don't call my boss an old boot!"

He frowned. "Loyalty to your boss? Has she brainwashed you?"

"Loyalty? Oh God, no. Nothing like that. You just need to call her The Curtain."

And that kept the chat going until we neared the dam. When we got our first glimpse of Lake Mead, we both shut up. It was breathtaking, or would have been, if the heat hadn't robbed the breath from us anyway. The thought of a reservoir of any kind didn't conjure up the most picturesque of images for me, but Lake Mead, the largest reservoir in the US, changed that presumption. It was a mass of blue, a palette of navies, taupes, and turquoises, a reflection of the beautiful day we'd been lucky enough to experience. As we approached Hoover Dam, I was transfixed at how still the gleaming lake appeared as it sat behind the dam, extending as far as the eye could see.

We pulled into a parking garage located near the dam's visitor centre. It didn't feel like we should be there already; the journey had flown by. And painlessly, at that, despite my reservations. Still though, the day was young – we were bound to have a row at some stage. It would almost be an anticlimax if we didn't.

The second we got out of the car, Colm was like a puppy unleashed after hours of being trapped in the boot. "Let's go down to the bridge to get a good look at the dam!" He was practically jumping up and down as he tried to contain his excitement. For pure devilment, I slowed down as much as possible, then waited for the onslaught of abuse – but no, he was too busy gawking all around him to rise to the bait.

"Pretty *damn* impressive, huh?"

I groaned. "Have you been waiting all day to toss that line out?"

"No. Just had a flash of inspiration there."

After ogling the dam from the vantage point of the overhead bridge for about twenty minutes, we went inside the visitor centre and bought our tickets for the tour, then made our way up to the first floor where we watched a film about the dam's contribution to the development of the Western US back in the 1930s. More than 20,000 men were employed in the project that would control flooding and provide water for Southern California and the Southwest, at a time when the US was mired in the Great Depression. I'm no engineer, but it was pretty obvious that building the dam had been one hell of an engineering achievement to pull off. When the film was over, and Colm had scrutinised each and every map and photo on the entire floor, we moved up to the exhibit gallery on the next level. The inspection process began again in earnest here, as we pored over models of hydroelectric turbine generators and suchlike. We spent so long examining the exhibits that daylight hurt my eyes when we finally went up to the observation deck. While Colm examined a model of the Hoover Dam Bypass Bridge, I went outside to admire the panorama of the dam, Lake Mead, the Colorado River and the Mojave desert. The expanse of empty desert space captivated me – the stillness, the immutability, the absolute freedom of it. You could stare at that panorama and feel, just for a few minutes, as if you didn't have a single problem in the whole world. It felt good to escape from the thoughts that were always haunting me. I don't know how long I stood there, hypnotised – it must have been a good fifteen minutes. I'd probably still be standing there if Colm hadn't come outside to find me.

"You okay?"

I mentally shook myself out of my trance. "Yeah, of course."

"You looked like you had a lot on your mind."

"The whole Leon thing is starting to wear me down." The words were out before I even knew I was going to say them.

"Oh?"

"Actually, forget I said anything. I don't want to go there right now."

He shrugged. "Fair enough. I could live with taking in this view for a while myself anyway."

"Let's do that, then."

We eventually walked back to the car, satisfied that we'd seen everything we could see and learned everything we could learn about the dam. I looked at my watch – it was only lunchtime. I didn't fancy going back to Vegas yet. The memory of the panorama of the desert was fresh in my mind, and all I could think about was being in the middle of it . . .

"Fancy a spin?" Colm must have read my thoughts.

"Where to?"

"Let's just drive, and see where we end up."

"Okay."

We took the road that would eventually lead you to the Grand Canyon.

"I was originally planning on doing a canyon trip after Hoover Dam and staying for the weekend," Colm said, "but I thought it better not to risk it after that whole sickness thing. Pity, because I even had the hotel picked out – a really cool place called Crumbler's Lodge. Before I go home though, I'm seeing the canyon, and that's that."

And that was that with the chat too. Colm had obviously reached his talk quota for the day – he didn't say a single word after that as we drove along. Strangely, it was a comfortable silence. Even the crazy 70s tunes that Colm had brought along for the trip seemed like perfect driving music. As we drove on, the vista became wilder and lonelier. It was perfect. I didn't know how far Colm was planning on driving, but I didn't care. It felt good to be getting further and further away from Vegas.

I didn't say a word for about half an hour, until something electrified me – something that wouldn't be very exciting by most people's standards, but it nearly made me jump out the window.

"It's a Joshua tree!"

"Want me to pull up?"

"Yes, please."

"Andie, I was joking. It's only a tree!"

"But it's the U2 tree! Pull over!"

Colm swerved the car off the highway. We parked on the hard shoulder, as close as possible to the tree. It was about thirty feet behind the rickety fencing that marked the boundary of desert territory. And though it was only a tree, spotting a real-life one felt to me like bumping into a pop star whose posters had been plastered on my bedroom walls for years as a teenager.

We climbed over the fence and made our way towards it.

When U2 released the album *The Joshua Tree* in 1987, I was too busy terrorising my brother, hiding buttons from my mother's overflowing "To Be Sewed Back On" family-sized Cara matchbox in her brown-bread mix, and generally keeping myself too busy with the whole business of being a seven-year-old to take any notice. But when I fell in love with their 1993 album, *Zooropa*, it led to what would be described by some (i.e. my family, friends, the neighbours who complained about the soccer-pitch-sized U2 flag that I painstakingly patched together from scraps of material and hung from the roof of our house, people like that) as an obsession. Of course, I made it my business to get the back catalogue, learn every lyric, pore over the meaning of every word of every song, and adorn my walls with posters of the band and the album covers. Then, I developed a fascination with Joshua trees – well, it was a natural concomitant of being U2's biggest fan *ever*, I suppose. (Of course, nobody had ever heard of them before I set my cap on them, oh no.) I scourged my mother to scour the library for books with information on the Joshuas, and she'd come home with the knuckles of her hands scraping the pavement with the weight of the bags of these big books she'd have dragged home for me. Then I'd disappear from the world for hours while I trawled through the books to see if there was anything I could learn from them. It was a great time for Adam, who I was still terrorising. When I eventually emerged from the cocoon of my bedroom, I'd be full of facts about the Joshers that I'd throw randomly into completely unrelated conversations.

Like the following very typical episode that sprang to mind as I stared with Colm at the real-live Joshua tree.

It was dinner time at the Appletons' circa 1994 and I was about fourteen.

"Yuck!" said Adam when my mother put a plate of congealed chicken, mushy broccoli and wet, sloppy potatoes in front of him (right before he proceeded to eat it anyway – he just had to get the point across).

I sidled across the table and said, "Did you say yuck? That reminds me of the *yucca brevifolia*. Do you know what that is?"

"One of those stupid cactuses you're always on about," Adam muttered as he got up for a steak-knife for his rubber chicken.

"A cactus? Any old fool can have one of those," I scoffed. Adam used to have one on his windowsill years ago. "You'd need to go to the US to see a proper Joshua tree. There's a Joshua tree national park in California, imagine that! There'd be some amazing ones there. Of course, you'd also see them at the side of the road if you were driving through the Mojave Desert. It's the Joshua tree's special habitat."

"Have we got someone in from bloody *National Geographic* for dinner today?" Dad said as he sauntered into the room, sniffing the air suspiciously to suss out today's servings. He threw an eye at Adam's plate, threw his eyes up to heaven, then adopted a resigned look. Hunger was the best sauce, after all.

"Well, if you ever find one of them yokes," he said, "cut off a few branches and throw them into your mother's dinners for a bit of flavour, like those cinnamon sticks she threw into that stuff that made us all sick."

Dad still wasn't the better of Mum's attempt to be cosmopolitan by cooking an Indian dish.

"You're encouraging her to do something that glued us all to the bog for a week?" Adam said through a mouthful of broccoli stalks. "It was those feckin' sticks that did the damage, I'd put the house on it!"

"Ah, anything would help at this stage. And don't you go putting my house on anything. Bad enough that herself out there in the kitchen tries to burn it down every few months." He turned to me.

I was expecting him to follow up with a reference to how *I* actually *did* burn down his house all those years ago, but he spared me the ignominy. "I've seen some quare-looking trees down by Madden's shed – are you sure one of them isn't a jostler?"

The slagging would always continue along these lines – oh yes, everyone wanted their two cents' worth of slagging – but I wasn't for turning when it came to something I was interested in. Usually, my barrage of facts would wear someone in the group down – usually Mum, even though she was the last to join in, but her burst of energetic jokes at my expense usually weren't matched by much stamina – and the radio would be turned on, at which point a new discussion would start up about which channel we should listen to. Discussion being a euphemism for argument, naturally. I smiled at the memory; they were the best of times.

"Are the trees telling a joke only you can hear?" Colm had spotted my smile. When I told him what I'd been thinking about, a strange look passed across his face.

"Are you close to the rest of your family?" I asked Colm. I hadn't mentioned his parents' death since he told me about it. The time had never been right. And yet, I felt I should say something. Maybe this was my segue . . .

"No." He stared away. Something in the tone of his voice made me too afraid to ask any further questions.

I had to admit, I was curious about his family situation. I would have thought that the death of his parents would have drawn him closer to his siblings – if he had some. But surely he'd have aunts and uncles? Wasn't he close to anyone? I had more sense than to ask any more questions and antagonise him, though – not now that Colm had let his wall down by a few bricks.

I was still shocked that he'd asked me to come on his desert drive at all, to be honest. It was weird. He was someone that people were drawn to, and yet the closer they came, the more he retreated. The combination of his ruddy hair and soft accent seemed to really work for him with the ladies in Vegas, but although he flirted with them, he would only take it to a certain point before running for the hills – or the desert, to be accurate. I was just surprised that he was bringing me along for the run.

My stomach growled, so loud that even Colm heard it.

"Time for lunch," he said, walking back towards the car.

Hungry and all as I was, I still didn't relish the prospect of getting back in the car and driving until we came across a service station. But we didn't need to. Just as I reluctantly began to trail after Colm, he whisked his backpack out of the car and walked back towards me. He sat down, unzipped the bag, and started pulling a cornucopia of goodies out of it – bread rolls, hard cheese (most likely smelly, both from the heat and naturally), crackers, crisps, candy (d'you hear me, with my 'candy'? You'd swear I was a local), cans of Cola that were probably at boiling point now, but who cared, and even a big check rug to put the whole kit and caboodle on. How he had fitted it all into the rucksack, I couldn't imagine – it was like a magician's hat, producing more and more every time he put his hand into it, even though it looked empty from the outside.

We didn't say a word for about ten minutes straight as we tucked in relentlessly. As soon as there was no food left to devour, I broke the silence.

"Have you done a lot of travelling?"

"I suppose. I went InterRailing around Europe for three months after I left college, then I moved to London and got a job as a photographer. Then the company I was working with asked me to relocate to South Africa for six months. Of course, I jumped at the chance. Then I did the year in Oz thing, which meant that I got to spend some time in South East Asia on the way back. I did a good bit of travelling all over Australia while I was living there, and New Zealand too. I've had stints of working in different parts of North America – never anywhere near here though – and I spent a year working in South America as well."

"You suppose? You could do a sideline in writing *Lonely Planet* guides after all that!"

He grinned. "What about you? Have you travelled much?"

"Most of my travelling has been done in Europe, really. I studied French at college, so I lived in France for four years. I taught English in a college near Paris. I guess asking you if you've ever been to Paris is a stupid question?"

"No, not at all. I've never been there."

"Did France do something to you to be left out of your InterRailing route?"

"It wasn't. I went all over France, actually – Lille, Nancy, Lyon – sorry to mention the war, I know you don't want to hear anything that sounds like his name at the moment – then down the coast to Marseille and Nice, then across to Toulouse and over to Bordeaux from there."

"But not Paris."

"No."

There had to be some story there. Nobody went all over France without going to Paris! I decided to let it drop, though. He obviously didn't want to explain why he'd boycotted the capital city – and, to his credit, he hadn't pushed me on the Leon issue earlier.

"You must have really loved Paris to have stayed there for four years," Colm said.

I shrugged. The truth was that I had sometimes been very lonely there. But at least it wasn't home. At that time, I had needed to stay as far away from home as possible.

"So is there anywhere left that you want to visit?" I was eager to change the subject.

"I've always fancied visiting the Galapagos Islands. Random, but if they were good enough for Charles Darwin, they're good enough for me. And I'll never get tired of visiting New York, no matter how many times I go there."

"True. I love New York myself. Who doesn't?"

We spent another while talking about various places we loved, until Colm eventually looked at his watch. "What time is this dinner Lindy has organised for you?"

"Six."

"Let's head back now so. We wouldn't want you being late for something so important, would we?"

"We totally would. I'm sick of the sight of that woman's face."

"You're not the only one." We both laughed. It was nice to have someone to share my dislike of Lindy with, terrible and all as it was to admit to that.

The drive back was full of convivial chat and banter, with Colm raving on about how great Pink Floyd's album *The Wall* was and how sorry he was that he hadn't brought it on this trip. He managed to pull me into his nostalgia buzz and we ended up discussing our favourite *Bosco* presenters back in the day, best and worst 80s adverts, and which 80s year showed the best movies on Christmas Day (seriously – he was able to name the feature films that were shown each year – the guy was one oddball). Colm was technically cheating on the 70s by such blatant adulation of the 80s, but I allowed him the transgression just this once. And it was a relief not to have to talk about Leon for once, terrible as it sounds. Much and all as I wanted to find him, I was really fed up of saying the same thing over and over again.

Before I knew it, we were back in Vegas. I was sorry that we were. Even sorrier when we had to return the car. I turned my back as I watched Colm hand over the keys – it was too painful. Still, though, I took solace in the fact that a day I'd expected to be hard work had actually been so much fun.

Everyone has a self-destruct button, but some people know how to not press it. I've never quite mastered that technique.

When we got back to the hotel, the words in my head that had been trying to gain a voice all day came tumbling out as I said goodbye to Colm at his bedroom door.

"Tell me one thing, Colm. The person I've been hanging out with all day is not the person I've come to know over the last few weeks. I see flashes of someone very different, but then you go back to being the person I first got to know. So which one of you is real?"

He fixed me with a glare. I returned it. Which was all very well in theory, but I was dealing with someone here who could seriously glare. The look went on and on. I was sorry now I hadn't looked away in the beginning, but it was too late to back out now.

When he finally opened his mouth, I expected an old-Colm type of barb – but what he said was far, far worse. "Why did you have to ruin a lovely day?"

I opened my mouth to protest my innocence, but realised there was no point. He was gone again. Whatever bridge we'd built today had crumbled, and he was back behind that wall of his. I stomped off down the corridor before I said something else that I'd regret. This was typical of Colm. He had ruined the best *craic* day I'd experienced since . . . well, since the night with Leon, which wasn't a day, so technically, he'd ruined the best *craic* day I'd had in years with his mood swings.

I headed straight for the minibar when I got to my room. A day in the desert is dehydrating work. And, who knew, the alcohol might give me the wisdom to interpret what the hell had just gone on there . . . but, as I flopped on the bed with a Coors Light, I knew I already had the answer. Yet again, I had touched a nerve, but this time it had been rawer than an abattoir. And, if I was honest with myself, I really wasn't angry with him at all. On some strange level, I understood him.

I'd been right about one thing, though – it had been only a matter of time before we'd had a row. Usually, being proved right made me feel great. So, I waited to feel great. It didn't happen. Somehow, I had known it wouldn't. Still, I'd managed to keep my mouth shut about what I'd found out about Colm, and that was something. Although, if today's performance was anything to go by, I was living on borrowed time before I blurted that out too.

Chapter Twenty-two

My phone rang at half seven that evening. Lindy. I hoped I wasn't going to be subjected to another round of Colm-grilling. It wasn't as if I would be much help to her – I certainly didn't know how to handle him or to act around him, if what had gone on earlier was anything to go by. It was my second call of the day from her – mercifully, she'd rung at twenty minutes to six to tell me that the dinner at six had been cancelled. It was perfect timing, as I hadn't even begun to get ready yet. Of course, that meant that Colm and I could have spent more time spinning in the desert instead of rushing back, but I should probably be thanking my lucky stars that we hadn't had the time to do that. If I'd opened my big mouth at the start of our journey home, asking Colm who he really was, I'm pretty sure he would have turfed me out onto the side of the road. I still wasn't sorry I'd asked, though. He'd got away with the whole split-personality thing for long enough.

"Hi, Lindy." I tried to make my tone suitably busy. I'd make up what I was busy doing as soon as she asked me. I hadn't thought that far ahead yet.

"What's the deal with the emails?" she said without any preamble.

"What?"

As soon as I asked the question, I realised what. Her words

could only mean one thing – there'd obviously been another email from Go Home. Damn it – I'd meant to check up on the email inbox last night! I should have known workaholic Lindy would check email over the weekend! But why had it been sent to the *Looking for Leon* account and not my personal mail?

"I'm going to read something out to you, and when I'm done you better tell me what's going on. It's a reply to a mail you sent to this person from your own email suggesting that they send you on their phone number. They've CC'd the *Looking for Leon* email address in their reply, before you ask." She cleared her throat, as if she was about to do a reading at Mass.

"*There is no point in us speaking or in me putting you in contact with Leon. He will never tell you to your face that he doesn't want you because he's too much of a gentleman to hurt your feelings. He's hoping that you'll just go away and leave him alone eventually. You need to listen to me when I say that you are causing so much trouble, and*' – this next bit is in capitals – 'you need to stop it straight away before you cause any more hurt!' Back to lowercase now – are you with me? '*Believe me, this is not what Leon wants or needs right now. If you don't have any respect for yourself, then I ask you, please have respect for Leon. If he means as much to you as you're telling the world he does, then do that much for him.*'"

I cringed. Hearing Lindy read out that Leon didn't want me was even worse than reading it myself.

"What's the story? This person has obviously contacted you before – why haven't you told me about this?"

"Because I didn't want you making a huge issue out of what's probably nothing when you could be focusing on more useful things instead."

I filled her in on the letter and the previous email as briefly as I could get away with.

"It's probably his ex-girlfriend," I ended. "Leon told me all about her, and it sounds like she's not over him at all."

"Or maybe *he* wasn't over *her* – why did he bring his ex up in conversation while he was chatting you up? They could be back together for all we know, which would pretty much throw this happy ending we're looking for right out the window."

"No way. The only reason I know about her at all was because I asked him how someone like him didn't have a girlfriend, and he told me that he wasn't long out of his relationship with Germaine. Believe me, he was so over that relationship – there wasn't a spark of enthusiasm in his voice when he spoke about her. It sounded like that relationship completely drained him." And then he'd said that nobody had caught his eye since he'd broken up with Germaine – until that night. Cue lots of bashful grins and cheeky smiles from both of us.

It already seemed like a lifetime ago.

"Hmm." Lindy didn't sound convinced.

"Or it could be just some random nutter who's bored and looking for someone to hassle," I said.

"Here's another theory. Maybe it's someone that Leon has asked to email you. Maybe they're telling the truth – he wants you to just crawl into a hole and die."

"Yes, Lindy," I said through gritted teeth, "I had considered that possibility too, but thanks for bringing it up all the same."

"It could even be Leon himself. Maybe he finds it easier to tell you to go away if he refers to himself in the third person."

"I don't think he'd be that cowardly," I said.

"You think, but you don't know. You have to admit that you really don't know a hell of a lot about him when all's said and done. If you did, you wouldn't be over here looking for him."

I decided to ignore her comment – a statement like that could only serve as an incitement for an argument.

After a few seconds of silence, Lindy spoke again. "This person could well know where Leon is, but if they do, let's hope their motivation is to stop you from getting to Leon for their own selfish purposes and not because he really doesn't want to see you. After all the time I've put into this, I want a knockout ending to this story."

"And maybe even a bit of happiness for me too?"

"Yeah, yeah. Even if you do get it together, you'll probably break up within a few months because of the distance or some crap like that – but the main thing is that we get things to the point where you're in a position to break up in the first place. Agreed?"

"Well, no –"

"Whatever. Now listen, if you get any more of these, you let me know, okay? You need to keep me informed about this sort of thing. It doesn't sound like the person is willing to give too much away, but the more contact we have from them, the more hints we'll potentially get. I'm going to go now and have a think about the best way to handle this."

"I don't know if there's much we can do if this person isn't willing to put me in contact with Leon," I said.

"You said yourself that the person behind this could be a nutcase who's just taken a dislike to you. I'm sure you realise that you can come across as very annoying sometimes, so it's an extremely real possibility that your personality has provoked someone. If you wake up in the middle of the night with some freak plunging a knife into your heart, your last thought will be that I was right. Now, let me go and have a think about what I can do to prevent that from happening."

On that happy note, she hung up.

Lindy had done her thinking. She'd also acted, so fast that I had no idea of what was going on until it was out there for everyone to see. I couldn't believe my eyes when I read the article in the local Las Vegas daily newspaper the next day.

> Andie Appleton's search for the man of her dreams has taken a nasty and potentially dangerous twist. The lovestruck Irishwoman who has been looking for Leon, a man from Arizona that she met on holidays, for the past few weeks has been receiving hate mail that warns her to stay away from Leon – or face the consequences.
>
> "Andie's received both physical mail and email from this person, cautioning her that she must stay away from

204

Leon. The mails would send a shiver down your spine," says a source.

Our source has also informed us that the police have been notified. "We're in the process of passing on all information, physical and virtual, to the police." As for the future of Andie's search, our source says it's business as usual. "It's going to take more than one psycho to scare Andie off. She has lots of new ideas to help her find Leon, so watch this space."

Trust Lindy to wring the maximum amount of exposure from this – and not to even tell me! Especially after the People Search lack-of-communication fiasco! It was exactly her style.

I picked up the phone to ring her and tear strips off her, but it instantly went to voicemail. I threw the phone on the bed and sighed. Even if I got through to her, she would be so utterly unrepentant that I'd get no satisfaction from her anyway. The whole thing was infuriating.

The hotel phone rang. I picked it up reluctantly.

"Hello?"

"Morning. I just read the evening paper, and it says –"

"I know, Colm, I know."

"Has Lindy been eating magic mushrooms again, or do we need to take out insurance on your life?"

"Lindy doesn't eat – surely you know that by now. But there is some basis to the story, albeit a highly exaggerated one." I briefly filled Colm in.

"I wish you'd told me," he said when I'd finished. "I can't imagine it felt great to be told Leon doesn't want anything to do with you. I'm sure you probably wanted to talk about it with someone."

His concern confused me. Yesterday, he'd been grumping and grouching at me, but now he was all worried about me! I said nothing, hoping he'd change the subject, but there was nothing but silence on the end of the line as if he was expecting me to say something else.

I didn't think I could stand going over the possibility of Leon being behind the mails again. I'd spent hours tossing and turning the previous night, wondering if I really was making a fool of myself and if I should call the whole thing off – or if I even could. I just felt like a bit player in the whole *Looking for Leon* juggernaut at this point. There was no way Isolde or Éire TV would let this go until they'd got everything they wanted out of it, and of course there was LVTV to consider as well. The whole thing was a mess that I'd never be able to clean up.

When Colm still seemed to be waiting for an answer, I decided to blame Germaine rather than getting into the ins and outs of who it could potentially be.

"Well, if it's her, she'll hopefully stop now that she's been exposed," Colm said when I finished speaking. "She, or he. Imagine if Leon turned out to be gay! Germaine can be a boy's name as well!"

"Oh, stop it! I never even considered that!" I chuckled. "We never actually even kissed, you know . . . oh God . . . now you have me worried!"

"Come on, admit it – it would be a brilliant twist to the story!"

"Well, it would certainly explain why he hasn't come out of the woodwork yet!" The more I thought about it, the more hilarious it was . . . this whole situation had been surreal from day one, and at this stage nothing would surprise me. I started to laugh, and once I started, I couldn't stop. Colm joined in on the other end of the line.

"I'm kinda relieved you found that funny – the minute it was out of my mouth, I said to myself that you'd probably eat the head off me!"

"What kind of an ogre do you think I am? Being grumpy is your job, not mine!"

"Okay, point taken – but I'm working on that, as they say over here."

"Ahem. Sure, Colm. Whatever you say."

"Listen, let me prove it to you. What are you doing this evening?"

"Trying to stop myself from hunting Lindy down and strangling her. Apart from that, there's nothing on the agenda."

"Well, there is now. Meet me in the lobby in ten minutes."

Chapter Twenty-three

Three hours later, I was sipping a tequila and feeling more relaxed than I'd felt in a very long time. I'd decided I liked the new, being-worked-on Colm a lot, lot more than the old one. If this was what getting sick did to him, then I was going to put a laxative into his food later – his illness had definitely marked a turning point in his attitude, even if yesterday had been something of a bump on the road. So far, neither of us had alluded to the conversation we'd had the last time we'd met face to face and, as the day was going so well, I was in no rush to do so either.

When I'd gone down to the lobby to meet him, he was at the reception desk. It looked like he was buying something.

"What's going on?" I said when he ambled over to me. He tapped his nose, and beckoned for me to walk with him out of the lobby and onto the Strip. Once we hit the street, he led the way towards a waiting bus. I peered at the writing at the front of the bus.

"*Las Vegas Helicopter Night Flight Transfer Bus*? We're going on a helicopter?"

"You really don't miss much, do you?" He roared laughing. "You sound like a kid!"

We got on the bus before I could say anything else.

"I don't know about you, but this is something I've wanted to do since we first got here," Colm said.

Twenty minutes later, the bus dropped us off at the helicopter terminal at McCarran Airport. Colm and I boarded a helicopter along with four others, a couple with two teenage children. We were handed glasses of champagne as soon as we were seated – even the teenagers, but their parents soon whipped them out of the hands of their children and into their own. I browsed the information leaflet I'd been given with my champagne. We would be going on a twelve-to-fifteen minute ride over the Strip and downtown, which promised 'spectacular' and 'mesmerising' views. I'm usually quite wary when I see those words, but for once the reality lived up to the promise. Vegas by helicopter at night was absolutely something else, primarily because all of the hotels were so distinctive. I could have recited the sequence of the hotels on the Strip from north to south in my sleep at this stage, but seeing them from this new perspective shook up my mental roadmap. I felt the thrill of seeing it all new again as the helicopter flew from the southern end of the Strip to the northern, just like when I landed in McCarran Airport for the first time and caught my first glimpse of the lights of the Strip. When we reached the Stratosphere, the helicopter dipped lower and began to circle the tower, then moved on to the glittering lights of the downtown area.

It would be a bad pun to say that those fifteen minutes flew, but honestly I couldn't believe how fast they went by. I had been so agog at the sights that I'd only taken a few sips of my glass of champagne, which was unheard of for me – I'd originally intended to drink Colm's too (if the parents in the family accompanying us didn't snap it out of his hands first, of course). All too soon, we were back in McCarran Airport and preparing to disembark.

"I'm so glad we did that," I said to Colm on the bus on the way back to the hotel. "When you wanted to meet up, I thought you were going to suggest going to a show, and I wasn't really in the mood for that."

Vegas was a city that bombarded you with advertisements for the bigger shows that had the budget to flash their ads up and down the Strip, and almost subliminally made you think you wanted to go to them just because you saw ads for them so often.

"Neither was I," said Colm. "The helicopter ride was amazing."

"Are you on a high after it? Sorry, I'm having a bad-pun night in my head. Don't mind me. It was amazing alright. It felt like it all happened too fast, though! I don't want the night to end yet!"

"Who says it's going to?"

The bus stopped at the MGM and I stood up to get off, but Colm caught the belt on the back of my cotton sundress and pulled me back down with it. "We're staying on for a while."

"Where are we off to now?"

"You know there's no point in asking, don't you?"

I shrugged. For once, I didn't mind not knowing. His last surprise had turned out to be a very good one.

We travelled down the Strip as far as the Venetian Hotel, then hopped out. Colm swept inside and went into full-scale organising mode, and within five minutes, we were sitting in a private two-passenger Venetian gondola, floating down the hotel's Grand Canal. I'd lost count of how many times I'd languished on the bridge overlooking the gondoliers serenading their charges in the gondola, making vague plans in my head to organise a gondola ride some day. Colm didn't know this, though. The gondolier sang his heart out to us, looking pained and joyful in equal measure. We drifted under a large arch as he sang, then on past a café and eventually past the bridge I'd supported myself on many times while idly daydreaming. There was something hugely romantic about the setting, and at some stage it hit me that all of this felt a bit like a date, but I put that thought out of my mind – that one was just too weird to grapple with on a lovely night like tonight.

When the ride ended, Colm suggested a drink in the bar in the Venetian. I saw absolutely no reason to say no – I rarely do when there's drink involved – so we made our way into the V Bar. I could see by Colm's face as soon as he walked in that he regretted his suggestion – the bar was uber-trendy and chic, and really not his type of place at all.

I grabbed the sleeve of his shirt and turned on my heel, dragging him along with me.

"What's the story?"

"You know there's no point in asking, don't you?"

"Touché."

We walked back onto the Strip, where I instantly hailed a taxi. We bustled in, and I gave the driver an address I'd memorised a few days before when I'd remembered the promise I'd made to Colm to coax him into staying at the MGM. It hadn't been important to me before to uphold it. That had changed.

"What's there?"

"Something you'll like," I said. "It's time for me to do something for you now."

Five minutes later, we arrived. I saw the shop I was looking for on the right-hand side of the street.

"Pull up in front of that costume shop, please."

A woman with a showgirl costume paraded the street outside the shop, and waved into the car with glee when she realised that we were potential customers. I filled the driver's palm with money, and we got out and made our way into the shop, escorted by our new showgirl friend.

"Hello, we're looking for 70s outfits," I said to the man in a gangster suit who came to attend to us.

"Hey, that's great!" The man looked Colm up and down, and it was so obvious that he was thinking that one of us had a 70s outfit already, but there was no way he would risk losing our business by saying any such thing. Good move, with someone as volatile as Colm around. "Follow me!"

Half an hour later I was decked out in a lime-green trouser suit, complete with huge bellbottoms and matching lime-green platforms. Colm was sporting a pair of canary-yellow trousers, a red and yellow shirt with swirly designs that reminded me of the carpet in Topple Town, and a bright red jacket. Of course, Colm was in his element, but I hadn't expected how much I'd enjoy browsing through the rails of miniskirts, tank tops and swingy dresses myself.

"Right, let's go," I said.

Colm didn't ask where – he'd given up inquiring. A couple of minutes later, we were in another taxi. As soon as I gave the driver the name of the street I wanted to go to, Colm's face lit up.

"What?" I asked.

"I know what's on that street."

"Oh, do you, now? Yes, I've wanted to go to bingo over here since the night we arrived. I hope you're ready for a night with the grannies."

Colm's smile screamed, 'Yeah, right!' He had my game well and truly busted – but I didn't care. His expression more than made up for any lack of surprise when we pulled up outside the 70s disco. I wasn't surprised he knew where we were going just from hearing the address – this was the biggest 70s club in Vegas. The only thing I was surprised about was that he hadn't gone there sooner. Then again, maybe he had – I wasn't his keeper, but it just seemed like we'd been hanging out pretty much every night since we got here.

The nightclub was exactly what I'd expected – non-stop 70s tunes. Everyone was decked out in 70s garb, but none of the finery was quite so impressively outlandish as ours, which surprised me – we were in Vegas, for God's sake! Of course, this only served to send Colm's happiness-rating through the roof.

"This has turned out to be one hell of a day," he said. "And I thought we couldn't top yesterday!"

"It beats sitting in my room painting my toenails, that's for sure."

"I'd imagine it does. And if we keep ourselves busy like this for long enough, we'll never have to talk about how yesterday ended, will we?"

I raised my eyebrows, then we both started to smile.

"I'm shocked you haven't brought it up already," he went on. "I thought it would be the first thing you'd say when we met earlier . . . it's not like you not to tackle something head on."

I shrugged. "Maybe you don't know me very well."

"Oh, come on. Ever since we came to Vegas, you've been

running around getting this, that and the other sorted, or confronting someone about something. What's different about this?"

What could I say? This is different because I decided to cut you some slack after what you've been through?

"You weren't comfortable with what I asked you about, and that's fine. You don't have to explain yourself if you don't want to."

"Well, maybe I want to." He pointed to a chill-out room, where people were sprawled about on blow-up sofas and sitting cross-legged on the floor. "Let's go in here."

We found two free gigantic green-and-purple beanbags, and plonked ourselves on them. The beans moulded around my entire body, and I instantly felt more at ease. Colm's beans obviously weren't magic, as he looked anything but relaxed.

"It was wrong of me to say you ruined yesterday by asking me that question about who I really am. You just took me by surprise, that's all. Okay, it's just a question, but it's a pretty fundamental one, when you think about it."

"Are you going to get all deep on me, Colm Cannon?" I laughed a fake laugh that didn't sound convincing even to me. "Look, it's fine," I said, trying to give him a get-out alley. Intrigued as I was about him and his circumstances, it was hard to watch him struggling with explaining where he was coming from. Besides, I knew what it was like to be stuck in a cul-de-sac you couldn't get out of . . . "You don't have to say anything else."

"No, really, I do." He looked down at his hands, then looked up and stared right into my eyes. "I know people think I'm distant. I've lost count of how many times people have told me I come across as arrogant – you weren't the first, and you won't be the last. But that's just how I seem to present myself to the world. That's not me."

Okay, he'd had his chance to get out of this conversation. He'd chosen not to, so it was time for the questions.

"So why do you project that image of yourself, in that case?"

He shrugged. "I'm not consciously trying to. That just seems to be how people see me. I'm fairly confident in most areas of life, and

I'm not afraid to pull someone up on something if they're in the wrong. That's often interpreted as arrogance. If that's how things are, then fine. I'm not bothered about what most people think. It would only worry me if people whose opinions I cared about thought that about me."

I left the implications of what he was saying unaddressed. I didn't want to get involved in a 'Does that mean you care about what I think?' conversation. That would just be too weird. And yet, if he did, I would be glad. I was starting to care about what he thought, too.

"You can do something about being distant, though," I said. "If you're removed from situations, that's because you choose to be."

"That's a force of habit, I suppose. Plus I have only-child syndrome – I keep to myself by nature." He ripped the label off his bottle of alcohol-free beer, then put the bottle down and looked over at me as I digested this only-child notion. "I'm just telling you this to try to explain why your question threw me. When you asked me which version of me was real, I was annoyed, but not at you. I just don't think anyone has seen me for who I really am for a very long time, if ever – and that's what annoyed me. I just hope it will happen some day."

"Of course it will . . ."

He shook his head. "Not necessarily. It certainly hasn't so far."

"Well, maybe it's just around the corner for you."

"So is a Lotto win." He gave me a rueful smile. "Anyway, I hope that explains to some extent why I said what I said yesterday."

I nodded slowly. "It explains a lot."

"Plus, I was in a shitty mood because I didn't want what was a great day to have to end at all. But hey, today's turned out pretty well too." He shook his empty alcohol-free beer bottle. "Anyway, enough serious talk. I'll get us more drinks."

I wasn't sure if I should have any more alcohol – I was starting to wonder if I'd already had too much to drink, because if I wasn't very much mistaken, I could have sworn that Colm Cannon had just opened himself up to me. Wonders would never cease.

Chapter Twenty-four

BB,

You have got me in SO much trouble. Remember Jane, that girl I was seeing a few months ago (the one that went off travelling for the summer not long after we met)? Well, she's back – and she's working in the same building as you. Her desk faces out to the front of the building. She can see everyone coming and going. Can you see where I'm going with this? Yes, she's been watching me hiding behind trees and popping up behind parked cars at lunchtime, and she thinks I'm stalking her! She rang me screaming down the phone at me, calling me an obsessive freak and saying she's lost a stone in weight because she's so afraid to leave the building at lunchtime to buy a sandwich. She says if she sees me there as much as one more time, she'll call the cops on me. I couldn't care less about the cops bit, but I'd kinda thought there might be some chance of us getting back together when she came back from travelling – looks like there's no hope of that now. (I suppose there probably wasn't anyway when she didn't even bother letting me know she was back in Ireland, but still, I'm pissed off with you for putting me in this position in the first place, so I'm going to blame you for everything. So there.)

You're on your own with this from now on, sis.

Adam

PS Send me on the address of your hotel there so that I can send my obsessive-freak therapy bills to you.

"Oh, God." I put my head in my hands. Poor Adam. He'd really liked that Jane girl. We hadn't seen him for weeks after she'd gone off to the States on her J1 visa. His sleeping habits had reached hibernation levels, and he stopped bothering to eat. Mum's food bill went down dramatically over the course of those few weeks, which was the only vaguely positive by-product of the whole debacle, but I got the impression that Mum would have preferred to have been stuck in the kitchen doing bouts of much-hated baking to entice Adam out of his hunger strike rather than seeing him fade away. It looked like she would only need to set the table for herself and Dad for dinner over the next while. Great. What a brilliant start to the day.

To make matters worse, I had a brainstorming meeting with Lindy to suffer through for the next hour. I hoped she had a few more tricks up her sleeve, because I was all out of ideas as to where to take this whole Leon thing. Much as we clashed on a personal level, I needed Lindy. Our programmes for Éire TV were practically making themselves, thanks to everything she'd thought up, even though her approach drove me mad most of the time. I just hoped she wouldn't mention the possibility of Leon having written those emails again though, or the only storming that I'd be doing was out of the room.

"Colm's just great, isn't he? He's like an undiscovered gem. Or a diamond in the rough."

"I suppose."

I suppressed a sigh. I should have been grateful really that we were on this topic again, with all of our ideas now in place for the next week. It turned out that Lindy hadn't been so much interested in brainstorming with me as notifying me about her already-formed plans, which suited me fine. There were more TV interviews lined up, there were more radio interviews, there was a magazine interview for one of the Sunday papers, that kind of thing. It appeared there was still a big appetite for the story in the States, despite the fact that I hadn't made much progress with finding any concrete leads. As for home, the third episode of the documentary had been broadcast, consisting mostly of coverage of the Leon Line-up and the subsequent date (Colm had cajoled Lindy into sharing it with him, in keeping with our usual LVTV/Éire TV tit-for-tat procedures), and Isolde reported back that the show was still a prominent talking point in the media. As for my columns, she hadn't given me much praise for them recently but hadn't complained either, so I could only assume she was reasonably happy with them.

"I realise I'm not talking to his biggest fan," Lindy continued, "but there's so much to him – he's fascinating –"

"Actually, we're getting on a lot better recently. He makes me laugh. Take yesterday, for example – he suggested that maybe Leon is gay, and that's why he hasn't contacted me – I laughed until I nearly turned blue, I can tell you. I never even thought of something like that! Imagine if he was!"

"Hmm." Lindy looked off into the distance.

"He's not, though. I would have known if he was. I'm not that bad with men!"

She raised an unconvinced eyebrow. We walked down the street in silence for a few seconds, then she rounded on me. "Tell me this straight out. Do you think he's interested?"

I shrugged. "I can only hope he is, otherwise, I'm going to look like an absolute idiot at the end of it all, aren't I?"

"Not Leon! Do you think Colm is interested in me?"

"Oh, we're back to talking about you. Sorry."

"Well? Is he?" She pushed her head forward and made her eyes bulge, all sarcasm lost on her as she waited for an answer.

"I have no idea. I don't know Colm well enough to be able to tell when he's interested in a woman."

"Does he talk about me much?"

Uh-oh. This wasn't going to be nice. Should I be honest or lie? I opted for somewhere in the middle. "Only when your name comes up in conversation for work-related reasons."

The truth was, Colm never seemed to have any interest in saying anything positive at all about Lindy. All he ever wanted to do was avoid her. In fact, the more I thought about it, the more I realised that Lindy was everything Colm wasn't into. They had absolutely no connection, and there was no spark between them at all when they did have dealings with each other.

"Hmm. There's a spark there. I can feel it. Maybe he's shy. He actually is shy, isn't he?"

I shrugged. It didn't matter what I thought or said. If Lindy wanted to believe he was shy, that was exactly what she would do.

"I mean, he comes across as all confident and bossy, but I think when it comes to women, he needs a little direction. And who better to provide it than my good self?"

"Indeed." The only direction Colm would be taking was the route to the airport to get away from Lindy. He was definitely the type of guy who would run a mile if someone came on too strong. Telling Lindy this was completely pointless, though. She'd probably accuse me of being jealous because I hadn't found Leon yet, or some such twisted logic.

"Anyway, I have to go," she said, gathering up her notes and adopting a self-important look. "I have an inspired idea rolling around in my head that I really need to work on straight away."

"Has it anything to do with Colm, by any chance?"

She laughed as she breezed out the door. "I suppose it has."

Colm had left the office after lunch to work from the hotel for the afternoon. Apparently, the noise in the office was too distracting, and he wanted some headspace. When I got back to the hotel after work, I flopped down on the bed and rang his extension as soon as I'd dumped my laptop bag on the table.

"Hey. Where do you fancy going for dinner this evening?"

"Oh, hi, Andie. Sorry, I can't have dinner with you tonight."

"Oh?"

"Lindy asked me to go for a drink with her."

"Oh."

'Oh' is what I said. What I actually wanted to say was, '*What? Why the hell did you say yes? I thought you couldn't stand her?*' But I held my tongue. With great difficulty.

I waited for Colm to elaborate, to explain, but he didn't.

"Right," I said then. "Well, enjoy your drink. Talk to you tomorrow." I hung up, confused as hell.

It was one of those evenings where I didn't fancy sitting on my own in a restaurant, so I ordered room service. Shortly after I finished eating, I was relaxing on my bed with a mud pack on my face when the hotel phone rang.

"Hi, Andee. I wanted to give you a call just to say 'ello."

"Oh, hello, Philippe. How are you?"

"I'm fine. The kesteeon is, 'ow are you?"

"I'm great, thanks! Why is how I am the kest-ee-on?"

"Because I am your friend, that is why. You sound very 'appee for someone who should be sad today."

"What are you talking about, Philippe?"

"Surely you must be sad that you were chasing after a gay man? It was never going to work out, no matter 'ow 'ard you tried. But you must not beat yourself with a stick about this, Andee. You were not to know. You –"

"Woah, woah, *woah*! Back it up there, Philippe. What are you talking about? Leon's not gay! Why are you saying he is?"

Colm. I'd kill him! Just when I was starting to think he was sound – him and his stupid sense of humour!

"I am not saying it. The paper is saying it!"

And then, the penny dropped. Lindy. I'd kill her! I'd really, really kill her!

"I 'ave a copee at reception if you want to read it."

"I'll be down in a minute."

And I was. Philippe thrust the paper in my hand as soon as I had taken my first step out of the elevator, wisely refraining from commenting on my mud pack. I scanned the paper hungrily.

> There's been a new twist in the *Looking for Leon* story. The elusive Leon might be *gay*, according to reports. Andie Appleton commenced a nationwide search three weeks ago for Leon, a man from Arizona that she met in Las Vegas last month, believing him to be the love of her life. However, the story is now swinging in another direction. A source close to Andie tells us that she has voiced her fears that Leon may not be interested in women at all. "It just hit her that this was one very obvious reason why someone wouldn't come forward if they were being searched for," a good friend of Andie's told us. "She actually couldn't believe she hadn't thought of it before. Now, she's so confused, and really doesn't know what to think. Leon is the only person who can tell us if she's right or wrong about this new theory of hers, though. She's just praying he'll come out of the woodwork soon – so to speak."

This time, Lindy had gone way too far.

"This is outrageous! She has no consideration for how this makes me look! It's a disgrace!"

"Calm down, Andee. You sound like me. And I like me, but me does not suit you."

"*I won't calm down!*"

Guilt engulfed me as Philippe actually recoiled from me. Adam always told me that I could be very scary when I was cross, but then, Adam is a bit of a softy, so I'd never really taken that seriously. But Philippe was now looking at me as if I'd hit him.

"I'm sorry, Philippe." I reached out to give him a hug. "It's not you I'm mad at." After some hesitation, he reluctantly stepped forward to accept my hug, despite the crumbles of mud pack that were falling from my face every time I said something.

"You must tell 'er 'ow angree you are, instead of telling me."

"Oh, I will!" I released Philippe. "The problem is, though, she won't listen! She just doesn't care! She's career hungry, Philippe, and very driven. She doesn't care who she steps on to get to where she wants to be." I picked up the paper and put myself through the torture of reading the article again. "She's made me look totally desperate by saying something like this."

"Why would she even think of saying something like this to the medeeah?"

"I repeated a joke Colm made about Leon possibly being gay to her, and she must have pounced on it. She wasted no time, did she? I mentioned this to her this morning, and it's now in the evening paper! And if you'd seen her at the time I said it, Philippe – she acted like she was totally disinterested! I actually wasn't sure she was even taking in what I said, that's how distant she was!"

"She is a sly one. She 'as the slitty eyes. And as for Col-um, he should not be stirring the shit in the pot by making those suggestions."

"Ah, no, Philippe. It was just a flippant comment he made to try to make me laugh."

"You are defending 'im? That is a new development for you!"

"Yes, well, we'll see how long it lasts. I'll tell you one thing, though. If he gets together with that Lindy, I'll never speak to him again. What a wagon!"

"A what?"

I smiled. I had often wondered how anyone who moved to Dublin could possibly have a clue what we were talking about half the time.

"Sorry, I meant she's a walking fucking bitch. Pardon my French."

"That kind of language is not sophisticated enough to be French." He winked.

"Listen, thanks for letting me know – at least now I'll know why everyone is looking at me with pitying stares today."

"No. They are looking at you thinking that maybe they 'ave a chance with you now that Leon is off the scene."

"For that, you get another hug." Philippe was wonderful; he knew exactly what to say when a girl was feeling down. "And now, I'm off to commit murder."

"You go, girl!" Philippe swayed his hips. And people thought Leon was the camp one!

Chapter Twenty-five

Lindy was nowhere to be seen the next morning. Apparently, Dave had her out reporting on something for a pilot of a new show he was working on. I would have accused her of running scared if I hadn't known that she wasn't one bit scared of me. Her drubbing would have to wait. My anger at her hadn't abated at all – if anything, it was escalating with every moment that passed.

I bet Colm knew where she was. Maybe she wasn't able to walk today after the rogering he'd given her the previous night, the big turncoat. He certainly looked tired himself today. I desperately wanted to find out what had gone on between them – and to find out where Lindy was, so that I could wring her neck – but I wasn't going to give Colm the satisfaction of asking. No way.

I needed to take my mind off Lindy before I went nuts. "Let's go for a coffee later this morning and thrash out this Isolde and Martin scenario," I said over the partition to Colm, trying not to hold his possible association with the enemy against him. Since Adam's mail, I'd been at a complete loss as to what my next detective move would be.

"Right, yeah." Colm didn't look up. For someone who'd come to me wanting to do something about this situation, he suddenly didn't seem too pushed any more. Maybe he was reliving last night's wild night of sex in his head.

"Eleven o'clock, so?"

"Yeah. Grand."

I sighed, then opened my inbox to work through today's email. Amongst the fifty-something emails, a mail from Adam caught my eye.

Subject: Thank you, thank you, thank you!

You are the best sister a man could have! Or a woman could have, if we had another sister! Or if I had another sister – for you, it would just be a single sister. I digress. I do that. You know that I do that.

Anyhoooooo . . . (actually, that wasn't very manly, and I'm feeling very manly today, so let me try that again . . .)

Oh, God, I thought. This could take a while. The other forty-nine emails didn't have much hope of being read today.

Anyhow, I'll move on by telling you there's been a development. After I emailed you telling you how you'd ruined my life, I looked up Jane on Facebook, found her and sent her a message explaining the entire situation. And what do you think happened? She rang me straight away, apologising and saying she'd only been such a bitch (her word, not mine – I think she's lovely – you know that – I'm doing it again, aren't I?) because she still wasn't over me. Yes, you read that right. She said she would never have gone away for the summer if I'd asked her to stay, but I hadn't, so she had thought I didn't care and just wanted to get rid of her. She said she never stopped thinking about me while she was away. When she saw me spying, she just saw red, but she said a part of her was thrilled to bits to think I was stalking her – she was actually a bit disappointed when she found out that I wasn't. (How brilliant is all of this? It gets better!) And then, she said there was nothing in the world she wanted more than to get back with me. Next

223

thing, I hear the doorbell going. Mum and Dad were out, and I'm there ignoring the fact that there's someone at the door so I can read her email over and over again. This person just won't go away, though. I'm thinking about calling the police when I hear someone shouting. "Please answer the door!" I instantly recognise her voice (pity she hadn't started shouting on the first ring – it would have saved her a lot of trouble). I open the door, and there she is. Now, I'm going to skip over what happened between then and now, but suffice it to say we're back together, and things are great.

Next time you have a problem you need to solve, definitely come to me. I think your problems give me luck.

From: **Andie.Appleton@hotmail.com**
To: **Adam.Appleton@gmail.com**

That's fantastic! I'm so happy for you! So, I guess you owe me then for reuniting you with the love of your life . . . ?

From: **Adam.Appleton@gmail.com**
To: **Andie.Appleton@hotmail.com**

Hint taken. OK. I'll do a few more days. Jane thinks it's all quite an adventure, so maybe I can incorporate a bit of quality stalking into our first official date tomorrow.

"Hey, Colm, listen to this." I briefly filled him in on Adam's email. "So we can cancel that coffee."

"Ah, no. I was so looking forward to it. Highlight of my morning."

"Yeah, you sounded pretty enthused about it." I looked around my desk for the nearest thing to throw at him, saw a pink stressball and chucked it over. He caught it mid-flight.

"You should take this back," he said. "You're the stress bunny out of the pair of us. Here!" He held it out.

I reached out to take it, but as soon as I did, he whipped it away.

God, he was childish! I went over to him and started to wrestle it out of his hands, but lost my balance and ended up falling right into his lap.

"Now look what you've done!" I said as I grabbed the desk and pulled myself back up into a standing position.

"Good job I'm used to women throwing themselves on me," Colm laughed.

"Ahem." I turned around to see Rachel standing behind us, staring and holding a bunch of letters out. "Sorry to interrupt the fun. Mail for you." She thrust the letters into my hand, then hurried away.

I returned to my desk. Colm followed me.

"What do you want?" I said.

"Go on, open it."

"Aren't you very nosey today?" I was feeling pretty curious myself though.

"I bet it's fan mail."

"Are you crazy? People email me through the website."

"There are still some people in the world who write letters. Come on, open one up and prove me wrong."

I ripped the first envelope open. Colm stood behind me to read over my shoulder.

Hi Andie,

You don't know me – my name is Oliver, and I live in Oklahoma. I've been watching you and your search on TV, and I wanted to tell you that Leon is a complete idiot if he doesn't contact you. You are so lovely and so beautiful, and the nicest thing of all is that you have no idea how gorgeous you are.

Just to tell you a little bit about me, well, I'm twenty-seven, five foot eleven, and I have brown eyes and black hair, just like you. I'm aware that I sound like a crazy guy who's trying to proposition you, but I just want to give you a picture of who it is that's writing to you. You're probably wondering why I'm writing instead of emailing. Well, it's for two reasons. I figure that you probably have someone else filtering your email for you, and you'll never get to see this message if I email it to you. The other reason is because you're so worth the effort of writing a letter. People just don't write them any more, do they? We're all so busy that we take the quickest option. This, to me, feels so much more personal.

I'm not writing to you just because I want to tell you how great I think you are, even though you are great. The reason I'm writing is because I've noticed recently that you seem more and more weary whenever I see any footage of you. I personally believe that you have started to feel that you won't find Leon. I even think you might be feeling a little bit lost yourself now. I hope I'm not crossing a line by saying this, but this is what I now see when I look at you. I wanted to tell you that if this guy does not (for some insane reason) want to meet up with you, then you have to understand that it is his problem and his loss. Please don't let this experience frame your future if it doesn't work out. I hope that it does work out, and I don't want to be negative, but I know what it's like to want something and not get it. I haven't exactly been lucky in love myself. Keep the faith, and know always how fantastic you are. And are you hot or what? If Leon doesn't show, you always have a date in me.

I'm going to stop writing now before I ruin the entire letter by sounding like an obsessive weirdo. I promise *that you don't need to worry about me showing up on your doorstep one day (only because you've been smart enough to keep your address a secret – ha ha! I'm kidding). Please just know that there are people out there supporting you and thinking that you are amazing. I say people, because I know I'm not alone in thinking this way. A friend of mine has even set up a thread on an Internet forum talking about how amazingly hot you are (I won't tell you where you can find it, though – I might not be a pervert, but my friend is a bit. . . overly descriptive sometimes. Sorry. Maybe I should have said nothing).*

Good luck with the search,

Oliver

"Hate to say I told you so . . ."

"My God. This is surreal . . ."

"As opposed to all the other completely normal things that have happened in the past few weeks?"

"Good point. Still, though – it's mad."

"Somebody loves you. I wouldn't like to be in Leon's shoes if this guy catches up with him and actually believes that stupid report about Leon being gay – he'll give him such a hard time for leading his favourite woman on. I'm sure he's probably read the report since he wrote that letter."

"Don't mention the war."

"Yeah, about that . . . listen, I never suggested anything like that to Lindy. I know I made a joke to you about it, but –"

I put my hand up to stop him and explained how I was the one who had inadvertently put the idea in Lindy's head.

He shook his head. "She really is something else."

I wasn't sure if he said it in admiration or disgust. I didn't ask. If he had any positive feelings towards her, I really didn't want to know about them.

Colm walked back towards his desk. "I'll let you read the rest of those in private."

"That's big of you!" I'd been so engrossed in reading Oliver's letter that I hadn't even thought about telling Colm off for reading the letter over my shoulder. I scanned it again before making any move towards opening the others. It was scary.

Maybe I was completely transparent, or maybe Oliver just noticed this because he'd been watching me very closely (which I tried hard not to get too freaked out about – he seemed like a decent enough guy), but either way, he'd hit the nail on the head about my feelings recently on this whole thing. I hadn't even admitted it to myself, but I'd started to feel like I was going through the motions. The excitement of the prospect of finding Leon had faded. Whenever I saw appeals for missing people on the news, I always thought to myself that if they weren't found within the first few days, they probably wouldn't be. Those stories usually ended in tragedy. My situation obviously wasn't anything near as serious or as awful as a missing-person scenario, but I couldn't help seeing some parallels all the same – if Leon hadn't come forward at the start, what could we do that would make him come forward now? The only information I could see us getting from here on was more of the same – people reporting that they knew who he was, when really they knew no more than I did. We had nothing to go on to suss out whether these people were genuine, or just looking for cheap thrills by taking the mick out of the crazy Irishwoman, and we'd had some so-called leads into the *Looking for Leon* email account before that had amounted to nothing. And Oliver was right – I was feeling lost. Lindy's insistence on charging ahead and doing whatever she wanted with this whole thing was making everything so much worse. I didn't know what my role was any more, and I certainly didn't feel like I was driving the situation. And yet, if it hadn't been for her, I wouldn't have got anywhere with this search, and would possibly have been out of a job when I had nothing to put on the table for Isolde. I had no doubt that she would have fired me in a heartbeat if this story hadn't been a runner – she was only looking for an excuse.

Problem was, I wasn't sure if I could do this for much longer.

Chapter Twenty-six

As Colm and I were leaving the office that evening, we met Rachel. She smiled a sweet smile and gave us a big hi. Although she seemed to be well in with Lindy, Rachel had always been friendly with me too since the minute I gave Dave a bit of lip – so to speak.

"Any plans for the evening?" I asked her as the three of us got into the elevator.

She snorted. "Not now, I don't. I was supposed to be meeting Lindy in Billabong – you know, that new bar that's opened up in the Golden Chip hotel on the Strip – but now Dave is coming in too, so I'm not going to bother."

"Yeah, I can understand why you wouldn't want to spend your free time in the same bar as him."

"Oh, it's not that so much as I don't want to spend my free time as a third wheel. Those two are unbearable around each other. They need to get a room."

Colm and I gave each other a look.

"Are you saying that Lindy and Dave are . . . ?"

"Making out like rabbits? You bet they are. Don't tell me you didn't know? Everyone does, except Dave's wife."

I threw a look at Colm. If there was anything going on between him and Lindy and he was upset at this news, he hid it well. If anything, he had the look of the village gossip about him, thrilled to have found out some dirt on Lindy.

"He'll get away with it too, though," Rachel continued. "Lindy isn't his first LVTV conquest, and she won't be his last. Not that she cares – she's only jumping into bed with him to try to further her career. It's not as if she has any feelings for him. But that's Lindy all over – she doesn't care about anyone but herself. I've lost count now of how many times I've made an arrangement with her, only to hear at the last minute that Dave's coming along too."

"Maybe you should reconsider whether or not she's really your friend," Colm said.

"I have," Rachel said, "and she's not. Why do you think I'm even saying all of this? I'd never have badmouthed her to anyone before, but now I just don't care. I'm sick of being used by her when she doesn't have anyone else to spend her time with."

The elevator reached the ground floor, and we walked through the revolving doors of the lobby.

"By the way, Andie," Rachel went on, "don't think for one second that Lindy is a friend of yours either. You should hear the things she says about you behind your back."

"Like what?"

"Well, 'basket case' is one of her nicer descriptions of you, put it that way. She thinks you're nuts to be on this search. It might suit her career purposes to work with you, but she's having a good laugh at you when you're not around."

"Tell me some of her less nice descriptions of me," I said in a low voice.

"Leave it, Andie," Colm said. "You're probably better off not knowing."

"No. Go on, Rachel. Tell me. I need to know what I'm up against here."

Rachel cringed. She looked sorry she'd opened her mouth. "Her nickname for you is Saddo Scarecrow because she thinks you always look so unkempt –" She paused as she saw my face go beetroot and then hurried on. "It's only because she's jealous that you can get away without wearing make-up every day and she can't. The Saddo bit is because she thinks you're a loser for needing to find a man this way. She's also called you a social reject a few times when she's been really annoyed at you, again in relation to you being on this kind of search for a man. Then there's spinster, shelf-girl and . . . you know what? I'm going to miss my bus if I don't run."

"Yes, I think we've heard enough," Colm said.

"Sorry – I didn't mean to upset you," Rachel said to me. "I just thought you should know."

"I'm not upset," I said. It was true. I was angry as hell, not upset.

"Anyway! Hope your evening is more fun than mine will be," Rachel said as she crossed the road to catch her bus home. She looked like she couldn't get away fast enough and was regretting having said anything.

"Oh, it will be," I said under my breath as I waved to her.

"Let's just forget we heard that. Where do you fancy going for dinner tonight? It's your turn to pick," Colm said as we started to walk up the Strip.

"I'm sure the Billabong serve bar food."

"Oh no, Andie. Just leave it."

"No. Don't even try to talk me out of it. I'm going there."

"She's not worth it –"

"I just want to have a calm chat with her, and point out the error of her ways. That's all."

"Andie, you don't do calm. You're shooting yourself in the foot when it comes to finding Leon if you burn your bridges with Lindy."

"Well, maybe I don't want to find him any more. My face has been plastered all over the country and he still hasn't come out of hiding. What does that tell me? Right now, I've nothing to lose."

"Except maybe your job . . ."

"You let me worry about that."

Sweat trickled down my back from the heat as we walked to the hotel – it seemed that no matter how long I spent in Vegas, my body

231

still refused to get used to the desert climate. By the time we arrived, I was feeling narky and fractious.

Colm was still on my heels when I located the bar inside the hotel.

"Don't follow me in here. I mean it. Don't."

He opened his mouth to argue with me, but something in my demeanour warned him off. He nodded, then turned away. I walked into the bar. Sure enough, Lindy was sitting in a booth with Dave, flashing a bit of immaculately waxed, tanned leg and looking ridiculously smug. I was such a whirlwind in my approach that they didn't see me until I was within touching distance of them. I didn't even need to stop to think about what I was going to do – sometimes, the old ways are the most satisfying. So I picked up her drink and threw it into her face, and I didn't even feel remotely guilty when an ice-cube hit her full force in the eye. Dave made a grab for his, but he was too late – whatever cocktail he was drinking looked like great chucking material, so chuck it I did.

"Andie! What the hell are you playing at?" Dave stood up and started fussing uselessly over Lindy while looking daggers at me.

"Don't even start, Dave." I turned to Lindy. "There is *no* way I'm working with you ever again!"

"Andie, calm down!" said Dave. Lindy was too busy with her eye to even look up as I spoke. "Why in a million years say that after the great job Lindy's done in getting you publicity for your search?"

"A great job? By making me look like a lovesick fool who has no chance with the gay man she's been stalking?"

Dave chuckled. "Oh, come on, Andie! Surely you can see the funny side of it. I thought it was an ingenious idea on Lindy's part –"

"In that case, you obviously don't have a clue what you're doing either."

Dave's face mutated into one gigantic snarl. "If this is your attitude, then LVTV won't be doing any further coverage of your search – so if I were you I would think very carefully before I opened that pretty little mouth one more time. You need us, Andie."

"That's where you're wrong. Oh, look. There's my mouth open. So what are you going to do about it, Dave?"

His face turned purple with rage. "That's it. You've talked yourself out of your relationship with us."

Lindy suddenly came back to life. "Did you think I ever actually imagined for one second that Leon was going to show up, you pathetic freak? I don't blame him for running a mile from you. He's clearly not interested."

I shrugged. "I suppose you'd know the signs after being dumped by Colm. Oh wait. You couldn't even get him in the first place." I didn't know if I was right about that or not when I said it, but her crushed face instantly told me that I was. "Does Dave know about your little crush? Sad, really. I almost feel sorry for you, Dave, being used by this career-hungry parasite."

"You little –" Lindy started.

"Despite that, though, you make a lovely couple. You're both as desperate for glory and as shallow as each other. Have a nice life together."

"You'll be sorry you did this! I'll make sure nobody in Vegas has anything to do with you again!" Lindy shouted after me as I walked away.

I stuck a finger up over my shoulder and walked straight on, ignoring her threats. They couldn't hurt me. I didn't care enough any more for them to have any power over me.

When I left the bar, I saw Colm sitting on a stool in front of a slot machine. He jumped off it when he saw me and made his way towards me.

"How did it go?"

"Well, I'd certainly give myself full marks. In fact, I think the whole thing couldn't possibly have gone any better."

Colm and I were in the middle of dinner that night when something hit me.

"Maybe Lindy wrote the letters!"

I couldn't believe I hadn't thought of it before. It would make complete sense that Lindy was the person behind the poison-pen letters! She was just biding her time, waiting to build up a history of communication, and then she had a story to go to the media with.

I explained my reasoning to Colm and pulled out my phone.

"No, don't call her," Colm said. "You've no evidence at all that she was involved."

"Were you listening to me at all earlier?" I'd recapped what had happened between Lindy, Dave and me line-by-line to Colm on our walk back to the MGM from the Billabong. "She never believed Leon was going to show up, so she had to come up with whatever she could to keep legs in this story for as long as she was tasked to do so by Dave."

He shook his head. "But that's no proof of anything. You haven't discovered anything new about Lindy today really, have you? You always knew she was out for herself and potentially capable of anything, but you can't pin this letter-business on her now just because you've had a row with her and it suits you to believe she was behind it."

"So if it's not her, who is it?"

He shook his head. "I don't know, and maybe you never will either. But if you've really had enough of looking for Leon, then there's no point in stressing yourself out over it any more. Walking away from the search means walking away from all that comes with it."

"I still think I should at least question her about it . . ."

"What's the point? This confrontation will just be an exact replica of the last one and the one before that. Even if it is her, it's her word against yours. My advice is to just let it go."

I sighed. Maybe he had a point. I hadn't a shred of proof that she had anything to do with it, and anyway, I always got that *Groundhog Day* feeling around Lindy – trying to reason with her was so utterly pointless. She just did not care about the repercussions of any of her actions, full stop. And if she *was* behind the letters, she'd be delighted to know that I was as mad as hell over it.

"Look, sleep on it before you decide what you're going to do, okay? In the meantime, I think you could do with another drink."

I laughed, despite everything. "Don't you get sick of looking at me drinking all the time?"

He smiled, a lovely bashful smile that made him look very young. "No."

We both stared awkwardly at each other for a few seconds, then Colm stood up. "Won't be long."

"Don't be," I whispered after him as he walked up to the bar. Suddenly, staying here in Colm's company felt a lot more appealing than having anything to do with Lindy.

Was it possible that I . . . I swallowed . . . was starting to have feelings for him? Good God, I thought, the stress was really starting to get to me.

I was starting to backtrack on my resolve to keep what I knew about Colm from him. Every time I spoke to him, I felt like a fraud. And the more time I spent with him, the more I knew I couldn't be that kind of a person around him. At least if he knew I knew, I could try to support him, try to help him. Whenever I looked back on the last few weeks, the one constant through them had been Colm's support through my various crises and run-ins with Lindy. I wanted to give him something back. I didn't know how I was going to tell him, and I didn't know when. I just knew that I would. As if things weren't complicated enough with the whole development of possibly having feelings for him . . . I pushed that to the back of my mind. Sometimes, the friends you made on the battlefields of work or any other intense scenario weren't necessarily the ones you'd choose in real life, and that applied to this situation too. We were two people who'd been thrown together and forced down each other's throats, that was all. We were just friends.

Chapter Twenty-seven

The next day, Colm and I spent the entire morning in my hotel room working together on the editing of the next show we'd be sending over to Éire TV. Although I would no longer be working with LVTV, there was still one show outstanding of the contracted four shows for Éire TV. My immediate thoughts after my altercation with Lindy and Dave involved walking away from everything, getting a plane home and accepting that my job at the *Vicious Voice* was dust. Sooner or later, I was going to have to accept that Leon wasn't going to come forward if he hadn't done so by now, and I really didn't know how much more passive rejection I could take. But as I walked back to the MGM with Colm and he listened patiently to my ranting, I thought about his role in all of this. I was sure he wanted to put an experience like this documentary on his CV, but it wouldn't be much use if the whole series wasn't delivered. Once I got used to the idea of potentially continuing with the search instead of running for the hills from it, I thought about my own career prospects. Isolde wasn't going to be impressed when she heard that I had cut ties with LVTV, but if I delivered on the Éire TV work, she wouldn't have as much justification to fire me – and there had been no talk so far of extending the contract. After talking it over with Colm the previous night after dinner, I'd decided to hang in there a little while longer and use my head instead of my erratic emotions for once.

As we worked our way through the show's contents, it soon became apparent that Colm didn't want me providing too much input and preferred to direct how things went himself, but we both laughed our way through the morning as we argued good-naturedly about what to put in and leave out of our half-hour slot. I hadn't seen Colm's bossy side in a while and, now that it was tempered with the knowledge that he was a good sort behind it, I quite enjoyed seeing it.

A few hours later, I felt much better about things. We'd contacted some newspapers and magazines directly and had secured two interviews. One was for a weekend paper's supplement, and the other was for a teenage fortnightly magazine called *Glamgirl*. Of course I was doing these interviews entirely for the purpose of giving us footage for the show – any hope that they would lead to Leon was now non-existent. He hadn't seemed like the type that'd read *Glamgirl* anyway. We'd agreed that we'd make no reference to LVTV and what had happened with them in the show for Éire TV. I'd contacted Rick and told him that I was no longer working with LVTV to see if that changed how he felt about me being the Face of People Search. He hadn't sounded impressed – LVTV had been very good for plugging People Search in features about me, and of course it had been free advertising for Rick – but he didn't seem to want to end my contract immediately either, saying he'd have a think about where we could take things from here. That meant that we could include any People Search activities I'd been up to since the last Éire TV show. Between it all, we had plenty of footage – but no satisfactory ending to the story. Eventually, I told Colm that the only way I felt we could end the last episode of the show was with the truth – I'd pulled out all of the stops to find Leon, but to date I hadn't heard from him and I didn't know at this point if I was going to continue with my search or not. Our final scene was to be of me putting a scrapbook together of all of the press cuttings I'd accumulated since I started the Leon search. As our Éire TV contract was open to being extended, this ending potentially allowed the story to be continued – but in my heart I knew that I was just going through the motions of trying to complete the show in the correct manner. There would be no more of me looking for Leon after this. And if Éire TV wanted more shows, I'd just have to try my best to make Isolde understand that it wasn't a runner. Of course, Colm had asked his boss Bea if it was looking likely that Éire TV would want to extend the run of shows, but she hadn't given him a straight answer. I was hoping that was a good indication that the answer would be 'No'.

Colm called to my hotel room that evening as I was putting the scrapbook together. He handed me a CD as soon as I answered the door.

I read the label: *The Wall*. "Pink Floyd?"

"I promised you that I'd get you into them, remember?"

"No, you *threatened* to get me into them."

"Give them a shot. You'll love them, I promise."

I shrugged. "Stick the CD into the laptop so, but I'm not promising anything myself."

The opening bars of a song that Colm informed me was called 'In The Flesh' filled the room. I was suitably underwhelmed. My thoughts turned to what they always do when I'm less than fully entertained – food.

"Have you eaten?" I picked up the room-service menu and waved at Colm. He shook his head.

An hour later, we'd finished eating and *The Wall* was still playing away goodo. "How long is this thing?"

"Not long enough. I could listen to it forever."

"You currently are."

I cleared the table, then moved all of my scrapbook stuff back onto it. Colm picked up one of the cuttings.

"Why do you do it, Andie?"

"Come again?"

He held up the article. "The attention seeking. Why are you never happy unless everyone is talking about you?"

I fiddled with a corner of the scrapbook. "I just fell into this, Colm. But when you think about it, it's the way of the world. Quiet people get nowhere. You have to make a fuss about yourself, or nobody else will."

"Is all attention good, though? I mean, I remember seeing pictures of you wearing tights on your head shortly before we came over here. Weren't you embarrassed when they were published?"

My cheeks blushed red. "People like me keep people like you in a job, so I don't know what you're complaining about!"

"I'm not complaining. I'm asking a question. I'm a cameraman by the way, not a paparazzi photographer."

Now he had me riled. "Same difference. You both make a living capturing other people's misfortunes. Not always, but it's a part of it, and you can't deny it! The juicier the pictures or the footage, the wider the audience."

"I don't take any pleasure from other people's misfortunes –"

"You seemed pretty happy to show me at my worst during that first Éire TV interview. The whole country knows how many hairs I have up each nostril now, thanks to you."

"Oh, come on. As if anyone was interested in looking up your nostrils!"

"Well, you evidently were."

"Zooming is part of my job. You're just splitting hairs now – so to speak. And that's more embarrassing than flashing your knickers, I take it? God, Andie, are you just looking for a reason to get pissed off with me?"

"I don't have to look. You just land them right in my lap time and time again."

There was silence for about twenty seconds.

"Okay. As a dumb guy who can't interpret the code of women who are pissed off with him, you'll have to tell me exactly what you mean by what you've just said. I don't know if I'm supposed to know or something, but I don't have a clue."

This was my chance to tell him what I knew. Here he was, giving out to me about being attention-seeking, when his own way of dealing with the bad things in life wasn't much better. He said I sought attention, but he ran away from it – who was he to say that one side of the coin was better than the other?

In the space of about three seconds, I ran through all the scenarios in my head for how to tell him. Straight out? He'd go spare. He'd obviously worked his entire life around trying to keep what happened a secret. There was only one other option, so no wonder it had only taken three seconds to brainstorm . . . but it wasn't an option I wanted to take. Colm wasn't the only one who'd put a lot of time into burying something.

"Andie, I know you think I'm a bit of a shit."

I opened my mouth to protest, but closed it again. In fairness, I had thought that about him more than once. But at least I was starting to see where the shit was coming from.

"Fair enough. I can be a shithead, but so can most people. But when I have good time for someone, I'll do whatever it takes to keep my relationship with them on track. We got off to a rocky start, but I'd like to think we're friends now – so if I'm doing something to annoy you, tell me. Well, maybe spare me the details of how you don't like how I eat chicken wings and stuff like that. I'd prefer to just hear the big stuff. Spare my feelings on the little things."

"I have good time for you too. Never thought I would – it's the whole shithead issue you mentioned – but there you go."

I paused, trying to get the right angle on what I knew I had to say.

"Which is why . . . if you had anything you'd like to share with me . . . anything that's on your mind that's bothering you . . . I'm always here to listen."

"Anything that's bothering me like what?"

"Oh, I don't know. The cost of wide-angle lens, tripods with one leg shorter than the other two, things like that. Maybe even the past."

His face instantly hardened. Either he was used to reacting like this whenever the P word was mentioned, or he was on to me. He said nothing. He looked up at me to see if I was going to say anything else, and when I didn't, he looked away again. I knew this trick – it was the get-information-by-saying-nothing method of finding out what was going on, which forced the other person to speak to fill the silence. After a few excruciating minutes of this malarkey, I realised that there was only one way to broach the topic.

"Colm." I moved over beside him and took his hand. He looked confused, but didn't pull it away, which I took as a good sign. "I know about the car accident."

For about ten seconds, it was as if I had said nothing. Colm stared expressionlessly at the ground, still holding my hand, looking like he was picking Lotto numbers in his head during a bored moment at work. In the eleventh second, it was as if a starting pistol had gone off in his head that finally allowed him to react. He ripped his hand from mine before jumping up off the bed and pacing to the other side of the room. A pink flush started to spread up his neck and onto his face.

"How?"

I had to admit, I was surprised – I had expected to have to go through the rigmarole of 'What are you talking about?' for about ten minutes before we got to this point. He was taking it well. Good.

"I read about it on the Internet."

"You read about it on the Internet." He nodded his head. "Of course. So, you just stumbled upon this information, did you? You were reading today's news, and a story from ten years ago – ten shagging years ago – just happened to pop up on your screen, did it?"

"Well, not exactly . . ."

"So how? How did you come across this story unless you were looking for it? Who told you about it?"

His face was now distinctly purple. Not a typical indication of taking something well.

"Nobody told me about it. I just happened to be doing some – research – about you and your awards, and I stumbled upon this link . . ."

"What's it to you about my awards?"

"Look, it doesn't matter! What I wanted to say to you was that you could talk to me about – what happened – if you wanted to. I can tell you're not happy, Colm. Something's bothering you."

"Oh, and you know me so well that you can tell that, is that it?" He shook his head. "Get real, Andie."

"I'm only trying to help . . . I thought we'd become friends recently . . ."

"Just because I've lent you an ear while you've been moaning about Leon doesn't mean you know me. You have absolutely no idea what's going on in my head."

"Maybe I understand more than you think."

"How?"

I shrugged. "The how doesn't matter. What matters is that you're pushing people away because you're living in the past. No wonder you're unhappy. You've never moved on."

"Bullshit!"

"Is it? Everything you love is from decades ago. The music, the clothes, even the biscuits! They're all from a happier time in your life, aren't they? Childhood . . . early teenage years . . . a time before you had to live with killing someone?"

He flinched as I said it. Maybe it was that he recognised some truth in what I said, or the bluntness of me saying that he'd killed someone, but he looked as if I had hit him.

"You have no idea what you're talking about." It looked like rigmarole time had come after all.

"It'll be okay, Colm –"

"It'll be okay? Have you ever killed someone?"

It was my turn to look at the carpet.

"Like I said, you have no idea what you're on about. I have to go." He was over at the door before he'd even finished the sentence.

"Colm!" I ran after him. "Wait!"

It was no use. He bombed it out the door, and by the time I reached the corridor, he had disappeared.

I should have been angry at him for running away, but I wasn't. I just felt sorry for him.

Chapter Twenty-eight

In the days after I told Colm what I knew about his past, he avoided me. I didn't take it personally at first when he refused to answer the hotel-room door to me, even though I'd seen him going in a few seconds earlier. My throat was raw from roaring in at him and my knuckles were turning skinless, not to mention the dirty looks I was getting from anyone who passed, but it was okay – it was hard for him to cope with the fact that I knew his private business, and I had to cut him some slack.

But when I saw him across the lobby of the MGM, rang his phone to test the waters, and saw him put the phone back in his pocket when he saw it was me calling, something clicked into place. Suddenly, things were very personal, and my pity for his plight turned to the rage of the ignored.

"Hey!" I yelled across the lobby at Colm.

He hesitated for a few seconds before turning around. I crossed to where he was standing, right in front of a clothes shop that opened onto the lobby. His face had the look of a Rottweiler about it.

"What's the deal?" I said.

"No deal. I'm just ignoring you. Or at least, I'm trying to. You're a bit slow about taking the hint."

"Why?"

"Probably genetic."

I chose to ignore that. "Why are you ignoring me? I'm not judging you on what happened. I only told you what I know so that I could support you."

He snorted. "If you've learned anything at all about me since we first met, you should know that I'm a very private person. Do you think private people want other people reading their private business?"

"It's on the Internet! Nothing that's on the Internet is private!"

"But you didn't just stumble upon the information – you were nosing into my business."

"Oh for God's sake, Colm! Get off the cross!"

"I'm not listening to this." He turned around and started to walk away.

"No! Come back here!" I walloped his back with my handbag. The wallop had the desired effect of making him turn around – although he looked even grouchier when he did, which I hadn't thought was possible.

"You have to face up to this! Are you going to spend the rest of your life hiding away from the world?"

"Mind your own business, Andie. Go off and have a dream about Leon or something." He turned to walk away.

I swung the handbag again. "Don't. You. Patronise. *Me!*"

The final swing must have hit a kidney, as he squealed with pain and held his hands to that general direction.

"Who are you – Miss Piggy? Give me that!" He grabbed the strap of my handbag and pulled the bag out of my hands. "You needn't think you're getting this back!"

Out of the corner of my eye, I spotted a huge handbag dangling from the arm of a display model near the entrance of the nearby shop. In one fluid movement, I lunged forward, ripped the bag off the model's shoulder and launched it at Colm's arm. It was all puffed out with paper, and swung well, as if it was complicit in helping Colm to see sense.

"Give me my bag back now! And stop talking to me like I'm a child!"

"Oh, I'm not. I'm talking to you like you're a clinically deranged madwoman. Look at yourself, Andie. This is exactly what I was talking about when I said you were attention seeking."

"Don't change the subject! This is about you, not about me looking for attention!"

"It's about to become about you. You've just stolen a bag from a shop to beat me with, the entire lobby is staring at us, and it looks like the girl behind the counter is calling security on you."

I looked up to see the shop assistant engaging in a frantic conversation on the phone while glaring in my direction.

"Is it any wonder I'm ignoring you?" Colm went on. "Not only do you wriggle your way into my private life, but then you turn the whole thing around so that it's all about you. You don't want to support me, Andie. You want to make my personal history into something you can solve. You want to fix me, and then it's all about you again – look what you did, aren't you so great, etc. And then, when I don't play ball with your plan, you have a hissy fit and make a show of both of us. So I think it's best to continue with this ignoring thing, don't you?"

I had no idea what to say. I suddenly felt very small.

"Colm, I'm sorry . . . I didn't mean . . ."

He held his hand up. "No. Just leave it for now." He dropped my handbag at my feet.

"Okay. But I am sorry. Just know that."

He nodded. He looked like he wanted to say something else, but couldn't get the words out. It suddenly seemed hugely important to me to find out what was on his mind, but my attention was diverted by the sound of a "*Hey!*" from an approaching security guard. Normally, I would have been worried, but it suddenly didn't matter that I might be plastered all over the news for shoplifting. There were more important things to worry about.

"I'll stay and tell them you didn't mean to take that," said Colm.

"No. You go. I can handle this."

He nodded. His face thawed. "For the record, if you need to use that on him to escape, it bloody well hurts."

I laughed in a nervous, high-pitched fashion as the security guard descended upon me, and Colm walked away to leave me to talk my way out of things.

I heard a knock at my door a few hours after I'd somehow manoeuvred my way out of the shop situation – Colm's knock. I got up and went to answer the door, bracing myself for the inevitable onslaught.

I opened the door to the sight of Colm's legs, his hair, his forehead and eyes, and a gigantic bouquet of flowers covering his entire torso. A box of chocolates was squashed between his left arm and his chest. A plastic bag containing a bottle of wine dangled from his right wrist, which looked like it was about to snap between the weight of the bottle and his attempt to hold up the bouquet of flowers.

I was shocked into silence. I pulled down the top of the bouquet to make sure that it was actually Colm standing behind the flowers – although the torn brown corduroy trousers had pretty much given the game away, but it was still hard to believe that he would do something like this.

"You're very quiet." A muffled voice came from behind the flowers.

"I'm just wondering how the hell you managed to knock carrying all that stuff?"

"Thanks. That was exactly the reaction I was hoping for."

"You should come in."

"I should." He shuffled in. "These are for you. You might have guessed that." He held out the bouquet of flowers, then fished out the chocolates and stuck them under my arm.

"I actually wasn't sure. It was quite possible you got lost on your way to Lindy's with these. I really wasn't expecting this . . ."

"Because I'm such a tosser, I suppose?" he asked as he freed himself from the bottle of wine.

"I just didn't think you were the type of guy to give flowers."

"I've never done it before in my life, so I suppose that means I'm not."

"So why now?" I threw the question out there as nonchalantly as I could, but my heart started pounding. It was a loaded question, and we both knew it.

The answer came in a format I didn't expect. Colm came over to me and took the flowers out of my arms, then cupped his hands around my face and stared into my eyes for what felt like forever. My initial reaction was shock, but within seconds, what shocked me was how right it felt.

He swept his hands down my cheeks, onto my neck and into my hair, staring at me in wonder. I stared back, drinking in this new, barrier-free person before me. I was almost afraid to breathe in case the interruption would startle him and send him away. And right then, I felt that I would die if he left my side. I slowly moved my arms up his chest, then rested them around his shoulders as I stroked the back of his neck. He closed his eyes, then rested his forehead against mine. We stood like that for an immeasurable amount of time, but when we finally looked up at each other, everything changed. Within seconds, he was kissing me with an intensity that made me melt into him. We tore at each other's clothes, stumbling backwards towards the bed. Once we got there, all I could think was that it was absolute madness that we hadn't done this before . . .

"What are you thinking?" Colm asked me as he snuggled his bare body against mine some time later.

I smiled, and kissed his neck. "Isn't that what the woman usually asks?"

"I know, I know. I'm just hoping you haven't already started to regret what we've just done."

"Of course I don't! Why would you think that I would?"

"I just can't believe my luck that you're actually interested in me," Colm whispered. "I've fancied you since the first time I set eyes on you in the Éire TV canteen, when you worked on that *Glitter* show."

"No way! I had no idea!"

"I used to spot you walking around the building, always in a hurry and looking super-confident, and glammed up to the nines, but I figured you never noticed me."

"But when we first met, you were so aloof and distant that I actually thought you hated me! I could never figure out what you thought about me!"

"I wanted to dislike you," Colm said. "I thought you represented everything I don't like. You seemed to be from a world that's a million light years away from mine. I looked at you and saw a leggy, skinny model –"

"Former model," I said. "And I'm not skinny."

"Ah, go away outta that! But let me finish. On paper, you had the potential to be a superficial celebrity wannabe and a drama queen. Sorry," he said when my face fell. "I just thought – and don't kill me for this – that you'd put on all that crying business during the interview when we first met, just so that you'd get publicity for the show. But once I got to know you, I knew then that you were genuinely upset during that interview."

"Damn right I bloody well was!" I said, feeling genuinely upset again.

"I know, I know." He stroked my hair softly. "I know what I'm saying sounds horrible, but I want to be honest with you about why I was so detached at times."

"Go on, so." I tried to put my indignation to one side.

"Anyway, this was all well and good until I started to develop feelings for you. Proper, strong feelings, not just fancying you. When we first met, I used to actively try not to be too friendly with you, because I had the impression that you thought everyone fancied you. Whenever I made a snide comment at you, it was because I was trying to pull you down a peg or two."

"So is that what that 'footballers are more your style' comment was about on the plane on the way over?"

"Yeah." He had the good grace to look sheepish.

"Well, you sure wasted no time in getting the knife in . . ."

"I know. It was nasty of me. But then I got to know you despite myself, with all the work we had to do together, and I realised that you're not like that at all. I knew I was falling for you before I got sick, but as soon as you gave up that George Clooney meeting to help me, I was goosed. I couldn't fool myself any longer – I had to admit to myself that I was crazy about you. Problem was, you seemed to be hopelessly in love with Leon. Even so, I had to spend as much time as possible with you after that – I couldn't help myself. Then, when Martin sent me that email complaining about Valerie, I had a cunning plan – you'd been so nosy about what was going on there . . ." He stopped and laughed when I thumped his arm.

"You meant to say 'interested', didn't you?"

"No, you were nosy, let's face it. But anyway. I thought it would be a good way to get to spend some extra time with you."

"I knew there was something behind all of that! At the start, you had no interest at all, and then suddenly it was a different story!"

"Andie, I was never in the slightest bit interested in what is or isn't going on between Isolde and Martin. It was just an excuse to have something to talk to you about. Things had been so frosty between us, then I saw an opening, and – I exploited it, being perfectly honest."

"No wonder you won all of those awards. You're quite ruthless in getting what you want when it comes down to it, aren't you?"

"Ruthless, no. Ambitious, yes – in most things. I really believed I had no chance at all with you, but that didn't stop me wanting to spend time with you. Actually, it wasn't even a matter of want – it was need. I *needed* to spend every spare second with you, because when I wasn't with you, I was thinking about you and driving myself crazy."

"I couldn't work out what you were thinking. I was actually afraid you might take Lindy up on her advances at one stage – you did meet her for a drink."

He laughed. "I only met her for that drink to have the opportunity to make it clear to her that I wasn't interested. I wanted to handle the whole thing as tactfully as possible before it got to a situation where she'd try to kiss me when we were out or something. I didn't want to embarrass her by rejecting her in front of lots of people or anything like that."

"That was nice of you. How did you do it, by the way? And how did she react?"

"I asked her for some advice. I told her I was in love with a girl from home, and didn't know whether I should make a move on her or not. I asked her what she thought I should do."

"No!"

"Yep. She got the message from that alright. Of course, she knew it was you straight away."

"So what was her advice? Or had she stomped out in a hissy fit by this stage?"

"Her advice was that I should forget this girl and look further afield."

"Crumbs. She really doesn't give up easily, does she?"

"No, but she eventually got sick of listening to me going on about how much I liked this girl. Once I mentioned that I thought this girl was my soul mate, I could see she'd given me up as a bad job. It was like a switch flicked in her head, and she wasn't prepared to waste any more of her time after that. She got up and left approximately three seconds later."

I barely registered anything Colm said after the words 'soul mate'.

"When I told you that I was meeting her," he continued, "I was trying to suss out if you were in any way jealous at the thought of it. You didn't seem to be, which was very disappointing!"

I zoned back in and found my voice. "I should've been an actress. There would have been more money in it than journalism."

He laughed. "But despite all that Lindy business, we seemed to be growing closer, and I started to wonder if maybe, just maybe, I had a chance after all. I could feel something happening between us, something amazing. For the first time in my life, I felt like someone 'got' me."

"That's exactly how I feel when I'm with you," I whispered.

"I thought it was real. But then, I found out that you knew about my past, and I felt that you'd just spent all that time being nice to me because you felt sorry for me. And that feeling I had of you 'getting' me – I wondered if it just seemed that way because you knew what you knew all along."

"That was never it," I said. "I only found out recently. Besides, there was always so much more to it – to us."

"I realised that once I had time to think," Colm said. "But when I found out that you knew, it nearly killed me. I kept thinking it would have been better never to have known how it felt to be this crazy about someone and to think you had a future with them, rather than find out and then have it torn away from you."

"So what changed?"

He shrugged. "I copped myself on, that's what. I realised I was being an irrational idiot. But hey, I have the excuse of having years of inexperience with women to fall back on. But that's a conversation for later. The bottom line was that if I was going to lose you, it wasn't going to be at my own hand. If you didn't want to be with me, that was your choice. But I've spent my life running away from happiness, and you were one thing that I couldn't run from."

"Please don't ever run away again."

"Oh, I'm going nowhere." He paused. "But, Andie, we need to talk about Leon . . ."

I nodded. I'd expected this. In fact, it was crazy that we hadn't spoken about Leon before now. At this stage, it wasn't so much an elephant in the room as an entire safari.

"How do you feel about him now?"

"He doesn't feel real to me any more. It feels like this entire experience of looking for him was predicated on a dream that I never really wanted to come true."

"If he showed up right now, what would you do?"

"I'd tell him I'm sorry for wasting his time, because I'm in love with someone else."

Colm's eyes widened. I nodded. He didn't need to return the compliment. I already knew he was in love with me too.

And it felt better than anything I'd ever felt before in my life.

Chapter Twenty-nine

Over the next few days, I found out all sorts of interesting things about Colm that helped me to understand him better.

After his parents were killed when he was twelve, he went to live with an aunt and uncle-in-law that he'd never got on with. His aunt was a detached and aloof woman, and his uncle-in-law resented his presence from day one. Colm knew they'd only taken him in out of a sense of duty, and fear of what the neighbours would say if they didn't. They had two girls in their late teens who were the lights of their lives, and they really weren't interested in having a boy too – in fact, Colm always felt that his uncle resented having another male presence in the house.

He'd never had a girlfriend since the accident. A lifetime of pushing people away from him had done nothing for his love life.

"I'd been seeing a girl called Sharon from home for two years when the accident happened," he explained to me over a room-service meal at four o'clock in the morning. We weren't getting much sleep these days, and had needed to refuel. "She was best friends with a granddaughter of the man I killed. She hadn't been in the car with me at the time of the accident – I'd been driving alone that night – but she knew it wasn't my fault, that I couldn't do anything to avoid the old man when he stepped out. That didn't stop the whole thing falling apart, though."

"Was she influenced by her best friend to give you a hard time? I mean, I presume her friend was mad at you, despite you not being able to stop the accident from happening . . ."

"Her friend was livid, as was her friend's entire family. They were a big family, and quite influential in the village in that they owned half of it – one of the pubs, a grocery store, some of the property on the main street, that kind of thing. They blackened my name to everyone who set foot inside the shop or the pub, even though they knew from the witness statement and the guards that I couldn't have done anything at all to stop what happened from happening."

"That was lousy of them."

"Yeah. A part of me understood it, though – they were angry, and who else would they take it out on, only the person who'd killed the one they loved? That didn't stop me feeling bitter about it all, though."

"I can imagine. And what did your girlfriend have to say about that?"

"My girlfriend always said to me that she was on my side, but I could tell she was doing it out of duty. She always looked mortified to be spotted walking down the street with me. She broke it off with me about two months after I killed the old man, and it destroyed me."

"You didn't see it coming at all?" I tried to phrase the question as gently as I could.

"I did, of course. The logical part of my brain knew a long time before it happened that it was over between us. I just fought those voices down so hard that when it did happen, I couldn't bear it. And I also knew that my relationship with my girlfriend wasn't the only thing that was over. My entire old way of life was gone forever."

"That must have been hard for you to come to terms with."

"It was. So I did the whole mature-guy thing and just went completely into myself. If nobody could get close to me, nobody could hurt me. So, as you've quite rightly pointed out, I push people away. I've been doing it for years, and I had no intention of stopping – even though I'm sick to death of doing it. I've known for years that it's time for me to get back to the real world. But then, when I actually felt ready to be with someone again, I just didn't know how to get back in the game. I know that sounds ridiculous, but it got to the stage where I felt like a freak. Imagine explaining to a girl that first of all you've killed someone, and then that you've never gone out with anyone else since. I'd sound like the biggest loser on the planet."

"Do you think I think you're a loser?"

"For some bizarre reason that I can't fathom, you don't seem to think that. But you're different, and that's why we got this far. If I hadn't met you, I'd probably have been alone forever – and possibly thinking that I was reasonably happy to be that way. But now . . ."

"Now?"

"Now that I've had a taste of what it's like to be with someone like you, I finally understand what all the fuss is about."

We indulged in a few seconds of goofy smiles before he continued.

"I've also managed to come to the realisation that I'm punishing myself – which might seem very obvious to you but, believe me, it took me a long time to realise that myself, simple and all as it is to grasp. Can you understand that?"

I nodded. I could, more than he knew.

"I know I couldn't have avoided hitting the old man that night, no matter what. But when you kill a person, you carry that with you for the rest of your life – a life that, in my case, was put on hold the day of the accident. The problem was that when I recognised what I was doing to myself, I was too entrenched in it to find my way back out. But then, you came bursting into my life, and – well, here we are."

"But what's so different about me?"

"What's so different?" Colm looked directly into my eyes. "Do you have any idea how amazing you are? I've never met anyone as full of life as you. You're vibrant, you're wild, you're – you're special."

I shook my head.

"You are. In the last ten years, you're the only person who's ever worked out that I've been carrying something around with me. You're the only one who's ever cared enough to even ask."

"But that's because you've never let anyone else in enough to see that something was up – and I only had the opportunity to get close to you because you were forced to hang out with me over here. That doesn't make me special."

"That's not true. I would have continued to push you away like I did at the beginning if I hadn't seen you for the caring person you are."

"You give me far too much credit."

"No. The problem is that you don't give yourself half enough. We'll have to work on that confidence of yours, Missy Appleton. Amongst other things. We've got a busy night ahead of us . . ."

He smothered me in kisses, and that was the end of that conversation.

It's always when things are going well that you need to watch out. Whenever I got one aspect of my life sorted, something else always got mucked up, just to keep me on my toes . . .

Colm and I had secured a new office for ourselves – the Internet café in the hotel. We had wireless Internet access in our hotel rooms, of course, but we both knew that we'd end up fooling around if we went to either of our rooms, and we'd make no progress whatsoever in planning the next episode of *Looking for Leon*. Philippe had pulled strings for us, and got us a daily Internet access rate for a dollar each. It was nine in the morning, and both of us were already ensconced in the café, bright-eyed, bushy-tailed and ready for a day's work. My inbox brought all of my good intentions to an abrupt end.

From: **Adam.Appleton@gmail.com**
To: **Andie.Appleton@hotmail.com**

Uh oh. I think every second mail I send you is bad news. That should give you a clue about what's to come.

Soooo . . . Jane seems pretty happy that we're back together – so happy, in fact, that she's been telling a few people – okay, the entire office – about how we got back together. It's a great story, you have to admit. Anyway, it's a big office, and you know how it is – you don't know who knows who. Long story short, tempted as

I am to make it long and postpone the bad news, it turns out one of the people she told knows Isolde. Jane hadn't mentioned the name of the person I was spying on, but she described Isolde as "the mad one in the office upstairs that wears the tents" and everyone knew who she was from that.

This is where it gets scary. So, Jane was leaving work yesterday when she was accosted by Isolde, who demanded to know the full details of my stalking attempt. Isolde knew from the office bigmouth that I was watching what she was doing because I suspected her of having an affair, but what she really wanted to know was who I was and why I gave a shit about her life. So Jane had no option but to tell her my name, and that I was doing a job for my sister, Andie. She had no choice, Andie – she was terrified. She said Isolde was ranting and raving and threatening police involvement if she didn't find out what was going on. Plus, Jane has just bought a new car, and Isolde threatened to scrape a new word into the side of her car every day until Jane told her what was the story was. You have a crazy boss – you mustn't know that, or you wouldn't have been messing with her in the first place.

I suppose you're wondering how Isolde reacted to hearing you were involved in this. Apparently, it was about as pretty as I'd imagine she is first thing in the morning. Or any time, really. Jane had been terrified before, but when Isolde started ranting about you, she actually thought Isolde was going to reach out and strangle her just to channel her anger somewhere. I wish I had some words of consolation for you, but . . . basically, you're fucked. Get the CV together.

Oh. My. *God!* Fear flooded through me. My face filled with blood. I would have left the country if I already wasn't in it. It didn't matter where I was or where I would go, though. Isolde would find me. She was probably on a plane to Vegas right now to strangle me with the hem of one of her curtains. I was *soooooooooooooooooooooooooooooooooooooo* dead.

Oh no! A box popped up on the bottom right of my PC screen. *Isolde has just signed in.*

Why, why, *why* had I set up Instant Messenger to log me in automatically?

I thought about signing out immediately, but no. I wasn't that much of a coward. I held my breath and waited for the onslaught to begin.

Ten seconds later, I had to exhale. Still no sign of her rant beginning. I was dead anyway, so there was no point in giving myself brain damage from lack of oxygen while waiting to be killed.

I spent a full half an hour staring at the screen, waiting for my bollixing to pop up. Eventually, I realised that she wasn't going to IM me. She was going to make me sweat. I had to try to do some work, so I went back to my inbox to deal with the messages that had come in while I'd been staring at the bottom right of my screen. Just as I did so, a new email came through from Isolde.

Oh God. I took a deep breath and opened it.

From: **Isolde.Huntingdon@vicious.ie**
To: **Andie.Appleton@vicious.ie**

Subject: I think you know what this is about . . .

. . . although your stupidity knows no bounds, it seems, so maybe you don't. So let me clarify. It's time for you and me to talk about you setting someone on me to stalk me. I haven't IM'd you because I don't want to hear your pathetic excuses. I'm the one doing the talking here, you understand?

You, Andie, seem to be determined to commit career suicide. Just when I think you can't surprise me any more with the lengths you will go to fuck up, you open my eyes once more to how self-destructive you are.

Let me tell you a little story. I'll tell you this as simply as possible, because it seems to be the only way to get things through to your thick skull. Once upon a time, there was a girl called Maud. She wasn't a little girl. She was fat. In fact, her entire family was fat. Her mother was fat, her father was fat, her brother was fat. Even the family dog had cholesterol problems. This was because they all ate too much. You with me so far?

Maud, the fat girl, grew up to be a fat adult. Maud's brother ballooned too. Maud and her brother were the best of friends in their fat bubble. This was because the fatties needed to stick together to deal with the world. Time went on, and fat brother met a fat woman and got married. Maud never met anyone, though. And eventually, she got sick of being fat. She decided to do something about it. She stopped eating badly and started doing lots of exercise. After a few years, Maud managed to become a thin person. She changed her name – her surname too – to suit this new person she had become.

Her brother stayed in the fat world, as did his wife. Maud suspected that her brother could be dragged out of that world, but his wife was putting up resistance. Maud had a feeling that the wife didn't have the motivation or the willpower to lose weight, and she was holding Maud's brother back. As time went on, Maud could see that her brother was growing more and more dissatisfied with accepting that he was a fatty when he knew he could do something about it, especially since his sister had done it and kept the weight off. But whenever he suggested to his wife that they should lose weight, she went ballistic. He told her he wanted to join a weight-loss group by himself, and that he wasn't trying to drag her into something she wasn't interested in, but she didn't want him doing it if she wasn't doing it herself. Things went on like this for years and years.

Eventually, the brother couldn't take any more. His health was suffering, and his wife had closed her eyes to the difficulties they both faced because of their weight. He went to Maud and begged her to help him before he became seriously ill. Maud was thrilled that he was finally willing to do something about his weight problems, and she vowed that if he tried to backtrack at any stage, as she knew he was likely to do through fear of his wife, she wouldn't let him off the hook.

Maud brought her brother to a weight-management support group and made him join up. Each week, they went to a meeting together where they attended a weigh-in. You see, Maud had been attending this very meeting for years, ever since she first lost the weight. As far as she was concerned, her addiction to food was like an alcoholic's addiction to the sauce. It was something she lived with every day, and managed through the support of her meetings and her group. She knew that if her brother gave the support group a chance, he would lose weight and learn to keep it off.

This is exactly what happened. And as for her brother's wife, Maud called around to her and explained to her that if her husband hadn't done something about his weight, his health issues would have killed him – and if she wasn't willing to do something about her own weight, she was the one who should start thinking about the kind of coffin she'd like. Maud was very scary when she wanted to be. Eventually, her brother's wife saw a bit of sense. Now, both Maud's brother and his wife go to the meeting with Maud every week.

All Maud is waiting for now is for the rumours of threesomes to hit the street.

Kind regards,

Isolde

Oh no. No. No. No. *No!* I was no longer frightened. I was deeply ashamed of myself, which felt even worse than fear. Colm and I had got it so, so wrong.

"Colm, Martin is Isolde's sister."

"What? That can't be – he told me once he only has one sister, and her name isn't Isolde, it's –"

"Maud." I finished his sentence.

"Yes, Maud . . ."

"Check your email." I forwarded on Isolde's email to Colm, then logged off, got up and walked out of the Internet café. There was no point in staying around to do any work when my career was officially over.

Chapter Thirty

I knew that being nosy would come back to bite me on the ass some day. Adam always said I would be a curtain-twitcher when I was an old lady – which is ironic, when you consider Isolde's choice of clothing. I was prepared for trouble, but what I wasn't prepared for was the embarrassment that haunted me for meddling in other people's lives. The only thing I could do was apologise. With my heart in my mouth, I went back to my hotel room and picked up the phone to ring Isolde. It rang out. I felt heartily relieved – then ashamed of myself all over again for being relieved. I decided to email her to apologise. It would mean very little to her, I assumed, but I had to address the issue in some way.

I wrote at least ten drafts of my email to Isolde, and discarded each and every one. Some journalist I was. Eventually, I decided to keep it simple and speak the truth.

From: **Andie.Appleton@vicious.ie**
To: **Isolde.Huntingdon@vicious.ie**

Isolde,

I know that no words can validate my behaviour. I was completely unfair to you, and I'm so sorry. I'll obviously understand if you're firing me – you would be completely justified in doing so.

Again, I am truly sorry.

Andie

It was only after I typed my name that I realised Isolde had called me Andie in her email, and not Andey. Nothing could have conveyed the gravity of the situation more than that.

The next few hours were unbelievably tense, as I perched on the edge of my seat in my room waiting to jump off it when Isolde inevitably rang me back. I also couldn't tear myself away from my laptop in case she was in a meeting and decided to email me instead – Isolde was one of those annoying people who typed noisily on her laptop all the way through a meeting, regardless of who it was with or what it was about. She'd been known to clear her entire inbox while talking non-stop for an hour in a meeting. She could type without looking at the keyboard, so she always managed to maintain her killer eye contact with everyone in the room. Still, nothing came.

Colm knocked on the door. I was so on edge that the sound frightened the life out of me. I briefly filled Colm in on what I'd been doing.

"Sitting here waiting for her to contact you won't make it happen any faster." He walked behind me and massaged my shoulders. "How about we do something to take your mind off things?"

He leaned down and kissed the back of my neck, just behind my ear. I didn't take much convincing after that to take up his suggestion.

An hour later, I got out of bed and checked my email again, as Isolde still hadn't phoned. My heart thumped when I saw a new email from Isolde sitting in my inbox. I double-clicked it straight away before my nerves got the better of me.

From: **Isolde.Huntingdon@vicious.ie**
To: **Andie.Appleton@vicious.ie**
Re: Looking for Leon

We need to wrap up the Leon story. It's run its course. If he was going to show up, he would have done so by now. What we need to do now is to work out how we can gain maximum exposure from ending the search. I want you to start working on how you're going to portray this to the media in Vegas. My advice is to take the sob-story approach as much as possible

– you're heartbroken, this isn't how you saw things ending, your life will never be the same again, blah blah blah. I'll start working on a press release for the Irish newspapers. Organise your flight home for the beginning of next week – that gives you time to make the most out of this. Make sure that publicist gets you as many TV, radio and newspaper interviews as possible, because when the word gets out that you're giving up on the search, there might be someone out there who knows something and will now come forward. We'd get a lot more out of all of this if we found him, you know, but if that's not going to happen, then there's no more for us to gain from this. I want you to email me tomorrow with a schedule of the interviews you've arranged to spread the word about this. Get off your email the second you've finished reading this and start organising things now. As for Éire TV, they've been humming and hawing about whether or not they want to extend the contract. I suggest you make sure everything you do is filmed between now and coming home so that your arse is covered either way.

As for the other issue, we'll talk about that when you get home. All you need to know is that Martin doesn't know about all of this. This is for his sake, not yours. Martin would be mortified if he thought anyone knew about his weight-loss efforts. Make sure he doesn't find out that Colm Cannon knows (as I have no doubt he does), or there will be serious trouble.

Isolde

PS If you tell anyone at work that my real name is Maud, then you really are fired.

I must have OD'd on the coffee earlier. Surely I hadn't read what I thought I'd just read. I skimmed the mail again, and to my disbelief it looked like I wasn't hallucinating. There were quite a few shocking things about those few paragraphs.

1) The Leon adventure was over. I'd been sure Isolde would have dragged it out a bit more.

2) Isolde wanted me to make a show of myself *again*. For heaven's sake! Could we not just finish this with a bit of dignity?

3) Where was my bollixing?

Then, I cottoned on to what she was up to. It was the making-me-sweat approach again. The bollixing I would get when she saw me face-to-face was going to be far, far worse than it would have been if she had poured out her frustration with me into an email. The whole thing of me having to do the boo-hoos on national TV again wasn't part of the punishment – she would have made me do that anyway – but God help me when I was in front of her. Her email was far, far worse in its own way than I had anticipated. Good thing she didn't know how I'd parted company with Lindy. That surely wouldn't help her mood. She didn't trust me to be able to give away water in the desert, never mind organise all of the Leon activities on my own.

"Colm, we're going home." I beckoned him over.

Colm came up behind me and read Isolde's email. "Hmm, you got away lightly!"

"No. This isn't all there is to it. I know Isolde."

"Maybe she'll surprise you. I see you haven't told her you're no longer working with Lindy though."

"Do you blame me? It looks like I have a bit of PR work ahead of me for the next few days if I'm to make it look like I took what she said seriously. Let's just hope she's not right and that me saying I'm ending the search won't make someone come forward with information about Leon. I don't know what the hell I'd do if that happened, now that . . ." I pointed to Colm, then back at myself, unable to say the words. It was really starting to hit me that it must have been so difficult for Colm to watch me try to move heaven and earth to find another man while he was developing feelings for me. I know that if I had been in his position, I wouldn't have handled it as well as he had.

"As you've said yourself, if it hasn't happened by now, it probably won't," Colm said. "Let's just try to enjoy our last few days here. I'm pretty happy to hear we're going home now though. I've enjoyed feeling like I've been living in Vegas for a while, but I think now the time has come to hit the road."

"What? The great explorer actually wants to go home? What's that all about?"

"It's about you," he said, stroking my hair. "I don't need to go travelling around the world any more to find what it is I'm looking for. Now, I have it. I want to go home and make you a part of my home life, and to become part of yours. The sooner that happens, the better."

"Oh, Colm, that's so sweet!"

He shrugged. "Besides, I'm starting to miss the simple things of home, like Cheese and Onion Taytos."

"Watch it!" I said, feigning indignation at having the same level of priority as a bag of crisps, but secretly thrilled at what he'd said before he'd made a joking comment to make himself look like a hard man. Becoming a part of Colm's life sounded damn good to me.

"Anyway, it looks like we should book our flights," Colm said. "Give me a second – I'll get my company credit card from my room, and we can book them now."

I turned my attention back to my computer as Colm left, and started to look for flights. As I skimmed the search results for flights, I went through a range of emotions. Relief was the dominant one. It would have been just typical of the way things worked out for me that Leon would come out of the woodwork now that Colm and I were together. What would I do then? Thankfully, it appeared as if Leon had absolutely no interest at all in ever having anything else to do with me. Blessings came in the oddest of guises sometimes.

Chapter Thirty-one

That Wednesday I made my way downtown after I finished work, armed with a hugely specific shopping list. I was a woman with a plan. Colm had done nothing since Isolde's email but talk about how he couldn't wait to go home and start enjoying life in Ireland for the first time in a very long time, even going so far as to say we should spend some of our own money on getting an earlier, pricier flight home on Thursday or Friday because we had no actual work commitments lined up after that – I vetoed that in favour of letting Éire TV pay, spending at least two full days in bed, and then enjoying a wild (70s) weekend in Vegas.

So I'd come up with the great idea of surprising Colm with a special Irish dinner to help speed up the time to our homecoming. He'd seemed a bit down the previous evening, and although he'd insisted he was fine when I'd asked him what was up, he wasn't himself. We'd been too busy all morning and afternoon doing our final interviews to talk properly, so I was looking forward to having a proper chat over dinner.

For the sake of my job prospects, I'd done as Isolde had asked and had informed certain members of the media that I was abandoning the search, but I'd kept it as low-key as possible. All of the local newspapers, some of the national ones and a few of the national magazines were interested and we filmed all of my interviews with them in case Éire TV came knocking on my door again looking for footage, but there was no longer the same mania surrounding it all since LVTV had pulled the story. I had to give Lindy one thing – she'd been damn good at her job. If news of my impending departure had reached Leon, it thankfully hadn't caused him to turn up in the MGM lobby. I'd felt horribly false during the course of the week's interviews, talking about how sad I was that things hadn't worked out differently while my lover filmed me saying these things. Colm had been understanding itself after each interview as I apologised over and over and assured him that he was the one I wanted, but I still felt like a cow about it. But at least now our work was done. I had nothing scheduled for the rest of my time in Vegas and could focus on nothing else but Colm from this point onwards.

I smiled at the thought of the evening ahead as I let myself back into my room. One of the beauties of a suite was having a kitchen and the ability to cook. Of course, I had no kitchen utensils, so Philippe had offered to lend me a rucksack full of pots, pans and all the paraphernalia. The plan was to cook a Sunday dinner for our Wednesday night meal: roast chicken, mashed potatoes, steamed vegetables, gravy, the lot. I was going to buy the cooked roast chicken in a nearby deli, so technically I was cheating, but the kitchen just had hobs and not an oven. Still, I felt content and domesticated a few hours later as I mashed butter into potatoes until they were as smooth as silk. It was going to be a plain dinner, as Colm wouldn't touch parsley or any of the other trimmings, but it smelled damn tasty. The pièce de résistance of the whole thing was that I'd managed to source some typically Irish things from a shop downtown. I'd bought Tayto crisps, Brennan's bread, Barry's tea and Kerrygold butter, which should please Colm no end. Okay, so we were going home in a few days, but it wouldn't be the same getting these things at home – everyone knew they tasted much better when you were far away, especially if you were dying to go home.

I'd told Colm to come to my room at seven o'clock as hungry as possible. I'd had to wash, chop and cook for an hour and a half, which was about eighty minutes more than I usually spent on preparing dinner, but it was worth it. I'd set the table in the sitting room with Philippe's fancy, flowery plates and champagne flutes. Scented candles were dotted around the room, their smell mingling with the medley of aromas coming from the kitchen.

At exactly seven o'clock there was a knock on my door. I put on my best domestic-goddess smile as I opened it.

Colm stood there with a face like thunder.

"Come on in!" The goddess smile faltered.

He marched in, the air around him charged with tension. If he noticed the Taytos and candles and thought there was anything strange about them, he didn't mention it. He was too busy circling the room, looking at the carpet.

I picked up a jug of water and posed like a 50s housewife. "Welcome to Irish night in Vegas," I said. "Tonight, we're having a typical Irish Sunday dinner on a Wednesday night, accompanied by a bottomless cup of tea. The smell of Barry's Tea brewing is the smell of home!"

My sales patter seemed to be falling on deaf ears. Colm was facing the window, seemingly determined not to make eye contact with me. Suddenly, he whipped around.

"Do you trust me?"

"What? Where is that coming from?"

"Yes or no?"

I frowned. "Of course I trust you. Why do you ask?"

"Do you think you know me well enough by now to share your troubles with me?"

"Well, yes." I frowned. "Colm, where are you going with this?"

"Who is Elaine?"

I froze. I racked my brains to think of how Colm could possibly know about Elaine. Nobody knew about that situation except my family and some old friends that Colm didn't know. How was this possible?

"Who is Elaine, Andie?"

I swallowed hard, my mouth suddenly dry. "Why do you ask?"

"You're not answering my question. Who is she? What happened to her?"

"How do you know about her?"

He shook his head. "Why don't you want to tell me about her?"

"There's nothing to tell." I felt the blood drain from my face.

"That's a lie."

"Where the hell is all of this coming from?" I slammed the jug of water onto the table.

Colm ran his hands through his hair. "When I was here yesterday and you went to the bathroom for a shower, I needed a pen and paper for something, so I picked up that battered-looking jotter that's always lying on your dressing table. You had a pen stuck into it, and that's the page it opened at . . ."

Oh God. "You read my diary?"

"I didn't know it was a diary! If I had, I would never have picked it up in the first place! I never dreamed it might be a diary – who even keeps one of those any more?"

"Well, me, for one, obviously! But you didn't just pick it up, did you? You read the damn thing! How could you do that?"

"I didn't mean to! Once it was open, the words on the page just jumped out at me! I swear, I didn't read more than a few lines. But what I saw was enough to tell me loud and clear that you're hiding something from me."

I said nothing.

He sat down on the couch and patted the space beside him. "So how about you tell me about Elaine right now?"

"Stop backing me into a corner! You read my diary, and then you think you have the right to know everything about me?" My voice rose with every word, and the end of my sentence wasn't much more than a squeak.

Colm stood up like a bullet and threw his arms in the air. "This isn't about your stupid diary! I've spent the past while telling you everything – every last little thing – about me and my life. I've never told one single other person the kind of things I told you. I completely opened myself up to you – and then, not only do I find out that there's something you're not telling me, but also that I'm some sort of pet project to you! I thought you wanted to listen to me because you cared about me, but from what I read, you're doing it for your own selfish reasons – to help you through whatever the hell this Elaine situation is. So what happens when you get over it? You'll no longer have any use for me, is that it? Well, you needn't think I'm going to sit around waiting for that to happen!"

"Colm, you have this all wrong –"

"No. What I got wrong was telling you everything in the first place. This is exactly why I kept my business to myself before. You've just proved that I was right to do that. And that's how I'll keep things in the future, too."

He walked towards the door.

"No, Colm! Come back here – we need to talk about this!"

"If you want to talk, tell me about Elaine. Right now."

"I will tell you, but just not now . . . it's a long story . . ."

He shook his head. "Forget it. It's over, Andie."

"No! Don't be ridiculous, Colm! Don't ruin what we have!"

"We have nothing. If we don't have trust and honesty, then we've nothing to build on. I'm just glad I found out now before I let you hurt me even more."

"Colm, don't go! The last thing in the world I would ever want to do is to hurt you – and if you did read my diary, you'd know how crazy I am about you –"

"I told you, I only read a few lines."

"What did you need a pen and paper for anyway?"

He threw his arms up in the air with a furious look on his face. "I had this crazy idea that it might be nice to write you little notes and plant them where you least expect it, just to brighten up your day – in the lid of your lipstick, inside your shoe, places like that. God, I really got all of this so wrong, didn't I?"

"No, you didn't! Oh Colm, that sounds so lovely!"

He crinkled up his face and sneered at me. "'So lovely'? A few seconds ago, you were tearing strips off me for reading your personal information. Well, I'm glad I did – if I hadn't, I'd still be like a sap thinking that you actually gave a crap about me. It doesn't matter now anyway. It's too late. It's gone."

"No, Colm! You can't just walk out when something bad happens in a relationship! You talk it through and you work it out – that's how these things work!"

"And I'd know that if I wasn't such a sad inexperienced twat, is that it? Don't patronise me, Andie. Go and find some other fool to make a project out of, and leave me alone."

He stormed out. After a few stunned seconds had passed I followed him, of course – what else could I do? Let the best thing that had ever happened to me walk out of my life? When he heard the door of my hotel room banging behind me, he whirled around. I ran up the corridor after him. Then, he started to walk back towards me. I halted, every tensed muscle in my entire body relaxing in relief. He was going to give me a chance to explain. Thank God.

He walked right up to me, and I mean right up – our noses were practically touching. I put my arms out to throw them around his neck. The look on his face when I did so was like a slap to the face.

"Don't you dare!" The disgust in his voice followed up the slap to the face with a thump to the side of my head with a blunt object. "Listen to me, and listen well, because this is the last time I'll ever speak to you. Don't ever come near me again. Do you understand me?"

My legs shook. For a few seconds, I actually thought I was going to faint. Nothing had ever scared me so much in my life as the hatred in his voice did right now. It was then I realised that the real Colm, the Colm that had been so hard to find under the façade, was gone. The mask that carried him through his life was back, and he wasn't going to take it off for me or for anyone from now on. I'd blown it.

"I asked you a question," he snarled.

Suddenly, I remembered the days when I'd found Colm vaguely

intimidating. Those days had nothing on how he was now. Tears instantly pricked at the back of my eyes. It was sheer willpower that allowed me to keep it together enough to turn my back on him and walk back to my room. I walked instead of running because some part of my brain had realised, between leaving the room and facing Colm, that I hadn't brought a key out with me. The tears dripped down my face, but I bit my lip and refused to allow a single whimper escape until I was sure Colm was gone – although I wouldn't have been surprised if he could see the trail of tears following me back up the corridor, if he'd been looking – it felt like I had a hose attached to the back of my corneas.

Of course, he wasn't looking. When I reached my hotel room and was forced to turn around, he'd gone. I leaned against the door of my room, slid down it and howled.

Eventually, I managed to pull myself together enough to go down to Reception and get another key for my room. I prayed all the way down that Philippe would be there to get the key for me on the QT, but in keeping with how my day was going, he hadn't started his shift yet. I had to go through the ignominy of explaining my locked-out predicament to a perfectly manicured and coiffed receptionist who just couldn't stop staring at my bulging eyes and violet cheeks.

I eventually got back into my room, where I stared down the barrel of a six-pack of Taytos that I knew would be devoured within the next hour just to get me through the trauma.

I opened my diary and read the words that had caused so much trouble.

Colm has a lot of issues, but I'm making it my mission to guide him through them. I've found that helping him has been helping me get through all the Elaine stuff that's rolling around in my head. Maybe if I can do something for him, it might bring me nearer to closure on Elaine.

Ouch.

Reading over what I'd written again and trying to see it through Colm's eyes, I could see why he was confused. My words actually made me question my own motives. Was he right? Was my anxiousness to help him really a bid to help myself feel better?

I did a lot of thinking over the next few hours, along with a lot of eating, and admitted things to myself that I hadn't dared to go near up until now. Colm *was* right. This was one of those situations where you try to convince yourself that you're doing something for someone else, but you know in your heart and soul that you'll get something from it too . . .

Yes, I loved Colm, and I wanted to do everything I could to make him happy. If encouraging him to share everything that he was carrying around with him would help him find the road to happiness, then of course I would do that. But I hadn't exactly found that path myself, had I? I'd veered off into a wilderness of my own a long time ago, one that ran parallel to the route Colm had been taking. Maybe there was a part of me that felt better about my own problems when I was trying to help someone else with theirs. It made me feel I wasn't alone, but not only that, it stopped me from having to face up to mine. At least Colm now wanted to do something about his, to move on.

A conversation I'd had with Leon decided to pop up in my head to say hello. My face burned with shame as I remembered what we'd said.

"It's been a tough few years."

"In what way?"

I shook my head. "I'm sorry. I don't know why I said that. Forget I mentioned it."

Leon sat back and regarded me speculatively. "Are you sure you don't want to talk about it?"

"No, but I'm sure you don't want to hear me moaning on about stuff I can't change."

"Maybe you can change it, though."

"Trust me, it's a situation I definitely can't change."

"Okay, but maybe you can change how you feel about it. Hey, how about this? Tell me what's bothering you, and I'll give you an outsider's perspective on it."

I frowned. "Why would you want to hear the problems of someone you've just met?"

"I haven't just met a random someone. I've met you. Go on, try me."

And try him I did. I told him everything about the Elaine situation, from start to finish. As I spoke, I couldn't quite believe that I was vocalising the story and the thoughts that had lived inside my head for years and years, mentioned to nobody until now. But that was Leon all over. His easy manner made confiding in him the most natural thing in the world. I'd never even considered sharing any of this with anyone before. It was buried away in my head, because bringing it up made it all real again.

"I don't know who I am any more since all of this happened," I said when I'd eventually finished recounting everything. "The me I knew has disappeared inside of myself."

"Everyone loses their way from time to time," Leon said. "The thing that's important is recognising the need to find your way back, and making sure you take steps to do just that."

"Easier said than done, I'm afraid."

"Tell me one thing. Have you forgiven yourself for all of this?"

I frowned. "So, you agree with me that it's all my fault, then?"

"No, I don't. I'm not assessing who's to blame in the situation you've just told me about. What I'm saying is that it's clear to me that *you* blame yourself for all of this. Am I right?"

I nodded.

"So when are you going to absolve yourself from the guilt you feel?"

"I don't know if I can, Leon . . ."

"Do you think Elaine would want you to be miserable?"

"Well, probably, considering that the last time she saw me, she thought I was getting it on with her boyfriend."

"Friends fall out all the time, then they make up. If she'd lived, would you guys have made up, do you think?"

I had to think about it. "I think we'd probably have had a lot of stuff to work through first – stuff that had been going on for a long time. But eventually, yes, I think we would have made up. For all our arguing, we did really care about each other."

"Well, then, there's your answer. Elaine would want you to move on. Just think about it, Andie. Nobody else can move you on past this point only yourself."

I sat on the bed for countless hours mulling over what I hadn't done. I hadn't taken Leon's advice. I hadn't moved on one centimetre from where I'd been when I sat with him in the bar all those weeks ago. Instead, I'd moved myself physically, chasing him, when what I was looking for could only be found within me. And another thing I hadn't done was that I hadn't been fair to Colm. Every bit of his anger was justified – I had been using his issues to try to make myself feel better. If I'd really wanted to help him, wouldn't telling him my story have let him know better than any other reassuring words that I truly understood where he was coming from? But instead, I'd tried to make myself feel like a bigger person by seeing this as a problem that Colm had, completely blocking out the fact that I was as culpable as he was – I was worse, actually, because at least he was ready to do something about his issues. All of this carry-on from me just rendered my so-called help attempts false and meaningless.

God, this was all a bit much for one night – when I got bursts of clarity, I didn't do them by halves. Good job they happened so rarely. That wasn't much consolation though as I stared at the empty space beside me that grew colder by the minute.

Chapter Thirty-two

I never know what to do with myself in the calm after a storm. It's a horrible period of time that reminds me of waiting in an airport with a hangover for a flight that keeps on getting delayed. I really wanted to do something to make the terrible feeling that was engulfing me just go away, but I couldn't make the plane come any faster, and even if I could, I wouldn't have had the energy to.

Colm had disappeared. We're talking vanished-off-the-face-of-the-planet type of disappeared. And the really frustrating thing was how easy it was for him to do. There was nobody that he felt he needed to keep in touch with on a day-to-day basis, nobody he needed to check in with to assure them he was alive and alright.

After my Think Tank, I called down to Colm's room with a pillow to explain to him that I'd finally woken up to myself, and to apologise (and possibly grovel). If he was in, I knew there wasn't a hope of him answering the door even if I knocked all night, so I was going to sleep up against his bedroom door – he'd be forced to talk to me when he finally left his room. If he was out, he wouldn't be able to get back into his room without waking me (I hoped), at which point he'd be forced to listen to me. I could hear his TV blaring inside the room, but that didn't mean he was in – he'd always leave the TV on when we went out. No amount of pointing out what a waste of electricity that was would change his ways – he did it at home to deter burglars, apparently, but now he was in the habit of doing it wherever he went – and he'd told me he sometimes left it on all night too and could sleep through the noise perfectly fine. I chanced a few loud knocks, but as expected they went unanswered. I settled myself outside his door and prepared myself to wait.

I'd woken up at eight in the morning with a severe crick in my neck, and a temper the size of Mount Everest. He obviously hadn't been out the previous night, so he was in there and just ignoring me. I'd been able to put up with that the night before, but the combination of not being a morning person, sleeping with a block of wood for the night and being woken up several times by loud scenes on Colm's TV had dropped my tolerance several feet below sea level.

I banged and banged on Colm's door until my knuckles bled – which coincided with a man coming out of one of the hotel rooms on the other side of Colm's, with his girlfriend or wife hovering in the background, and eating the head off me for making such a racket. It was alright for him, waltzing out into the corridor with nothing but his boxers on – from the looks of things, his love life was going just fine. The noise from Colm's TV the previous night probably hadn't helped the man's mood though.

I ran down to my own room, collected a book and camped outside Colm's room again. He'd have to leave sooner or later. Besides, I hadn't had much chance to read since I came to Vegas, and now was as good a time as any to catch up. Except I discovered after about two minutes that I couldn't read. No, I hadn't somehow lost the ability to do so, but the combination of passing people and staff staring at me, asking me if I was locked out and just plain laughing at me, proved something of a distraction, not to mention the fact that I was far too engrossed in listening for any signs of movement on the other side of the door to concentrate on more than one line at a time.

After a while – okay, after a couple of hours – it dawned on me that Colm wasn't coming out. Why? Because he wasn't in there. There was no way he'd still be in his room close to ten o'clock. He wasn't happy unless he was up and about doing things before he'd even gone to bed the night before. A cold sensation crept over my entire body as I entertained the notion that he'd stayed out for the night. Where could he have spent the night – or, worse still, with whom? He knew nobody in Vegas, except . . . Lindy. No. Surely he'd never go there, no matter how mad he was with me? But, suddenly, anything seemed possible. He knew how much she got on my goat – what better way to get back at me?

Wild visions of Colm and Lindy together flooded my mind. I almost vomited, and would have, except I hadn't eaten anything since those Taytos the night before. I got up and shuffled my way back to my room. I was almost paralysed with fear at the thought of Colm with someone else. Even if he wasn't with Lindy, who was to say that he hadn't just gone out to a bar, met someone and gone home with her? I hadn't thought it was his style, but maybe I was wrong. It seemed I was wrong about a lot of things recently.

I sat on the bed and hugged my knees to my chest, paralysed by how upset I was. I felt powerless. My initial anger at myself for not being honest with Colm about Elaine turned to disappointment at the way Colm had handled the situation. Yes, I'd messed up big time, but Colm's reaction to it had been a bit excessive too . . . and while I didn't blame him for feeling let down by me, I felt he should have given me a chance to explain my side of the story. If he couldn't do that, what hope would we have ever had? Would he have walked away from us the first time we ran into a roadblock, regardless of what it was?

Once I started questioning everything, I just couldn't stop. Was he really in love with me? Did he just think that he was because we'd been thrown together over here? If he really loved me, wouldn't he have listened to what I had to say before ending things? Wouldn't he have done everything he could to keep us together, instead of breaking it off? Had he just been looking for an excuse to get out of our relationship?

The thing that bothered me the most though was that, for all his talk about facing up to his past and moving on, he'd just brought himself right back to square one by running away again like this. He was really just going around in circles. I hadn't been fully honest by concealing my past issues, but he certainly hadn't either. His weren't the actions of someone who had any intention of moving on. He was just falling back into old, comfortable patterns. Was he always going to do that as soon as life threw something at us?

It was scary to realise that I actually had no idea how Colm was going to handle the situation we found ourselves in. It was even scarier to admit to myself that I wanted to spend the rest of my life with this person whom I barely knew, and who barely knew me. There was very little I knew for a fact any more, but that much was enough. If I knew he felt that too, all of the rest of it could be worked out. But it didn't look like he did feel that way, did it? The first sniff of trouble, and he was out the door and hitching a ride to the moon.

I sat on the bed for so many hours that my bum turned to jelly – it pretty much was jelly anyway with all the eating out I'd been doing since I came to Vegas – but the pins and needles were a sure sign that my body wanted me to get up and actually do something. But what could I actually do that would be in any way constructive? I sighed, and made a mental note to rejiggle the top three on my pet-hate list. Firmly occupying the Number 1 position from now on would be 'Trying to find people'.

I grabbed the phone again and rang Colm's extension, knowing that there'd be no answer. I half-hoped that someone would pick up, because that would at least mean that I'd know that he'd checked out. Okay, so it would present a whole new set of problems relating to where the hell he actually was, but right now I knew absolutely nothing. That thought made me wonder if Reception would tell me if Colm had checked out or not. Philippe would have been able to find that out for me, no bother, but he wasn't working today.

I picked up the phone and dialled Reception. "Hello, could you put me through to Colm Cannon, please? He's a guest at this hotel, but I don't know his extension." The sly approach was probably the best way to go in this instance. If he'd checked out, the receptionist would have to tell me that there was no such guest.

"Andie, is that you?"

Damn it. It was Nicole. She and I had always shared a quick chat whenever I walked past her in Reception since the day I'd received the letter from my unknown number-one fan. As Colm was usually with me whenever I walked past Reception, she now knew him too.

"Ah – yes, it's me."

"Okay – has Colm changed his room or . . .?"

I sighed heavily. "I'm too stressed to even think of a plausible excuse for what I've just asked, so I'm going to tell you the truth. We've been seeing each other, but we had a blazing row last night and now he's vanished."

There was a long silence. "How long have you two been together? And what about Leon?"

"Not long and, as for Leon, he's clearly not interested."

"I see." The disapproval in her tone was obvious, but she reverted into professional mode. "What can I do to help you here?"

"I was wondering if you'd be so good as to see if Colm has checked out. He's been saying all week that he wanted to change his flight and go home today because we had nothing planned to do. I know I shouldn't be asking you to do this, but . . ."

"Just say nothing to anyone about it, okay?"

I heard her tap-tap on her keyboard for about fifteen seconds, then she said, "He hasn't checked out . . . but there's something you should know."

"Oh?"

"I was working overtime last night when Colm walked past. Things were quiet here and he looked really upset, so I called him over and asked if he was okay. He said he wasn't but didn't want to bore me with the details, but he'd be fine soon because he'd be going home to Ireland first thing in the morning and getting away from all the – horseshit, I think he called it – here."

I nodded slowly. It made sense. And while it was far preferable to him spending last night making Lindy squeal with pleasure, it also meant he hadn't cared enough to stay around and sort things out.

"Nicole, thank you so much for being so kind to me."

"My pleasure," she said, but her voice was slightly colder than it had been in the past. She wasn't impressed that I'd been with Colm while the Leon search was going on, that much was clear – but at least she'd had the goodness to tell me what Colm had said, regardless of her disapproval.

I put down the phone and thought about what I'd just heard. Okay, so he hadn't checked out, but those kinds of formalities were never important in Colm's world. It would be just like him to pick up his bag and go, then phone the hotel later when he'd cooled down and instruct them to take his room payment from the credit-card details he'd given at check-in.

So, where did that leave me? My flight wasn't until Tuesday as we hadn't been able to find anything to suit the Éire TV pocket until then. I couldn't spend the time between this and then sitting here thinking about everything.

I willed my legs to flip off the bed and for my feet to meet the carpet. There. That wasn't too hard. I put one foot in front of the other and walked to the window. If I hadn't been on my own all day staring off into space, I would have sworn that someone had injected my legs with lead (the guy in the 70s hotel immediately came to mind as a suspect). I walked to the desk and turned on my laptop, opened a website and pulled out my credit card. Within a few minutes, I'd bought what I was looking for. I ran to the shower, got dressed, then got out my cases and packed like a lunatic. I was just about to leave the room when the phone beside my bed rang. I pounced on it.

"Colm?"

"Andee, it's Philippe. We must talk!"

My heart sank. Much as I loved Philippe, he and his inflections were all I needed now. I'd be on the phone until the end of his shift.

"We must talk!" usually meant he fancied a catch-up call to ask me where things were with Leon or to complain about one of his colleagues who would invariably be sitting right beside him as he spoke.

"I'm sorry, Philippe – can I ring you back later?" And I would – from the airport, to say my farewells to him. Philippe had been nothing but welcoming to me from the day we'd met, and while I would have loved to have said goodbye face to face, I just wasn't able for it while my mind was in such turmoil. I'd end up a crying mess, he'd try to convince me to stay until he lost his voice, and neither of us would be any better off at the end of it. Of course there was always the hazard that I might run into him on my way out.

"No, Andee!"

"I can't talk now, Philippe – I'm really sorry." My voice caught. "Please try to understand," I said tearfully before I put down the phone. I felt awful for hanging up on him, but I had to get away before my sanity packed in.

I threw my room-key on the table with a note to say I was checking out and to charge everything to the credit-card details I gave upon arrival, loaded myself up with my belongings and left.

Chapter Thirty-three

Ten minutes later, I was standing in a queue outside the hotel for a taxi to the airport. I'd had to travel through the hotel and go out a side entrance to avoid being seen by Philippe, which had cost me time – but I would have lost a lot more if he'd seen me leave. My thoughts wandered relentlessly as the queue shuffled forward. The facts that I'd been forced to face over the past while kept slamming from one side of my brain to the other. Some were harder to accept than others.

Fact 1: Leon didn't want to be found.

There, I'd said it. No maybes, no logical reasons or justifications for why he hadn't come forward – he just didn't want to. He didn't want me. End of story.

Fact 2: This wasn't just about finding Leon.

Okay, Fact 2 was ever so slightly harder to admit to myself. Leon was the dream, the utopian way of escaping from all my problems. No conversations about my penchant for flashing my knickers on nights out, no seeing Johnny Meagher's face peeking through my food when I got my Friday fish and chips (fish and chips that are thrown onto paper are on my "Things I love" list – I'm old school about things like that), and most importantly, no proximity to the place where I was responsible for someone else's death.

Fact 3: If I had found Leon, I wouldn't have known what the hell to do with him.

And if I thought 2 was a hard one to swallow, 3 was just plain embarrassing. I couldn't pick up a magazine without reading about how I was dying of heartbreak over my lost love, but if he'd been found, there wouldn't have been a happy ever after. What I'd said to Colm when we'd spoken about Leon summed it up – if Leon had showed up, I would have told him I was in love with someone else. What would have happened then? I suppose we would have had an awkward moment where I would have had to get rid of him as politely as possible, or he would have found some excuse to leave abruptly. Nice.

Fact 4: Fact 3 is because of Colm.

Fact 5: If I lost Colm forever, I didn't think I would be able to bear it.

Which was why I had to get home as soon as possible. Wherever he was, I would find him – I wouldn't rest until I did.

"An-*deeee!*"

The voice from the end of the queue carried on the warm desert air to where I stood, now first in the queue for the next available taxi. Oh God. I whipped my head frantically in the other direction to see if there was any sign of a taxi approaching. Naturally, the lane remained ominously empty.

Philippe ran up to me, his face a picture of indignation. "You are lee-ving Vaygas? But why?"

"I'm not leaving, Philippe. I'm just – taking a trip to – LA, for an interview."

He shook his head so vehemently that it looked like he'd just received an electric shock. "No, you are not going to LA."

"Of course I am!"

"You lie." He said this with the absolute certainty of someone who was convinced they were in the right. "You know why I know you lie? Because I called to see you after I rang you. You didn't answer the door. I was concerned. So I got the key to your room from reception and let myself in –"

"You what? Philippe, I could have been stark naked inside that room for all you knew! That's such a breach of guest privacy –"

"No. You sounded too sad to be naked. Naked is good, no? I thought I would find you in a puddle of crying with the chocolate stains all over your face and clothes, too sad to answer the door to a good friend, but instead, I find a note saying you're leaving. And I say to myself, Philippe, that means she didant even want to say goodbye to you. That was hurtful."

"I did, Philippe, but –"

"No. We will deal with your 'orrible friendship etiquette later. But me, I am a good friend, and that is why I have been trying to find you . . ."

A taxi rounded the corner and stopped in front of me. I lunged for the door, and hurled my hand-luggage into the back seat while the taxi-man put the rest in the boot.

"I'm sorry, Philippe. I really need to go. You've been a wonderful friend, and I'm sorry I have to leave this way. I'll ring you later."

"No! You are not leaving!" Philippe grabbed my arm and tried to pull me way from the taxi.

"I bloody well am! Stop this, Philippe!" I just about managed to shrug him off before yelling "The airport! Quick!" at the driver and throwing myself in beside my bags. I looked up to see Philippe running around the car to get to the front passenger seat. "*Lock the doors! Quick!*" I yelled at the driver, but it was too late.

Philippe was in.

"Throw him out! He's not coming with me!"

"Yes, I am!" Philippe turned to the driver. "I am 'er friend. She does not understand the friendship, but I persist in being 'er friend because I am a caring person."

"You won't change my mind, Philippe! I'm leaving Vegas and that's that!"

The driver looked suitably impassive. "Are we going to the airport or not?"

"You and I are. He's not! Get the hell out, Philippe!"

"No. I am not lee-ving."

And he meant it. Fine – he could have it his way. If he wanted to pay for another taxi back from the airport, that was his business, but I wouldn't be coming back with him. "Let's go to the airport, please."

The driver shrugged, and edged the car forwards.

"*No!* Stop the car, *now!*"

The driver ignored Philippe, and increased his speed.

"You must stay, An-dee! there are things you do not know!"

"Drive!" I hollered at the driver. "Faster!"

"Did you hear me? Don't you want to know what these things are? I will tell you whether you do or not. You must know." He turned to the driver. "I told you to stop the car! It is important!"

The driver drove on as if Philippe had never spoken.

"Are you deaf?" Philippe put his hand on the steering wheel. "You must pull over!"

The driver swerved to the left. "What the hell – let go!"

"Philippe, stop! You'll kill us!"

"And if I do, it will be your fault for not listening to me!"

The driver pulled up abruptly with an almighty screech of the brakes. "Get out of my car, you madman! *Now!*" The driver didn't wait for Philippe's protests, but instead got out of the car, opened Philippe's door, grabbed him by the lapels and hoisted him out onto the side of the road in one fluid movement.

"Stop it! I will sue you for the man'andlement!"

"I'd rather be sued than dead." In a fraction of a second, the driver had ensconced himself behind his seat again and driven off. He shook his head. "This place makes LA look normal."

I had to stifle an erupting giggle as I waved out the window at Philippe, who was running after the car and shouting God only knew what. Had all of that really just happened? What the hell had got into Philippe?

I had to admit, I was curious about what this news of his could have been . . . but then again, he could have just been making that up to get me to stay. He'd romanticised the idea of me finding Leon from day one.

The driver was silent all the way to the airport, but occasionally shook his head and muttered something that sounded undeniably like "Nutcases". I tried not to take offence at the plural. All that mattered was getting my flight home.

I kept expecting a siren to go off as I checked in, flagging to someone somewhere in the city that I was trying to escape, but it passed without event. Bags dispatched, I did a quick 360 and spotted the only free seat in the entire heaving airport, so I dived on it, only to discover when I shifted my bum to make myself comfortable that I was already stuck to the seat. Christ, things were bad when I was the only person in the entire airport who had fallen for the chewing-gum trap. There was undoubtedly some kid watching me from behind a seat somewhere, and laughing his chewing-gum-free ass off. You had to hand it to me – when I did something, I did it properly, but this was taking the whole being-blind-to-what-was-in-front-of-me thing a bit too far.

I looked up, mumbled "Okay, I've learned my lesson – leave me alone!" at the Man in the Sky, and hoped I could get through the rest of my flight-wait unscathed.

I decided to stay where I was – my trousers were ruined now anyway, so no point in standing up and showing them to the entire world until I really had to – and to check my phone. Just to make sure that everything was alright at home, and that there hadn't been an emergency that anyone was trying to contact me about . . . Oh, okay. To see if Colm had contacted me. There, happy now?

Two hours later, I was still there. I had another hour to kill before my flight, but my thoughts were more than enough to keep me occupied, and I had yet to make the journey to my departure gate. Then my peripheral vision picked up on someone walking towards me, but I didn't pay much heed until the person's feet stopped right before me. I shifted my gaze from my phone to the sensible shoes in front of me. They were a flat, brown leather lace-up affair, pristine and unscuffed. Above them was a pair of brown slacks with a perfect crease running down the middle. Higher up, I wasn't surprised to see a beautiful brown cashmere jumper finishing the look to perfection. The head of the lady who wore this outfit with endless aplomb was also groomed with precision. Her make-up was light, with that barely-there effect that took so long to pull off, and gave her skin a glowing appearance. Her short hair was lightly curled, its copper highlights complementing the shade of her foundation. I had no idea who she was, but I couldn't help thinking that someone should snap her up for an ad for make-up aimed at women in their fifties – she was the most stunning-looking woman of that age I'd seen in a long time.

"Can I help you?" I asked when she said nothing.

"Andie, I need to speak to you. It's about Leon."

I resisted the urge to sigh heavily into her face. It was sweet at first when all of these lovely ladies in their fifties came up to me waxing lyrical about how Leon and I were destined to be together, and how they were certain that he was travelling around Europe at the moment looking for me, and it was only a matter of time before someone got in touch with him and let him know that the woman of his dreams was waiting for him back in the States, and we'd live happily ever after yadda yadda yah. But not only was it now very draining, but it was really getting to me how people thought they could just come up to me whenever they felt like it and interrupt whatever it was I happened to be doing at the time to give me their blow-by-blow account of what they thought of the situation. They knew nothing about the shagging situation. If I knew nothing about it and I was slap-bang in the middle of it, how could they assume they knew better than me? And what was worse, in this case, was that I was sure I could detect an Irish accent in her voice. It was barely there, the accent of someone who had lived in the US for a long time, but detectable nonetheless. I'd met a few Irish people over here, and they were the worst of the fifty-somethings. Not only were they willing to tell me in excruciating detail where I'd gone wrong with Leon, but they all had single sons or friends with single sons or divorced sons or reformed alcoholic sons who were looking for a woman, and they'd be more than happy to set me up with them when I got back home, seeing as I wasn't managing my love life very well on my own. Nobody could put you down while trying to make it sound like they were trying to do you a favour quite like your own people.

"I've nothing to say about Leon." I looked back down at her shoes again, not just because I wanted to break eye contact, but because I was vaguely mesmerised by how immaculate they looked. She surely must have just bought them in one of the airport shops while waiting for her flight. I was sure I could even get the smell of new leather if I sniffed hard enough.

"Well, I've plenty to say about him, and I think you should listen."

The tone of her voice shocked me. It was impervious, commanding, and utterly patronising. Something snapped inside me. Who the hell was this woman to tell me to listen to her as she gave out to me? Enough was enough. If this lady had to take the brunt of my anger at all the elderly ladies who were in love with Leon, so be it.

"No. You listen to me." As I listened to myself, I realised that I sounded pretty scary. Good. I stood up for added effect. The lady was as tall as I was, so it didn't really have much impact, but I felt better for it. "I've had it up to here with listening to everyone going on about Leon as if they know him. I'm sick of hearing people say that if I'd done this, that and the other, I'd have found Leon by now. And most of all, I'm sick of people like you coming up to me and telling me what I should and shouldn't do. What makes you think you have the right to approach me – to *interrupt* me – to tell me what you think I should do? Who are you to think your opinion is the one I should follow?"

She looked at me as if I was a bug that had flown into her tea. "Good grief. What did I do to deserve that? I'm not sure what he sees in you."

"And I'm not sure what business my love life is of yours!"

"If you'd give me half a chance, I'd tell you. Perhaps you'd like to leave your anger aside for one moment and listen."

She stared challengingly at me. Something about her demeanour raised my curiosity. I couldn't honestly say she was anything like the grannies I'd met so far. I raised my eyebrows at her to encourage her to go on.

"Do I look familiar to you?"

"No. We definitely haven't met before." She was the type of woman that you'd remember meeting.

"We haven't, but that doesn't mean I couldn't look familiar."

I wasn't sure what she was getting at, but I looked her over again to see if I could make any sense of it. I wondered briefly if she was some former model and was big back in her day – maybe she expected me to know her – but she just didn't seem like someone who would be crass enough to even mention it if she had been.

"I'm afraid you don't."

"That's disappointing. I'd expect someone who is supposedly in love with my son to be able to see the family resemblance."

Her words were like a boulder coming down a hill towards me at speed.

"You're Bridget?"

"Well, you know my name. That's something."

"But you – you don't look like someone who'd turn a hose on someone else." It was all I could think of. I suppose I could have said worse.

"My, it sounds like you and Leon had some strange conversations."

"I'm just shocked, that's all . . ."

"Well, you're not going to stop feeling like that any time soon. Let's get the shocks over and done with. Have you received any nasty letters and emails recently warning you off Leon?"

My stomach lurched at the mention of the letters. I nodded slowly.

"Me. All me."

There was no head-hanging as she said the words. In fact, she looked downright proud of herself.

"Why did you write them? Why is it so important to you that I would stay away from Leon?"

She smiled. "You're getting me to my destination too fast, Andie. This is something I was hoping I could build up to slowly." Her hard-faced look was suddenly replaced by one of sheer vulnerability, almost of devastation. "Could we go somewhere to have a coffee, perhaps?" She walked away without waiting for a reply. She knew I'd follow, much as I was tempted to stay sitting down just to thwart her.

Thankfully, we found a free table in a nearby café within seconds. We didn't order coffee. Whatever this was about, it wasn't about coffee.

"First of all, you shouldn't take my letters personally. I'd have written the same thing to anyone. There was no you involved in this – just a template in my head for any person I would perceive to be a threat to my son's welfare."

"How exactly did you see me as a threat to Leon? All I wanted to do was to be with him." Which was true at the time, if not now.

"You couldn't be with him. Nobody could. Him meeting you made a bad situation a million times worse."

I instantly pictured seven kids huddled together on a couch, watching Leon and the wife he hadn't told me about arguing over the Irish girl who was looking for him.

"Look, if I've broken up a home or something, I apologise, but as far as I knew, Leon was single."

She shook her head. "If only it was something as delightfully simple as a broken home." She looked down at the table and traced circles on it with her index finger. She didn't seem like someone who would ordinarily circle.

"Please, just tell me. Whatever it is, it can't be that bad."

She looked at me with pity. The look was worse than any words, and said more.

"Leon is dying, Andie."

I felt my heart actually clunk. I never knew hearts could do that, but mine did. It clunked until it felt like it was no longer there.

"He's got prostate cancer, and it has spread all over his body. He's only got days to live."

"But . . . but he was fine when we met only a few weeks ago!"

"He wasn't fine. He just put on a good show."

I started to tremble so violently that I must have looked like someone who was using an electric drill on a hole in the road. Leon's mother picked up on it straight away. What was worse was that she looked like she was about to join in but at the last minute she regained control of herself.

"Right, let's go. We're heading to the bar."

I shook my head. "I don't want alcohol."

"Well, I do. You're not the only Irish person around here." She grabbed my elbow and yanked me away before I could say another word.

Chapter Thirty-four

"Vegas was his last big blast. He wanted to say goodbye to the world in style, so he dosed himself up on painkillers and hit the road. I was worried sick about him going on his own, but there was no persuading him to bring friends along – he said he just wanted to please himself, and see where the week took him. As it happened, it took him to you."

I thought back on how Leon looked that night. Certainly not like someone who was sick – or at least, not at first glance. His shaved head suited him, and I never once thought it was for a reason other than style. He was thin, but not painfully so. His suntan had eliminated any traces of a possible pallor. Ironically, he'd looked the picture of health, a walking advertisement for the value of a week in the sun. Maybe it had been the happiness he must have felt at being released from the shackles of his sickness, if only for one week, that had lent him a look of wellbeing.

"I had no idea. We talked for hours, and he never mentioned a thing."

"Why would he? The whole idea of the holiday was to get away from it all. To get away from himself, really. He just wanted to be the person he used to be for the last time, before he got too sick to do so. As it happened, his timing was perfect. A few days after he got home, he took a turn for the worst. And ever since then, he's been suffering horrendously."

"And here am I, drawing attention to him at a time when he needs to be left in peace. If only I'd known . . ."

"Attention isn't the issue. Not many people have even realised it was him. He told nobody about going to Vegas in case his friends insisted on following him there to look after him, so very few people have made the connection at all." Some of her whiskey sloshed over the side of the glass as she slammed it down on the table after a quick gulp.

"Yeah, but he knew, and he had enough on his plate – which, I assume, is why you sent me those letters."

"Yes. That kind of thing isn't my usual style, but I had to do whatever I could to protect my son. I'm sure you think I'm a witch for trying to keep you away from him, all the same."

I shrugged. Now wasn't the time to start throwing insults, or agreeing with them.

"Oh, come on!" she said. "Leon told me you had a bit of fire in your belly."

Or maybe it was. "Yes, a witch is probably a euphemism."

"Good. That's the spirit." She smiled.

I smiled back, then a hush fell on our table as I digested what she'd just told me. My whole world had changed since those brown shoes had come into my line of vision.

On the way to the bar, Bridget had explained that she'd booked into the MGM to find me (as my tenure at the MGM had been mentioned in several interviews – my whereabouts were no secret) and phoned down to Reception to request to be transferred to my room number, whereupon she'd encountered "an extremely loquacious Frenchman" who'd questioned her on who exactly he was putting through to me. Bridget had sensed he was the type of person she'd be better off to have onside rather than off, and had told him she was Leon's mother in the hope that he was aware of my search and would move things along. When I'd refused to speak to Philippe when he phoned my room, he'd told Bridget that I was unavailable at that moment but he would see to it that I'd make myself available. After his bid to stop me leaving had failed, he'd called to Bridget's room and insisted she travel to the airport immediately. It was down to sheer luck – and chewing gum – that I hadn't gone through the departure gates and Bridget had been able to spot me. She'd been certain that her arrival at the airport would be too late, but had felt compelled to try. Funnily enough, asking her how she'd located me had been way down my list of priorities, so she really could have spared herself the bother of relaying her lengthy explanation. All that mattered was the bombshell she'd just dropped.

I had visualised the Leon story ending in many different ways at very different times. When I'd gone looking for him immediately after losing him in the fire drill, I'd indulged myself in ridiculous thoughts of fate bringing us back together. I'd be going up an escalator in one of the hotels when I'd spot him coming down the corresponding one, and he would jump over the handrails and land perfectly on the step below mine, whereupon we'd be consumed with joy at our reunion and commence a bout of feverish kissing. Or I'd put my hand out to press a pedestrian light on the Strip, only for him to reach out at exactly the same time, at which point we'd fall into each other's arms and celebrate our reunion right there and then on the Strip. That kind of Hollywood nonsense.

After we launched the search for Leon, it was inevitable that I'd engage in idle daydreaming about what would happen after he'd been located – but, as time moved on, I'd accepted that the most likely scenario would be that he wouldn't be found. I'd go back to my life, he'd get on with his, wherever it was. All of this would be an anecdote that would be brought up at dinner parties in years to come. Never in a million years could I have envisaged this outcome.

I broke the silence. "I can understand now why he never made any attempt to contact me. I'd imagine the last thing on his mind was me when he has such a huge health issue to contend with."

Yes, I was digging. I wasn't lying when I said that I understood why he hadn't contacted me, but I wanted to hear more of the story.

Had he thought I was a nutcase for having even tried? If he hadn't been sick, did Bridget think he would have been interested, or would I have just been making a fool of myself one way or the other? I willed Bridget to say something – anything that would give me an indication of how Leon had felt about the whole thing. But she didn't. She stared at the table instead.

I exhaled slowly, feeling frustrated at the lack of information. But something more urgent was gnawing away at me too.

"Bridget, why exactly did you come here today?"

She raised her eyes to meet mine, then dropped them again.

"It wasn't for my sake. You didn't come here to explain to me why Leon hadn't contacted me, surely? Why would you go to all the effort to leave your dying son for the sake of someone who means nothing to you? You wouldn't. So that only leaves one possibility. You need me for something. Am I right?"

She didn't look up as she nodded. When she spoke, it was to the rim of her glass.

"I told him to forget about you. When he saw you on TV, he'd just had his latest round of treatment. It hadn't gone well. He was in agony, and it was all for nothing – it hadn't worked. It had been his final hope, and now, there was none. Just when he was at his lowest point, you were beamed into our living room. It didn't take long for me to piece the story together."

"And you weren't too happy about it . . ."

"I wasn't. The last thing he needed was a reminder of what could have been when he knew he had only weeks to live. I wanted his last few weeks to be as comfortable as possible."

"Bridget, I hope you're not telling me that you stopped Leon from contacting me if that was what he wanted?"

"No, no, no – absolutely not!" Back to the annoyed look. "The lack of contact was his decision. He said the time you spent together in Vegas was really something special, but he couldn't bear having your memory of that tainted by seeing him as he is now. He was talking about you as if he'd met the woman he would marry in other circumstances."

"Really?"

"Yes. He was heavily drugged at the time – he wouldn't have told me anything otherwise, you know how lads are – but he seemed pretty adamant that in another world, you would have been the one. How you can know that after only one night, I don't know, but it must have been one hell of a good night." She looked at me as if she was wondering what sort of wild sex acts I had performed on her innocent son. "Before you say anything, he knew it was unfair on you. He said plenty of times that you'd be wondering why he hadn't gotten in touch, after you'd gone to the ends of the earth trying to find ways to find him. He thought about ringing you and explaining the situation to you, but he was terrified that if the story got out, he'd have a camp of reporters and cameramen on our doorstep. He needed to be left to die in peace." Her voice wobbled a bit as she said the world 'die'. "But he never forgot you, and never stopped watching the coverage of you on TV."

"What did he think of it?" I braced myself for something I wouldn't like.

"He thought it was gas. He said it was typically 'you' stuff."

Phew! "He knows me well."

"So he says. And he was delighted for you when you became the Face of People Search. He knew that a job like that was a real coup for your profile."

Hmm. Lindy would have loved to have heard something like that. "But what's changed? Has he decided he wants to see me now, after all?"

"No. I've decided he wants to see you. Or rather, he needs to see you."

She ordered two more drinks from the hovering barman with a nod of her head and a flick of her wrist towards our glasses. He seemed very interested in our conversation, the nosy git.

"Andie, you cannot fathom how much pain Leon is in. Once the edge wears off the painkillers, he's howling. Our doctor said Leon should have died weeks ago. And yet, he's still here, still fighting every day. Do you have any idea why?"

I didn't dare say anything.

"He can't let go of you. Mentally, he's holding on for you. He doesn't want you to see him as he is now, but he can't let himself die either because of you. And that's why I'm here. That's why I've sacrificed precious minutes away from his bedside to come here, that's why I've practically given people Chinese burns today to get them to tell me where you were, and that's why I'm sitting here in the airport with you now with another round of alcohol on the way. You can't take that flight home, Andie. My job now is to persuade you to stay, no matter what I have to do to get you to agree to it. I know it's a big ask, but please stay. Just give me the chance to persuade you."

"No." I stood up.

"Ah, Andie!" She suddenly sounded a lot more Irish-mammy-esque. "Will you at least think about –"

"If Leon needs me, the last thing I'm doing is spending another minute here drinking. Quick, let's go. Take me to him."

Bridget instantly charged from her seat, grabbed my arm and led me away, as if she was terrified that I'd change my mind. I suddenly saw a glimpse of the woman who went mad with the hose pipe – she definitely had a manic edge to her.

I tried to force all thoughts of Colm (and my already checked-in baggage no doubt winging its way to Ireland) out of my head as I booked a flight from Vegas to Phoenix.

Chapter Thirty-five

The flight seemed to pass on fast forward, and Bridget drove like a rally driver from Phoenix Airport to her home, with me praying that all the whiskey had left her system. Along the way, she explained that Leon had lived in New York for the past ten years, but had moved home when he discovered he had cancer and had put his New York home up for sale. As we pulled up to Bridget's house, I couldn't help but admire it, inappropriate and all as house-spotting was at this time. When I thought about houses in Arizona (which wasn't very often, or ever, before I met Leon), crumbling brickwork and arid gardens came to mind, surrounded by thirsty land that stretched into infinity, and looking progressively more parched the further away it was from the only house in a ten-mile stretch. In contrast, Leon's parents lived in a gigantic, sprawling detached house relatively close to Phoenix, surrounded by other houses dotted on the landscape in a haphazard fashion.

As we got out, I fought between the urge to throw myself in the front door and get this over with and the much more pressing need to find something, anything, else to do rather than go inside. I spotted some flowers. They'd do.

"Are they . . . begonias?"

Bridget looked in the direction of what was evidently a much-loved and tended-to flowerbed, even in these difficult times, then looked back at me with the appropriate level of contempt that my comment deserved.

"Those are roses, Andie."

"Ah. Yeah. They are, aren't they?"

Her face softened as she sussed my game. "You've made it this far. You can go the rest of the way, surely?"

I hoped I could. But the fact was, the man I'd spent so long obsessing about had been dying behind the walls of this house, while I'd been falling in love with the cameraman who'd been dispatched to capture our reunion. The whole thing had been a complete sham, and I felt like I'd been making a mockery of a dying man.

I took a deep breath, and braced myself for the worst. I hadn't seen a dying person in a very long time. I'd seen a dead person, of course, but . . . No, now wasn't the time to think about that.

I tried to imagine what lay ahead. The Leon that I knew was so full of vitality that it hurt to even dilute his presence in my head. I dreaded seeing the ravages of the disease on him in reality as Bridget led me through the front door into a wide, gleaming hall. I shook my head at the sight of it – somehow, I had known that Bridget's house would be immaculate, regardless of the awful situation she found herself in – but I shook it in a good way. I almost felt affectionate towards her, even though she had such obvious potential to be a total cow – but our shared troubles were bonding us together, however briefly, and she suddenly felt like an old friend as she guided me on my wobbling legs down the hall. Although, I wasn't sure if an old friend would manhandle me as if they were steering a rickety old wheelbarrow, but now wasn't the time or the place to bring that up.

I'd expected Leon to be in bed somewhere off the hall, and was building myself up to entering a dark musty room when he just suddenly appeared in front of me. A man who could only have been Leon's father had pushed him out of what must have been the sitting room into the corridor. Yes, pushed him. It came as a shock, although I should have expected it. But any surprise I was feeling was nothing compared to what registered on Leon's face as he looked up at me from his wheelchair.

"Andie! Jesus Christ!" He looked at Bridget.

She was smiling confidently, not a hint of worry on her face about her decision to bring me here.

"You should know Andie well enough by now to know she won't let you away with that Jesus Christ comment," Bridget laughed, as if me turning up in Leon's hall in his last days on earth was the most normal thing in the world. "It won't have escaped her notice that it's a very Irish thing to say."

"You might let me away with my Plastic Paddy ways just this once, Andie. I'm a bit under the weather at the moment . . ."

"Just this once, so. And besides, it's nice to hear your Irish streak coming out. All you need now is a big thick accent, and you're there." I was surprised at how casual I sounded.

"I've been trying to help him out with that for years," said his dad in an accent so thick he needed to hang cards around his neck to communicate effectively. I knew his name was Liam, but it didn't seem like a great time to introduce myself. Besides, it wasn't as if he didn't know who I was, after the past few weeks.

"Any idea what he just said there?" Leon asked me. "You might let me know if you do." He threw back his head and laughed uproariously.

I could only manage a screechy, nervous giggle in response. This was going far too well.

"Okay, time to address the elephant in the room and all that," Bridget announced importantly in what could only be described as a state-of-the-nation tone. "Leon, I know you didn't want Andie to see you like this, but we've all had to accept that you're dying, and you've accepted it yourself. Now, we need to give Andie the opportunity to accept it too. I didn't bring up any son of mine to be the type who doesn't finish what he starts . . ."

"You only have one son," Leon interjected. "Or are you about to spring someone else on me now? Or even wheel me onto the set of *This Is Your Life*? And yes, Andie, I was forced to watch that shit too growing up!"

"And if you'd let her go back home without saying goodbye to her, you would have regretted it. It's only fair and right that you swallow your pride and let this woman see you before you pop your clogs."

"Bridget! Good God!" I couldn't help it – the words flew out, as my words are prone to do.

"Why are you both so taken with profanities?" Bridget shook her head. "Well met," she said to her husband.

"Mom doesn't do sugarcoating," Leon said to me. "You'll get used to it sometime around the time she'll pass you the brochure for the best coffins over dessert. I'm toast, and I know it. Apparently, you had to know it too."

I took a nervous breath. "I hope you're not angry at us – at me – for coming here and –"

He waved away the rest of my sentence. "No. It's . . . pretty damn amazing to see you again. In the flesh, I mean. I've seen plenty of you on TV."

"In every sense," Bridget said. I hoped she was referring to the horrible knickers pictures that had surfaced on some awful entertainment show, and not something else that I wasn't aware of . . .

"Hey, quit it, Mom. And when I said I wasn't mad, that was addressed to Andie. You are a whole different story. I'll deal with you later."

"I did the right thing, and we both know it. You, my darling, don't have time left to be faffing about when it comes to making decisions."

I threw Bridget another horrified look, but Leon just smiled at me. "The terrible thing is, she's right. And I don't have much energy for arguments these days, so I'm not exactly a formidable adversary."

I smiled politely, trying to get my head around the dynamics of this family. Liam just stood there, periodically staring up at the ceiling and frowning at it when he spotted cracks or cobwebs (or possibly nothing – since he was looking over my head, this was pure speculation on my part). Leon and Bridget seemed to have decided that the best coping strategy was to make light of it all, while I . . . well, I was tempted to make enquiries about where they'd bought their rather elaborate coat-stand, just to keep the conversation flowing.

Thankfully, Leon stopped me from saying anything too stupid about coat-stands, or the various other silence-fillers I'd spotted and was about to pounce on.

"So, are you shocked?"

"Not as much as I thought I would be. You look – fairly okay, actually!"

"And you lie quite well."

"No, you look much better than I'd expected, if I'm being honest."

"Would I make a good poster boy for the sick and dying?"

"You'd be about as good as they'd get, I'd say."

"Again, I can see why you two got on so well," Bridget said wryly.

"Do you want to come into my room, before these two relics drive you mad?" said Leon. He raised an eyebrow over his shoulder at his father who grinned back at him.

"Yes, go ahead," said Bridget. "I'll leave out some drinks and sandwiches on the kitchen table – Andie, pop out in about ten minutes, and they'll be ready."

Liam wheeled him off to his room. I followed obediently. What lay ahead was the last thing I expected. I'm ashamed to admit to yet another clichéd expectation related to the sick and dying – this time, the Bedroom of the Dying Person – but I honestly had expected drawn, heavy curtains, dank air, a musty smell, and a low bed with a bedpan and bucket beside it. Leon's room was a sunburst of almost blinding light, with one wall entirely made of glass. The nearest curtain to this room was back at home with Isolde, and so it should have been. The wall of glass opened onto a glorious garden, full of cherry-blossom trees with petals dancing in the air, sturdy ash trees, and the obligatory palm trees. The entire garden was framed by rows of uniformly planted foliage that I suspected were orange trees, and was dotted at its corner points with silk-floss plants.

"This is why I never bring women in here," Leon said to his dad. "They just ignore me, and zone in on the garden instead."

"Back home, we call this a football pitch. Wow." It was a suitable garden for this abode, though. Everything about the house screamed luxury.

I looked around the room. Leon's bed was a huge mass of white pillows and a pristine duvet cover – wholly unlike any of my hospital-bed scenarios. I felt like whipping my sunglasses out of my bag as I took it all in.

My eyes fell on his overflowing bookshelves. "Oh, you're a fan of Daniel Larch too!" I walked over to his extensive collection of Daniel Larch books. It looked like he even had copies in different languages. I guess Leon also spoke Spanish, German and French, then. Wow.

"I'm a big reader. Care to go outside?"

I nodded. Liam slid a pane of glass back, and wheeled Leon onto grass that had evidently been freshly cut only that morning.

Liam muttered something completely incomprehensible, then went back inside. "Gone to help Mom," Leon said by way of explanation. "Aka, giving us some space."

I pulled out a seat from a set of patio furniture, and brought it over beside Leon's wheelchair. "Probably not a bad idea. We should really talk about this whole thing."

"Probably. You first."

"Why me?"

"Oh, come on. Don't make me pull out my 'I'm dying' card!"

I must have looked suitably horrified, because he instantly changed tack.

"Oh, don't mind me and my warped sense of so-called humour. It's just my way of getting through this. How about we start by me telling you how I'm thinking? Let's face it, I could pop off at any minute, so time is of the essence."

He looked exhausted before he even got into it. He took a long, shaky breath.

"My first reaction is: total mortification. I'm mortified that you're seeing me like this." I opened my mouth to refute his words, but he held his hands up. "No. Don't tell me I'm looking really well. I'm clearly not. I'm in a wheelchair. I've lost three stone in three weeks. I've already got the pallor of a dead person, with the chalky skin and the black bags under my eyes. And now I feel like a woman for saying something so totally girly like that – and here was I, thinking I was mortified before!"

I had to laugh as a blush coloured his face. "Well hey, that's one way to get rid of the pallor issue," I said. "Every cloud and all that . . ."

"Yep. But let's be honest – I'm not the person you met a few weeks ago. And I didn't want you to meet this new person. Can you understand why? Or do I have to embarrass myself any further?"

"I understand." And I totally did. He thought my illusion of the Leon I'd met had been shattered. He was worried now that I was looking at him as a sick and dying person, and I'd no longer be attracted to him the way I was in Vegas.

"Phew. That's good, because I think I've reached my redness-in-the-face quota for one day. But, now that you're here, I have to admit that it's pretty nice . . . you have no idea, none whatsoever, of how the thoughts of you kept me going in the worst of times . . . but I was too afraid to let you become anything more than a thought. After we were separated in the fire alarm, I was so sick from the drink as soon as I went outside and air hit me – and that was when I realised that no matter how much I wanted to, there was no way I was able to stay on my feet any longer, still less spend any more time with you even if we had met up again. I went back to my room in the Tropicana hotel and spent the night being sick. Maybe the fire alarm was a blessing – I would have been so embarrassed if you'd seen me in that condition. So you can understand that the reality of having you here, seeing me like this, wasn't one I could even consider. But now, it's done, you've seen me in my infirm state, and I'm still alive. That's a big achievement for me, these days."

"So, you don't regret your mom bringing me here?"

"No. I would never, ever have asked you here – but now that you're here, I know that she did the right thing. Thank God for the people who know us better than we know ourselves, sometimes."

As soon as he finished his sentence, Leon's face contorted in pain.

"What's up?" I said. "Can I get you anything?"

He waved his hand, and closed his eyes. "It'll pass."

I felt like time stood still as I sat there watching him struggling with the pain. My overriding feeling was one of complete uselessness as I watched the battle waged between him and the disease.

"Can you get me some water?"

"Sure." I bounced out of my seat, glad to be able to do something constructive. And, if I'm totally honest, I was glad to move away from his pain too. I just didn't know how to handle it.

It seemed I wasn't the only one. I walked into the kitchen to find Bridget face down on the kitchen table, crying her eyes out. Liam sat beside her, murmuring incomprehensible words of comfort, but looking like he'd prefer to join in. There wasn't a sandwich in sight. I tried to make myself scarce as I tiptoed to the sink to get the water, but Bridget and Liam were so immersed in their grief for what could have been, and what was to come, that they didn't even look up as I scuttled past them. Truth be told, I was half hoping they'd pull up a chair for me as I returned to Leon with the water, dreading the second when I'd have to resume watching this beautiful man die before my eyes.

Chapter Thirty-six

"So, have you forgiven yourself?"

He caught me completely unawares. I walked back with his glass of water, expecting him to be slumped in the chair and exhausted. Instead, he was sitting upright, looking alert, and ready for answers. I didn't need to ask him to clarify his question. I knew exactly what he was referring to.

"I thought I had. But no. I haven't."

"Andie." He shook his head. "If I could get out of this chair and kick your butt, I would. What happened? After all our talk in Vegas, I really thought you were going to try to move on . . ."

"I did try, but in completely the wrong way . . . I tried to help someone else with a problem they had, and it went totally, totally wrong . . . oh, Leon, I've made such a huge mess of everything."

Then I shut up, realising how whiney I must sound to someone who had a hell of a lot more to worry about than I did.

"Well, come on. You can't leave it at that."

"You don't want to hear it . . ."

"Look, I haven't much time left, madam, as you well know. Don't make me wait for information."

"But . . ."

"No. You can't argue with that. It's a dying person's prerogative to press home their advantage when needs be – you just know it'll work – evil, yes, I know, but tough. Spit it out."

I took a few seconds to try to formulate the best way to tell the man I'd told the whole world I was in love with about how I'd tried to solve the problems of a guy I actually was in love with while really trying to solve my own. It was a tricky one.

As I told him how I'd gone to such great pains to get through to Colm and help him through what was eating him up, I tried so hard to keep any feeling for Colm absolutely out of my words.

"You're crazy about him." It wasn't even a question.

Of course he must have seen Colm and me together at the Leon Line-up and the reward dinner. He wouldn't have known who Colm was at the time, but had he now joined the dots? I cringed at the thought. How awful for him.

There was nothing I could say.

"But that's neither here nor there," he went on. "You're still running away from your past, Andie. When are you going to deal with it?"

I shook my head. "I just don't know."

"I do. You're not. You're going to put the rest of your life on hold while this thing eats you up. You'll waste all the potential you have to really get where you want to be in life, because you're so busy dragging around a sack of shit with you and it's slowing you down. We've been through this before. It's weeks later, and you've done nothing about it."

"Hey, where has the Leon I knew gone to?"

"I gave you a sympathetic ear in Vegas, and then gave you my advice on the situation. Clearly, my advice meant nothing to you, as you haven't acted on it. So I'm sure you can guess what kind of message that gives me . . . you mustn't have respected my opinion much."

"That's not true! I thought the world of you . . . I still do . . ."

"Please, Andie. Don't say things like that – they're not true. You know, since I first saw you on TV looking for me, I've done a lot of thinking about what it was about me, about us, that made you go on this hunt. Yes, we got on great, we really clicked, we had something special – but was that enough for you to go on a global hunt for me? Or were you doing it for another reason? And the more I thought about it, the clearer it became that this was never about me. It was about you, and how I made you feel about your problem. Well, this time next week, Andie, I probably won't be here. So you'd better work out pretty damn fast how to be at peace with yourself. Nobody can save you from yourself only you." He looked up at a clock on the wall. "Thanks for coming. It was good to see you again . . . and to get some closure."

He was kicking me out. It felt like a physical blow.

"Leon, please . . ."

"My mom will sort out your transport back to Vegas. Take care, Andie, and thanks for coming to say goodbye. I wish you well – and I hope you get your closure, too."

With great difficulty, he manoeuvred his wheelchair so that he turned his back to me. Of course, I could have undone all of his hard work in two seconds by simply walking around the wheelchair and making him face me, but we both knew I wouldn't do that.

"Thank you, Leon."

"You've nothing to thank me for. Whatever I did to try to help you didn't work. You should go now."

I nodded, but of course, he couldn't see that. He was too busy staring straight ahead into the depths of the garden, steadfastly avoiding looking at me. His disappointment in me, his disapproval of my ability to waste opportunities when there were none left to him, seeped from him.

He was right. It was time for me to go.

Chapter Thirty-seven

That was the last time I ever saw Leon. After Leon's dismissal of me, Liam kindly dropped me to a train station to get a train to the airport. I scribbled my mobile number on a piece of paper and handed it to him before I bade him goodbye, asking him if he'd be kind enough to keep me updated on how Leon was. He nodded, and then tried to press several hundred dollars into my hand to cover my expenses. After a lengthy discussion, I eventually convinced him that I wasn't willing to take a single dollar of it, but the sentiment alone meant a lot to me.

I returned to the MGM after I touched down in Vegas, not knowing what else to do with myself. I couldn't face another flight, especially a transatlantic one, after what I'd just found out. Nicole was on the reception desk when I arrived. I tried to book in again, only to find that there was no record of me having checked out despite me leaving a note saying I wanted to do just that. Not only that, but Nicole informed me that Philippe had "found" the key to my room, which she said I must have lost, on the floor near Reception and had left it in an envelope for me to collect. She asked no questions and acted as if we'd just had a perfectly rational conversation instead of one full of glaring inconsistencies. I could only conclude that Philippe had kept the option of my room open in the hope that Bridget would catch up with me and I would need a place to stay if a meeting with Leon was to take place in Vegas – although why Philippe would do that for me after how I'd refused to listen to him, I didn't know. I asked Nicole for a pen, paper and an envelope, wrote a grovelling apology to Philippe for my behaviour mingled with copious references to how appreciative I was of him, and asked her to pass it on to him.

The shops in the MGM were thankfully still open, so I did a quick tour around the hotel and bought the things I'd need to keep me going now that my luggage was Dublin-bound without me. I fell into a coma-esque sleep as soon as I entered my room, a sleep that kept me sheltered from the world for a good fourteen hours. When I awoke, I saw a missed call on my mobile from a number I didn't recognise. I'd obviously slept through the call in my exhaustion. I dialled the number for voicemail. Bridget had left a message, saying that Leon had passed away in his sleep during the night.

For the first few seconds, I felt a glorious numbness, and I thought I would be okay. All the way back from Arizona, I had tried to make myself accept the fact that Leon was going to die, and soon. Admittedly, it had happened sooner than I expected, but at least his pain was over.

Those few seconds passed fast, and were soon obliterated by a yawning chasm of time that I felt I was never, ever going to escape from for the rest of my life. Facts started to hit me in the face, coming so fast and so hard that it felt like a tennis-ball machine had been given drugs and aimed right in my direction. You went to see Leon, and he died right afterwards. *Pow!* He was in good form when he first saw you, but you upset him so much that he couldn't bear to look at you. *Bam!* You didn't do what you promised him you would do – and he was rightly disgusted with you for it. *Boom!* My head was like an episode of *Batman*. And then, just to completely finish me off, another tennis ball hit me just when I thought the machine had been turned off. And Colm doesn't want anything to do with you either. *Bang!* He still hadn't contacted me. Maybe he would when word got out about Leon's death, just to do the honourable thing, but that wouldn't be good enough. It shouldn't take a death for him to get in contact.

I dialled Bridget's landline number. Liam answered with a grunt that might have been "Hello".

"Liam, it's Andie. I'm so sorry. How . . . I mean, he seemed okay when I was there . . . did he take a turn after I left?"

"No, he was in great form all evening," Liam said slowly – which was how I knew what he was saying at all. "Your visit must have buoyed his spirits. I hadn't seen him that content in a long time. He spent a few hours on his laptop, then watched some TV with us before he went to bed. Then Bridget went to check on him in the middle of the night, as she always does, and . . . he was gone." He cleared his throat. "It seemed that he hadn't been in any distress. He just slipped away."

I had no idea what to say when Liam finished speaking. "How is Bridget?" was all I could think of.

"She's in a bad way, but happy that he went peacefully at the same time. The doctor gave her something to help her sleep." He paused. "She's so grateful to you. If you hadn't come to see Leon with her, he would have gone to his grave unhappy."

"It's me who should be grateful, Liam." And I was. Not only for Leon's love, but also for Liam's words.

"Andie . . . have you seen the news today?"

"The news? No." For a few seconds, I couldn't for the life of me work out why Liam was bothered asking me such a question at a time like this. But then my preoccupied brain kicked into gear just as Liam spoke again.

"There's been another development."

I didn't like Liam's tone. This was bad. "Yes?" I could hear the nerves in my voice in that one-syllable word.

"The word is out here that our Leon is . . . was . . . your Leon."

"What? How?" I hadn't told a soul what I'd found out about Leon.

"From what we've pieced together, someone recognised my wife with you in the airport and identified her."

I shoved the phone closer to my ear as I strained to decipher his words. "Bridget has a very high-profile job in a government department. She's often called on to do interviews on TV while representing her department." In contrast to Liam's mumbling voice, Bridget's was crystal clear, and I could easily see a woman as confident as her speaking articulately on behalf of the government. "The person who recognised her must have known who you were too, and contacted someone in the media about it."

The face of the barman who was eavesdropping on my conversation with Bridget instantly flashed into my mind.

"She got a call from someone late last night, some journalist, asking her why her son had been hiding away from you. Not asking if he was the right Leon – they just assumed, hoping they'd catch her off the hop. She said she hadn't a clue what they were talking about and hung up, but it wasn't enough to throw the journalist off track. There's a big write-up in one of the papers today about how they've found the right Leon at last – and the story is even bigger now because Leon's mother happens to be a public figure."

"Oh, good Lord."

"Yes. Of course, all of this was before he . . ." Liam couldn't bring himself to say 'died'.

I was glad. I wouldn't have been able to hold it together if I heard that word again.

"Do they know about . . . ?"

"The media? Not yet. It won't be long before they do, though. Some of them have just set up camp outside our house to try to interview Leon. They'll soon work out what's happened with all the comings and goings here."

Oh my God. This was so much worse than I could ever have imagined. "Liam, I'm so sorry to have dragged you into this mess of a situation."

There was a pause, but he eventually said, "Sure how could you have known things would work out this way?"

"I'm sure you and Bridget never want to see me again . . ."

"Don't be daft. We actually want to ask you to come back down here again today. The funeral will be on Sunday, and Bridget wants as many of Leon's friends and family around as possible between now and then."

"Liam, I wouldn't dream of imposing myself on you at a time like this."

"You'd be helping." He lowered his voice. "Bridget needs everyone to rally around her now. She has it in her head that she wants you here because of what you meant to Leon, and she's always like a hen with an egg if her plans don't work out. You don't have to stay here if you're not comfortable with that – I'll pay for a hotel for you, and your travel expenses, of course . . . but just having you around the house tomorrow would help her. It'd help me too – I'll only have to listen to her if she doesn't get her way." He forced a chuckle out.

"If I'd be helping, Liam, then of course I'll come – but I won't hear of you paying for anything. I'll go now and sort out a flight and hotel online, and I'll ring you back with the details."

Thirty minutes of laptop-pottering later, I'd booked a flight to Phoenix that would leave in three hours' time, a hotel to stay in that night and the following night and a hire car to get me from the hotel to Leon's house. I rang Liam back to let him know I'd be at their house the next day at midday. I just couldn't face going around to Leon's house tonight – it was too soon. By tomorrow, I'd surely have pulled myself together a bit more.

Once I'd sorted everything out and had nothing immediate to focus my mind on, the sense of loss devastated me. I turned on the TV, dreading what I would see but powerless to stop myself. Sure enough, on the LVTV ticker was: '*Mysterious Leon believed to be government minister's son.*' That ticker was about to go on fire very soon when the parasites found out the rest of the story.

At a loss for anything else to do to kill the time until my flight, I packed my carry-on bag and left the hotel to go to the airport early. Guilt would eat me up unless I kept moving and tried to keep myself busy. Although Liam's words had helped, I couldn't stop

313

feeling in the wrong for keeping Leon alive longer than he should have been, then breaking his heart and killing him. By anyone's standards, I had really knocked the ball out of the park this time.

While I was waiting for my flight in the airport, I sent Isolde a text informing her of Leon's death. About a minute after I sent my text, she replied.

Ring me straight away.

The familiar fear rippled through me. What now?

I selected Isolde's number on my mobile and pressed the call button. My heart thumped as I waited for her to answer.

"Yeah."

"Hi, Isolde, it's Andie. You asked me to ring."

"Yes, I know I did. I don't need you to tell me that."

"Em . . . what can I do for you?"

"Nothing. Not much new about that, is there?"

I had no clue where this was going. "So . . . why are we talking right now?"

"I wanted to pass on my condolences to you on Leon's death, of course. I'm sure it must be hard on you."

"Oh . . . em . . . thanks, Isolde. I appreciate that." Well, that certainly wasn't what I'd been expecting.

"You don't have to sound so shocked, you know. I am human."

News to me. "Em . . . yeah, I know . . . I'm just kinda . . . shocked in general, and a bit out of sorts." I knew Isolde knew a fudge when she heard one, but hopefully she'd let it pass this time, given the circumstances.

"Yes, it's an unexpected climax to the story," Isolde said. "Personally, I thought he'd been hiding out until you gave up – that's what everyone thought."

"Yeah." I was too depressed to challenge her on that, or to defend myself. The little things like that didn't seem to matter now anyway. I silently prayed that Isolde would hang up now, her good deed for the decade done.

"I also rang because I can do something for you. It might help to ease the pain of Leon's death somewhat. I don't know if you deserve it after the carry-on you put me through over Martin, but I'm a generous person."

I stifled a snort. "Oh?"

"That was where you should have said 'You are, you are indeed, Isolde.' I'm not sure I want to help you now." She made a strange sound that I'd never heard from her before. It sounded like a very small, very short, *normal* laugh. Not her usual patronising cackle, but a genuine, empathetic laugh.

Now I was really confused.

"I got a call earlier today. It was from someone you know."

Long pause. She seemed determined to drag this out as much as possible. I obliged with an "Oh?" when it didn't seem like she was going to continue without one.

"Yes. The cameraman rang me for a chat. Any idea what he might have wanted to chat about?"

"No!" Colm rang Isolde? If I thought my heart was thumping before, it was nothing compared to the golf-ball-in-a-washing-machine feeling I had now.

"You. He talked about you non-stop. I hadn't taken him for the talking type, but I couldn't shut him up."

"What did he say?"

"He was mostly repeating what he'd said in an email he'd sent me –."

"He emailed you?"

Isolde sighed. "Will you let me finish?" said the woman who had been waiting for me to feed her lines only a few seconds ago.

"Yes, he emailed me yesterday saying it was all his fault that you set your brother on me. He took total responsibility for the invasion into my life, the stress you caused me, the downright trauma . . ."

A busload of Rottweilers being released into Isolde's back garden while she was sunbathing in a bikini wouldn't traumatise Isolde. Talk about hamming it up. I knew that saying nothing would be a wise move, though.

"And he begged me not to let it cost you your job. Then he rang and begged again. I could tell it was killing him to do it, though. He must really like you."

I was stunned into silence. My heart started to beat faster again, but this time it was out of excitement.

"I'm telling you this for a few different reasons. Number one – I owe you. The sales of *Vicious Voice* have been phenomenal since we started looking for Leon. Number two – I may be a tough bitch – actually, no, there's no may about it – I *am* a tough bitch – but I'm not a heartless one. If I can help two people to get together and be happy, then I will. And number three – you won't like this one – you are absolutely useless with men, from what I've seen in the time I've known you. I'm afraid you'll let a good man slip through your fingers – even if he is an interfering one with an overactive imagination. He seems okay apart from that. So if you can't see what's right under your nose, then you need someone to hang a banner from a helicopter for you. I'm not wasting my money on something like that, so that's why I asked you to ring me. Number three isn't entirely altruistic, if I'm honest . . . if you're a happier person, you'll work better. Plus, I'm sick to the back teeth of looking at your long face every Monday morning."

"Can I just check I have this right, Isolde – Colm emailed you yesterday, then rang you today?"

"You remembered two consecutive pieces of information correctly, Appleton. Impressive."

I started to giggle nervously. Colm had faced the wrath of Isolde for me! Surely that could only mean very good things for us – that he'd forgiven me – and although I felt guilty for feeling a twang of happiness when Leon had just died, I couldn't help it. It didn't mean that the pain of his death hurt any less. But it did give me hope for the future at a time when I'd thought I had none.

"Did Colm say where he was ringing from?"

"Of course not. Do you usually start your conversations with 'I'm ringing from Vegas, Isolde?' What are you getting at – is he not in Vegas or something?"

"No. He's gone missing. I think he might have taken a flight home. We had a row, and he hasn't spoken to me since . . ."

"I remember the call came from an Irish mobile, but that doesn't tell you where he rang from when you've been using Irish mobiles all along. And, as you know, our phone system here always shows the full international code even if you're ringing from a mile up the road."

"Okay." I tried to swallow my disappointment and focus on the call. "What about the column? I'm not sure I'm up to writing about Leon's death just yet . . ."

There was silence for a few seconds. "Okay. Here's what we're going to do. Forget about the column for the next few days. I'll write an article saying that Leon has died, and you'll be unavailable for a while as a consequence. I'll run that in the next edition. And in case you're wondering what will happen with Éire TV– well, you were commissioned to produce four shows, and you've done that now. You don't owe them anything any more. My guess is that the story of Leon's death is going to be all over the place for the next few days, so they'll have more than enough footage of various celebrity-watcher type of twats giving their opinions on the whole thing to fill a half-hour. If they had an interview with you on their show, it'd be a major scoop for them, but if you're not up for it, don't do it. Send them my way if they give you any hassle."

"Wow. Thanks, Isolde – that'd be a big help. And, I must admit, I'd expected you to argue with me about not writing my column, so thanks for understanding where I'm coming from."

"I won't lie, Andie. If you did write a column to wrap this whole story up as soon as the funeral is over, it would mean good news for our sales. But that's your choice, and I won't be forcing you to do so. I'll leave it with you."

"Thank you, and thanks for everything you've told me. You have no idea what it means to me."

"Don't underestimate me. I have a fair idea. I was young once too, you know."

For a few seconds, I was bold enough to contemplate asking her if there was anyone in her life. There could well be, for all I knew –

perhaps she was just very discreet. But I got a bit of sense at the last minute before I opened my mouth. Best to leave well enough alone.

Isolde started talking again. "You've done well with this project, so when you get back, we'll look at having you branching out a bit – maybe dealing with some of the more hard-hitting stuff. I might give you some of the stuff Jason usually works on. He could do with having his toes stepped on. Take him down a peg or two."

I didn't comment on that – I'd think about it later. Meanwhile, there was one other thing that was nagging at me. "Isolde . . . I appreciate you telling me about your weight issues. You really didn't have to do that, you know. You could have just fired me straight away and given me no reason. It was what I expected."

"I know it was. That's as close to an olive branch as anyone has got from me in a long, long time."

"But why? I don't mean to be offensive, but being nice to people – especially me – is not really your thing."

"You keep telling me things I already know. No, I'm not particularly nice to people generally, but, as I've already told you, I'm not heartless. I can recognise when people are going through a rough patch. Your rough patch has gone on a while, and it's time it ended. Now, I'm never going to do the touchy-feely stuff with you or with anyone else on the team, but if I can help anyone out in my own way, I will. And I think all of this falls under that category. Now, scram, before you destroy my hard-woman reputation entirely."

"Thanks again, Isolde . . ."

"Shut it. Way more thanking going on here than I'm comfortable with. Oh, you gained a lot of brownie points by not calling me Maud, by the way. And, as I warned you before, keep that to yourself. It wouldn't be good for my professional image if I didn't have a name suitable for the industry."

"Umm." I was trying not to laugh.

"Seriously, if that ever comes out, I'll burn your house down, just like you did all those years ago. And don't think I won't do it, because I will."

"Oh, I know you would."

We both laughed, the first time we ever both laughed at the same time.

About a minute after my call to Isolde, she texted to say she'd forwarded Colm's email on to my account. I raced to the nearest Internet kiosk and accessed my work email through a remote web browser.

Hello Isolde,

Colm Cannon here, the cameraman for Looking for Leon.

I'm sure you're wondering why I'm emailing you, so I'll get straight to the point. The situation of Andie getting her brother to spy on you was completely my fault. I was the one who convinced her there was something going on between you and Martin. The reason I did it was because I needed something to connect with her about, some shared interest. Sometimes, people are the most obvious thing to talk about. Unfortunately for you and Martin, you got caught in my crossfire.

Andie tells me that you're an exceptionally clever lady, so I'm sure you're sharp enough to have worked out why I needed that connection. And I'm writing this email to you because me falling in love with her means that she's going to lose her job because I was too stupid to realise that I should have just asked her out, instead of finding pathetic excuses to spend time with her and pretending to be Sherlock Holmes.

If I have to beg for her, I will. So, here goes. Please don't make her suffer the repercussions of me being an idiot. I'm happy for me to lose my job instead. Go directly to my boss – Martin can give you her number – and make an official complaint about me and my unprofessionalism. But I'm pleading with you to leave her out of this. She only tolerated my antics because she's too nice a person to tell me to get stuffed.

I know I am in no position to ask for favours, but if you're happy to move the needle of blame over to my side and to let Andie keep her job, then maybe you could keep the contents of this email to yourself. I know I don't have a chance with Andie, so I'd prefer to keep my feelings to myself. You're the only other person in the world who knows about this. I'm very good at messing up, and I really don't need any help, so if you could take pity on a loser who is useless with women, I would forever appreciate it. Andie is too special for me to risk having her running out of my life as fast as her legs will carry her, which I know is exactly what she would do if she knew just how strongly I feel about her.

I really am very sorry that I got you involved in the mess that is my world. Love makes people do crazy things, as I am finding out. All I can do is apologise. I'll respect whatever decision you make on this.

Regards,

Colm Cannon

I was very, very glad Isolde hadn't respected Colm's request to keep the email contents to herself. A warm, glowing feeling spread all over my body. If it wasn't for the fact that I was on my way to Leon's funeral, I would almost have felt happy for the first time in days.

Chapter Thirty-eight

I knew the funeral was going to be bad, but never in my wildest dreams could I have anticipated just how bad.

Looking back, it had a sense of inevitability about it. Things started off okay – or as okay as a funeral can ever be, which is unbearable at best. Bridget, who was taking a stiff-upper-lip approach to dealing with the day, had welcomed me into the mourning party with open arms – which I felt was very generous of her after I had killed her son. When I'd told her as much between great shuddering blubbers the previous day after I landed at her and Liam's house, she whooshed my fears away with a window-wiper-style wave of her hand.

"Andie, he was ready to go after seeing you. You did him the biggest favour in the world, one that I, or anybody else, couldn't do for him. Whatever you two spoke about, it was obviously a form of exorcism for his soul. My little boy is finally at peace now." Her voice caught in her throat, but she rallied within seconds and carried on as if it had never happened. "So cop on, will you?"

I copped on and pulled myself together. I'd spent six hours at the house the previous day meeting Leon's friends and family, the family from Ireland (FFI) having arrived in the middle of the night before. Bridget had tried to keep the atmosphere as light as possible and nobody had dared do anything that might darken it. It was her way of coping, and we all did whatever we could do to fit in with that. Meeting everyone the previous day should probably have made this day slightly easier but, as we walked into the cold church, I realised that nothing could ameliorate what lay ahead of us.

The presence of the media all around us was never mentioned or acknowledged. Bridget insisted that I sit with the family, which made me feel like a fraud as the thought of Colm popped unbidden into my head, but now was not the time to disagree with Bridget about anything. I didn't dare cry during the ceremony – Bridget's rigid head served as a warning to me to keep it together. I didn't understand her way of coping, but I owed her enough to respect it, difficult and all as it was. If pretending it all wasn't happening was helping her, then so be it.

The priest had known Leon for all of Leon's life, so it wasn't a struggle for him to speak about him. It was definitely a struggle to listen, though. His warm words of praise for all that Leon was as a person filled me with endless regret that I hadn't had the opportunity to get to know him better. Regret was soon suppressed by guilt that I'd made such a song and dance about finding him, and yet I'd fallen for someone else. And I won't even get started on how I felt about how my actions had forced Leon into hiding at a time when he should have been trying to enjoy his last days. By the time we stood up to walk Leon's coffin out to the waiting hearse and bring him to his final resting place, I was shaking so much that I was sure I must have looked like I was having some sort of spasm.

I walked – or rather, shook – down the aisle, keeping a deferential distance behind Bridget and Liam but still feeling like an intruder. When the doors of the church were opened for Leon's coffin to be pushed through, a dead heat flooded in on top of us, and I thought I would faint. Afterwards, I fancied that it might have been a warning sign from Leon, but I didn't pick up on it.

I heard the sound of a flashbulb before I saw anything. I had walked with my head held low on my journey to the exit, examining the tiles on the church floor, the gnarls of the wood in the pews, the weekly newsletter and holy-water fountain – anything but the coffin. But, even buried so far inside my protective cocoon, the sound registered with me as very bad news. The last few weeks – had it only been weeks? – had taught me that much.

"Andie, how do you feel about Leon's death?"

An overweight man shoved a camera into my face. I was too shocked to respond at first as I looked around and saw a sea of reporters and cameras gathered around the door of the church.

The overweight man's words opened the floodgates for a deluge of other questions, all moral qualms about invading a funeral gone out the window.

"Are the rumours of a reunion with Leon true?"

"Were you with Leon when he died?"

"Andie! Is it true that you and Leon returned to Vegas to marry before he died?"

The last question was asked in an Irish accent. And what was worse, I was sure I recognised the voice. I knew I shouldn't turn around to see who it was, but just like Lot's wife couldn't resist, nor could I. And with all the strange things that had happened to me in the last few weeks, being turned into a pillar of salt would probably feel entirely normal.

"Andie!"

The voice belonged to Sadie, an ex-colleague of mine from the *Glitter* days whom I'd never liked. She waved excitedly at me as if she had just spotted me at the other side of a swimming pool in a holiday resort.

She'd always been a career-hungry, overly ambitious cow who would stamp on someone's grave to get what she wanted – which, it seemed, was exactly what she was sent over here to do. I glared at her as she tried to approach me, but she was soon jostled out of position by the crowd, all of whom were desperate to throw more questions at me.

I had to bite back the obscenities that rose to my lips in response to the vultures' insistence. I had enough respect for Leon's memory not to drag myself down to their level, hard and all as it was to resist flying off the handle at them.

Not everyone approached things in the same way, though. It might have taken a lot to make Liam speak, but this was one situation that could certainly be classed as a lot.

"Have you no pride in who you are, that you won't let a man go to his final resting place in peace? You should be all ashamed of yourselves. You're disgusting, every last one of you!"

Murmurs of "Yeah" and "Disgraceful" rippled along the crowd of mourners. I was tempted to join in, but I had a feeling that me opening my mouth for any reason at all would not be a good thing, and would only serve to encourage the baying mob. Liam's words seemed to have the desired effect, however. The reporters remained silent as Leon's coffin was carried into the hearse.

Bridget and Liam inched their way reluctantly into Leon's uncle's car, which was parked directly behind the hearse. This was it – Leon's final journey. Bridget and Liam were clearly not ready for it, and yet, they knew they had to do it. Nothing could ever possibly make them feel ready for this awful moment. And now, my presence had made everything feel a hundred times worse. I cursed myself, cursed the reporters and cursed God as I walked on to my own hired car. All in my head, of course – it would have been pretty pointless holding back at the reporters and then turning into a Tourette's sufferer at this juncture.

"Where are you going, Andie? Come with us," Bridget said to my back.

I frowned. "I can't – I – surely you don't want me around, not after what's just happened?"

"Will you get in and don't be daft, like a good girl," Liam said.

As I got in, Iceberg Bridget held out her arms and pulled me to her. I bit my tongue so hard to stop myself from crying that my top teeth were practically grinding off the bottom ones somewhere in the centre of my tongue. It wouldn't be fair to fall apart on Bridget now, not when she was trying so hard to keep up the hard-woman act.

"I just can't believe they'd sink so low as to do that at a funeral," I said.

"I can. Human life means nothing to those people. Leon's not a person to them – he's just a story. As are you, as I'm sure you're starting to realise." She stroked my hair to take the sting out of her words. "Stick with us. We'll protect you from them."

Liam reached over and squeezed my hand. I couldn't believe how charitable they were both being to me. These were good, good people.

I was starting to realise a lot of things other than how I was just a story. The truth was, I was being hung by my own petard. I was employed by a paper that did exactly the same thing on a day-by-day basis. The name of the paper said it all, really. Isolde was vicious, albeit a little bit less so since her bout of compassion, but her fundamentals weren't going to change. The paper was vicious. Would I become vicariously vicious if I stayed working there? Was I vicariously vicious already? Isolde would wear me down sooner or later. She'd said she wanted me to start working on some more hard-hitting stuff. It'd start out with articles that named and shamed the local people who'd been caught without a TV licence in the previous year, but before I knew it I'd be invading some poor family's most private moment, just like what was happening right now. And, while I'd always had a problem with Isolde's ferociousness, what had I actually done about it? I'd given up confronting her, tamed by the failure of my previous attempts to wear her down.

These thoughts whirled around in my head as the funeral procession came to a halt outside the graveyard. I felt Bridget's entire body tremble against mine as Leon's uncle parked the car and turned off the engine. I wanted to run a million miles away from here, but there was nowhere to go, no option other than seeing the funeral through.

I took up my stance behind Bridget and Liam again before we trudged into the graveyard. I didn't once look behind to see if the reporters were lurking. I didn't need to – I knew they were – but I couldn't bear to see them.

When I think back on the burial now, I can barely recall a thing about it. I was too lost in thoughts of that night in Vegas, sifting through a lifetime of what-ifs and what-could-have-beens. I think it was some sort of twisted survival mechanism that my brain switched on to get me through the burial – while these thoughts made no sense when I knew that Colm was the one I was in love with, they were easier to manage than to focus on the reality of putting Leon in the ground forever. There was no logic to my thought process except to move from one second to the next, and to do whatever it took to make the agony of the burial pass. I know there was a lot of wailing done by Leon's extended family, but I couldn't fully hear the sound in my head. I know that Bridget and Liam remained completely immobile throughout the ceremony, but that Bridget fainted as soon as the ceremony ended. I know that I helped Liam to pick Bridget up, and that we carried her back to Leon's uncle's car, but I can only remember snippets of it. But I also know that every second of that ceremony is etched onto my brain forever, and right now I'm just blocking it out. One day, I'll unlock it, and make myself relive every horrible moment in an attempt to get over it. But that day was not the day to do it.

Of course, the blasted photographers captured the moment of Bridget's faint, and although Leon's family formed a protective barrier around her as Liam and I carried her back to the car, pictures of us still ended up in the papers the next day. I never felt such intense anger in my life as I did when I saw a zoom of Bridget's crumpled face on the cover of a newspaper. Of course, I knew some of my anger was directed at myself for being the catalyst of these innocent people's involvement in a world that had nothing to do with them. But it was too late to change that now.

Leon's uncle drove us back to Leon's home, while one of the FFI brought my car back. Liam and I helped Bridget into the house. By this stage, Bridget had adopted her own coping mechanism of retreating inside herself to block out what was happening. She wouldn't speak, she wouldn't look at us when we were talking – it was as if her soul had left her body. Her stillness was far more terrifying to see than any hysterics could ever have been.

Bridget and Liam had invited the mourners back to the house for some food and tea after the burial, and cars began to pack up the driveway. I was glad of an opportunity to make myself useful.

"Bridget, I'm going to get started on the sandwiches and tea now. You stay there. It's all under control."

"Good girl, good girl," Liam answered for Bridget and nodded his approval.

"Make the tay nice and strong now, none of that watery shite," one of the cousins piped up. "That lot will go to town on you if you don't make a good cup of tay."

"In other words, it's you that wants strong tay," a cousin of the cousin said.

"You know and I know that strong tay would be good right about now."

"Tay's on the way," I said, running to the kitchen to escape the madness. Displacement was a wonderful thing in times of crisis. The anticipation of tay, the talking about tay and the drinking of tay could always be relied upon to see the Irish through the worst of times.

At least half of the mourners at the church had made their way back to the house. Thankfully, but not surprisingly, there wasn't a photographer amongst them. They might as well have been there, though, with all the talking that was done about them. My mortification increased with every new mention of "Disgraceful", "Parasites", and my own personal favourite on the morto scale: "shaming the memory of a good man." After a while – and it wasn't a long while, I'm not that slow – I realised that although Bridget and Liam weren't holding what happened against me, there were plenty of other people who were – and, not only that, but they were enjoying doing so. Under the circumstances, I couldn't really fault them for it.

As soon as I had buttered my last sandwich and filled every cup, bowl, saucepan and flower-pot in the house with tay, I sought out Bridget and Liam to say my goodbyes. I didn't have to do much seeking – Bridget was still on the couch, exactly where Liam had put her, and Liam was still hovering over her, exactly as he'd been doing an hour before.

"Liam, I'm going to drive back to Vegas now, and leave you all in peace."

"Ah, no. Sure stay around here for a while . . . you don't want to be on your own at a time like this . . ."

"No, honestly. It's time I went. But thank you."

"Well, if you're sure . . ." I could see relief pass over his face. Although I knew he wasn't holding any grudges over what had happened, my presence, and the whispers it was producing, wasn't making things any easier.

I twined my fingers around Bridget's. She continued to stare off into space.

"I'm leaving now, Bridget. Thank you for finding me, and for bringing me to Leon."

As soon as I mentioned Leon's name, Bridget came alive again. Her hands were the first bit of her to react – she squeezed my fingers so tight that I had to stop myself from crying out in a mixture of surprise and pain – then she turned her face to mine and smiled.

"Thank you, Andie, for making Leon happy. Goodbye."

Then she dropped my hand and resumed her space-staring, thinking, no doubt, about her boy.

I shook Liam's hand, thanked him, and left as discreetly as possible. It was entirely probable that FFI would be asking me about the next batch of tay if they spotted me. Besides, I really didn't want to hear the rasp of a "Good riddance" echoing in my wake.

The relief that flooded through me as I got into my rented car and drove out of the driveway was like nothing I had ever experienced before. It only lasted a few minutes, though. Without the distraction of Bridget and sandwiches and tay, the reality of everything that had happened crashed on top of me, and I had to pull into the hard shoulder before a crash of another kind happened. Leon's disdain for me and my lack of action was justified. He'd given me good advice that I hadn't acted on. And then, to make a bad day worse, Colm somehow managed to find his way inside my head. Colm had met me halfway and had been honest with me, and yet I'd just continued hiding myself. Before long, I was so guilt-ridden about the whole thing that I had to turn the key in the ignition and drive again to focus my thoughts on something else.

One thing was for sure – I had a long journey ahead of me, and it wasn't just the drive to Vegas that I was talking about.

The papers the next day were every bit as bad as I thought they would be. Pictures of Bridget, Liam and me were plastered all over every publication I picked up. I knew I shouldn't even look at them, but it was impossible not to. It would have cost me a month's wages to buy every newspaper that I was in, so I hunched down in a corner of a bookstore with a handful of them and sifted my way through the articles. They were painful to read, but it was better to get it over and done with . . . even if I was reading the same old thing over and over again. A few papers in, though, something new caught my eye.

> Directly after the burial, a scuffle took place between a photographer from the *Mail* and an as yet unidentified man, believed to be Irish. The photographer, Bill Bayside, was allegedly hit by the Irishman when Bayside tried to take pictures of Andie Appleton leaving the church with Bridget and Liam O'Reilly, Leon's parents. Both men are currently being questioned in relation to the incident.

Oh, God . . . it had to have been someone from the FFI . . . I tried to sweep the cobwebs off my brain to try to remember if everyone from the contingent from Ireland had come directly back to the house after the funeral, but it was impossible to say with that lot – they were no sooner in the front door than they were out the back one, smoking fags and what have you. Still, it was nice to think that someone had tried to defend my honour, especially when they hadn't seemed to be too happy with me back at Bridget and Liam's house. I just hoped whoever it was wouldn't get into too much trouble for it.

I finished my review of the papers and left the bookstore. I was thrilled to get back to the refuge of the MGM. The previous day I had thought about going straight to the airport after Leon's funeral and just getting the hell out of that city, especially now that I had absolutely no reason left to stay, but I was too mentally and physically exhausted to face the prospect of a flight home until I'd recovered a bit. Oh, and there was the other small issue of needing to see if Colm was still around Vegas . . .

Colm still hadn't made any contact. I was desperate to do something constructive, so when I got back to the hotel, I rang several airlines to see if a Colm Cannon had taken flights home with them over the last few days. I was told very little, and put down the phone none the wiser as to his whereabouts.

I thought about ringing Éire TV to ask to speak to Martin until I remembered the Martin/Maud debacle, so that bright idea was going nowhere.

I went to my laptop and logged into my email, hoping that there'd be a message sitting there waiting for me from Colm, and knowing there probably wouldn't. Sure enough, none of the new emails that awaited me were from him.

I decided to work my way through the rest of my emails to keep me occupied. And, just as I was replying to the first of the new ones, a box popped up at the bottom right of the screen notifying me that there was a new message in the LookingForLeon mailbox. I clicked on the link to direct me to the new email. What I saw who it was from I nearly had a heart attack. It couldn't be . . . this just wasn't possible . . .

Chapter Thirty-nine

I rolled my chair back from the table, the laptop and most of all, the offending email. Someone was playing a sick joke on me – the sickest joke imaginable. Why would anybody be so cruel as to do this?

I was afraid to open it. If someone was willing to do something like this, then God only knew what the message would contain. And yet, how could I not open it? It felt like I was going through the whole GoHomeAndie saga again. But, just like those emails, not opening this one was not an option.

I took a deep, scratchy breath, and sat back at the desk. I opened it quickly before I lost my nerve.

From: **Leon.OReilly@hotmail.com**
To: **LookingforLeon@hotmail.com**
Subject: Things we need to talk about . . .

Dear Andie,

One of the things we never got around to talking about was how much of a computer geek I am. My geek-rating stood to my advantage when I was thinking about the best way to explain everything to you after I'd gone off to this better place everyone talks about (hopefully, somewhere that has a room full of PCs for dead computer geeks). You see, there's a lot I need to tell you, but I need to make sure I'm dead when you read this. Otherwise, I'll just present you with the dilemma of whether or not you should contact me again, and I really think you have enough on your plate to sort out at the moment. Or maybe you have it all sorted out by now, who knows. I knew I needed to tell you so much stuff, but couldn't do it while I was alive – and the whole thing of being impossible to be on the computer writing emails after you're dead was a bit of an issue for me, so I've set my email to send this mail on a date that I'm projected to definitely be dead by, according to my trusty doctors. Cool, eh? Of course, you don't need to be a computer geek to know about that – anyone who's ever used an email application knows it, but I was rather proud of my idea and wanted to show off a little bit. Actually, now I feel like a bit of a fool, as it really isn't all that clever when you see it written down – but it took ages to type all that, so I'm not going to delete it all now.

You may, at this stage, be slightly curious as to what exactly I need to talk to you about. Only natural – I'd be the same. I'm tempted to draw this out just to tease you, but with the way my health is right now, I could well kick the bucket in the middle of writing this email, so I really should get my skids on. Besides, no offence, but writing an email isn't exactly how I've planned to go, even if it is an email to you. I'm hoping for a rather picturesque death in my wheelchair watching the wind blowing through the cherry-blossom trees while I watch rabbits jumping around the garden (rather like Molly's death in Home And Away – except she had children frolicking around the garden instead of rabbits) until my internal screen fades to black (just like Molly's screen did).

So . . . here's the thing. I was kinda, just a little bit, a smidgen, besotted with you. Just a tad totally head over heels. Phew, it's a relief to finally be able to say that to you, after all of these weeks of holding myself back from contacting you and telling you this. And as for when you came to visit . . . well, you might not have gathered that from the way I treated you that day, but I can explain. I'll probably lose every bit of dignity I have in the process, but thankfully, I'm dead now, so I won't have to worry about it. (It has its advantages.)

When I saw you walking into my hall, my first instinct was to run away as fast as I could so that you wouldn't see me. I couldn't run, of course – I couldn't even frigging-well wheel myself away. And that should tell you everything you need to know. Would anyone really want the woman of their dreams to see them as diminished as I was on that day? I wasn't the guy you fell for in Vegas. It's amazing the effect a few weeks can have on a body that's determined to let you down – even I am shocked by how fast this thing has eaten me alive, so I can only imagine the impact it had on you, seeing me so shrunken and dependent in that wheelchair. All I needed was the colostomy bag for the full effect. Can you imagine how demoralising, how frigging soul-destroying, that was? Not to mention mortifying. I was afraid to look into your eyes in case I saw disappointment, disgust, disdain. It was bad enough to lose you first time around and this time I knew I'd lose you again as soon as you clapped eyes on me. There was only one way to make it easier on both of us, and that was to do nothing.

Mom was right to bring you to me. I know that after today. I wouldn't have been able to die in peace without having seen you, just one last time. I couldn't mentally say goodbye to you. I couldn't let go of that amazing experience we'd had together. That night in Vegas was the first night in my life where I'd really understood the connection that everyone talks about. You were finishing my sentences, I was finishing yours. I could have said anything in the world to you, and you'd have known where I was coming from. I've never had that with anyone before. At least now, I can die knowing what that feels like.

But it wasn't just about seeing you. I was reluctant to let you go because I wanted – I needed – to do something for you. Why? Because you will never, ever know how much you've done for me. I'll be honest about this. It did my dying ego a lot of good to see this beautiful, wild girl that everyone has fallen in love with professing her undying love for me – little old me, the guy who couldn't get through an ad break without sicking up his dodgy medicine. It was like a warm blanket that I could hug around myself when I felt at my lowest. In the moments when the pain consumed me so completely that I wished I was dead rather than have to take the agony for one second longer, the sight of you messing around on TV always pulled me back from the brink. And it made me feel good to think that someone amazing like you – a fun person, but most importantly, a good person – wanted to be with me. It's a strange old business, this dying. It can make you feel worthless. You made me feel like I had a value. And because you did so much for me, I had to do something for you too.

You told me you'd never told anyone about what happened with Elaine before. I'm glad you told me. I would say that I don't know what it was about me that made me so special, but it wasn't me that was special, it was us. And because of how we were together, I know why you told me. If you told anyone how amazing those few hours together were, they would never get it. Only you and I will ever know. When someone you feel so strongly about is upset, you'd do anything in the world to help them, and that's how I felt when you came to visit me and I found out that you hadn't made any progress in moving on from what happened.

The being-understanding approach hadn't worked, so I had to try a new tactic. I'd imagine you thought my change of behaviour was down to me sulking over you falling for this Colm guy, but it wasn't. Well, there may have been just a little bit of sulking involved – yes, I'm jealous as hell about the guy, but if I can't be around to make you happy, I want somebody else to. Anyway, I took the tough-love approach with you to try to make you realise for once and for all that you weren't to blame for what happened to Elaine. I also realised that if you're still this hung up on blaming yourself for Elaine's death, you're doubtless going to find some way to be hard on yourself for mine too. And not only that, but if I hadn't sent you away, I know you'd have felt like you had to stay around until I took my last breath, because you'd have considered yourself a bad person otherwise. I was very tempted to let you – very, very tempted. But Andie, I knew you weren't mine to have at that stage. I had to make you feel like I wanted you to go, because I wanted you to work on sorting out the rest of your life. I'm hoping that you've done a lot of thinking since you visited me. You've wasted enough time on things you can't change. If I came across as a bastard, I apologise. And yes, I did kick myself after you left for sending you running off into the arms of another man, but I have a feeling you would have gone there sooner or later anyway.

So, there you go. I'm almost done, but I have one big ask of you before I go. If this guy Colm means something to you, if what you have with him is anything near as special as what you and I had, tell him about Elaine, if you haven't already. And then, will you for the love of God get over yourself and forgive yourself? Now, and you thought I was a bad cop the day I sent you packing, huh? I mean it though, Andie. Stop putting yourself at the centre of what happened to Elaine. None of it was about you. You can tell yourself for the rest of your life that it was, or you can find the nearest beach and draw a line in the sand under this. You choose. Either way, you won't get her back. Elaine is gone, but you're still here. So do her, and yourself, a favour. Live your life as best you can. She didn't get that opportunity, and if you're her friend, you owe it to her. And for God's sake, do it for me, while you're at it.

Now, I just hope my nerdy skills don't let me down, and this email actually gets to you – I've practically written a new testament of the Bible at this stage. I hope it's of some use to you, beautiful one.

Goodbye, Andie. Thank you so much.

All my love,

Leon

The tears had begun sometime after 'Dear Andie'. By the time I'd reached the end of Leon's email, they'd formed sprawling pools on the table.

What had I done to deserve such love?

I re-read the main body of the email again and again. I'd known from the start that Leon was an amazing person, but this was incredible, even by his standards. His generosity of spirit when his death was impending was mind-blowing. I closed my eyes and let an image of Leon walking towards me in the MGM wash all over me.

"Thank you, Leon," I whispered before I opened my eyes.

And when I did, I realised that after eight long years, I was willing to allow myself to move on.

Chapter Forty

It was shortly after reading Leon's email that I found Colm's passport on the top shelf of my wardrobe.

I stared at it, wondering if I was going mad from the stress of the past few days. My life was becoming a study in surrealism. This, of course, meant that Colm definitely hadn't gone home to Ireland. That fact was completely eclipsed by the notion of me having his passport in the first place . . . how in the name of all that's holy did it come to live in my wardrobe?

I racked my brains, and eventually I came up with an explanation that seemed plausible. I had no idea whether it was the real story or not, but the only thing that made sense was that Colm gave me his passport for safekeeping some night that we were out, and just hadn't asked for it back yet. I didn't remember it because I was blind drunk. Yes, that definitely made sense. I thought back to the night we went for the dinner Colm had won in the Leon competition (which hurt me to even think about now – it must have looked so crass through Leon's eyes). Colm had his ID out that night, because despite being in his thirties, he looked much younger and was always asked for ID (I was never asked – maybe I should devote some time to being concerned about that at some stage, but as I was slightly busy with a million other neuroses, now wasn't that stage). He wouldn't have been drinking himself, of course, but he'd bought a few rounds for me when we went to a bar after we'd dragged the arse out of our free dinner for as long as we could. I had ended up blind drunk, so that was that box ticked. Why he'd never asked for it back though, or even made any reference to it in the interim, I didn't know, but then, it was Colm we were talking about. Since when did he ever do anything that was expected?

Still, at least I had something to go on now. After reading Leon's email, I'd promised myself that I'd do whatever it took to sort things out with Colm. I owed it to Leon. And there were plenty more things I had to make good on as well, but this needed to be dealt with first. And I wouldn't rest for one minute until I'd found him. This time, I was determined to find what I was looking for.

On impulse, I grabbed the swipe for my door and made my way back down to Colm's room. He was still in the country, so he could well be staying in the hotel – and it wasn't as if he could leave the country without me, so surely he wouldn't go too far away from here?

I stopped outside his room, and just as I was about to knock I heard feet trundling inside the door. The relief I felt was overpowering. But soon, all too soon, fury rose in me for how Colm had handled the last few days. And doubtless he was going to put me through the whole rigmarole of knocking my knuckles raw all over again right now. It was too much.

"*Open up!*" I slapped the door with the palms of both of my hands. "You have some neck, do you know that? Do you think you can just disappear off the face of the earth whenever you feel like it? Did you ever stop to think that I might be worried? *Did you?*"

Some glimmer of self-awareness warned me that I sounded like a total psycho, but it was too late.

"Fine! If you haven't the guts to speak to me face to face, I'll say what I have to say right here!" I was shouting at the top of my voice now to make sure he heard me. "I made a mistake, and I'm sorry. I should have been honest with you. But I'm not the only one who messes up, am I? Why did you have to run away the first time we hit a wall? But I can forgive you for it if you can forgive me. Please, stop shutting me out!" There wasn't so much as a scuttle on the other side of the door, so I continued unabated. "You have yourself so convinced that you're alone in the world and that nobody cares about you, but that's just not true! You're not alone – you have me! Didn't you listen to me before? *I'm in love with you!*"

There was silence at the other side. I oscillated between embarrassment and anger at the lack of response.

"And now that you know that, surely you'll open the door like any man worth his salt!"

I heard footsteps approaching the door. My feelings swayed from relief to fear that Colm might open this door and just tell me to go away. What would I do then?

"Thanks for your declaration of love, but I think my wife might have something to say about it."

A middle-aged man in a suit stood in front of me. Judging by the look on his face, he wasn't sure if he was amused or annoyed by my interruption. His suitcase stood upright not far behind him, and he hadn't even taken his suit jacket off.

"Oh, I'm so sorry – I was looking for someone else, obviously – he must have just left this room. As in, checked out earlier – I'm not suggesting he was hiding under your bed up until a few minutes ago or anything –"

"Hmm. I think I'll check under the bed after you've gone, just in case."

"Ah ha ha ha!! Yes – yes, good idea – right – well, I'll just go then. Sorry about all that." I cringed as I backed away from the door and ran down the corridor to my own room.

Good God. All of that emotion had taken it out of me, and it had all been for nothing – not to mention the mortification – I couldn't take the time to indulge in my embarrassment, though. It was time to think. So, Colm was no longer in the hotel. Unless he'd changed rooms to get away from me? I'd get Philippe to check that out, but surely that was unlikely. Assuming he wasn't in the hotel, he must still be in the country, given the whole passport issue. He hadn't palled up with anyone since we came to Vegas, not surprisingly for Colm, so he wasn't hanging out drinking beer and eating pretzels in someone's sitting room. The only other avenue of possibility was that he was avenging himself with Lindy, but I refused to seriously consider that. Even though I had given the thought some headspace when he'd first gone missing, I'd considered it on the way back from Arizona, and realised that I had more faith in Colm than that.

I sighed. Perhaps Vegas wasn't exactly a lucky spot for me. I seemed to spend all my time here looking for a man.

A short while before I had reasoned that he would stay close by – close to his passport at any rate – but now I was suddenly convinced that I could comb the length and breadth of each hotel in Vegas and I still wouldn't find him. He'd never expressed much interest in being here, after all.

So, left to his own devices, where would he go?

Then it hit me. We went to Hoover Dam because Colm hadn't felt well enough to make the big journey to the Grand Canyon. He had been determined to go there before he left for home. My mind went into overdrive as I tried to formulate the best plan. I could pack a bag, hire a car, drive to the Canyon and be there before the end of the day – but then what? I hadn't managed to find Leon after a fire drill. I sure as hell wasn't going to be able to find Colm hanging around the Grand Canyon late at night with only a pair of binoculars to help me out. The whole world knew that finding people wasn't my forte.

I'd have to work out the specifics later. For now, it was time to visit Reception. There was only one man for the job of helping me out with my next move.

Philippe looked up suspiciously when he saw me. We'd had a chat before I'd left Vegas for the funeral and he'd forgiven me for giving him such a hard time when he tried to stop me going to the airport, but he'd seemed slightly apprehensive of what I was going to do next ever since. I didn't blame him. I felt exactly the same way about myself.

"What drama is going on now?"

"The one that's the soundtrack to my life, Philippe. Missing men."

"Poof!" He made a French-sounding sound. "Perhaps they go missing because they are chased away."

I hadn't time for philosophy, but I had to tread carefully so that I didn't annoy him again. But before I could say what I had in mind, he opened his mouth.

"And–ee, did you see the entertainment news last night?"

"No – I'd never watch that shite."

Philippe didn't get my attempt at sarcasm, and just threw me a confused look. "I've been slightly busy with funerals and the like, Philippe. Why do you ask?" I had a horrible feeling this wasn't going to be something I wanted to hear.

"Lindy had another trick up her sleeve. It is now down."

"What do you mean?"

"She did a report on her show about how you and Colm had been together all the time you were pretending to be looking for Leon."

"Oh my God." The cow. The sad, pathetic, vindictive cow. "Has she no respect for the dead? That's a total lie, Philippe. Colm and I only just got together!"

"I know that. You know that. The rest of the world won't believe that for a second, though."

He was completely right. My thoughts instantly turned to Bridget and Liam. Would they believe it?

I'd have to deal with that later. Time was running out.

"I need your help just one last time, Philippe. I know it's getting kinda old, but this truly is the last time I'll ask you for anything."

"Hmm. We'll see about that. But go on. I am bored and 'ave nothing else to do."

I glanced over at the queues of people before the reception desk, and the other busy staff members diligently processing requests.

"I need you to check on your computer system to see when Colm checked out of his hotel room, and if by any chance he checked into another room in the hotel instead."

"So, you are asking me to violate customer privacy."

"I hate to ask you to break the rules, but Colm's missing and there's no way I'll find him without some more information."

He shrugged. "If you know me at all by now, you will know that I do not care about breaking the whules. Whule-breaking is the making of my day. I go out of my way to break at leest one whule every day."

"Good – then maybe I'm helping you out too!"

He gave me a slanty look. "I've already reached a respectable quota of whule-breaking today, so I can take or leave this one. Also, you asked Nicole to do exactly the same thing for you when Colm went missing. This does not make me feel very special."

When she's told me to keep schtum about that, I'd assumed she would too! I took the moving-on-swiftly approach.

"Philippe, please! Don't make me beg."

"I think you just did, achshuly . . ."

"Philippe, please, don't be an asshole."

He smiled. "That is more like it. My fiery And–ee is back. Now, we can talk business." He hauled himself up from the depths of his armchair and went out to Reception to disturb one of the staff that was actually working so that he could take over their computer.

"He checked out of his room at nine this morning. He is not in another room," he said upon his return.

"This morning!" What? He'd been here all the time? "Thank you, Philippe." I stood up.

"Where are you going?"

"Next door, to check with the rent-a-car crowd if Colm rented a car from them this morning, and also to rent one myself."

"Where are you going after you get that information?"

"The Grand Canyon."

"Please, Andee, don't do a *Thelma and Louise* over a man!"

"No, no." I filled Philippe in on my theory.

He shrugged when I finished speaking. "I suppose it's as good a place to start looking for him as any ozer. You do know that the rent-a-car crowd probably won't give you details on who has rented their cars? Not everybody is as relaxed as Nicole and me, you know."

My thoughts again turned to the harassed workers at the reception desk who could have done with a bit of help from their relaxed colleague, but Philippe had been so good to me that it would have been rude to have even made a joke.

"It doesn't matter if they don't tell me. I'll just check the forecourt to see if the red Alfa Romeo Spider is missing. If it is, Colm has it."

"What about accommodation? You will not sleep in the car, surely?"

"Possibly. I've done a lot of strange things in cars." I smiled, thinking of Leon and me in the car in the MGM. Philippe gave me an odd look, and I suddenly realised what he was thinking. Time to swiftly move the conversation along again. "No, I'm joking – I'm going to stay in a hotel called Crumbler's Lodge. Colm mentioned it before. I'd bet the arse of my trousers that he's there."

"Ah, yes, I 'ave 'eard of that 'otel. It is in a good location."

"It seems to be, but that's completely incidental. Knowing Colm, he wouldn't care if it was a ten-mile uphill trek away from the Canyon as long as it was a cool hotel."

Philippe smiled. "And will you be returning 'ere with the car or dropping it off in a branch closer to the Canyon?"

I shrugged. "No idea. I haven't thought that far ahead. Depends on the outcome, I suppose."

His face softened. "What I was really asking you, Andee, is when I will see you again. Or if I will."

I jumped off the desk and ran over to hug Philippe.

"You know what, Philippe – right now I have no idea where all of this is going, where I'll end up, what I'll be doing this time tomorrow. But one thing I do know is that you're a great friend, and regardless of what happens, you and I will be staying in touch." And I meant it, too. Philippe had a heart of gold.

He patted me on the back when the hug finally ended. "We 'ad better. And if you 'ave any problems at all, you ring me. It gives me something to do, your problem portfolio. I might even have to work now that you're leeving. That would be 'orrible."

I smiled as I walked away. When I took one final look back, I saw him wiping his eyes. Great. Now I was making grown men cry.

Chapter Forty-one

I spent the drive to the Canyon swinging between memories of the last time I'd travelled this road to Hoover Dam with Colm, and thinking out how I'd go about looking for him. I really didn't know where I would start – I just knew that the Canyon was the only hope I had of finding him. I fought down the voice in my head telling me there was no sense at all to what I was doing. That voice had been getting louder since I noticed the red Alfa Romeo Spider sitting pretty on the forecourt when I went to collect my hired car, but I was trying my very best not to listen to it. He probably just wanted to try out another car, that was all. But if I stopped what I was doing, then I would have no plan at all, and that thought terrified me much more than being wrong.

I landed at the hotel just after three o'clock. It was perfectly located just beside the north rim of the canyon. The joys of travelling in low season meant that when I checked in, I was told that my room would have stunning panoramic views of "the vast depths of the Canyon". The place was falling down around itself, but it was exactly Colm's style, and I felt closer to him just by being in such a place.

I plastered my biggest smile on my face as the hefty receptionist handed the big heavy key to my room to me. "Could you tell me if you have a Colm Cannon staying here at the moment?"

She gave me a sly smile. "Oh, I'm afraid some guests like to keep their whereabouts to themselves, madam. We like to respect that."

She certainly was discreet. She must have recognised my name (the whole of the US did by this time to say nothing of just Arizona) but she had made no comment.

"Yes, I understand. But . . ."

I launched into my story, and the lady – Cassie, according to her nametag – nodded, frowned and smiled at all the right places. She peppered my dialogue with uh-huhs and oh mys, patting her permed hair occasionally.

"That's quite a tale, young lady." She smiled widely.

I congratulated myself for having connected with her.

"Yes, and that's why I'd really appreciate it if you could help me out here."

"You know, I'd absolutely love to." She titled her head to one side and smiled beatifically.

"Great!"

The smile vanished. "But I can't. As I explained, it's a matter of client confidentiality."

Someone had been watching too many legal dramas. She smiled again but the look in her eyes told me that I would be getting nowhere. I wondered whether she was another ardent Leon fan like Nicole and whether that was affecting her behaviour. I said thanks as sarcastically as I could and made my way up to my room, resolving to ask another member of staff later.

As soon as I'd deposited my luggage in my room – a rainbow of multicoloured bedspreads, blue curtains and wine carpets – I went back downstairs to check the facilities for any sign of Colm. Cassie threw a look my way as I passed through Reception on my way to the dining room. She narrowed her already squinty eyes when she saw me, as if to warn me not to even try her again. It didn't matter – I would knock on every door of the hotel to see if Colm was in any of them if I had to. Cassie had no idea what she was up against with me.

I walked around the restaurant and the bar, but there was no sign of Colm. That was pretty much the extent of the facilities, so I wandered back out to Reception, trying to decide what my next move would be. Cassie was tapping behind her desk, yawning, as I passed by again. I figured her shift would be finishing up soon, if her tired face was anything to go by. I'd noticed when speaking to her that her heavily caked make-up had started to fade around her eyes, and her lipstick had vanished completely – all that remained was the outline of her lip pencil. I'd work on her replacement then.

I briefly considered setting off a fire alarm to get Cassie out from behind the reception desk so that I could check the room records, but had enough sense to realise that if I didn't start growing up, I'd end up with a criminal record. That was something the old Andie would do, the Andie who couldn't face up to the hard stuff. The new Andie was going to start doing things the mature way like every other grown-up. She was going to go to the bar and have a drink.

Things suddenly seemed much better with a frozen margarita in my hand. They mustn't have looked that way, though.

"Excuse me, darlin', but I couldn't help noticing that you don't look too happy. Anything we can help you with?"

A lady with a Southern accent and a kindly face was looking over at me. Behind her, a husband and three children were peering over too.

"I'm fine, but thank you for asking." I smiled back as genuinely as I could. She didn't seem nosy – more the mammy-hen type, which was quite nice in my book. I really didn't feel like telling my story yet again though.

"You coming on this four o'clock tour?"

I shook my head. It was only then that I noticed their backpacks under the table, no doubt bulging with mammy sandwiches and two-litre bottles of drinks.

"Maybe you should. You look at a loose end."

"I can't. I'm hoping to meet someone tonight."

"But the tour is only two hours, so you'd be back in time."

I hadn't expected that answer – the bags suggested they were going away for several years. I thought about it. There was no sign of Cassie making a move, and it would take me the guts of two hours to go knocking on every door in the hotel anyway. Besides, I'd probably still be sitting in the bar in two hours' time trying to work out what else I was going to do to find Colm, and still be none the wiser, so I might as well do something worthwhile. Waiting for someone else to come on duty was the only plan I had.

Twenty minutes later, I was sitting on the bus beside one of the kind lady's children, a monosyllabic eleven-year-old called Agatha. The kind lady herself was called Charlotte. She'd got a good deal in the world of names, so I thought it was rather mean of her and her husband – Jack, another inoffensive name – to saddle their child with a burden of a moniker like Agatha. Possibly not so kind.

Luckily, none of the family seemed to recognise me so I could relax on that count.

The tour was a helicopter trip over the Grand Canyon. Strangely enough, I'd never had one single thought about seeing the place itself as I drove out – it was just the place where I hoped Colm would be, nothing more and nothing less. But boy, was I glad I hadn't wasted the opportunity to see the Canyon. After we were picked up at our hotel, we were brought to the Grand Canyon National Park Airport for check-in. Only minutes later, we were sitting on a helicopter that would take us on a sixty-minute panoramic tour. As I looked out the window at the Kaibab Plateau and forest in the heart of the Canyon's vast, endless depths, the beauty of the vista before me wiped all of my troubles out of my mind for a few precious minutes. The Colorado River glistened up at me as it wound its way far below. It almost looked as if it was winking at me, giving me a sign that everything was going to turn out okay . . . or perhaps that margarita had been a strong one. Our guide peppered the beautiful sights with facts and figures about the canyon's geologic history. The sheer scale of it was overwhelming, and for the first time I really understood why Colm was so anxious to spend time here and really see it properly.

When we returned to the hotel, exactly two hours after we'd left it, Cassie was still sitting behind the reception desk. She now looked like a pudding that had been left out on a dinner table for too long and was slowing melting and congealing. Her make-up had completely disappeared at this stage, and her perm had flattened and was sticking to her head, despite the air con. She suddenly whipped out a make-up bag and started to repair her face, as if she had read my thoughts. To my surprise, she looked up in the middle of her plastering and smiled at me. I gave her a reluctant smile back, wondering if she was taking the mick – but, in fairness, it looked genuine enough. Maybe she was feeling bad about refusing to help earlier.

I declined the kind lady's kind offer to have dinner with her and her family. It looked like I was going to be busy knocking on doors for the rest of the evening. As I bade the family goodbye, I felt a sense of dread as I thought of the hours ahead of me. I was as moorless as a boat in the middle of the ocean. Of all the crazy things that had happened to me in the past few months, this was the most extreme in its lack of foresight. At least before, there was some plan, some aim behind my actions – it all went towards finding Leon. Now, I was in a place that Colm could possibly be in, but might not be. If I got through the door-knocking experience without dying of humiliation, what happened then? I had absolutely nothing else to go on.

I took a shower, then decided to go for a walk – ostensibly to think, but I knew I was just procrastinating. But what if I knocked on the door of a serial killer? Or someone thumped me because I'd interrupted them getting lucky?

I sighed. The whole thing was ridiculous. I was trying to move away from acting the eejit, after all. There was no way I could do it. But what would I do instead?

Music drifted towards me from the bar – U2's "Where the Streets Have No Name" – and I was drawn to it. I went to the bar and ordered a glass of water to clear my head. The bar was a mixture of high tables and chairs, long, sprawling tables for groups, comfy couches and corner booths. I spotted an available booth to the left of the bar, headed over and sank into it. The curved edges of the booth completely obscured my view of the rest of the bar, which suited me fine. The last thing I needed now was any distractions when I had so much to think about.

Suddenly, the music changed to something much slower – something else that I recognised.

"Oh, Jesus."

I put my arms on the table and rested my head on them. Why was God taunting me? As the opening cords of Pink Floyd's 'Wish You Were Here' filled the room, I couldn't stop tears running down my cheeks and onto my arms. It was like a sign that things with Colm were over for good.

The tears escalated into great big heaving sobs that wracked my whole body. Within about twenty seconds, I felt someone touch my shoulder.

"Please leave me alone," I said into my arms, hoping that whoever it was would just go away.

"You still don't like Pink Floyd, then, judging by the effect they're having on you. After all my hard work . . ."

I whipped my head up. Colm was standing beside me, smiling shyly.

I bounded out of the booth and threw myself into his arms. He clasped his arms around me and buried his head in my neck, squeezing me tight and holding me as if he never wanted to let go.

Eventually, we drew apart.

"I *knew* you were here somewhere!" I said.

"Oh, did you now?"

"Yes! It was the only thing that made sense! Well, thank God I have my instincts to fall back on, that's all I can say – I knew if I relied on them I'd find you!"

He smiled sympathetically. "Sorry to burst your faith in your instincts, but I actually wasn't here. I left the hotel this morning with the intention of renting a car and just driving off into the desert somewhere, but in the end I couldn't leave the place I thought you were. I spent this morning circling the streets of Vegas, trying to decide what to do about us, then I went back to the MGM to talk to you. The minute I walked through Reception, Philippe jumped on me and told me you'd come here."

Philippe. Darling, darling Philippe. He'd be getting a trip to Paris on me after this.

We slid side by side into the booth and I snuggled up to him.

"But why didn't you call?" I asked.

"I wanted to surprise you." Colour rose on his cheeks. "And I thought the first conversation we had after everything that's happened should be face to face, and not over the phone." He kissed my cheeks. "But now that you're here in front of me, talking isn't actually what I want to do at all – but I'll try to behave. Anyway, I went around the corner and got the car we brought to Hoover Dam. I got here and checked in and the minute I said my name was Colm, Cassie in Reception said to me 'Are you Andie's Colm?' The relief I felt! I was also startled by 'Andie's Colm' – it's always been 'Andie's Leon', you see. Anyway, as soon as Cassie explained that you'd told her about us, she said she'd seen you going on a tour earlier and would be happy to ring me when you arrived back. She did and I've been sitting over at the other side of the bar ever since – I knew you'd come in here eventually. I hadn't expected you to be drinking water, though – that was a bit of a shocker."

"I know – I can't even use alcohol as an excuse for the tears!"

We laughed, but then Colm's face turned serious. "Andie, I'm so sorry I reacted the way I did. I shouldn't have."

"Where did you go? You just vanished."

"I went to stay at a cheap hotel downtown – but without actually checking out of the MGM. Getting a hotel wasn't as easy as it sounds, seeing as I'd forgotten that you've had my passport since the night of the dinner date – but one eventually let me check in with my driver's licence as ID. Actually, my first thought after we fought was to go straight to the airport and go home, until I remembered where my passport was, but then I realised anyway I couldn't run away. I've spent my life running, and it has to stop. But

I needed some time to think, Andie. I knew if I stayed in the MGM, I'd be tempted to call to you to try to sort things out. I needed to put some physical distance between us."

"But didn't you realise I would be worried sick?"

"If I'm honest, I hoped you would be . . . I know it's awful, but I was testing you. I wanted to see what lengths you'd go to in order to find me. You were happy to do whatever it took to find Leon, and I needed to know if that was the case for me too. I'm sorry, Andie – I know I have no right to play God. But you kept the truth from me, and that hurt me so much. I was so angry that you hadn't been honest with me, and it clouded my judgement – and what was even worse was the feeling that I was just a pet project for you, something you needed to use to get you through whatever this Elaine situation is. But after mulling it over all day Thursday and Friday, I eventually came to my senses and realised I wasn't being fair – I didn't even listen to your explanation. Just when I was ready to climb down off my high horse, though, I turned on the news and found out that Leon had been located, and that he'd died. That was a shocker, I can tell you."

"I figured you would have heard. But when you didn't get in contact with me . . ." I trailed off. "I didn't know what to think."

"I tried, believe me. The second I heard about Leon, I went straight to the MGM and called to your room – but you must have left for the funeral by then. I scoured the place for Philippe to try to get some info – you always said he was the man in the know – but he was nowhere to be seen."

"But why didn't you ring me?"

"Frankly, I was afraid of how you might react. It seemed better to talk to you face to face. And so . . ."

"So?"

Colm had gone a peculiar shade of red. "Okay. I was trying to suss out if you knew what came next, but I'm thinking you don't. Am I right?"

"Colm, what are you talking about?"

"I'm right." He nodded. "Shit."

"You're starting to freak me out . . ."

"I was at the funeral, Andie. I found out the details from Leon's local newspaper and I went."

"What? Why?"

"I had to be there in case you needed me. The last thing I wanted was to be disrespectful to Leon, so I made sure to keep my distance from you in the church out of respect to his family – but I just couldn't stay completely away from you when something like this had happened. And, as I said, I was hoping we might be able to have a word after the funeral, but it didn't work out that way."

"I can't believe you were there and I didn't notice you!" I threw my arms around him. "But why were you worried about telling me that? That was such a sweet thing to do . . ."

"There's more."

I removed my arms from around him while I waited for him to elaborate.

"Those bastards outside the church were like vultures, taking pictures of you and Leon's family. I was standing near one of them, waiting for an opportunity to catch your eye, when he started roaring your name and papping furiously. I just saw red, and told him to leave you alone if he wanted to see his next birthday. He responded by transferring his camera to one hand, and decking me full force with the other, then turning around and papping away again as if nothing had happened. So I'd no choice but to bury a fist in his stomach."

"I don't believe it . . . *you* hit the photographer?"

"Yeah, that would have been me."

"Did you get in trouble with the police?"

"Nope. Luckily, the idiot that hit me had enemies. He started ranting on about how he'd have me up for assault, but then a few journalists from a rival newspaper came over and said they saw how your man had hit me first, and they'd be happy to tell the police just that if vulture boy wanted to get them involved. The story made the paper, but things didn't go any further than that."

"Did you leave after the church part of the funeral, then, to get away from all of this?"

"No. I went to the graveyard." He shook his head. "There was no way I was going to just pop up on top of you though after Bridget fainted. The poor woman. I couldn't believe it when the baying mob practically jumped on top of her to capture pictures of her at the worst moment of her life. Believe me, not all photographers would do that – there are some left in the world with morals and ethics."

"Yeah, well, not in Vegas." I shuddered at the memory.

"I know you're probably disgusted with me for brawling at Leon's funeral . . ."

I shook my head. "Those photographers and journalists made a mockery of his funeral, not you. And I can hardly fault you for defending my honour, can I?"

"You can fault me for a lot of other things, though, Andie. I've handled everything that's happened very badly."

"Well, that makes two of us. I wasn't honest with you, and that wasn't right . . . but it was because I hadn't been honest with myself either. I thought I'd moved on, but I was just standing still."

"And now?" he asked.

"Now . . . now I need to spend a lot of time sorting myself out. And I think I should start that process by telling you what I should have already told you a long time ago. Let's order a drink. This'll take a while."

Colm snuggled me against him while I told him the story of what had happened with Elaine from start to finish, and what Leon had said to me in Vegas and in his email. Then, Colm told me every last detail of the night he killed the elderly man. I could see him reliving it as he said the words.

"It wasn't your fault," I whispered when he'd finished.

"Elaine's death wasn't your fault either, but we both know that doesn't stop us from feeling responsible. But Leon was right. There comes a time when everyone needs to let go and move on. And . . . I was really hoping we could help each other do that by moving on together. What do you think?"

"I think I've finally found exactly what I've been looking for."

His face lit up.

"And I also think it's time you stopped behaving yourself," I added slyly.

His eyes widened, and he furrowed his brow in enquiry. I nodded.

As we passed through Reception, hand in hand, Cassie raised a make-up brush to us in salutation and whooped like a cowgirl.

Chapter Forty-two

Colm woke up when his alarm went off, and looked around the room in shock.

"Jaysis, Andie, the cleaners came in while we were asleep and tidied up the place. And look, they packed your bag too. Wasn't that very good of them?"

"Hilarious. Don't give up the day job."

"What time did you have to get up to do all of this? The room was a bombsite when we went to sleep!"

"A few hours ago." I swung my desk-chair around to face him. "And it would be a bombsite when you insisted on tearing my clothes off me and flinging them around the room, wouldn't it?"

"You love it. And I love doing it, so we're both happy." He raised one eyebrow at me speculatively.

"Not a hope," I said to the eyebrow as I swung back around to my laptop. "I've more work to do this morning and we're leaving the USA today, which is why I packed so early. I'd suggest you get back down to your room now and get your stuff together."

"You're a hard woman," he said as he dragged himself out of bed and looked around for his clothes. I'd put them in a neat pile beside one of the bedside lockers, which was the last thing he expected. It took him a good minute to find them. (Attempting to be tidy was part of the new me.)

"I thought you'd be up early yourself, actually. Why aren't you whizzing around the place working as usual?"

"One word. Unemployment. Or unemployed, if you'd prefer. Either works."

It took a few seconds to sink in. "Oh no! Were you made redundant? When did this happen?"

He shook his head. "I quit. I actually have given up the day job."

"*What?* How come you never told me?"

"I was keeping it for the journey back to Ireland. I thought it'd be a good time-passer for that part of the flight where you feel like you're never going to get home. Oh, well, we'll just have to do a crossword."

"But why quit now? It doesn't make sense . . ."

He shrugged. "It just wasn't worth it any more."

"It hasn't been worth it for a long time, in your eyes, but it's never been enough to make you quit before," I pointed out. "So how about you tell me the real reason?"

"Oh, Bea-tch just got too much to bear. No big deal." He looked away.

When you first start seeing someone, you learn new things about them several times every day. I'd just learnt something very important about Colm. He was a hopeless liar. Not only was he making furtive eye contact with an art-nouveau cat-esque creation in a painting on the wall rather than looking at me, his cheeks had flushed so fast after he spoke that it was as if someone had held a hoover up to them and sucked all the blood to his face.

I walked around in front of him and stood in front of the hideous painting. "Our first row was a humdinger, but I can promise you that our second will be even more spectacular if you don't tell me right now what the story is." I folded my arms in front of my chest and put on my best no-nonsense, bordering-on-threatening face.

"You look like you have a glucose barley stuck in your throat. Have you been digging into my sweet stash again?" Colm looked more amused than threatened.

"Colm! What's going on? Why did you leave?"

He took a deep breath and exhaled slowly. "She wanted me to film the funeral."

That shut me up. My tough face dissolved.

"She rang me to ask me about the funeral. When I said I'd be going she instantly assumed I meant I'd be there as a cameraman and not in any other capacity. When I explained to her that I was going out of solidarity with you and there was no conceivable way that I would do such an unthinkable thing as shoot footage of his funeral, she went ballistic at me for wasting what to her was an opportunity. She tried every angle you can imagine to get me to do it. It started with her being 'disappointed', then she reminded me of the obligations of my contract, followed by a guilt trip on how I was letting the team down if I didn't do this. I told her to get stuffed. And that's when things got a bit ugly." He shrugged. "As you said, I haven't been happy in that job for a long time. I've told Bea-tch countless times in the past that I'm not happy to film funerals – of course, that didn't stop her assuming I wanted to film Leon's, just because this one is so high profile – she's sickening. Invading on people's grief is not my idea of a good day's work – everyone should be allowed their privacy at a time like that. I don't want to be in a job that has that level of disrespect for others."

"But what will you do now?"

"I'll live a happier life. It was a joke, anyway. I was hired as a cameraman, but I ended up doing a full-time job as a project manager as well as the full-time job I was employed for, just because they were too tight to pay someone else to do it. That place was taking advantage for a long time. Enough was enough."

I must have looked worried, because Colm got up and put his arms around me. "This is going to work out fine. I'll freelance – there are always plenty of jobs available for weddings and corporate events. I'm not selling my soul to a life I hate any more."

"Well, that makes two of us, then." I extricated myself from his arms and pulled up my sent items on my laptop. "Read the last mail I sent."

He read it in a few seconds. "I didn't see that one coming," he said then.

358

"You know what, neither did I. But now that I've done it, I can't understand why I didn't do it a long time ago."

He took me in his arms again. "I won't even ask you right now what you're going to do – knowing you, I'm sure you have a plan up your sleeve. And whatever it is, it'll all work out fine."

"For both of us," I smiled. "Now, I'm going to have to kick you out, I'm afraid. I have to finish my final column."

"Diligent to the last." He planted a long kiss on my lips. "How long will it take?"

"Give me half an hour. I have it all written in my head already."

"Okay. That gives us time for breakfast before we start out for Vegas."

As soon as he'd left, I turned my attention to my laptop. I re-read the email I'd just sent to Isolde before starting my column.

Isolde,

The final column that I'll be sending on to you later is exactly what you told me not to write when I first set out to find Leon. But that's okay, because I'm handing in my notice. We both know this isn't the job for me. I know you'll be happy to get rid of me too, so I don't feel too guilty. Let's face it, the post-Vegas success buzz would have worn off soon, and we'd be back to killing each other.

If you wish to use the column, that's fine. If you don't, no bother. I won't be writing this column for the readers, or for anyone other than myself. It is going to be my way of saying goodbye.

Thanks for everything, Isolde. You've been a total pain to work with up until a few days ago when I started to like you, but it's been a learning experience all the same. And I promise you, I will go to my grave keeping your real name a secret (as long as you give me a glowing reference).

All the best,

Andie (A-n-d-I-E)

PS Don't forget to test the interviewees' sheep impressions when you're recruiting my replacement. We all know you secretly love your shepherd's role.

As I clicked back into my inbox, a new mail popped in. It was from Bridget. I'd left my love-nest in the middle of the previous night to email her and refute Lindy's claims that Colm and I had been together when I'd started my search, and to inform her that the fact we were together now in no way diluted the high regard I held Leon in. I had no idea how she would react to it in her reply. I gulped as I opened her email.

Two minutes later, I was fighting back tears. In Bridget's reply, she not only dismissed Lindy's ramblings as "pitiful and inconsequential", but also thanked me again for all I'd done for Leon, and had wished Colm and me every happiness for the future. And most importantly, I could tell that she meant it. With parents like Bridget and Liam, it was no wonder at all that Leon had grown up to be the person he was.

I took a deep breath before I started my second task. This wasn't going to be easy, but I had to do this. It was time.

Dear Leon,

The moment has come for me to say goodbye to you. Not long ago, this would have destroyed me. You see, I wasn't very good at letting go. But that's hardly news to you, seeing as you're the one who opened my eyes to that very fact. You opened my eyes to a lot of things, Leon.

I believe in luck, but I also believe in fate. I know that our eyes were destined to connect through the crowd in the MGM on the wonderful night that we met. I now also know that we were meant to be separated too. You were sent to me to take me on a journey, one that's opened my eyes and shown me the direction my life should take. You said that our time together was a source of solace to you in your final weeks, which is something I'm deeply grateful for. I'd hate to think you did so much for me without me being able to give something back. Because of you, my life has changed in a way it never would have – never could have – without your influence.

I went looking for you, and I found you. But I also found a whole lot more that I didn't even know I was searching for. You changed my life, and I'll never forget that. I'll never forget you.

Rest in peace, Leon.

All my love,

Andie

Chapter Forty-three

Four months later

"'Allo?"

"Ah, Philippe, is it yourself?"

There was a pause. "Well, of course it is, And-ee – you rang me, so you must know it is me, no?"

Now wasn't the time to explain Irish sayings, so I continued on with a "How are you doing?"

"I am fantasteek, And-ee. It is lovely to 'ear your voice! It feels like so long ago since you were here in Vaygas."

"Four months is a long time, I suppose! We have a lot to catch up on! I hope you're not too busy there at work?"

"Listen to you. Already taking the peas out of me. I will fit you into my 'ectic day, And-ee. Tell me, 'ow are things going between you and Col-um?"

"Great. We moved in together, and it's all going so well . . . things are just perfect." I knew the smile on my face was embedded in my voice as I spoke.

"Ah, that is lovelee to 'ear. And I suppose you both are working like lunateeks as usual?"

I filled Philippe in on how I'd left the *Vicious Voice*.

"I bet your boss was sorry to see you go."

"Oh, she's doing just fine without me. She started writing

362

columns herself until she found someone to replace me, and they went down a treat with the public, so she's now my full-time replacement. They're really snarky columns, complaining about everything and everyone you can imagine. It seems to be what people want, and she's even been getting invites on to TV shows on the back of them to defend her position about this, that and the other – which she seems to love."

"So she's essentially become you, then! A nasty version of you!"

"Yes, except she thrives on all of this kind of thing. Me, I'm happy to be relatively anonymous again."

"And are you anoneemous? Surely people still recognise you?"

"Yes, but I've deliberately been keeping a low profile since I left the *Vicious Voice*, and the fuss has died down." And thankfully, I hadn't become the hated figure I'd feared I might as a result of Lindy's rumour. The whole thing never really came to anything; interest in the story died with Leon's death. "There's always someone new to talk about. I'm old news now, and I'm happy about that."

"But what about work? Did you find another job?"

"Freelance work has been flooding in. That was one advantage of having my face plastered all over the place – my name is out there. I just don't do any articles about Leon. I still have money left from that People Search contract anyway." Rick had launched People Search in Europe shortly after I returned home, and he got me to do a few appearances in various capital cities, but we parted company amicably as soon as my three-month contract was up. "As for Colm, he set up his own videography company. He does videos of weddings, mainly, but he also gets freelance camerawork gigs. He's so busy that he's had to employ someone – Adrian – to take on some of the wedding jobs."

"Ah, that ees good to 'ear. So are you looking for another job in a paypear, or will you continue to freelance?"

"Actually, neither, if all goes to plan. I've decided to apply for a teacher-training course next year. It's something I've wanted to do for a long time."

"Really? That's wonderful! What will you teach? Drama?"

363

I had to smile. "No, although I can see why you would think that. I'll hopefully be an English teacher."

"Oh. Well, you 'ave good Eng-leesh, so that is a good start. And you are very brave to do such a thing at your age."

If anyone else had said it to me, I might have taken it up as a snarky comment. Coming from Philippe, I knew it was a case of what you heard was what you got – and he was right. Most people my age would have considered leaving a job and re-training for something else at thirty a big step, but most people hadn't met and been inspired by Leon. And what I had found out about Leon's career after his death had blown me away.

Leon hadn't told me what he did for a living on the night we met. When I thought back on it, we'd spent most of our time talking about me. I would have felt guilty about that except that I knew, looking back, that Leon had wanted it this way. Mostly, when I made any enquiries on that night about his life, he'd deflected them and turned the conversation back to me. And when I went to visit him, his career path was never going to be on the conversation agenda. So when I found out that Leon was a very successful author with an endless string of books behind him, I can safely say that I hadn't seen that one coming.

"Leon was the author of a prominent series of fantasy books for teenagers," Bridget had explained when she last rang me. Bridget and I had kept in constant contact since I'd returned to Ireland, something that seemed to be helping us both. "He wrote under a pseudonym – Daniel Larch. You may have heard of him?"

"Heard of him? I've read every single book he's ever written!"

Although Daniel Larch's books were ostensibly for teenagers, they'd achieved the arduous task of also speaking to an adult audience, and successfully crossing over into that market too. Part of Daniel Larch's rise to prominence was the mystery surrounding the real identity of the author. It was widely known that the name was a pseudonym, and his publishing company had made it known that the author refused to give up his or her real identity.

"Yes, he did very well for himself," Bridget said with more than a hint of pride in her voice.

"Why didn't he want to write under his own name?"

"Fear. Unfounded fear, of course – he was an amazing writer, but there was no convincing him of that. He was determined to be a writer, but when he was offered a publishing deal on the strength of his first book, he got cold feet. He was afraid that if the book didn't sell well, he'd never be taken seriously as a writer. I was dead set against him creating Daniel Larch – I knew the quality of his work was outstanding – but he didn't have the same belief in himself."

"But when the books became a phenomenon, why didn't he take credit for being Daniel Larch then?"

"Fear again. Leon was a shy man. He kept to himself, and he led a very peaceful, laid-back existence. He was concerned that once his face became public property, he'd never be able to reclaim his privacy. As Daniel Larch, he had the best of both worlds – he was able to make a living doing what he loved doing, but also keep his low-profile lifestyle. As long as the books were selling, the publishing company didn't care."

After what I'd experienced in Vegas with the media, I could completely understand Leon's perspective.

"It's all about to come out, though. Leon was in the middle of finishing the third book in his latest trilogy, which of course can't be released now. It was due out next year, and the publishing company asked Liam and me if they can let the public know why they won't be able to deliver it. Daniel Larch has a huge fanbase who are hanging on for the final book in the trilogy, so they'll be demanding answers from the publishers. Leon had seen this coming, and he'd discussed his options with us. He eventually decided that he didn't have an issue with his identity being made known after he'd passed away. He was just sorry he ran out of time and couldn't finish the final book. God knows, he tried – he wrote 50,000 words of it after he got sick. But eventually, he just had to accept that he needed to put his energies into getting from one day to the next. Even the toughest of fighters have to know when to let go."

"I can't believe it," I said. "Leon was Daniel Larch!" I had so many questions that I didn't know where to start. "He's produced over twenty books – he must have been writing for years!"

"He gave up his job when he was twenty-three to write full-time. It was quite a risk – he'd moved to New York and taken on an amazing job as a stockbroker after he graduated from college. He was on a great salary, and the bonuses and incentives he was receiving at the time were phenomenal – but he walked away from it all after two years and started writing full-time." She sighed. "His father and I gave him a hard time about it – no, to be fair, *I* gave him a hard time about it – but it certainly worked out for him financially."

I thought back on some of the articles I'd read online about Daniel Larch over the years. The man was one of the highest earners in the literary world. Leon had been very, very rich.

"He spent a third of his life doing something he adored. That's more than a lot of people do," I said to Bridget.

I thought about what I'd discovered only the previous day. I had been tidying up my email inbox – a long overdue task – and I'd moved Leon's email to a special to-be-kept-forever folder before I deleted all the rest of my emails. Of course, as I'd moved it, I'd had to open it up to read it again. And it was then that I noticed for the first time that when I reached the end of the mail, the scroll bar on the right-hand side still had some scrolling space left. I scrolled down, expecting to see his email signature, if anything at all. But instead there was this.

By the way:
Make that career move you spoke to me about. And don't be afraid. I made a risky career move once, and it really paid off. You will never know what you are capable of unless you take a chance.

It was yet another legacy from Leon to me. How strange that I had missed it the first time! But, in any case, his message was waiting for me to find it at a time when I really needed it. Now, I was ready to listen to what he had to say, and to act on it.

For the millionth time since I left Vegas, I wished Leon could have been granted the chance to live. While I knew he and I would never have ended up together, I also knew he had so much to offer someone else. But even though the cruelty of his death affected me every day, the warmth of the experience of knowing him dulled the pain somewhat. I felt privileged to have crossed paths with him, however briefly.

"It's all talk about me here," I said. "So what's going on in Vegas? Any gossip?"

"Well, achshully, I 'eard something recently that I thought would interest you. I noticed Lindy had not been on the entertainment slot for a while, so I made a few discreet enquiries."

That probably meant he put an ad in the paper asking for information, but I let him continue.

"Lindy was fired last month, And-ee! If that is not karma, I do not know what is!"

"What? But – that one is so smart, she'll have Dave up for unfair dismissal!"

"No. She cannot. I was told that Dave followed all the correct procedures. Lindy was given several warnings about her be'aviour, both verbal and written. She was not a permanent staff member, just on a six-month contract that was renewed a few times. When she came to the end of her latest contract last month, Dave did not renew it. And she 'adn't any comeback after all the warnings he had given her."

"Oh dear. Well, who knows, maybe she'll learn from the experience. It's definitely about time for her to grow up, that's for sure." I couldn't feel too smug about Lindy's misfortune – she wasn't the only one who'd needed to grow up. But at least now, I was working on it.

"That is all that is happening here, And-ee. I miss you, but I am sure you are not planning on coming to Vay-gas anytime soon. You are probably glad to be back at 'ome now and to not 'ave to travel any more."

"Actually, I'm planning on doing a lot more travelling soon. But I can't tell you too much about it right now – it's a secret."

"Ooh! Now you have me intrigued. Can you even give me a hint?"

I smiled. "Well, all I can say is that I'm not going back to Vegas, yet I might be in your neck of the woods sometime soon . . ."

Chapter Forty-four

The anticipation of Christmas hung in the air as I made my way down Grafton Street. Groups of people were moving in throngs into nearby pubs and restaurants, laughing and joking, whilst others flooded into the shops, attracted by the shimmering fairy lights that glistened invitingly at them. I've always found the lead-up to Christmas to be more exciting than the day itself. And, if things went according to plan, this year's lead-up would be more exciting than most.

I crossed Dame Street and made my way towards O'Connell Bridge. I walked as one part of a human tidal wave over the bridge and onto O'Connell Street, where a Christmas festival was taking place. The Friday before Christmas was the day when most people would be finishing up in work, and the festivities had been organised by a group of nearby retailers to get people in the spirit to spend as much as possible. The centre of the street had been transformed into a mixture of the North Pole and the front of a Christmas card, with plastic fir trees, Santa's grotto and reindeer providing the backdrop. The plan was working, if the number of bags swinging from the arms of almost every person that passed was anything to go by. I had no bags. I'd learned to let go of a lot over the past few months, and I no longer carried baggage with me

369

wherever I went. I was happy to leave everything behind me for the journey I was about to take.

The collective sound of a group of carol singers in front of the Spire resounded in my ears as I made my way towards Clery's clock, winding my way through fir trees and stands of free mulled wine and mince pies as I crossed the road. I couldn't see whether Colm was waiting under the clock or not as I made my way down the street. As I approached, I noticed a number of other men standing aimlessly in front of Clery's. I wondered if they were waiting for their girlfriends or wives to leave Clery's with their shopping, or if they were up to the same thing that I was. Clery's had always been the traditional place for couples to meet in Dublin, but I'd never once met a date there. I'd always thought it was too clichéd, or so I had told myself. Now, I realised it was just because I'd subconsciously been waiting for the right person to meet there.

I felt like I was in Vegas all over again as the endless lights of the shop displays dazzled me, trying their best to seduce me. But the competition was far too stiff for them to even be in the running. Within seconds, they were rendered invisible, and there was only one thing I could see.

I caught Colm's eye. He broke into a huge smile, which gave me the incentive to propel myself into his arms. He bundled me into his open coat – a long, black, 70s-style thing that screamed cosiness, and wrapped it, and his arms, around me so tight that I could barely breathe. And then he kissed me, so urgently and yet so tenderly that my breath was completely taken away, as if it had been years since we'd last met instead of only hours.

I had no idea how long we stood like that, completely oblivious to the world around us. All I knew is that I could have stayed in that moment forever, if it hadn't been for what I had planned. A plop on my nose brought me back to reality. I looked up, and felt a sense of wonder envelop me.

"I can't believe it! Do you know how long it's been since it snowed at Christmas in Dublin?"

"The last time I remember it snowing at Christmas, I was living at home in Kerry. And a lot of time has passed since then."

"Which is a good thing, right?"

"Absolutely. So, maybe the snow marks the beginning of a new chapter . . ."

"I think so. One thing's for sure – we certainly couldn't get more of a contrast with Vegas if we tried!"

"When we were first in Vegas, I wasn't allowed to do this." He pulled me to him again. I allowed myself one last snowflake-mingled kiss before I pulled away.

"We have to go."

Colm raised his eyebrows. "Where?"

"Do you trust me?"

"Of course . . ."

"Then don't ask me any more questions. Just go with this. Promise?"

"O – kay . . . but . . . I do have one little comment to make. This place that we're going to that I'm not asking anything about at all whatsoever . . . can we walk there?"

"That's a question, not a comment, but I'll answer it. We could walk, but we don't have a spare ten hours, so we're not going to do that. We'll get a taxi."

"Right. I'm not raising an objection to the plan I don't know anything about, but I have to say that we'll never get a taxi from anywhere near here – all of the streets around here have been closed off."

"I have a plan." I beckoned him to follow me. We walked up the street to where a group of rickshaw sleighs awaited to take customers to their favourite store, a free service that enabled customers to empty their pockets even more.

"We're going to a shop on the North Circular Road, please," I said to a driver who looked annoyed at being disturbed. I guessed he was being paid a flat rate for tonight.

"Wha'? What the bleedin' hell do ya want to go to a shop up there for? Have you noticed how many bleedin' shops there are around here?"

I flashed a fifty-euro note at him. "The North Circular Road shops are better." There weren't very many shops on the North Circular Road – it was mostly pubs and restaurants – but it didn't matter.

He pocketed the fifty. "Dead right, luv. In ya get." Within seconds, he was rocketing past the nativity crib at the top of O'Connell Street, as if he was afraid I would change my mind and demand my money back.

He deposited us in front of one of the few shops on the North Circular Road – a bridal shop.

"Before you ask, we're on this street so that we can get a taxi. We'd never get one in the city centre."

It was as if the mere mention of the word had summoned it. I looked to my right, only to see a taxi stopping at the lights right beside us. I ran over to check if it was available. It was.

"The airport, please," I said as Colm and I shuffled into the back seat.

"The airport?"

"No questions. You promised, remember?"

"Yes, but I don't have my passport."

"I do."

"You having yours is no good if I don't have mine."

"No, I have your passport. And my own too, before you ask."

"How is it you always seem to have my passport?"

"Ah-ah! 'How' is a question."

"We're heading back to Vegas, then. And that's a statement, not a question."

"Good guess, but no."

"Phew! I'm kinda done with Vegas."

"Me too. Now, no more questions or statements."

I cut Colm off at the pass every time he attempted to say a word on the way to the airport. He eventually gave up. I ignored his quizzical looks for the rest of the journey.

Even though the airport was busier than ever, a feeling of goodwill engulfed me as I led Colm to an Aer Lingus check-in area. The sparkling lights of the gigantic Christmas tree in the departures area seemed to wink at me, as if they were complicit in my plan and approved wholeheartedly of it. I winked back at them, not caring who saw me. After all of my escapades in Vegas, it was a bit late to be worrying about people thinking I was a bit batty.

"When does the embargo on the questions end?"

"Who says that it does?"

"Okay. But I should point out that I have to film a wedding on St Stephen's Day."

"You're not working on St Stephen's Day. Or the day after, or the day after, or – well, for quite a while. Adrian is taking on all of your jobs for the next few weeks. He's delighted to get the work, so don't worry about it – your company is in good hands."

"What are you talking about? And don't tell me not to ask any questions! What's going on, Andie?"

I thought about keeping the guessing games up, but the queue to the check-in desks was moving fast, so I relented. I dug into my handbag and handed a printout of the holiday details to Colm.

He quickly scanned the information, the expressions on his face flitting from confused to excited to an even deeper level of confusion.

"The Galapagos Islands, New York and Paris? How can we be going to all those places?"

I looked around. "I could go to town on you with that answer, but I'll refrain."

As we edged forward in the queue, Colm stared at me for a long time before breaking into a huge smile. "I can't believe you remembered . . ."

"I can't believe you'd think I wouldn't have. When you're in love with someone, you remember every little detail . . . even if you haven't admitted to yourself at the time that you love them."

Colm said nothing. He just stared at me.

"What? What is it?"

"There's something I have to tell you . . . I have a big problem with going on this trip."

My blood ran cold. I felt mortification flush my face as I took in Colm's serious expression. Had I got it all wrong?

"You see, I had a more specific reason for not going to Paris than what I told you."

He didn't continue. I looked up, and saw him waiting for me to say something.

"Well, come on! Out with it!"

He grinned. I didn't know whether to feel comforted by that, or furious. "Before I tell you, let me just say that I know it's a cliché . . . but . . . Paris has always been my planned proposal city."

His grin spread into a full megawatt beam, brighter than all of the Christmas lights in the entire airport put together. I was so on edge that it took me a second to realise what he'd just said.

"We need to end the embargo on the questions now," he went on, "because I have a few very important ones to ask. First of all, in light of what I've just said, do you still want to get on this plane? Because you know what's going to happen if you do . . ."

My voice caught in my throat. I was so happy, I thought I would burst if I spoke a single word. I managed a nod, sending happy tears flying down my cheeks.

"You'll get the next question when we're in Paris." He bent down and kissed away the tears, then lifted me up and twirled me in the air. I never wanted the moment to end – but I knew that when it did, I had a lifetime of other special moments to look forward to. It felt amazing.

"My turn to ask a question now," I said when my feet finally hit the ground again. "But it's a bit personal, so please don't take offence . . ."

"Ask me anything."

"Can we *not* have Marietta biscuits served at our wedding reception?"

THE END.